Lynda La Plante was born in Liverpool. She trained for the stage at RADA and worked with the National Theatre and RDC before becoming a television actress. She then turned to writing – and made her breakthrough with the phenomenally successful TV series *Widows*. Her novels have all been international bestsellers.

Her original script for the much-acclaimed *Prime Suspect* won awards from BAFTA, Emmy, British Broadcasting and Royal Television Society as well as the 1993 Edgar Allan Poe Award. Lynda has written and produced over 170 hours of international television. *Tennison* has been adapted by ITV and was broadcast in March 2017 in the UK; international broadcast will follow.

Lynda is one of only three screenwriters to have been made an honorary fellow of the British Film Institute and was awarded the BAFTA Dennis Potter Best Writer Award in 2000. In 2008, she was awarded a CBE in the Queen's Birthday Honours List for services to Literature, Drama and Charity.

If you would like to hear from Lynda, please sign up at www.bit.ly/LyndaLaPlanteClub or you can visit www.lyndalaplante.com for further information. You can also follow Lynda on Facebook and Twitter @LaPlanteLynda.

Lynda La Plante

WIDOWS

ZAFFRE

First published in Great Britain in 1983 by Sphere.

This edition published in 2018 by
ZAFFRE PUBLISHING
80–81 Wimpole St, London W1G 9RE
www.zaffrebooks.co.uk

A CIP catalogue record for this book is available from the British Library.

Trade Paperback ISBN: 978–1–78576–331–1
Ebook ISBN: 978–1–78576–333–5
Paperback ISBN: 978–1–78576–332–8

also available as an ebook

1 3 5 7 9 10 8 6 4 2

Typeset by IDSUK (Data Connection) Ltd
Printed and bound by Clays Ltd, St Ives Plc

FSC www.fsc.org MIX Paper from responsible sources FSC® C018072

Zaffre Publishing is an imprint of Bonnier Zaffre,
a Bonnier Publishing company
www.bonnierzaffre.co.uk
www.bonnierpublishing.co.uk

For Ann Mitchell, who was Dolly Rawlins
and will always be

Prologue

London 1984

The blueprint for the raid was immaculate: Harry Rawlins would not have had it any other way. He was a wealthy antique dealer specialising in high-priced artwork, silverware and jewellery, and he and his wife Dolly made a formidable couple. But there was another side to Harry Rawlins. An accomplished criminal and money launderer, he drew from his men a deep respect and loyalty – but he was a cold, calculating and lethal enemy. And although the police suspected him of being heavily involved in crime, Harry Rawlins had never spent a single day behind bars.

The plan was simple and, as ever with anything Harry Rawlins led, had been rehearsed over and over again in every detail. Four of them, wearing balaclavas, would hold up a security wagon at a pre-set marker on the dual carriageway Strand underpass. A bread truck in front of the security wagon, driven by one of the gang, would act as a blocker by slamming on its brakes. As soon as the security wagon ahead halted, the three men following in a Ford Escort van would take up position. One would hold up the traffic behind at gunpoint while the other two, using blasting gelatin with a wired detonator cap, would blow open the back doors of the security wagon. The driver of the bread van would join them and each man would fill the others' rucksacks with money bags before three of the armed raiders ran the last fifty yards to the exit of the underpass to a waiting getaway car.

The fourth raider, covering their escape, would then drive the bread truck to a prearranged hideout.

As the bread truck, the security wagon and the Ford Escort van entered the Strand underpass, everything seemed to be going to plan. The raiders, all seasoned villains, were prepared for the next phase. But then, suddenly – the unexpected happened. A short distance behind them, a police car appeared, heading down the underpass in pursuit of two young joyriders.

As the sirens blared, the driver of the Ford Escort van turned to look behind him in panic – and in that same split second, the driver of the bread truck, continuing with the raid as planned, slammed on his brakes, forcing the security wagon to do the same. By the time the driver of the Ford Escort van turned back, it was too late. He ploughed into the back of the security wagon and the joyriders ploughed into the back of him.

The almost simultaneous impacts caused the raider in the front seat to lurch forward. The blasting gelatin flew out of his hand and hit the dashboard, setting off an explosion and fireball that engulfed everything inside.

The three armed raiders were trapped inside their own vehicle; the flames and smoke making it impossible for anyone to wrench open the driver's door. No one could reach them, no one could help them, but everyone could hear their screams as the petrol tank finally exploded and blew what remained of their van apart.

In the awful confusion that followed, no one noticed the driver of the bread truck. He watched in disbelief for a few seconds, then ran back to the bread truck and drove out of the underpass.

* * *

All three charred bodies from the Ford Escort van were taken to Westminster Mortuary. Two days later, the forensic pathologist completed his examination and identified them officially as Harry Rawlins, Joe Pirelli and Terry Miller.

As the driver of the Ford Escort van, Harry Rawlins had taken the full impact of the gelatin explosion. The upper part of his body had been literally blown to pieces, the skull so badly fragmented it couldn't be reconstructed, and both legs were charred down to the bone. However, still attached to the wrist of a burnt and mutilated left forearm was a gold Rolex watch with the now blurred inscription: To Harry – love, Dolly – 12/2/62

Although police had suspected from the first that the second body was Joe Pirelli, the face was too badly burnt down one side to be 100 per cent certain. He had a criminal record, but no fingerprints could be taken, as neither hand was found intact. In the end, a forensic odontologist had to be brought in and eventually identified the body from dental records to within reasonable doubt.

With three previous convictions, Terry Miller was identified by a partial thumb and forefinger print on what remained of his burnt left hand.

All three men had been married. All three wives were now widows.

CHAPTER 1

Dolly Rawlins stood in her kitchen ironing the shirt collar and cuffs she had carefully starched, just the way Harry always liked them. Beside her, the laundry basket was piled with ironed sheets and pillowcases. Wolf, the little white poodle Harry had brought home after Dolly had given birth to their stillborn baby boy and their hopes of a family were dashed, sat at her feet, his head drooping. Always alert, every time Dolly moved he padded after her.

Dolly had been washing, ironing and dusting since she had returned from the police station. It was now after 1 p.m. Sometimes she would stop and just stare into space, but then she would feel the pain building up, and she'd begin working again; anything, anything to stop that pain inside her. The police wouldn't let her see Harry's body as it was too badly injured, and part of her refused to accept what she had been told. They were lying to her, she was certain. Any moment Harry would walk back into the house.

* * *

Linda Pirelli had stood frozen to the spot in the cold mortuary, her long dark hair framing her ashen face. She wished she had someone with her, she wished for a lot of things but, right now, she wished that this was a bad dream and any second she'd wake up.

'Dental records suggest this is your husband, Mrs Pirelli, but, as we didn't find all the teeth, we'd like you to take a look as well,' the mortician said. 'One side of his face is not too badly burnt, so if you remain standing where you are, you'll be fine. Ready?' Before Linda had a chance to answer, he'd pulled the white sheet back.

Linda gasped, held her hand to her mouth and froze. She felt something warm trickling down the inside of her leg.

'Toilet, I need the toilet . . .' she started to mumble softly.

'Is this your husband, Joseph Pirelli?' the escorting policewoman asked.

'*Yes*, yes, it is. Now please get me out of here,' Linda pleaded.

The policewoman gripped Linda's arm, and gently guided her from the mortuary to the toilets in the corridor.

* * *

Audrey, Shirley Miller's mother, was worn out and fed up. She glanced down with distaste at her old shapeless, woollen dress, her bare legs and her ankle boots. Catching a glimpse of herself in the kitchen window, Audrey saw the grey roots were showing in her dyed orange hair; she needed a tint to feel human again. As she stared at her haggard reflection, she could hear her daughter sobbing her heart out upstairs.

Shirley lay on her bed, her eyes red-rimmed from weeping. Every time she wiped her eyes she started crying again, repeating his name over and over.

'Terry ... Terry ... Terry ...' Shirley screeched, clutching a framed photo of her husband to her chest.

Audrey bustled in carrying some hot milk and buttered toast on a tray, but Shirley couldn't touch it so Audrey polished it off instead. As she ate, she looked at the small silver-framed photograph of Terry clenched in Shirley's hand.

Sitting back on the edge of the bed, Audrey considered her beautiful daughter, the pride of her life. Shirley was a stunning young woman, with a curvaceous figure and long natural-blonde curly hair reaching to below her shoulders. She had the sweetest, most trusting temperament and had only ever gone against Audrey's wishes once, and that was to marry Terry Miller. *She'll get over him*, Audrey thought to herself. *In time she'll be herself again.* But for now it was best just to let her cry.

* * *

At 2 p.m., Dolly dragged herself and the ironing up the stairs of her immaculate Potters Bar home. Wolf followed sleepily behind. Wolf's normal sleeping spot in the living room was on the thick Persian rug in front of the ornate fireplace. The mantelpiece displayed a lifetime of photographs of Dolly and Harry: their wedding at Chelsea Registry Office, with Dolly in a Chanel suit, carrying a small bouquet of white roses, their honeymoon in Paris, and then from every anniversary, Christmas and charity ball after that. In the winter, the open log fire warmed Wolf's little body and in the summer he enjoyed the cool air circling the room from the open sash windows. When Harry was away on business, however, Wolf always curled up next to Dolly on the sofa – plush red velvet with gold tassels.

Dolly opened the bedroom door. Inside, the bedside lamp gave a soft warm glow across the spotless room, the matching draped curtains, bedspread and scatter cushions were all neat and tidy; nothing was out of place. After putting the ironing away, Dolly dug her hand into her apron pocket and lit her hundredth cigarette of the day. As she gulped in the smoke she felt her heart heave heavily inside her.

Back downstairs, Dolly opened the mahogany doors of the stereo cabinet, switched on the record player and gently placed the needle on the LP that was already on the turntable. She had played it over and over since she got home from the police station: the deep rich tones of Kathleen Ferrier singing 'Life Without Death' seemed to soothe her.

Dolly sat in the living room smoking, with Wolf curled up at her side. She sat there all night. She didn't cry, she couldn't – it was as if someone had drained every emotion from inside her. She thought back to the morning two days ago, when Harry had kissed her goodbye. His business trip to buy some antiques should only take a couple of days, he'd said. She'd missed him every moment he was gone and last night had been preparing lasagne for dinner on his return home – Harry liked it with the cheese crisped up over the pasta – when the doorbell rang.

She had wiped her hands on a dishcloth as Wolf yapped and bounded towards the studded mahogany front door. She went to follow him into the hallway and froze. There, outlined in the stained-glass panels, were two dark figures. The doorbell rang again.

The two detectives had shown her their warrant cards and asked her whether her husband was at home. The law had come knocking a few times in the past, so Dolly was immediately guarded and non-committal, telling them Harry was away on business. They had then told her to get her shoes and coat on and accompany them to the station to identify something they believed belonged to her husband. They were unhelpful in the patrol car, refusing to answer her questions, which scared her. What if they had arrested Harry? She decided not to say or ask anything until she knew more.

At the station they took her into a cold, bare room with a Formica-topped table and four matching hard chairs. A uniformed policewoman stood beside Dolly as a detective handed her a plastic property bag containing a gold Rolex watch with a diamond encrusted face. When she tried to open the bag, the detective had snatched it away.

'Don't touch!' he snapped. He put on white forensic rubber gloves, removed the watch and turned the face over to reveal the faded inscription.

'*To Harry – love, Dolly – 12/2/62,*' whispered Dolly. Somehow she managed to maintain control. 'That's my husband's,' she said. 'That's Harry's.' And her world collapsed.

'We took it from the wrist of a dead body.' The lead detective paused to gauge her reaction. 'The charred, dead body of a man.'

Dolly grabbed the watch, backing away from the detective until she hit the far wall of the room. The female officer came after her, hand held out.

'That's evidence!' she said. 'Give it here!'

Dolly held on to the watch with all her strength. Shock had made her lose all inhibition. 'You're lying!' she screeched. 'He's not dead.

He's not!' As Harry's precious watch was prised from her fingers, she hissed, 'I want to see him. I *need* to see him!'

The female officer had had enough. 'There's nothing left to see,' she said coldly.

All the way home in the police car, Dolly kept telling herself that it could not have been Harry, even though the voice in her head kept whispering to her . . . She'd given that watch to him on their tenth wedding anniversary. He'd kissed her and promised that he would never take it off. Dolly had loved the way he would glance at it; would hold his arm out straight, turn his wrist and watch the light catch the diamonds. He was never without his Rolex – even in bed. For their next anniversary, she had bought him a solid gold Dunhill cigarette lighter engraved with his initials. He'd laughed and told her that, like the watch, he would always carry it with him.

But, even so, she could not accept that he wouldn't be coming home.

* * *

Audrey had arranged Terry's funeral. It was a quiet family affair, just a few drinks back at the house, nothing special; besides, Shirley was still in such a state that it was all Audrey could do to get her dressed.

Greg, Shirley's punk brother, helped out as best he could, but he was still very young and couldn't cope with his older sister's outpourings of emotion. When Shirley had tried to jump into the grave on top of the coffin, he'd been so embarrassed he'd walked off and attached himself to a completely different and far more dignified funeral party.

No headstone had yet been ordered because Audrey hadn't liked to ask for money, but she planned to arrange something as soon as Shirley was back on her feet. She had high hopes of Shirley going back onto the beauty queen circuit; with her stunning looks,

Audrey thought her daughter could make it through to the Miss England heats. In fact, she had already put her down for Miss Paddington . . . she would bring that up later, when Shirley wasn't crying so much.

* * *

Linda was in the living room of the crowded Pirelli family council flat. All Joe's relatives had been invited to the funeral and wake and were howling and carrying on in voluble Italian, dressed from head to toe in black. Her mother-in-law, Mama Pirelli, had been cooking for days, preparing a feast – pasta, pizza, salami – you name it, it was on the table. Linda was an orphan and had no family of her own to invite. As for friends, the lads from the arcade where she worked never really knew Joe, so, Linda was getting very drunk on her own. She could sense the guests watching her, shaking their heads at her bright red dress. She didn't care.

Looking round the sea of tearful faces, Linda suddenly spotted a woman at the far end of the room and recognised the little blonde slag she'd seen with Joe a few weeks ago. Blazing with fury, she pushed her way through the guests towards the weeping woman.

'Who the hell invited you?' Linda screamed. She'd give her something to remember him by! She threw her glass of wine over the girl and would have laid in to her if Gino, Joe's younger brother, hadn't pulled her away in time. Holding Linda tight as she sobbed, Gino whispered soft comfort in her ear, and casually placed his drunken hand on her right tit.

* * *

Consumed by grief, Dolly Rawlins had barely eaten. She felt as if night and day had blurred together, but somehow, on autopilot, she had agreed to bury her husband. She sat in the living room wearing a neat black suit and black hat with a small veil. She smoothed her black kid-leather gloves over and over, feeling her wedding and engagement rings through the soft leather. Wolf sat on the sofa beside her, his little warm body pushed against her hip.

Even today, Dolly was a strikingly composed figure; her sandy hair was immaculate, her make-up was discreet and her manner was businesslike. She was a woman determined to let no one share her very personal and very private grief. They couldn't possibly understand and the last thing she wanted was anyone suggesting that they did.

* * *

Dolly's partnership with Harry had been a very special one. They had met when she was running her late father's antique and junk stall in Petticoat Lane, but it wasn't Harry's flash E-type Jag, his good looks and charm that had drawn her to him, although of course she noticed them. No, the connection went much deeper than that.

When Harry proposed with a solitaire diamond ring, he took Dolly's breath away. Harry's mother Iris had been equally breathless, but for very different reasons. She couldn't believe that her son wanted to marry a girl she saw as a common money-grabbing little tart. Iris had brought up her only son single-handedly after his father was imprisoned for armed robbery and died of cancer shortly after his release. She established a very successful – and apparently legitimate – antique business, made sure Harry got a good education, and saw that he travelled extensively to further his knowledge of antique art, silver and precious stones. By the time he took over the business, Iris was struggling with arthritis and blinding migraines and ready to retire. Her final ambition for her only child was to see him married to a rich young woman with class and social connections. It was the first time Harry had ever defied his mother.

Dolly never told Harry about the day she had called on Iris in the elegant St John's Wood flat her doting son had bought. Not exactly elegant in those days, Dolly was nevertheless not quite the brassy blonde that Iris had envisaged. She was attractive, broad for a woman and with hands that had seen hard work, but she was demure, feminine and quietly spoken. Iris had gathered herself and offered tea.

'No thank you, Mrs Rawlins,' Dolly had replied. Iris winced at the girl's East End accent. 'I just want you to know that I love Harry and whether you like it or not, we are going to get married. Your constant disapproval and threats only drive us closer, because he loves and needs me.'

Dolly had paused for Iris to respond – to apologise if she had any sense. Instead, Iris slowly looked Dolly up and down, sneering at her ordinary clothes and unimaginative flat shoes.

Dolly shrugged and went on. 'My dad was a dealer in the antiques business and he knew your husband, so don't give me all your airs and graces. Everyone knows he fenced stolen goods and done ten years in Pentonville for armed robbery. Everyone knows you used the proceeds to run the business while he was inside. And let's be honest, you were lucky to get away with it.'

No one had ever talked to Iris like that before. 'Are you pregnant?' she asked, gobsmacked.

Dolly smoothed her pencil skirt. 'No, Mrs Rawlins, I'm not, but I do want a family, and if you want to be a part of it then you should zip your mouth. Harry and me are getting married, with or without your permission, and threatening to cut him out of the business is just cutting off your nose to spite your face.' Dolly turned to leave. 'I'll show myself out.'

'If it's money you want,' said Iris. 'I'll write you a cheque here and now. Name your price.'

Dolly held out her left hand with its diamond solitaire engagement ring.

'I want the gold band to go with this, cos you don't have enough money to pay me off. He's all I want and I am going to make him happy. Like I said, you can be part of our lives or not, it's up to you.'

Once again, Dolly headed for the door. Once again, Iris's words made her pause.

'If you're thinking of running the antique business with Harry you'd better lose that common East End accent.'

'I intend to, Mrs Rawlins.' Dolly glanced over her shoulder and looked Iris square in the eyes. 'Just as you managed to lose yours.'

* * *

Eddie Rawlins, the cousin Dolly couldn't stand, breezed in with his cheeks flushed from the cold, and interrupted her thoughts. He was similar in looks to Harry, but whereas Harry had been strong and muscular, Eddie seemed like a weak version.

He rubbed his hands and gestured out of the window at the funeral cortege. 'They're all here,' he said, beaming. 'Hell of a turn out. The Fishers are here, not to mention the law watching in a car down the road. You can't even see the end of the line, there must be fifty cars out there!'

Dolly bit her lip. She hadn't wanted it this way but Iris had insisted: Harry was an important man who had to be buried in style. Dolly knew how much Iris must be hurting too, so she had given her what she wanted. She'd never be thanked for it, but it would make Dolly's life less stressful in the long run.

Collecting her black leather handbag, Dolly stood and smoothed her skirt, checking herself in the hallway mirror on the way out. Just as she got to the front door, Eddie stopped her and took a small brown packet from his pocket. He leant forward and spoke in a hushed voice even though they were completely alone.

'This is for you, Dolly. I know it's probably not appropriate right now, but the law's been sniffin' round my place and Harry gave me this to pass on to you if anything ever happened to him.'

Dolly stared at the package. Eddie shifted his weight and moved closer.

'I think it's the keys to his lock-up,' he said.

Dolly slipped the packet into her handbag and followed Eddie outside. She couldn't believe she was about to bury Harry. All she wanted to do was lie down and die. Her little dog was all that kept her alive now.

The neighbours were out on their driveways and, as Dolly walked down her front garden path, she could feel everyone watching her. Car after car was lined up, waiting patiently to follow the hearse, which was weighed down with wreaths and bunches of flowers. Dolly had never seen so many hearts and crosses; the splashes of colour standing out in contrast to the line of black cars.

Eddie ushered Dolly into the back of a black Mercedes-Benz with dark tinted windows. As she bent her head to step into the car she saw her mother-in-law in the Rolls-Royce behind. Iris mouthed the word: 'bitch'. Dolly ignored her, just as she had done throughout most of her married life.

Once she had settled herself, Dolly gave the nod for Eddie to follow the slow-moving hearse. Through the driver's mirror, he saw the trickle of tears start to run down her ashen face. She made no effort to wipe them away as she spoke in a tight voice.

'I hope you told them I'm doing nothing back at the house after the funeral . . . nothing. The sooner this is over the better.'

'Yeah, I did,' Eddie replied cautiously 'But I think Iris is havin' a few folks back at her flat. She asked me to go and said she's paid for everythin'.' Dolly closed her eyes and shook her head. Iris hadn't been financially self-sufficient since retiring so 'paying for everything' actually meant that Harry was paying. Or, more accurately now, Dolly.

Harry Rawlins was buried in the style his mother wanted, with hundreds gathered at the cemetery, and even more flowers surrounding the graveside. Throughout the ceremony, Dolly remained solitary and unmoved. She was the first to leave the graveside and the nosy, intrusive crowd of mourners raised their bowed heads to watch her go.

Among the mourners was Arnie Fisher, in his navy cashmere coat, immaculate tailored suit and shirt. As soon as Dolly's car moved off he nodded to a huge bear of a man standing at the back of the crowd. Boxer Davis pushed his way forwards. Boxer's suit, in comparison, was shoddy and threadbare and even his shirt was grimy and stained. His big stupid face appeared moved by the ceremony, and he wiped his flattened nose – dripping from the cold – with the back of his hand. Arnie Fisher flicked a look at Dolly's slowly retreating Mercedes and nodded for Boxer to follow. Boxer shuffled, slightly embarrassed.

'Don't you think I should wait a few days, boss? I mean, she only just buried him.'

Arnie stared at Boxer for a couple of seconds, jerked his head towards the Merc again, and turned away. Conversation over.

Standing a few feet away from Arnie was his younger brother, Tony, who towered above everyone, making even Boxer look small by comparison. The cold sun glinted off the diamond in his right ear as he fingered it while he chatted to some friends. He came to the end of some joke he was obviously telling and they roared with laughter. Unlike his brother, Tony was a handsome man; in fact, the only similarity between them was their steely blue ice-cold eyes. Arnie was short-sighted so he wore rimless glasses – but there was something about those unfeeling, unemotional eyes they both shared. Boxer looked from Tony back to Arnie and obediently made his way through the dispersing mourners to follow Dolly back to the huge, empty home where she and Harry had been so happy for so long.

A short distance from the main crowd, Detective Sergeant Fuller leant against a tombstone, making a mental note of everyone there. *My God*, he thought, *it's like looking at the mugshots down the Yard*. All the lags were there – the old timers and the new blood. A diligent young officer out to impress the powers that be, Fuller was pissed off to have been sent on what he considered a fool's errand. His boss, Detective Inspector George Resnick, had been obsessed with catching Harry Rawlins for longer than Fuller had been alive. 'There'll be something, Fuller,' Resnick had barked to Fuller and Detective Constable Andrews that morning. 'Every criminal in London will be in that graveyard today, either to pay their respects or to make certain Rawlins doesn't come back from the dead. So, there'll be something. And I want to know what.'

DI Resnick had always believed that Harry Rawlins was the ringleader behind three armed robberies on security vans. His attempts to prove it became an overwhelming obsession – and had been a constant irritation to Rawlins. Eventually Rawlins took action. Resnick was photographed accepting an envelope from a known criminal and, when the story was leaked to the *News of the World*, he had found himself under investigation for corruption. It took him months to prove his innocence, and by the time Resnick returned to work, the stigma had ruined any hopes of promotion. The irreparable damage to his career fuelled Resnick's festering hatred for Rawlins and he swore that one day, no matter how many years it took, he would see Harry Rawlins behind bars. Death had beaten Resnick to it, but it was an obsession that seemingly extended beyond the grave.

Fuller didn't care about Resnick because he didn't believe for a second that Resnick cared about him – he had put nothing and no one above catching Harry bloody Rawlins. However, they both cared what the Fisher brothers were up to and who they were talking to, so Fuller watched them like a hawk. Fuller was ambitious to climb the ranks; and the Fishers had been on every copper's 'most wanted' list ever since he was a uniformed recruit. They'd be the catch of the century, now Rawlins was dead!

After the mourners dispersed, Fuller threaded his way between the gravestones towards the exit. He was about to get into the waiting police car when he noticed the mud on his forty-pound shoes and, irritated, wiped them on the grass verge. DC Andrews grinned at him from the driver's seat. Fuller was not amused, particularly as he also had mud on the hem of his best trousers.

Fuller opened the car door and sat down heavily inside. He took a clean, white, perfectly ironed and folded handkerchief and spat on it before wiping the mud from his right trouser leg.

'See anything interesting?' Andrews was making conversation. He'd watched Fuller looking bored shitless for the past hour.

'That prick Resnick can ruin his own career if he wants to, but he's not ruining mine,' Fuller snapped back.

'I remember reading about him in the *News of the World*.' Andrews was on top of all the gossip. He thought it impressed the female officers at the station. 'Suspended from duty for taking bribes. The crooked cop who took a pay-off.'

'Am I supposed to care?' Fuller snarled. He slammed the car door shut and jerked his head for Andrews to drive.

'He got two Commissioners' Commendations for bravery before he was even a sergeant,' said Andrews as he put the car in gear. 'He was a good officer.'

'Well, he's not now!' Everyone knew that Resnick's chances of promotion were scuppered – he'd kept his rank as DI by the skin of his teeth but, every time his name was mentioned for promotion, someone dragged up the dirt and he was passed over. It was only recently that DCI Saunders had persuaded the CID commander to let Resnick have an operational posting again, and he had been reluctantly given a small cold crime investigation team to run.

'Every copper associated with that chain-smoking dinosaur is seen as just as big a joke as he is. I'm not taking that lying down, Andrews, I can tell you that much.'

Fuller flipped open his ever-present notebook and stared down at the list of names he had taken at the funeral. 'Now, he's a fool chasing ghosts. Our attentions should be on the living.' As the car moved off, Fuller turned and stared at the throng of people waiting in the car park, looking for Arnie Fisher, but he had already left. Fuller frowned and tapped his book.

'Let's take a look at Rawlins' old lady's gaff, see who's at the wake to pay their last respects to that bastard.'

CHAPTER 2

Dolly sat in the plush velvet chair watching Boxer carefully pour her a brandy. He was drinking orange juice, trying to make a good impression no doubt. Why on earth had she let the big stupid idiot in? Why him, of all people? But she found his presence strangely comforting; in his own funny way he seemed genuinely moved by Harry's death. She slipped her hand down to touch Wolf, sitting as always close to her side. The tiny dog looked up and licked the tips of her fingers. She felt lonely, terribly, terribly lonely.

Boxer was a waste of space, but he'd thought a lot of Harry and considered him to be a friend. Harry wasn't Boxer's friend of course, Harry had simply chosen to look after Boxer and give him the odd handout, not because he liked him, but because he could manipulate him. Boxer followed Harry like Wolf followed Dolly; the difference was that Wolf was smart enough to realise he was truly loved back.

They drank in silence. Boxer, who was still standing, seemed ill at ease, as if unsure whether he should move his bulky body into one of the chairs. Dolly nodded and he sat down, holding his now empty glass on his knee. Dolly was tired, her head ached, she wanted him to go, but he just sat there. Eventually he coughed and touched his collar.

'They want Harry's ledgers,' he blurted out.

'They?' Dolly hid her frown as she looked at him. She was giving nothing away.

Boxer got up again and paced the room nervously. 'I'm working for the Fisher brothers now, Dolly . . . They . . . they want Harry's ledgers.'

'I don't know what you're talking about,' she replied.

'They'll pay good money for them.' Boxer's voice trembled slightly. He was trying to sound serious, but not demanding.

Dolly's apparent lack of interest was making Boxer anxious. She knew him well enough to know that making him anxious also made him careless. He'd tell her everything without even realising.

'Harry's ledgers,' Boxer continued. 'He was famous for them. He named names, Dolly, you know he did. Every lag he ever came across and maybe some he hadn't yet, but knew he would. If the filth gets hold of them ledgers, there won't be a decent villain walking the streets of London.'

'I told you, I don't know—'

Quick as lightning, Boxer was beside her, bending down, his big moon face close to hers as he pointed at her with his index finger. Dolly didn't flinch. He wasn't angry – he was frightened.

'Yes, you do! You do know! So, where are his ledgers, Doll?'

In a flash of uncontrollable anger, Dolly sprang to her feet. Boxer backed away. 'Don't you call me that, you hear me? Only Harry ever calls me that! I don't know nothing about no ledgers! And what's it got to do with the Fisher brothers anyway?'

Boxer gripped her upper arms as he desperately tried again. 'The brothers have taken over his patch. They sent me and if I go back empty-handed it'll be Tony visitin' you next, so do yourself a favour and tell me where they are!'

Dolly stepped back, face twisting with rage as she clenched her fists, nails cutting into her palms. 'I only just buried him, for Christ's sake!' For a split second, Dolly's grief surfaced at the thought of Harry being replaced so quickly by lowlifes like the Fishers.

Boxer recognised her grief instantly because he felt it himself. Suffused by guilt, his face softened. 'I'll come back.'

'I don't want nobody round here! Nobody! Get out!'

'It's all right, Dolly, don't worry. Just don't go to anyone else, OK? The Fishers wouldn't like it. I'll come back.'

'GET OUT . . . GO ON, GET OUT NOW, BOXER!' she shouted and hurled her glass at him. He ducked just in time and it shattered against the door. Raising his hands in surrender, he turned and made a hasty retreat.

As soon as the front door slammed, Dolly went over to the record player. As the heavy beautiful voice of Kathleen Ferrier filled the room, she felt her anger calm. She sang along to the record: '*What is life to me without thee? What is life if thou art dead . . .*' Suddenly she remembered the package that Eddie had given her before the funeral. Picking up her handbag, she tipped out the contents onto the floor in a jumbled mess. Dolly fell to her knees, scrambling to find the piece of paper wrapped round a set of keys, hoping and wanting it to be a message from Harry. Quickly unwrapping the note, she instantly recognised his neat writing.

Bank vault – H. R. SMITH – PASSWORD – 'HUNGERFORD'.
Sign in as Mrs H. R. SMITH

There was more written below.

Dear Doll,

Remember the day you signed at the bank with me for the deposit box? It's all yours, now. The keys are to the lock-up near Liverpool Street. You'll find some things there, but you need to get rid of them.

Harry

Dolly knelt on her plush cream carpet with Wolf by her side and clutched the paper to her chest. She read and reread it, trying to make out when it was written. There was no date, no message of love, just simple instructions. The bank vault contained the ledgers, she was sure of it. She'd always known they existed because Harry was always making lists. His mother had taught him that without the trust of contacts – criminal or legitimate – any business would fail. She had shown him how to keep a ledger, recording names, dates and purchases made, legitimate or illegitimate, and insisted he keep the ledgers safely locked away; they would be insurance against anyone who turned against him.

Dolly memorised the letter before burning it, and slipped the keys onto her own key ring. Harry would have been proud of her. As she carried Wolf up the stairs, she repeated the password over and over to herself: '*Hungerford, Hungerford.*' The name was easy to remember and the sign-in at the bank was simple, too: 'Mrs', then Harry's initials and then 'Smith'.

As she got ready for bed she wondered how much money the Fisher brothers would give to get their hands on the ledgers. She brushed her hair and then went over to the bedroom window. An unmarked police car was parked a little way down from her front gate, waiting, watching. 'Bastards,' she muttered to herself, and pulled the curtains.

CHAPTER 3

A crowd of police officers had been at Dolly Rawlins' place for nearly two days, searching every inch of the house. They had even stripped bare the little cot in the nursery and slit open the tiny mattress with a penknife. *And they think we're the animals*, she thought to herself as she held back the tears. Their dead baby's nursery, the untouched, sacred reminder of the little boy she and Harry had lost, was now soiled, tainted and dirty. She felt as if she was losing her baby all over again, but although the callous disregard for her feelings wounded her deeply, she didn't show it.

After the police had finished inside the house, they moved outside. Nothing was left unturned. The garden was dug up, the plant pots were emptied and the soil sifted through, but they found nothing. Not even a stray dry-cleaning ticket was unaccounted for.

In the lounge, all the drawers from Harry's desk had been tipped out on the floor, every letter and envelope, every picture frame pulled open. Dolly watched as they mutilated her beautiful home. She didn't speak, just watched, her body tense with anger; she knew they would find nothing. Harry was too clever, far too clever for the filth. At the sight of DC Andrews, sitting on her upturned sofa taking apart a photo frame he'd picked up from the fireplace, Dolly snapped.

'You leave that, you bastard!' She made a grab for it.

Andrews looked to Fuller, who was standing reading Dolly's private letters. Dolly turned to him.

'Tell him not to take that! It's the last photo we had taken together, on our anniversary.'

Fuller continued reading. 'Take it down the Yard,' he said to Andrews, without looking at Dolly. 'We need a recent shot of Rawlins to show the victims of this and every other unsolved armed robbery in London.'

Dolly had had enough. She picked her way through the debris strewn across her lounge, to the telephone.

'This is harassment!' she barked at Fuller. 'I want to talk to your commanding officer. What's his name?' There was no reply. 'I'll have you for this! And I want my husband's watch back . . . you hear me? I bought it for him and I want it back! It's the only thing I have left of him.'

Fuller continued to ignore Dolly, which infuriated her further. She picked up the phone. 'Your commanding officer! Who is he? I want his name!'

Now Fuller looked at her. 'Detective Inspector George Resnick,' he said with a smirk.

Dolly replaced the receiver as if it had burnt her hand. The only time she had ever seen Harry bothered was over Detective Inspector George Resnick. Determined to prove Harry's involvement in a security van raid, Resnick had turned up at the house to interview Dolly. Resnick threatened that no matter how often Dolly lied, one day he would send Harry Rawlins down for life.

Dolly had warned Harry that he needed to get Resnick sorted. 'Wouldn't it be funny,' she had said casually, 'if Resnick was the one stitched up? Imagine if everyone thought he was taking bribes and the press got hold of it?'

The following Sunday at breakfast Harry had dropped a copy of the *News of the World* on the table. Resnick's career lay in tatters on the front page. Harry had smiled at his wife and opened a bottle of champagne. They had toasted seeing the last of him.

But now it seemed Resnick was back on Harry's case, determined to sully his name now that he wasn't around to defend himself or to protect her.

'My husband's dead,' Dolly said to Fuller. 'Isn't that enough for you?'

* * *

The short squat figure of Detective Inspector George Resnick thudded down the station corridor, the inevitable cigarette stuck in his mouth, his overcoat open and a battered hat perched on the back of his head. Resnick carried a thick heavy folder under his arm and, as he passed the main detectives' offices, he flicked doors open and barked his orders without breaking stride.

'Fuller, my office pronto, bring the reports. Andrews, get me some coffee! Alice, I want those forensic reports back today!' Resnick didn't actually catch sight of anyone he shouted at – but he knew they were there and he knew he'd get what he wanted. Reaching his own office, he took his key, opened his door, entered and kicked it closed behind him, causing the already cracked glass to shudder.

Alice hurtled out of her office clutching the requested forensic reports, just as Andrews collided with Fuller in the corridor.

'The coffee machine's broken!' she said.

The colour drained from Andrews' face. This wouldn't go down well with Resnick. He scampered down the corridor in search of another one.

It was already 9.30 a.m., Fuller had been waiting since nine for his orders and, feeling tetchy, he straightened his already straight tie and tapped on Resnick's door.

'Enter!' Resnick bellowed.

Resnick's office was in its usual state of confusion. Every available surface was crammed with used coffee cups, paperwork and ashtrays full of discarded cigarette stubs; even the floor had piles of files stacked in lines. The drawers in the filing cabinet were open because they were crammed too full. Resnick stood in the centre of the chaos smoking his tenth fag of the day, coughing his lungs up and reading a file at the same time.

Alice began sorting out the mess on his desk. She worked fast, tipping cigarette stubs and ash into the bin and collecting screwed up bits of paper from all over the room. She was there to restore order to Resnick's disordered life so that, each day, he could see the woods for the trees. Without her, he'd simply drown in files and cigarette ash and piss everyone off even more than he already did. Alice had been with Resnick a long time and she knew the torment he'd been through; she'd been right by his side through every moment of his investigation, she'd seen him in those quiet vulnerable moments late at night and she understood exactly what he had lost when Rawlins set him up and then grassed him to the papers. Above all else, he lost his dignity and standing as an officer – and that was impossible to get back no matter how hard he tried. Most people in the station thought Alice was an angel to cope with Resnick's mood swings and foul habits on a daily basis, but she loved working for him. He went from role model to embarrassment in the blink of an eye and, although everyone else seemed to have forgotten his spectacular early years in the force, she never would. She would be loyal till the end. And she was the only person he ever said 'please' and 'thank you' to.

'Alice is taking my rubbish down to the incinerator to burn, Fuller,' Resnick said. 'I don't allow cleaners in here as things may go missing, be seen by the wrong people or get into the wrong hands.' Fuller blushed, wondering if Resnick was implying something.

As Alice cleared a space on the desk for the phone, it rang.

'What?' barked Resnick. He listened, growing redder by the minute, and then slammed the phone down. 'Criminal Records,' he spat. 'Up in arms cos I've "removed files without permission and without filling in the proper forms".' Resnick threw a crumpled piece of paper at Fuller. 'Fill that in and send it back to the fuckin' arseholes! And get the rest of the lads in here!'

As Fuller left the office to summon the rest of Resnick's men, Andrews arrived with the coffees. Resnick grabbed one, lit another cigarette and began his daily routine of filling his newly emptied and cleaned ashtray. Within seconds, Fuller was back with Detectives Hawkes and Richmond. As everyone settled, Fuller completed the backdated records request sheet and handed it to Alice; she'd go down there in person and smooth things over . . . again.

Resnick pulled up his chair, plonked himself down in front of his 'lads' and spread out the contents of a file on to his clean and tidy desk. Next, he opened an envelope from Forensics and tipped out a bunch of large colour photographs of the dead bodies from the raid, horribly mutilated, their faces burnt and contorted. The worst of them showed the charred remains of Harry Rawlins, unrecognisable as a human body, apart from the bit with the watch on it.

'She didn't need to have him cremated, did she?' Resnick quipped as he laid out the photographs on his desk. Leaning back in his chair he noted that Andrews looked shocked. Fuller wore his usual arrogant, unperturbed expression. Fuller was a good officer, but there was something about him that got right up Resnick's nose; even now he was sitting there as if he had a red-hot poker up his arse. Andrews, on the other hand, who was perched on the end of a desk because he couldn't find a chair, was an idiot. Hawkes and Richmond he knew of old; good, hard-working coppers but nothing exciting. Since returning to work from suspension, the top brass had not been so willing to entertain his officer selection requests, so he'd had to take the ones he was given.

Resnick eased his chair forwards, opened the previous night's reports and glanced over them. He lit yet another cigarette, inhaled deeply and blew the smoke out towards Fuller. Tapping the report, he picked up an enlarged photo of Rawlins' forearm and wristwatch. 'Says here, Fuller, you think we're spending too much time on this Rawlins business. That correct? That what you think?'

Fuller bristled and looked to Andrews for support. Resnick was on him like a flash.

'Oi, Fuller, it's you I'm talking to, not him!' He stood up. 'You think I'm wasting your time do you, Fuller? Well, let me tell you this, you narrow minded little . . .' Resnick stopped himself from swearing and leant his clenched fists on his desk to steady his anger. 'We've got the case of the century, right here, and if you can't see that then you're even more stupid than I think you are.' Fuller rolled his eyes and Resnick flew into a rage. '"Here we go again!" is that what you're thinking? You're all told within minutes of joining up, aren't you? "That's him. That's the poor sod who was framed!" Castrated more like and who did it to me, eh?'

Fuller didn't like being the target of Resnick's anger. 'One of Harry Rawlins' mob apparently, sir,' he said, through tight, angry lips.

'That's right. And not one of Harry Rawlins' mob does so much as fart without the nod from him. It was Rawlins that did me in! And now it's my turn to get him by the balls and wipe him out.'

Fuller looked Resnick straight in his raging eyes. 'It'll be a bit difficult now the man's dead.' The silence in the room and the stare between Resnick and Fuller seemed to last forever. In Fuller's opinion, Resnick was a wreck and a has-been. A bright boy, groomed for promotion, when Fuller was told he was being moved to work under Detective Inspector Resnick, he'd felt shafted. Everything about the man annoyed him; his scuffed, filthy shoes, his stained shirts, the constant smell of BO, his cigarettes and yellow smoke-stained fingers . . . Fuller had decided he'd try and sniff out anything he could on him. It shouldn't be difficult: everyone knew the fat man's history. Mud sticks, Fuller thought to himself.

Resnick rammed his hands deep into his pockets as though restraining himself from thumping this insolent subordinate. When he spoke again he was calm and quiet. 'I'm not talking about Rawlins himself, I'm talking about his system. His ledgers . . . which I'm well aware you don't believe even exist, Fuller.'

Pacing up and down behind his desk, Resnick spoke fast, spitting out his words while simultaneously gulping smoke into his lungs and blowing it out through his mouth and nose.

Resnick slapped file after file of unsolved robberies onto his desk. 'The A3 Raid, the Euston Bypass Raid, the Blackwall Tunnel Raid.' His stubby finger prodded each file as it landed. 'Take a look at the formation on the suspect vehicles, Fuller, each one's identical, and each time the men got away. We've got nothing on any of them, not a single bloody thing.' Resnick's tirade was interrupted by a coughing fit, the jowls on his face shaking, a puce colour rising upwards from his neck. 'An' you can bet your sweet life, all of 'em, every single one, was instigated by Harry Rawlins! And do you know why I think that?' Resnick paused, staring daggers at Fuller, waiting for the arrogant prick to say something smart. Wisely, Fuller chose to say nothing. 'Cat got your tongue, Fuller?' Resnick taunted. 'Let me help you out. I think Harry Rawlins was behind every single one of these unsolved armed robberies, because the MO is exactly the fucking same as the job that blew him sky high! And I also think that all of these robberies will be detailed in his ledgers.' Fuller's greedy eyes flicked from the mess of files on the desk, to Resnick's red, sweaty face. Resnick smiled. 'That's right. Dozens of crimes, just waiting to be solved. How would that look on your prissy bloody starched and ironed CV, eh?'

Resnick waddled over to a whiteboard with a sheet over it and jerked his head. Like a bunch of schoolboys, they hurriedly clustered around him.

'We solve one, we solve them all,' Resnick announced as he pulled the sheet away like a magician, revealing a detailed drawing and crime scene photographs of the failed robbery in the Strand underpass. With a red felt-tipped pen Resnick ringed a picture of a bread truck. 'A truck like this was seen by a witness in front of the security wagon.' Next he ringed the raiders' Ford Escort van. 'This is the van that exploded, killing the three men inside.' Jabbing the circled bread truck with his finger, he hammered his theory home. 'In every single one of these robberies –' Resnick pointed to the scattered files on his desk – 'they use that same formation: four men. The solo driver up front – that's the man we want. He's our link to everything else.'

Feeling Fuller's watchful eye on him, Resnick had a sudden desire to belt him one, but controlled his urge and stepped aside to leave the other officers absorbing the crime scene photographs. Helping himself to the remains of Andrews' coffee, he watched Fuller making copious notes in his CID issue pocket book, failing to notice the coffee dribbling down his own shirt front.

'Why haven't we found that driver, Fuller? Or the bread truck? It can't be difficult to trace a vehicle that size that delivers in the West End,' Resnick said. He was enjoying watching Fuller's mouth twitch with anger.

Fuller knew Resnick was trying to rile him. He struggled to hide his resentment. 'The lads have been searching night and day,' he said. 'The fact is, we only got a sketchy description of the truck from one witness. It might not even have been a bread truck – could have been any large white delivery vehicle. And, more to the point, it might have had nothing to do with the robbery.'

'Didn't you hear what I said about MO? And if you'd bother to read all the statements from the failed raid, you'd see a witness who was driving in the other lane thought the large white vehicle in front of the security van suddenly stopped. Now, why do you think that might be, Fuller?'

'Well, maybe the car in front of the supposed bread truck stopped suddenly and in turn—'

Resnick cut him off. 'The bread truck driver's our link, our only link – the one that got away! Mark my words, Fuller, that driver is part of the whole thing. He deliberately stopped suddenly to block the security van.'

Fuller wasn't going to get into an argument. 'If you say so . . . sir.'

Resnick detected the beat before Fuller said 'sir'. He let it ride but frowned. 'My gut feeling says so, Fuller. The driver of that bread truck will know everything and everyone involved, even the back-up team. Harry Rawlins was rumoured to keep details of all his crimes and associates in ledgers. If it's true, then whoever drove that truck away has to know about them and maybe even where they are. We find those ledgers and we'll clear up God knows how many robberies, and make a shedload of arrests. I want every man that ever came into contact with that bastard Rawlins questioned, along with anyone who comes within pissin' distance of his wife. I want round-the-clock surveillance on Rawlins' widow. Get it organised pronto, Fuller.'

'What about the other two widows?' Fuller asked.

Resnick caught the twitch at the right side of Fuller's mouth, but chose to ignore it. 'They're not worth following for more than a couple of days. I can't see them knowing anything of any use.'

'And the Rawlins antique shop?'

'Bollocks to it! That place is a cover, a front for funding the robberies and laundering the proceeds. The business ledgers from that place will be squeaky clean. It's his criminal ledgers I want!'

Resnick strode to his office door and farted loudly as he left, imagining that stiff prick Fuller's face twitching. Bellowing with laughter, Resnick stomped off down the corridor as they all rushed out of his office after him, holding their breath.

Back in the main CID office, Fuller grabbed hold of Andrews. 'You know Rawlins never spent a single day in the nick or got charged with anything while he was alive? All we know for sure is that he was running a legit business. If he was the man behind all those armed robberies, where's the dough? We searched Rawlins' house, we got his and his widow's personal bank details and there's nothin' – not one thing that puts him in the frame.'

Andrews nodded. 'Maybe Resnick's wrong about the bread truck driver. We've made loads of enquiries at bakeries, shops and supermarkets, so it seems strange that we haven't traced the van or its driver.'

'Course he's bloody wrong!' Fuller exploded. 'But we have to prove it to him – so get Hawkes to carry on with that and you get yourself and Richmond settled outside the Rawlins home. See what the widow's up to.'

CHAPTER 4

From behind the lace curtains of the master bedroom, Dolly checked herself in the dressing table mirror one last time. Her immaculate appearance hid a variety of emotions, all of which she had brought under control in order to do what she needed. The police in the unmarked car in the street outside couldn't see her anywhere near as well as she could see them, but right now, she needed to lose them and get to Sloane Street. Harry's safety deposit box was waiting for her. She resented their constant intrusion, their self-righteous assumption that she'd slip up in her 'weakened state' and lead them to something that could ruin Harry's name and reputation. In fact, their presence ensured the exact opposite: although Dolly was dying inside, Harry's instructions had galvanised her. By following them, she was keeping him alive.

Dolly set off confidently on one of her regular journeys to Myra's hair salon on St John's Wood Road. A glance in her mirror en route confirmed she was being followed by the unmarked car from outside her house. When she parked her Mercedes near the salon and walked down the road, she recognised Detective Constable Andrews, stuck in the middle of two women arguing as to who had seen a free meter first.

Myra's was a boutique place frequented by a very regular, well-to-do clientele. The atmosphere was 'home from home' and Dolly loved being pampered here on her twice-weekly visit. The decor was plain and elegant, and the mirrored walls allowed for easy socialising without turning your head. Myra herself was a very astute businesswoman underneath her rather brassy appearance, and Dolly was happy to pay over the odds for her service. Myra knew that cups of tea and coffee, biscuits and the odd glass of wine turned a cut and blow into an afternoon out – she earned loyalty from her clients and, in return, they earned loyalty from her.

Today, when Myra greeted Dolly at the door as she always did, Dolly got straight to the point.

'Can you do me a favour?' She handed little Wolf over. 'Take care of him for me for an hour.'

'What about your tint, Mrs Rawlins?' Myra asked.

Dolly smiled and kissed Wolf on the head. 'Don't worry. I'll pay you.' And with that, she took a headscarf from her handbag and slipped out of the back door.

At the end of the alleyway, Dolly hailed a cab on the main street. DC Andrews was still trying to find a parking space with a clear view of Myra's salon.

* * *

The corridor that led to the safety deposit boxes seemed to go on forever and every pair of eyes seemed to be on Dolly. Unnerved and strangely excited, she found herself almost swaggering along the marble floor, eyes fixed on the sharp-suited young man waiting for her at the other end. She needed to convince him – and herself – that she belonged to this world of locked-away secrets. That's all anyone ever really put into safety deposit boxes – secrets.

Dolly had only been to the bank once before, with Harry. This time she had a nervous tickle in the back of her throat as the straight-laced young clerk took her details. She was so nervous, she nearly signed her real surname by mistake.

'This way, Mrs *Smith*,' the clerk said. Dolly detected the heavy, knowing emphasis on the surname. Reaching the lift, he handed her a key and pressed the button for the basement.

When the lift doors opened, she was met by a security guard who guided her through a series of four heavy, lockable doors, each of which he locked behind them, before they got to the vault. The final door had a barred gate on the inside, which had to be unlocked separately. As the outer door was opened and the security guard searched for the key to open the internal barred gate, Dolly thought of the prison life which Harry had always so adeptly avoided. He'd been so clever and they'd been so lucky to have the life they did. For a split second, grief rose from the pit of her stomach and stopped somewhere in her throat. She felt sick. *Hurry up*, she thought to herself. *I need to sit down.*

Ushering her into the vault, the security guard showed her the bell on the desk, which would summon him when she was ready to leave. Dolly waited for him to leave the vault before she pulled out the key Eddie had given her. She slipped it into the numbered safety deposit box on the wall, and turned it. Inside was a heavy strong box.

Ten minutes later, the contents of the box were strewn on the table in front of her. She'd not had time to count the vast bundles of bank notes, although they must have totalled tens of thousands of pounds, and she left the .38 revolver concealed under the cash, untouched. It was Harry's ledgers that fascinated her.

The ledgers were bound in heavy brown leather like ones she'd seen in a Dickens play on TV. Each page was neatly handwritten, dated and labelled, with entries going back for almost the whole of her twenty-year married life. As she flicked through the pages she realised some of the names recorded were of people she knew to be dead, but it was the most recent ledger that stunned and amazed her. Page after page was filled with copious lists of names and the monies paid out to them, as well as monies stashed here, there and everywhere. The back of the ledger was filled with pasted and neatly aligned newspaper cuttings, resembling something like a film star's scrapbook of reviews. But these cuttings were detailed articles on various armed robberies Harry had obviously committed and, next to the articles, were names that Dolly suspected referred to those who had been involved in each robbery. No wonder the Fishers wanted these ledgers! They could put all the competition away for a very long time and acquire a very tidy sum of stashed cash from Harry's old jobs.

Dolly shivered slightly. She hadn't realised that Harry had organised and committed so much heavy crime. Looking at the dates, she realised that most of the robberies had taken place after her third miscarriage; then there was a lull before they picked up again after her baby boy was stillborn. This hurt her deeply, but she also understood. The untouched nursery had been a sanctuary for Dolly, who suffered bouts of depression, but Harry had never once set foot inside the beautiful, cornflower-blue room. She knew he had distracted himself from the traumas of their personal life by throwing himself into his work; but she'd thought he was away at antiques auctions. He hadn't exactly lied, but he had allowed her to misunderstand exactly what 'work' he was throwing himself into.

Dolly continued to flick through the last ledger – and stopped, shattered. There, in Harry's neat, immaculate handwriting, were the detailed plans for the raid in which he died. Dolly saw the number of guns required, the vehicles to be used and the names and contact numbers for Joe Pirelli, Terry Miller and the security firm insider. The names Pirelli and Miller both rang a bell with Dolly. They'd been at some event or other with their respective wives – respective widows, now. For a second Dolly wondered what the two women were doing right now, subconsciously allowing herself a smile. *Well, they won't be doing what I'm doing*, she thought to herself.

The meticulously detailed plans, drawings and directions for the robbery read like the script for a play. She couldn't quite believe that a man so reluctant to pick up his dirty clothes from the bedroom floor could be so organised when it came to robbing an armed security wagon . . . but then, there was nothing life or death about laundry. Suddenly she remembered Harry's blackened wristwatch. Feeling sickened, she slowly shut the book. Within seconds, she'd opened it again, now turning the pages rapidly to see what Harry had planned for their future, desperate to find out all the secrets she could about the man she loved.

'My God,' she whispered to Harry as she read his words, 'you even worked out crimes as far ahead as '86!' As the scope of his plans sank in, Dolly looked at her watch. An hour had gone by since she'd left the hairdressers and she knew she had to go.

In the taxi on the way back to Myra's, Dolly made copious notes in her small black Gucci diary of what she had read in the ledger about the failed robbery. She used her own shorthand, just in case the coppers watching her ever fancied a random 'stop and search'.

Dolly snuck back into Myra's the way she had gone out. From inside the salon, she spotted one of the detectives approaching the front door. Thinking quickly, she pulled off her coat, grabbed a magazine and sat down under the hairdryer just as the officer entered the salon. Dolly smiled sweetly at him then, as he walked out looking embarrassed, got out the diary to read over what she'd written.

CHAPTER 5

Arnie Fisher was in a fury, the sort of fury that used to get him shut in a cupboard as a little boy. His hard blue eyes flickered with anger, and spittle foamed at the side of his thin lips as he paced around his enormous desk. He wore a pale grey suit, immaculate, handmade grey shoes and a silk blue-grey tie, which was now pulled halfway round his neck. He pulled out one of the desk drawers and threw it across the room.

Arnie had just had his Soho office on Berwick Street redecorated; the velvet wallpaper and plush carpet were now a matching snooker-table green. He'd also ordered new furniture: two heavy brown leather sofas, a brown mahogany bookcase and a matching cabriole-legged coffee table. The log-effect gas fire was half in, half out of its hole, waiting to be connected to the gas supply. A chandelier, yet to be fitted, balanced precariously on the edge of the coffee table, and stacked on the floor next to it was a collection of sporting prints waiting to be placed on the green walls. In his efforts to be tasteful, Arnie had created a hideous, gloomy room. He'd even had an en suite bathroom fitted with a dark green bath, green wash basin and gold taps. The bidet he'd wanted had had to be abandoned because there wasn't enough room. Arnie was moving up in the world: new office, new patch – once he'd got his hands on the Rawlins' ledgers, there'd be no stopping him.

The en suite toilet flushed and his brother Tony came out, doing up his flies and rearranging his balls. He never washed his hands.

'Who did you get to do this?' Arnie asked, pointing to his desk.

'Do what?'

Arnie slapped his hand down on the desk. 'I said I wanted it French polished! It's a bleedin' antique. Some ham-fisted git's only gone and bloody varnished it!'

Spittle shot out of his mouth and he dabbed it with a crumpled silk handkerchief. He repeatedly banged his hand on the desk, venting his fury. Then, he removed a biro from his pocket and, gripping it like a knife, scratched a deep mark across the surface.

Tony shrugged, unmoved by Arnie's rage. 'It only cost a ton to do up,' he said. 'You should be grateful!'

Arnie pulled out another drawer and flung it across the room, missing Tony's head by inches. Tony didn't give a toss. He never worried when Arnie threw a right old wobbler. It always blew over. The only time you needed to be worried or cautious where his brother was concerned was when he was nice to you, when he smiled that strange, thin-lipped, tight smile. Right now, his teeth were chomping up and down like a donkey's. Tony left the room as Boxer entered.

Arnie got himself back in control, rubbing his hand gently up and down the varnished antique desk. 'Look at this, Boxer. This desk is inlaid and that idiot gets some . . .' Arnie stopped himself before he got angry again. 'He's got no class, my brother. No eye for beautiful things.' Boxer was just as ignorant as Tony, of course, but at least he had the decency to look sorry. Arnie sat back in his leather-studded chair and folded his arms behind his head.

'So, what've you got for me, Boxer?' he asked.

'Not a lot, Mr Fisher. I told her you were willing to pay good money for Harry's ledgers, but she didn't even flinch. If you ask me, she doesn't know where they are.'

'I'm not asking you!' Arnie snapped. Tony slipped back into the room to see if everything was all right.

'If you give me a bit more time, Mr Fisher, I'll try again. She's still very upset. It'll be easier to talk to her when she's calmer.' Tony was standing very close to Boxer's right shoulder now, practically staring down his ear as he listened to Boxer's feeble excuses. He was dying to interrupt, to intimidate and bully this weak and pathetic man. Boxer stood with his head bent, shuffling his feet.

'Is that it?' Tony asked as he closed in even further on Boxer.

Arnie raised his hand – just a flick, but it was enough for Tony to keep quiet. Then he jerked his head. Tony was about to stand his ground, but he saw that tight nasty smile, thought better of it and left the room.

Boxer shifted his weight from one foot to the other. He was scared of Arnie; he hated himself for it, but the nasty little queen gave him the runs. You just never knew where you stood with him. Tony was different. A real womaniser who would screw anything if it had all its limbs, he was quick to use his fists if he felt it necessary. At times he was punch-crazy – but at least you could see it coming with Tony. Arnie's stare was far more terrifying.

'Time, Boxer, is something I may not have,' said Arnie. 'You do understand what might be in those ledgers, don't you?'

'I do. I do know, Mr Fisher, and I am doing my very best for you.'

'Your very best is shit. When exactly did you have this pointless conversation with Dolly Rawlins? I sent you there days ago.'

Boxer stuttered his way through another excuse. 'I didn't want to come back with nothing, Mr Fisher. I was trying to think of another way to get her to co-operate, you see. I didn't come up with nothin', so I thought I'd better come round and tell it like it is. I told her straight though . . . I said: "Don't you go to anyone else cos Mr Fisher'll be very angry." She won't do anything stupid, honest she won't.'

One raised finger from Arnie and Boxer fell silent, like a terrified dog with a bullying owner.

'You're gettin' your knickers in a right tiswas, ain't ya, Boxer? Job too much for you, is it? Can't you handle it? Want Tony to take over with Dolly Rawlins, do you? Eh?'

Boxer knew exactly what Tony would do if he got given the job of getting Dolly to talk. 'No, don't do that, Mr Fisher. Let me speak to Dolly again. Please!'

Arnie removed his glasses and began polishing them slowly. 'You asked for more time and I'm going to give it to you. You got two weeks, my old son, two weeks. If you don't come up with the ledgers by then I'll send Tony in to see to the widow, an' you know how Tony likes the ladies, don't you?'

The phone rang, Arnie picked it up and instantly went all coy, wriggling his body. 'Hello, Carlos. I'm fine, darlin', I'm fine. Hang on a sec – piss off then, Boxer, and remember this: if anyone's named in them ledgers for sure, it's you. You used to work for the bastard. Now get out before I set Tony on ya.'

As Boxer scurried across the office, his slow brain churned over what Arnie had just said. He was right. It would be in his interest to get those ledgers. He'd acted as a 'hammer man' for Harry on a couple of robberies. Boxer decided that he'd go and see Dolly again that night, whether she liked it or not. He quietly closed the door to Arnie's office and moved down the staircase into the club. It was dark, seedy in the daytime as well as at night; the strong smell of stale cigarette and cigar smoke mixed with beer clung to the red velvet curtains. It was pungent and sickening.

Tony Fisher loitered at the bottom of the stairs. He'd have a bit of fun with poor old Boxer. 'Arthur Negus of the *Antiques Roadshow* calmed down, 'as he?'

Boxer started to skirt round Tony nervously. Tony stepped in front of him and put his fists up in a boxer's stance. 'Come on, Boxer, come on . . . show me your mettle!'

Boxer put his fists up half-heartedly, Tony slammed him one, hard below the waist. He buckled, holding his belly and gasping for air.

Tony leant over him menacingly. 'You're losing your touch, sunshine,' he said, and laughing his guts out, he ran back up the stairs. Boxer felt like puking his up.

CHAPTER 6

Dolly stood behind the net curtain in the darkness of her bedroom, once again watching the filth watching her. The same unmarked police car that had followed her to the hairdressers was parked not far up the road. She smiled to herself and looked across at Wolf, who was curled up on the bed watching her. 'Fancy parking under a street lamp,' she cooed at her little baby. 'We can see his stupid, bored face, can't we?' One of the plain-clothed men got out of the car and walked off, leaving Andrews slumped in the passenger seat. Dolly's smile dropped and she headed downstairs, Wolf at her heels.

DC Andrews desperately tried to focus on Dolly as she left the house. With just a coat slung over her shoulder and no handbag, she was obviously taking her little dog for a walk. Andrews yawned. Surveillance was tiring. Ahead of him, he could see Dolly as she strolled along the pavement, repeatedly stopping while the tiny dog cocked his leg on every tree, wall and lamp post. Reaching the corner, he turned right out of sight. Dolly stood, hands on hips, with her back to Andrews. She clapped her hands: 'Come here! Wolf – come here!'

Andrews smiled to himself. Dolly wasn't exactly the commanding voice of Barbara Woodhouse, the TV dog trainer. 'If you're the wife of a master criminal,' he whispered, 'I'm a monkey's uncle.'

Dolly followed the dog round the corner. Andrews thought briefly about getting out and following her on foot, but it was cold, and she was just fetching the dog. However, when she had still not returned after a minute, he became alarmed, got out of the car and ran to where he had last seen Dolly. 'Christ!' he said, squeezing the word out through clenched teeth. Dolly and Wolf were nowhere to be seen. He ran back towards the car just as his colleague, DC Richmond, approached with two cheeseburgers and milkshakes.

'You seen her?' Andrews was flustered.

'Who?' Then Richmond realised and sniggered. 'Don't tell me you've lost an old woman and a pooch?'

'Do you think Resnick'll give a shit which one of us was watching her and which one was taking an unscheduled burger break?'

Richmond got the message loud and clear, threw the incriminating food and drink into the nearest garden and jumped in the car. 'I'll drive,' he said. 'We'll find her.'

* * *

Dolly and Wolf had melted into a stag party crowd at the top end of Barnet Road and then she'd hailed a cab towards Liverpool Street Station. As the cab drove south, Richmond's unmarked police car passed them going the other way, doing a circuit of the immediate area. Dolly smiled as she stroked little Wolf, who was curled up by her side. She could feel the adrenalin coursing through her body. She liked the way it made her feel close to her Harry.

In the rear-view mirror, the cabbie watched the way her eyes had followed Richmond's car as it passed. He'd had enough people in the back of his cab to know that Dolly was either on the wrong side of the law or was on her way home to her husband after an evening with her lover – and Dolly's age suggested to him that she was dabbling in criminality.

Unaware of being watched, Dolly was mumbling to herself: 'We showed him, Wolf, didn't we, darling? Yes, we did. We showed him!'

At Liverpool Street Station, Dolly paid with the exact change, cash she'd put into her coat pocket for speed. Preparation would be everything from here on in. After a quick look round to make certain she hadn't been followed, Dolly carried Wolf down the backstreets to the big arches behind the station. Here, there was a row of lock-ups, mostly used by British Rail for storage, but others hired out to car mechanics for repairs and MOTs.

The alley was dark and dingy with no external lighting, and cold, each building shading the next from natural daylight. Dolly slowly progressed down the line of archways. She took her time; she couldn't see what she might be stepping in, and her eyes had to adjust to the darkness. She was looking for number fifteen. Some arches had no doors on them and the insides were huge caverns of dripping water, cold, damp and musky-smelling like underground cellars. Old, wrecked and rusting cars stood silent like ghosts of the past, windscreens shattered, wheels gone and doors left open. She passed wrecked car after wrecked car, getting more and more filthy, and laddering her tights on a jagged old bumper. In one unused archway, a group of winos lay in a drunken stupor by a makeshift fire in an old dustbin. They remained oblivious to her presence as she walked past.

Eventually Dolly stopped by a green sliding door. Removing the keys Harry had left her from her coat pocket, she tried one of them in the padlock. She almost dropped Wolf when the doors suddenly moved towards her an inch or two and a dog with a terrifying growl and a high-pitched bark slammed into the door from the inside. Wolf began to bark, making the dog behind the doors even more aggressive. Dolly covered Wolf's mouth with her hand; she could hear the dog's chains rattle as it continued to hurl itself frantically against the door. She peered upwards and realised she was at number thirteen. Scuttling towards the next archway, she hoped the dog hadn't attracted attention.

A faded and grimy number '15' was scratched into the paintwork of a small entrance door built into the larger wooden doors of the lock-up. Harry's secret place. Dolly tried one key, then another and the small door swung open.

Inside the large, cavernous room, it was eerily silent until the echoing thunder from the trains above filled the space. Dolly closed the door behind her, put Wolf down and switched on a small pocket torch.

By the light of the thin beam she slowly edged forwards and, as Wolf sniffed about by the old ghost cars, wagging his tail, she felt sure he could smell Harry. He seemed so excited at the prospect of seeing his master again. When Wolf looked up at her as if to ask: 'so, where is he?' her heart sank and she felt Harry's loss all over again.

This was a 'man's place', a million miles from the pristine opulence of their Potters Bar home. She could almost smell the sweat and the hard work and the testosterone as she imagined Harry's men hanging on his every word while he held court. For what seemed like an age, Dolly couldn't move; she'd never been to this lock-up and she was frightened of what she might find hidden deep in the darkness. Dolly had lived with the knowledge that she'd find out some secret about Harry one day, but she always imagined it would be a younger lover. He was so incredibly handsome and even the best men in the world are suckers for flattery. But what was inside this lock-up . . . this was a big secret to keep.

As she ventured forwards, eyes focused on the furthest dark corner, she didn't see the puddle filled with thick, slimy, oil-streaked mud and swore as she felt some of the brown water seep onto her feet. She looked down at her ruined shoes and saw Wolf sitting in the middle of the puddle, tail wagging. His little paws now had black, oily 'socks'.

Dolly made her way to the back of the garage, towards a set of large wooden interior doors, also with a smaller interlocking door. Opening it, Dolly switched on the overhead neon strip lights. As they blinked into life, she was surprised to see the annexe was much cleaner than the rest of the lock-up. A couple of old wrecks had been pushed against the wall and, in the centre of the room was a medium-sized van covered with a tarpaulin. As she pulled off the tarpaulin her hand slipped and she winced as she broke a nail. Wolf darted under the van and began frantically digging at the floor – Dolly knelt beside him, ripping her tights again, and looked where he was digging.

Below the loose concrete were slats of wood. Lifting them away, she revealed a two-foot by one-foot hole in the ground containing something wrapped in brown sacking. She hauled the package out and opened it to find two sawn-off shotguns. The handgun in

Harry's safety deposit box was the first time she'd known for certain that he'd used guns, but it hadn't been a shock to her. In fact, her pulse had raced at the thought that he'd left her something to protect herself with, even after he'd gone. But these guns. These guns were different. These guns weren't for protection, they were for committing armed robberies. In that moment, Dolly felt closer to Harry than she'd done at any other moment since his death. He'd given her the keys to this place and was allowing her, at long last, to know everything. What Dolly now did with all of this information was up to her and her alone.

Without touching the shotguns, Dolly wrapped and replaced them in their hole in the ground. She slowly stood. *It's all here*, she thought as she looked around; everything Harry used in his robberies – the cars, the vans, the cutting tools, the gloves, the shotguns. This was all hers now. Dolly reached into the pocket of her oil-stained coat, brought out her diary and opened it to the page of shorthand notes she'd made after leaving the bank. Everything Harry needed to commit the next robbery was in those ledgers, in her diary and in this lock-up. She clicked her pen open and drew a strong, bold tick next to her note, '2 S-O'; two sawn-offs. As she smiled down at that tick, she could almost feel Harry smiling with her . . . 'that's my girl,' he'd say.

Dolly walked through the cavernous, dank, warehouse. It was enormous. She headed towards a small room at the far end, which looked as though it had been built out of old partitions from a legal office. The once polished wood was now badly peeling and the cracked windows were cobwebbed and dusty. She turned the handle on the grubby door and stepped inside. Looking down at her hand, she saw that she'd picked up oily fingerprints in almost the exact same pattern as her own. She imaged they were Harry's actual fingertips touching hers.

The office was stark: a sink and a small Calor gas stove, a desk, a couple of wooden, mismatched chairs and numerous girlie pictures stuck to the wall. Used mugs and mouldy half-eaten biscuits told Dolly that this was where Harry and his team must have planned the robbery that went so terribly wrong. Dolly picked up the dirty mugs and took them over to the filthy sink. She turned the taps on and they made a knocking sound as the pressure built, trying to force the water through the pipes. Suddenly a brown rusty liquid spurted out, bouncing off the porcelain and onto her coat, causing her to jump back. She dropped the mugs into the sink, cracking two and snapping the handle off the third – three broken mugs: Harry's, Terry's and Joe's. The tears Dolly had held just beneath the surface for so long welled up and, in the privacy of Harry's office, she allowed them to flow. The relief was so overwhelming that she felt lightheaded and weak, gripping the sink for support. She fought the emotions but it was no good, the floodgates were opened and there was no closing them. Her devastating sadness at losing Harry was sapping her strength and she struggled to keep herself upright as she gripped the cold porcelain sink. With her head bowed, she could see Wolf sitting at her muddy, oily feet and she suddenly remembered a moment when Boxer had been at his lowest ebb, living in the gutter, and Harry had pulled him out. 'All I see is dog shit,' Boxer had said to Harry through his drunken haze. 'Wherever I look, all I see is dog shit.' Harry had lifted Boxer's head and replied, 'Then look up, Boxer, my old mate. If your head's down, dog shit's all you *can* see. So, look up.' Of course Harry hadn't been Boxer's mate at all, but he always knew the right thing to say.

When Dolly finally lifted her head, the tears had stopped and Wolf was on his feet waiting for her next move. She glanced one last time at the three broken mugs, picked up her little dog and squeezed him tight, ignoring his dirty, muddy, oily fur. 'All right, darlin',' she whispered. 'Mummy's all right now. Everything's all right now.'

CHAPTER 7

Linda arrived on the dot of ten at the Sanctuary health spa in Floral Street and instantly realised that her very best clobber, which she'd ironed specially after getting Dolly's phone call, didn't even come close to the fabulous clothes the other women were wearing as they floated by. *They've probably never done a day's work in their lives*, she thought and was just about to walk out when the snooty receptionist asked if she was the guest of a member. When Linda mentioned the name of Mrs Rawlins, she was welcomed with open arms.

On the obligatory guided tour, Linda didn't know where to look. She'd never seen so many half-naked women before and she didn't like it. The changing rooms were the worst: everything came off in there and people just strolled about as though they were at home. In fact, Linda didn't even walk around naked at home in case the window cleaner saw in through her nets or the bailiffs knocked.

The prices in the food bar were extortionate and she thought about nipping out to the cafe opposite for a bacon sarnie and coffee, but the assistant told her that all she had to do was mention the name of Mrs Rawlins and anything could go on the tab. Linda shrugged. She wasn't used to getting something for nothing.

'Go on, then,' she said, pointing at a sandwich. Cheese would have to do.

Sandwich in hand, Linda was led back to the dreaded changing rooms, where she was left to fend for herself. She stood there, fully clothed, feeling like a right idiot, trying not to look at all the bums and tits brazenly walking by. She couldn't cope for long and, head down, she walked swiftly out.

As she wandered round the gym, Linda glanced over at the exercise bikes. At first she hardly recognised Shirley, she looked so thin and worn out, but it was her all right. Linda started to wander over but was stopped by one of the attendants who informed her she was not allowed in the exercise area without the right clothes.

'Oi!' Linda shouted at Shirley. 'Feelin' peckish?'

Shirley turned and, recognising Linda, stopped pedalling. Linda bustled past the attendant. The women didn't hug as neither seemed certain that was the right thing to do, so Linda just said, 'Been a while, ain't it?'

They quickly established that they had last spoken at a cocktail party somewhere or other about two years previously. Linda's memory of events was nowhere near as clear as Shirley's due to the free bar, but Shirley filled in the blanks. The bottom line was that the cocktail party had been a Harry Rawlins do – and it was Dolly Rawlins who had called them both out of the blue and told them to meet her here.

Neither Shirley nor Linda knew exactly why they'd been summoned, but they both hoped it was to do with a handout of cash; they couldn't even begin to imagine what else it might be.

'Well, whatever the reason,' said Shirley, 'I'm going to enjoy the spa facilities while I can. Come on!' She headed for the changing rooms, coyly followed by Linda.

Shirley quickly changed into the fluffy white towel provided while Linda, trying and failing to look at ease, focused on her chipped nails, avoiding eye contact with anyone and everyone. Shirley handed her a towel. 'Relax – Dolly's paying,' she said kindly.

Linda had forgotten how beautiful Shirley was, how easily elegant and womanly. Even under a square towel, Shirley was a stunning shape, with her hair and make-up immaculate. Linda wasn't going to let Shirley see how insecure she was so she attempted to make a joke.

'I don't want to drive the fellas wild by exposing my body, Shirl.'

'It's only women here.'

Defeated, Linda snatched the towel from Shirley. 'Well, I'm not taking my bra and knickers off. They might get nicked!' she snapped as she bundled into a cubicle for some privacy. When Linda bent to remove her shoes, she could see the now seated Shirley looking in at her. 'Bleedin' 'ell!' Linda's dulcet tones echoed round the changing room. 'What's the point in having a soddin' door that stops two foot off the ground!' When Linda stood back up, she was head and shoulders above the top of the door and Shirley couldn't stifle her giggles. 'It's like getting changed behind a postage stamp! I might as well be out there with you!' Linda draped her arms over the top of the door and the two women howled with laughter for the first time since they'd heard the news.

By 11.30 a.m., Shirley was relaxing with her eyes closed in the bubbling, milky water of the jacuzzi and Linda was sitting on the edge, warming her feet and ankles. Her red satin bra was visible above the white towel and she'd dropped crumbs into the water from the cheese sarnie – but she didn't care.

'A good screw is as good as an hour's exercise, did you know that? And it don't cost you an annual membership fee, I can tell you,' Linda laughed at herself as she stuffed the last of her sandwich into her mouth and washed her hands in the jacuzzi. 'Course you can't just lie there and take it, you've got to do some of the work.'

'Don't you ever talk about anything else?'

'Well, I'm not getting any, am I? Me and Joe were at it pretty much every night.' Linda's mood dipped as she remembered her husband. 'There's a lot of adjusting to be done, I can tell you.'

Shirley opened one eye and glared at Linda. Was being celibate for a month really the biggest adjustment after your husband's been blown sky high in a botched bank job?

By midday, Dolly still hadn't appeared and Linda was getting tetchy. Shirley was now naked on the sunbeds and Linda was sitting by her side sipping coffee, eating a chocolate bar and moaning about the money.

'If she's a no-show, I've spent a bloody fortune on food I didn't even want! I'm fatter now than when I arrived! Some bleedin' health spa this is.'

'She'll be here. Keep your voice down,' Shirley whispered. She'd forgotten quite how embarrassing Linda could be sometimes, even when she wasn't drinking. In fact, Shirley had wondered if Linda had sneaked a drop of vodka into her coffee because she was definitely getting louder. Twice she had fed bits of biscuit to the parrots that were in cages hanging from huge fern plants. The attendants had asked her not to, but she'd ignored them. She'd also been making loud remarks and laughing at some of the women's figures, calling them 'stick insects'.

Linda hadn't meant to embarrass Shirley, but could see that she had. The truth was that Linda felt totally out of her depth in these elegant surroundings. She looked around: these women were all self-indulgent, toffee-nosed, snooty, skinny bitches with more money than they knew what to do with. She was about to leave when she saw Dolly walking casually towards them wearing a matching bath towel and turban. Dolly nodded her acknowledgement to a couple of attendants as she moved up the steps towards the sunbeds. 'Gawd almighty,' Linda snorted to Shirley and jabbed her with an elbow, 'Lana Turner's alive and well and living in London – take a look.'

'Hello, Linda, hello, Shirley. I'm sorry I didn't send no flowers. Not in the rule book,' Dolly said with a smile. Linda chewed her lip. Dolly's *Watch with Mother* voice and glib reference to their husbands' funerals instantly annoyed her. It was hardly appropriate as an opening line. Linda would have preferred: 'How are you?' or, 'Long time, no see,' or, 'So sorry that my husband got your husband killed!'

'Let's go into the sauna – we won't be disturbed there,' Dolly said and walked off ahead of them. Shirley and Linda followed Dolly in exactly the same obedient manner as Wolf – as though they instinctively knew that following would be more beneficial to them than not.

Linda had never been in a sauna before. She was sweating profusely and worried that the colour would run from her red satin bra and show through the pristine white towel. Shirley, who was well used to saunas, immediately lay flat out along the top bench.

'How are you both?' Dolly asked, as though it was the most innocent question in the world. Nothing Dolly did was innocent anymore – and knowing what she did now, she wanted to find out a little more about these widows before sharing her latest thoughts. Dolly had also remembered the cocktail party from two years ago. It had been brimming with villains from the four corners of London. If she was totally honest, Dolly hadn't remembered Shirley and didn't recall her saying a word all night; Linda, on the other hand, had been entirely memorable.

'Terry didn't leave any cash for the mortgage, so if I don't win Miss Paddington next week, I'm going to have to get a job.' Shirley seemed genuinely distressed by this; but then she was a girl in her mid-twenties with no education and no real life skills. She'd always been looked after and had no clue how to survive on her own.

'My heart bleeds,' Linda mocked. 'Try doing three jobs at once. That's how many I had when Joe was inside the last time. And what the fuck is Miss Paddington?'

'Oh, it's a beauty contest!' Shirley beamed as she explained. 'Mum entered me for it. I was ever so mad at her at first, cos of just losing Terry. But there's a thousand pounds prize money for first place and a holiday for two in Majorca. And the winner goes forward into the next Miss England competition!'

'Then Miss World I suppose?' Dolly said, her sarcastic tone unnoticed by Shirley.

'That's right.' Shirley's eyes glazed over as she dared to dream. 'This could be the start of something big for me.'

Dolly turned her attention to Linda. 'And how are you now?'

'Well, you know Joe. Easy come, easy go. God, it's bleedin' hot in here.'

Dolly poured more water on the coals, adding to Linda's discomfort. 'Sit low down. It's hotter if you stand or lie on the higher seats.'

The casual chat was over. Dolly moved on to why she had brought them both here.

'You know the Fisher brothers have taken over Harry's patch, don't you?'

'I heard the rumour,' Linda panted as she began to overheat.

'You had any trouble from them?'

'Not from them, no,' Linda confirmed. 'The pigs did my place over though and they're a real pain in the arse, keep hanging round the arcade. If they don't leave off, I'll get the sack.'

Dolly glanced at Shirley and raised her eyebrows.

'They've done my place over four times,' said Shirley. 'I've not seen the Fishers though.'

Linda, for now, wasn't remotely curious about Dolly's questions. She was just focused on not melting. 'God, it's boiling in here. Is it meant to be good for you?'

Shirley wasn't good with many topics, but she knew about spas. 'Saunas are designed to sweat out all of the impurities from your body,' she explained.

'I can think of a better way—' began Linda. Dolly held up her hand to interrupt.

'Now look – I want to talk to you both. The Fisher brothers and the law are sniffing around for information.'

Linda tried one last joke. 'And I thought they just fancied me . . .' She saw a tiny, split-second smile appear on Dolly's face before it disappeared again behind tight lips and unreadable eyes.

'You know how Harry worked,' Dolly continued. 'He kept records of everyone who ever worked for him. He listed names; informants, gun merchants, bankers. Money in, cash paid out. All logged and dated. He used his books, his ledgers, as protection if anyone grassed or cheated on him.'

'I dunno what you're talking about, Doll,' Linda said, feeling a bit dizzy from the heat.

'Then listen!' Dolly snapped. 'And don't call me that. I don't like it. The Fisher Brothers want Harry's ledgers.'

'Why?' Shirley asked.

'I reckon it's cos they're named inside, along with their dodgy deals, and they're scared that if the law gets their hands on 'em they'll be in big trouble.'

'Who's got them?' Considering that Shirley wasn't the sharpest girl in the sauna, Dolly was impressed that she was the one asking the sensible questions.

'I have,' Dolly said calmly. As she began to explain, she spoke slowly and deliberately, emphasising every word so the women couldn't possibly misunderstand. Shirley visibly hung on Dolly's every word, while Linda tipped her head back, closed her eyes and quietly listened, still panting a little in the unbearable heat. 'Harry always said that if anything ever happened to him, he wanted me to be all right. He wanted his team to take over and look after all of us. One time he joked that if he died, as long as his team had the ledgers they could run the business without him. But Joe and Terry went with him, so it's up to me now. I'm going to look after us. I'm going to look after all of us. Just like Harry wanted.'

Dolly, with hardly a bead of sweat on her, looked at Shirley's attentive face. She wasn't entirely sure if Shirley knew what on earth she was talking about, but at least she seemed to be listening. Then Linda sat bolt upright.

'I can't stand this heat much longer, I'm flaking out!' she said.

Dolly glared at Linda, a look of seething fury on her face. Here she was, bearing her soul and Linda didn't even have the decency to listen. She got up, gathered her towel around her and stormed out before she did something stupid, like shove Linda's head in the sauna coals.

'What did I do wrong?' Linda asked Shirley. But the look on Shirley's face was just as angry as Dolly's.

'Can't you see she's upset?' Shirley said. 'It must have been terrible for her, even worse than it was for us. Her old man was blown to bits and unrecognisable. They'd been married for twenty years.'

Linda jumped up from the bench. 'An' I ain't upset, is that it? Just cos I don't show it, don't mean I don't feel things.'

Shirley tried to calm Linda, but she wasn't having any of it, pacing and threatening to give Dolly a piece of her mind. She could easily have left the sauna and gone after Dolly, so Shirley thought it was all bravado – and then suddenly Linda stopped shouting and crumpled up on the seat, hugging her knees and burying her face in her hands. She spoke in a muffled voice.

'I had a shower this morning and got soap in me eyes. When I tried to grab a towel from the hook on the door I picked up his dressing gown instead. I could smell him, I could still smell his body, it was as if he was right there with me again, but it was just his dressing gown . . .' Linda broke down and sobbed.

Shirley's mouth twitched as she felt the tears welling up in her, and the next minute she too was sobbing, thinking of all the things in her flat that reminded her of Terry.

When Dolly re-entered she found the pair of them in floods of tears, hugging each other. Dolly tried to keep herself in check, but then she started crying too. This was the first time Dolly had cried properly in front of anyone, but she didn't care. It seemed OK to share her grief with the other widows; she wasn't embarrassed or worried that they'd see her as weak. She instinctively trusted them, and this was a momentous thing for Dolly to do with anyone. Trust. This was what she needed.

The tension eased and Dolly started the conversation again.

'When I asked you here, I wasn't sure how much I was going to say. But now I am. We've got two options regarding Harry's ledgers—'

'We?' Linda interrupted. At Dolly's slight smile she quietened down and began to listen.

'Harry planned jobs months in advance, all written down, so if the Fishers got their hands on the ledgers, they could stay on top. Just like Harry did. So, option one is that we sell the ledgers to the Fishers and they would offer us a percentage of anything they make. Or option two, if we don't sell –' Dolly took a deep breath as Shirley and Linda leant in closer – 'we pull the big job Harry had lined up.'

Linda started to laugh hysterically. Shirley sat with her mouth open.

'You are joking?' Linda stuttered.

'If you don't want to do it, that's fine. But I can't do it on my own, so I'd have to sell and the Fishers are cheap double-crossing villains and will no doubt stitch me up.'

'We can't do an armed robbery, Dolly,' Shirley whispered.

'Yes, we can. We can finish what our men started. It was a good plan that would have worked if they hadn't used explosives.'

Linda and Shirley glanced at each other, not knowing how to respond. Was Dolly mad? Had grief tipped her over the edge?

Dolly continued, slowly and calmly, 'I could have sold the ledgers without telling you and avoided a three-way split, but I want to do right by you as Harry always did right by Joe and Terry . . . And this job is right.' Dolly hit them with her killer blow. 'If you don't want to do it, I understand. I'll do my best to get a couple of grand each for us off the Fishers. Then they can do the job Harry was planning and pocket the million quid.'

'A million quid?' Shirley shouted before slamming her hand over her mouth.

Linda, streetwise and sharp as a tack, knew that if something sounded too good to be true, it probably was. She was married to Joe long enough to realise that a million-quid job would be dangerous. She smiled and shook her head. 'Do us a favour, Mrs Rawlins, what do you take us for . . . a pair of mugs?'

'Far from it,' said Dolly. 'We're more similar than we are different, Linda. I know what you're feeling inside right now and I know how to make that better. One last job. For our men, yes. But for us, more. This is your ticket out of struggling in shooting galleries for less than half you're worth, and you –' Dolly said, looking at Shirley – 'you'd never have to work a day in your life.'

A panicked Shirley piped up, 'I don't want to leave London.'

'You won't have to, love. No one will know it's us. I know exactly what to do.'

Dolly could see Shirley and Linda faltering, so pushed them a little closer to the decision she wanted. 'You think your Terry and your Joe left you with nothing? They didn't. They left you with me. Me, the ledgers and their next job. We were never just the little women sitting at home. We know what they did. We know why they did it. Harry led me to his ledgers for a reason – and that reason is us. He didn't want us to be alone and he didn't want us to struggle. We deserve this, ladies.' Dolly stood up. 'Just think about it. I wouldn't have suggested it if I didn't think we could do it. And I'll pay all your outgoings before the job in ready cash.'

Linda and Shirley sat open-mouthed and mute. Dolly could almost hear the cogs turning as they weighed up their options.

'I'll contact you again in two days,' she said. 'Don't try and get in touch with me. I'm being watched by the Old Bill and they might have my phone tapped. They're the reason I didn't turn up here at the same time as you. I don't want us seen together, so make sure you leave separately, and at least twenty minutes after me.'

And she was gone.

Linda and Shirley sat in exactly the same position, wearing exactly the same vacant facial expressions, for what seemed like ten minutes. Then Linda spoke.

'She's off her trolley.'

'Should we tell someone?'

'No one would believe us.'

CHAPTER 8

Dolly had been driving around for ages, to White City and back, trying to lose the plain-clothes officers in their unmarked car, but they were still on her tail. 'Damn you!' she shouted out loud as she looked again in her rear-view mirror. No matter how many turns or side roads she took, she just couldn't lose them. When she'd called a couple of days after the spa, both Linda and Shirley had agreed to meet up and hear more. And now all three of them had planned to get together. Dolly didn't want to be late – but what could she do? Unless she was 100 per cent certain that she wasn't being followed, she simply couldn't risk meeting or contacting the other widows in any way.

Dolly remembered a film she'd once seen and smiled to herself wondering if maybe, just maybe, the same ruse would work for her. She started to accelerate and sped round Shepherd's Bush roundabout, then headed along Notting Hill Gate, straight down Bayswater Road towards Marble Arch. They were still there, still behind her. She zipped in and out of the line of traffic, then took a right turn towards Hyde Park, keeping in the inside lane. Glancing in her rear-view mirror, she could see the police tail about four cars behind. She overtook a heavy goods vehicle that was on her inside, then nipped in front of it and turned sharply into the drop-off entrance of the Dorchester Hotel. She was out of her car in seconds with Wolf under her arm. She handed the doorman the keys and a £10 note.

'Park it, darlin'. Be back in an hour or so after dinner.' And she whisked into the Dorchester.

The doorman went over to the Merc, got into the driver's seat and was about to start the engine when he saw a blue flashing light in the front grille of the car behind him. DC Andrews jumped out of the still-moving police car, ran over to the Merc, pulled open the door and grabbed the doorman by his lapel. 'Where did she go? Which way?' Terrified, the doorman just pointed to the hotel entrance.

Andrews ran inside the lobby and began frantically looking around for Dolly, but she was nowhere to be seen. And no one, even the receptionist, had noticed her. He was in for another bollocking from Resnick, who was still pissed off about the hamburger incident.

Andrews got back in his car, slammed the door and found a parking spot. He was hoping beyond hope that Dolly was simply in the hotel somewhere, so he decided to stay with her car. It's all he could do.

* * *

Linda had arrived at the Liverpool Street railway arches fifteen minutes early. It was bitterly cold and she was freezing. She hadn't realised the area would be so dark, and hadn't brought a torch, so was having difficulty in finding lock-up number fifteen. She'd not been surprised when Dolly called; agreeing to meet up with her and Shirley again was an easy decision. What else did she have to get her heart racing these days? Since Joe's death, Linda's life had been horrible, truly horrible. The half-empty bed was impossible to get used to, the people who came into her arcade disgusted her and the police treated her like shit on their shoe. Above all, life was boring as hell – and Linda hated boring. Whatever Dolly thought she was doing, Linda was happy to tag along, catch up with Shirl every now and then, and maybe make a bit of money out of Dolly along the way.

She approached one of the premises and, peering through the crack between the large wooden doors, nearly jumped out of her skin when she saw a huge Alsatian pounce towards her, snarling and barking. She quickly scurried one door along, raised her fist to knock and—

'You're early,' Dolly said from behind her.

'I wasn't sure where it was and I don't like being late.'

The cold had put Linda in a grumpy mood, which Dolly sensed immediately. Fortunately, Dolly was feeling cheerful after losing Andrews and her comfy cab ride over. She smiled at Linda as she unlocked the door. 'It's a good way to be.'

Inside the lock-up, Dolly calmly lit a cigarette as Linda stepped from foot to foot trying to warm up. She could murder a cuppa, but Dolly just sat on a packing case, got out her black leather diary and reviewed her notes while they waited for Shirley. Linda was no good at being silently irritated and, eventually, her under-the-breath mumblings made Dolly speak.

'Kettle's in the back, darlin'. Mine's black coffee, no sugar. Keep yourself warm, eh.'

Linda pulled a face and went into the annexe, where three brand-new mugs, a new kettle and a packet of unopened custard creams were waiting for her. 'Come on then, tell me the plan,' she called.

'We wait for Shirl,' Dolly said without looking up. 'It's her Miss Paddington thing tonight so she'll be another twenty minutes.'

'You might have told me!' Linda shouted from her tea duties.

'Why, what were you doing?' This was hurtful. Dolly knew full well that Linda would have been doing nothing of any interest. 'We're a team, Linda. We wait for Shirley.'

* * *

Shirley could feel one of her false eyelashes coming loose as she sat in the taxi with her mum, but she didn't have the strength to fix it. She was wearing a stunning black glittery evening gown, high heels, fake tan and enough hairspray to sink a ship. She also still wore her Miss Paddington number stuck to her shoulder. She looked a million dollars – apart from the make-up running down her tear-streaked face.

There was an awkward silence. Eventually Audrey decided to speak first.

'I didn't mean to imply you were turning tricks, darlin',' she whispered, hoping the cabbie wouldn't hear. 'I just wanted to know where you got the money for that dress.' Shirley stared out of the side window of the taxi, trying not to cry again.

Shirley hadn't been able to concentrate at all during the pageant, even though she was by far the most beautiful girl there and should easily have won. Audrey was so incredibly proud and just knew it was 'in the bag', but then, when Shirl took off her coat and revealed her brand-new dress, Audrey had made the clumsy comment about her daughter being a prostitute and things had gone downhill from there. Audrey had tried to redeem herself by giving Shirley a great big hug just as she was lining up to go on stage. 'You go out there and steal the show, my girl. You're beautiful and you're lovely and you're a winner.' Then she said the second stupid thing of the night. 'Terry and me will be front row, centre.' She'd meant to say 'Greg', but it had come out as 'Terry'. Audrey could have kicked herself as she watched Shirley's eyes widen and her lower lip tremble. She'd wanted to apologise to her daughter, but didn't have the opportunity as Freddie, the compere, called Shirley's name and the floor manager shoved her on stage.

As Shirley had stepped out into the spotlight her mind was so far away that, when Freddie asked her what her hobbies were, she'd mumbled something about liking vegetables and books.

Audrey had taken full responsibility for the whole fiasco. Shirley had let her, but in fact other things had been on Shirley's mind. As the cab dropped Audrey off and continued on to Liverpool Street Station, Shirley began to pull herself together and thought back to a week ago.

She had been waiting in the ladies' toilet in Regent's Park for over half an hour when Dolly had eventually breezed down the steps and calmly started to touch-up her make-up in the cracked and peeling wall mirror.

'You give them the slip?' Shirley had asked, referring to Dolly's constant police escort.

'No,' Dolly replied through her stretched lips as she reapplied her lipstick. 'DC Andrews is outside, looking after Wolf.'

Dolly put her make-up away and handed a stuffed envelope to Shirley, who was still trying to figure out whether or not Dolly was pulling her leg. 'There's enough in there to cover your mortgage for a few months and more besides. You'll get that every month. We'll meet again next Thursday after Miss Paddington; details are in the envelope.'

'Dolly, I . . .' Shirley started, 'I'm not sure I can handle it. There'll be shooters, won't there?'

'It's all right. Listen, if you don't come, we'll know you're not up for it, OK?'

Shirley squeezed the envelope and could feel the wad of money inside.

'You'll just have to pay me that back, no harm done, all right, darlin'?' Dolly said with a knowing smile. Then she walked out.

When Shirley had finally dared to pop her head out of the ladies' loo, she'd just managed to catch a glimpse of a man in the distance walking to his car, glaring back at Dolly walking off in the opposite direction with Wolf by her side. Balls of steel, Shirley had thought to herself. Bet he doesn't put that in his daily report!

* * *

Linda was on her second tea when she and Dolly heard the banging on the main garage doors. Shirley bundled in, clip-clopping across the uneven floor in her stilettos, banging her suitcase into everything and apologising for being late.

Bleedin' 'ell, what you come as?' said Linda. 'Look at her, Dolly, all dressed up like a dog's dinner. You wearing false eyelashes?'

Shirley dropped her suitcase on the floor straight into the oily puddle, which splashed all over her newly tanned legs. She jumped backwards, snapped a heel, stumbled and ended up seated on the bonnet of the dirtiest car in the lock-up. Tears instantly welled in her eyes.

'I come eighth! I made a right fool of myself and I was awful to me mum.'

Linda spoke again, but more kindly this time. 'Eight's not bad, Shirl. How many of you were there?'

'Ten . . .' Shirley mumbled pathetically, and Linda turned quickly away in order to hide a smile.

Shirley stood up straight and brushed her backside down. When she looked at her hand, it was covered in oil and she could only imagine what her tan coat looked like from behind. The final straw was when she noticed that she'd broken a nail. The tears came and she said, 'I wasn't going to come.'

'Did anyone see you?' Dolly asked, secretly very relieved to see her. She needed to get things back on track.

'No, I got off at the station, like you instructed.'

'Did you see anyone?"

'Well, course I did! It's a bloody station at kicking-out time!' Shirley snapped, then immediately checked herself.

Dolly settled Shirley down, patting and stroking her head like she did Wolf's. She ordered Linda to make some more coffee.

'I've been here half the night and all I've done so far is to act as a bloody waitress,' Linda muttered, stomping off in a huff.

Ten minutes later, the three women were seated round a large crate, stocked up with tea, coffee and biscuits, looking at the maps and drawings Dolly had laid out for them. Linda was nibbling the top off a custard cream, Shirley was nibbling her broken nail into some sort of acceptable shape while wafting Dolly's cigarette smoke away from her face, and Dolly was hunched over the plans, writing copious notes in her diary – things they needed to buy, to do, to learn.

'Our main problem is going to be the weight we got to carry on our backs from here –' Dolly added a neat line to her drawing of the Strand underpass – 'right up to here. That's where we'll have the getaway car parked. It's a run of about fifty yards.'

Dolly looked up to see Linda scraping the custard out of her biscuit with her bottom teeth. 'You listening?' Dolly demanded.

Linda confidently recapped everything Dolly had been saying. 'Nicked van up front to stop the security wagon in the underpass. Nicked van behind to block it in. Shooter keeping cars in check. Shooter getting the guards to open up. Rucksacks full of money.'

'Very heavy money,' Shirley corrected.

'Very heavy money,' Linda repeated. 'Fifty yard run to nicked getaway car.' Linda was clearly very pleased with herself.

Insubordinate bitch, Dolly thought. She'd have to tame her before the big day but, for now, she let it go. 'One of us will have to learn how to use a chainsaw as well and that's really heavy,' Dolly continued.

'I've got no strength in my arms,' Shirley said. 'My legs are OK so I'm not worried about the weight of the money.'

'You've carried a third of a million in notes, have you?' Dolly snapped.

Shirley fell silent. She was too tired to care how much this mythical third of a million weighed so she changed the subject. 'What happens if we get aggro from anyone in the cars behind us?'

Linda butted in. 'Weren't you listening?! I just said: "shooter keeping cars in check" – that's me. Don't you worry your pretty little head. There'll be no have-a-go heroes on my watch.' Linda grabbed another custard cream. 'What about explosives?'

Dolly glared at Linda – one long, cold stare that said it all. *If looks could actually kill*, Linda thought, *I'd be dead on the floor.*

'Sorry, Dolly,' she said and reached a comforting hand across the crate.

Dolly moved her hand away and changed the subject. 'I'm arranging a meeting with the security contact soon. We know from the ledgers that the wagon always uses the underpass, but that the runs vary in the time and exact route they take. Once a month there's a big run with extra cash – we'll go for that one about four months from now. The contact will confirm the exact date and give us the route map – and we'll need every minute to prepare.'

As Dolly reached down to her bag, Linda and Shirley rolled their eyes at each other. Two months, four months, six months – did Dolly honestly believe they could pull off an armed robbery?

Dolly sat upright again, two large brown envelopes in her hand. 'Get yourself wheels,' she instructed, handing them over. 'Pay cash and make sure they're taxed and MOT'd, then, after the job's done, we'll ditch 'em.'

Linda opened her envelope and swallowed hard, eyes glinting. She tingled all over – there had to be two grand inside! She was grinning like the Cheshire Cat as Dolly handed her a set of keys to the lock-up and brought the meeting to a close.

'From now on, this'll be headquarters. Be careful how you come and go.' Dolly held up another set of keys for Shirley. 'Now's your chance, love,' Dolly said. 'You in or out?'

Shirley squeezed the envelope full of cash, looked at Linda who eagerly nodded – and she took the keys.

Dolly stood up, pleased with how well the evening had gone. 'That's it for tonight,' she said. 'Golden rule is you two never call me at home, I'll get in touch with you as and when I need to. Inside your envelopes is a list of details of what each of you have to do. We take this in stages. Stage one is to get the motors sorted, and for you, Shirley, to get all the clothing gear I've put on your list.'

Dolly didn't wait for confirmation; she didn't need it. They'd taken her money and they'd taken her keys. As far as she was concerned, they were now a team and she was in charge. They'd do as she said, just as Joe and Terry had always done what Harry said. 'You two can lock up. Don't leave together, just like at the spa.' And she was gone, with Wolf quick on her heels.

Linda and Shirley still sat at the crate, their envelopes of money in front of them. They listened to Dolly's footsteps echo out of the lock-up, heard the Alsatian barking like a lunatic, then nothing.

It was Shirley who broke the silence.

'You scared, Linda?'

'If I believed that this was for real I'd be shitting myself, darlin',' Linda laughed, taking her money out of the envelope to count it.

Shirley agreed, but she was genuinely concerned for Dolly. 'She's not right, is she?'

'Not even close! Look, I dunno why she's doing this, Shirl, but it seems to be helping her. Making her feel better. And I have to admit, talkin' about it makes me feel alive, like I'm tingling all over.'

'So you're just going to go along with it?'

'I'm not proud. I need the cash. Joe left me broke and I know your Terry did the same to you. Dolly'll come to her senses eventually and we'll all just go back to our lives but, for now, I'm going to keep on taking the money and Dolly can live in her little fantasy world with us for company.' Linda could see that the decision to play along with Dolly was nowhere near as easy for Shirley. 'We're actually doing her a favour, Shirl. We're looking after her, giving her something to aim for . . . making sure she doesn't end up naked in Trafalgar Square with a traffic cone on her head.' Linda reached across the crate and put her hand on Shirley's.

Shirley looked down at Linda's comforting hand and noticed that she no longer wore her wedding ring. Then she looked at her own long, slender fingers. They were shaking and her gold wedding ring glistened. She didn't feel elated, or as Linda had put it, 'tingling all over'. If this was all just part of Dolly's grieving process, then Shirley felt terribly, terribly guilty. And if this was really about three widows getting together to commit their dead husbands' armed robbery, then she felt petrified. But the envelope of money under her hand was lifesaving. Without it she'd lose the house and everything in it.

'Come on,' Linda said, helping Shirley to her feet. 'Let's go home.'

* * *

As Dolly walked along the street towards the Dorchester, she could see Andrews in his car outside. He was every bit as predictable as she'd thought he was; a foot soldier, nothing more. As she passed his window, she couldn't resist giving him a small smile. She tipped the doorman when he returned with her Merc, and then drove off like a cat who'd got the cream.

Back home, Dolly locked the garage doors from the outside, allowing Wolf to have a pee in the front garden before heading in for the night. Usually she would have entered the house through the connecting door in the garage to the kitchen, but she couldn't resist toying with Andrews, who had parked up in his usual place outside her house. As she took out her front door key and let herself in, Dolly smiled to herself, thinking how adept she was becoming at losing her police tail. But when she opened her front door, her smile turned to shock, a chill ran through her body from her head to her toes, and her eyes stung with anger as she took in the mess before her. The hallway carpets had been lifted, vases and figurines were knocked over, the upholstery had been slit open, houseplants upturned and the soil tipped out.

Noticing the light coming from the open lounge door, she moved slowly and quietly forward, tiptoeing over the broken debris.

Dolly froze as she heard the click-click of a record dropping down onto the turntable, then the eerie silence was broken by the words of her song filling the room. '*What is life to me without thee, what is life if thou art dead?*' She slowly pushed open the lounge door and held her hand to her mouth – the room was destroyed, the stuffing hung out of her beautiful sofa, pictures were smashed.

She had only just straightened everything out after the cops had turned the house upside down – and now this! Anger flooded over her and she kicked the door, causing it to swing open and slam against the cabinet behind it.

Boxer Davis jumped, dropping the framed picture of Harry he held in his hands. His suit and hair were covered in the fluff from the sofa stuffing and he looked so ridiculous she was suddenly not afraid anymore. Without a word, she walked over and lifted off the needle from the record on the turntable. Wolf whimpered, not knowing what to do, running round the room, getting tangled up in the torn cushions.

'It wasn't me, Doll, honest,' Boxer whined nervously.

Dolly turned on him and screamed, 'Don't you dare call me that!'

Boxer was nearly in tears as he begged Dolly to listen to him. 'There was nothing I could do. I couldn't stop him. If you'd been here, Dolly, he'd have done this to you. I'm so glad you was out! I really truly am glad you was out!'

'Who?' Dolly said through clenched teeth.

'Tony, Tony Fisher. He thinks you know where Harry stashed those ledgers.'

'You stood by and let him do this? Watched him do this to my home!"

Boxer hovered around her, almost crying with the shame of what had happened, repeating again and again that he had nothing to do with the damage. 'I'm trying to do you a favour, gal. I'm worried for you. They're not offering money any more. They want those ledgers.'

Dolly sat on her torn velvet chair and Wolf jumped up beside her. 'I've told you! I don't know where the ledgers are. I've told you and I've told the law.'

'But they don't believe you. I do though, Dolly, I believe that you don't know. But they still have to be somewhere, don't they? So maybe you and me could take a little look round? And Tony Fisher wants to pay the other widows a visit an' all.'

Dolly felt her insides tighten. 'Why the bloody hell would he want to do that? If I don't know anything, they're not going to, are they?'

'Tony doesn't think like that, Dolly. He just wants to hurt someone till he gets what he needs.'

Dolly sat with her head in her hands, desperately trying to work out if Tony could possibly know about her meetings with Shirley and Linda. She was always so careful, but she worried nonetheless.

Boxer was now sitting on his haunches in front of her, patting her knee like a great ape, his eyes blinking repeatedly. She wanted to hit him. She couldn't take on the Fishers without a plan and she had no one to turn to. She needed time and she needed somehow to keep the Fishers' away from the other widows. Her head was spinning.

'How did Tony get into my home?' she demanded.

Boxer smiled, pulled an old plastic card from his jacket pocket, holding it up for her to see.

Dolly stared at him. 'You do know the police are watching me, don't you?'

'You're not going to get me into trouble, are you, Doll?' Boxer was clearly unnerved. He hadn't known. Would Dolly have him arrested for breaking and entering?

'*Don't* call me Doll! And I think you're in enough trouble without me adding to it, don't you? Working for the Fishers is a dangerous move, Boxer. They're not smart, see, not like my Harry was. I mean, if the Old Bill did my house over and couldn't find the ledgers, what makes Tony Fisher think he's going to do any better?'

Boxer sat there on his heels, looking at Dolly for guidance. His poor brain couldn't work out how to speak at the same time as think.

'Leave me alone now, Boxer. Come round in the morning, help me tidy up and we'll see if we can find any hiding places that the coppers and Tony might have missed.'

Boxer's eyes widened and his face lit up like a child who'd just been given the biggest ice cream in the world. 'I will!' He beamed as he stood up. 'I'll be here at nine, shall I?'

'Seven.'

'Seven's better. Yes, I'll be here at seven. I'm meant to report back to the Fishers this evening, so I'll let them know you're co-operating and tomorrow we'll look properly and everything will be all right.'

Dolly couldn't believe how gormless Boxer was. She watched him trot off out the front door, with a renewed bounce in his step. She then bolted and double locked every door in the house before tidying the kitchen a little. All her food from the freezer lay on the floor defrosting and her beautiful china and cutlery was smashed and strewn everywhere. She didn't have the strength to tackle this tonight, so she made herself a coffee and sat back down in her ransacked living room, on her ruined sofa.

Dolly knew she had to start thinking the way Harry would have done, but it was hard as she looked around the room at the collection of Capodimonte figures Harry had bought her, smashed to bits. She looked at Wolf. 'What would Harry do? Eh, darling? What would Daddy do?'

She thought about the police car outside and was tempted to call Resnick and tell him how his idiot men chose to follow her to the Dorchester instead of stopping Tony Fisher and Boxer Davis from breaking in and destroying her beautiful home. She went to her window and peered out through a rip in her thick velvet curtains. 'Idiots!' she seethed. 'You've just watched Boxer Davis leave my home and it doesn't even cross your mind how or when the hell he got in here in the first place.'

Dolly turned to survey her living room. Amid the horrific mess, the broken framed photograph of Harry dropped by Boxer stood out as clear as day. At first, she felt sad seeing Harry's handsome face smiling up at her through the cracked glass, but then she felt he was trying to tell her something.

'What is it, Harry? What should I do?' Dolly said softly as she knelt on the floor and picked up the broken frame. She stared at his face and with her whole heart and soul whispered, 'I loved you. I loved you so very much. Dear God, Harry, I still love you. You would never have let those Fisher bastards do this to us.'

Then, as if Harry was suddenly there standing by her side, she suddenly felt comforted. He would guide her through the next few months, through the robbery, she was certain. She was doing it for Harry, after all. She truly believed that he would watch over her now, and wouldn't let anything go wrong.

That night, with little Wolf curled up on Harry's pillow next to her, Dolly had her best night's sleep since she'd heard the terrible news.

CHAPTER 9

Dolly had been up since 6 a.m., tidying and cleaning. At first, she hadn't known where to start. Usually, she'd run the vacuum round but this morning she couldn't even see the carpet under all the debris.

By the time Boxer strolled up the driveway, she was dressed in her oldest clothes, apron and headscarf and was throwing away yet another bin bag full of broken memories. Seven a.m. was clearly way too early for Boxer. He looked like a zombie as he shuffled past her; although he seemed enthusiastic enough to get on with the search for Harry's ledgers.

The second zombie in the street was the very tired young officer in the car parked six houses down. 'You're not paying any attention, are you?' Dolly said. She glanced down at Wolf. 'Silly policeman.'

In the lounge, Boxer was assessing the situation.

'What shall I do first?' he asked. Housework, especially after a ransacking, wasn't something he was going to take to easily.

'Right,' said Dolly. 'Throw anything that's broken beyond repair, but bag the sofa cushions and curtains, they can be fixed. And, once you can see the carpet, the vacuum's in the cupboard under the stairs.'

'Right you are, Dolly.' Boxer beamed. With idiot-proof instructions, he was far happier. 'We'll have this place spick and span in no time.'

Dolly watched Boxer as he bagged her last few broken Capodimonte figures. The damage wasn't as bad as she had originally thought, and it was mostly downstairs. Once everything was cleared, her sofa was probably reparable and she'd no doubt be able to scrub the carpet clean from the mud and grass stains that had been trampled in from her back garden. It was the intrusion that hurt her the most. The police, the Fishers, they each seemed to think that they could treat her with such disdain and get away with it.

Upstairs, the beds were stripped and the third wash load was already on. As she began to collect the strewn clothes from the floor, Boxer appeared in the doorway.

'Found anything?' he asked, his usual big stupid grin on his face. He was acting like her best friend, as if nothing had happened, as if he wasn't responsible for all of this mess in the first place.

'Let me salvage what I can first, eh, Boxer? I can't see the wood for the trees right now.'

'Sorry, Dolly.'

'As we get things tidied, we'll search every nook and cranny – don't you worry.' She gave him a reassuring smile and Boxer lumbered back downstairs. Her smile disappeared as soon as Boxer was gone. Dolly knew he'd be useless at the tidying and cleaning, but she also knew that she needed to keep him sweet. She had a plan and Boxer would be a big part of it.

* * *

Linda was down at the yard well before the auction had even started. Flicking through the brochure, she paced along the rows of cars for sale, inspecting one after the other, unsure what she was looking for. She knew bits and bobs about cars . . . what a good engine looked and sounded like, what safety checks to do on a new buy, and how to hotwire one. Joe had taught her a thing or two about what goes on under the bonnet of a car – and on the back seat . . .

Eventually she decided she liked a used red Ford Capri and she began chatting up the dealer. He was very helpful and obviously thought she was a sexy little thing and definitely up for it, giggling at his bad jokes and letting him put his arm around her. He agreed to take a look at the engine for her; Linda rubbed her body against him and smiled. She was so busy getting the lowdown on the Capri, she failed to notice Arnie Fisher arrive in a silver Jag.

Arnie, carrying a leather briefcase, bustled his way through the maze of cars towards the auction room. He stopped when he saw Carlos leaning on the bonnet of a Rolls-Royce he was there to bid on. Arnie straightened his silk tie. 'A real nice looker . . .' he whispered and winked.

Carlos liked it when Arnie was obvious with his affections; it made him feel special and a man like Arnie didn't consider many people in his life to be special at all.

Carlos was wearing a nice suit. *The boy's learning fast*, thought Arnie, assessing him with his ice-blue eyes. Arnie didn't go for rough trade; he liked his boys neat, tidy and with a bit of class – although Carlos had a bit of the animal in him as well. He noted that perhaps Carlos had on too many gold necklaces. He'd speak to him about that later, when they were alone.

Carlos started enthusing about the low-mileage Roller, one of the best he'd seen. All it needed was the odd touch-up and an engine tune to make it perfect. Carlos lifted the bonnet and leant into the engine. Arnie hadn't the foggiest about engines, but he followed suit, so he could press his body against Carlos. He noted that Carlos had made an effort to clean his nails; yes, the boy was going to go places. He was getting very fond of him.

Arnie handed over the briefcase and patted Carlos on the cheek. 'There's enough in there to buy the Roller.'

'How high do you want me to go?'

'It's all sorted, Carlos, darlin'. It'll not go higher than the reserve price. They know I want it. There won't be no other bidders.'

Arnie was right: the auction on the Roller was done and dusted in a flash. Carlos bid, bought, paid in cash, and they were on their way for a slap-up lunch in less than thirty minutes.

Linda, with the aid of the over-amorous dealer, got a good price on the Capri. As she counted out the cash, he moved in with a sleazy grin. His arm slipped beneath Linda's coat. She gave him an icy glare.

'Piss off or I'll start screaming,' she hissed.

He got the message loud and clear. As she walked away with the keys to her new car, she heard him muttering: 'Soddin' bitch!'

* * *

Shirley's brother, Greg, was adamant that everything was legit and he hadn't nicked the car he'd got for her, but she still wasn't sure, even though it was a good price and she liked it. Audrey, on her fifth cup of tea, chipped in that Greg must have nicked it cos according to *Exchange and Mart* the motor was worth twice what he'd paid for it. Greg and Audrey were going at it hammer and tongs when Shirley dropped a bundle of cash on the kitchen table. They both fell instantly silent. Audrey gasped, missed her mouth with the cup and dribbled tea down her chin. Greg grabbed for the wad of notes, but Shirley got there first, peeling off the £750 she owed him. Handing over the keys and log book, he legged it before anyone could have another go at him.

Shirley knew exactly what her mum was thinking. 'The money was in a suitcase belonging to Terry,' Shirley lied. 'Or do you think I can make a grand on the game in less than a week?'

'A grand?' Audrey screeched. Shirley wasn't a natural liar. 'In a suitcase? The coppers missed it, did they?'

Shirley held her ground. 'Yes! It was hidden in the seam of the case and they was too busy flirting with me to notice.'

'And when exactly did you find this grand? And why didn't you tell me?'

'It's nothing to do with you, Mum!' Shirley snapped.

'We're all hard up, my girl! That washing machine you gave me didn't walk round to mine on its own, you know. I had to hire a van. They don't cost peanuts! I'd like to have known is all I'm saying. I'm your mum after all.'

Shirley pulled fifty quid from the bundle of notes and handed it to Audrey. 'I'm sorry my washing machine cost you money, Mum, I really am,' she said sarcastically.

If Audrey had been a better person, she'd have walked away leaving Shirley embarrassed at thinking her mum could be so easily bought. But instead, she took the fifty quid.

'Let's take your new car for a spin to the pub,' she suggested. 'Your round, Shirley.'

* * *

The little Mini estate wouldn't start first time, or the second, but eventually it fired up on the third, then spluttered and kangarooed down the road. Shirley said the brakes seemed a bit stiff, and then swore as the windscreen wiper fell off.

'Greg had better fix it, or else,' she said furiously.

'It might be your drivin',' love,' Audrey remarked.

'Terry taught me how to drive and I passed me test first time,' Shirley replied heatedly.

After a run round the block, Shirley decided the car wasn't so bad after all. She dropped her mum off at the pub and said she was taking it for a longer test drive. She'd agreed to buy it because there was plenty of space in the rear to stash all the gear needed for the robbery and the inconspicuous colour wouldn't stand out in the traffic afterwards. She'd have picked a canary yellow car if the choice had been hers – but she could do that easily enough with her third of a million. Shirley laughed at herself – fancy buying a car for its robbery qualities!

As she trundled along, Shirley was beginning to feel more like her old self again. Her thoughts turned to having her hair done, maybe she'd get some streaks and go a bit blonder, and maybe even have a nice massage . . .

* * *

Linda put her foot down on the Capri's accelerator and watched the speedometer move quickly upwards . . . seventy . . . seventy-five . . . eighty. It felt exhilarating, a quick look in the mirror and no one behind, so she put her foot down further: eighty-five . . . ninety. This motor was a good buy, she thought – and then, suddenly, a small plume of smoke wafted from the bonnet, and began to billow out, flowing over the windscreen so Linda could hardly see the road. She pulled the car over onto the lay-by, got out, kicked the front tyre and swore at it.

As she perched on the bonnet of her smoking car, she couldn't help but smile. 'What the hell am I doing?' she said out loud. One of Linda's duties on Dolly's list was to learn basic car maintenance – and here she was at the side of the road having just bought a shit-heap of a Capri.

Car after car drove by; men honked their horns but didn't stop to help. Linda didn't mind. As she sat there, she felt incredibly strong – she had money in her pocket and a brand-new second-hand car. She'd learn how to fix it properly, just like Dolly asked. She'd call Gino and get the name of his car mechanic mate from the pub. She'd learn hands-on, not from a book. She'd learn quick and she'd learn right. Not for Dolly's stupid, pie-in-the-sky robbery, but for herself. Linda couldn't remember the last time she achieved anything really – but that was all going to change.

CHAPTER 10

Boxer was sitting at Dolly's newly cleaned dining table stuffing eggs and bacon down his face as if he hadn't eaten in weeks. He wiped a slice of bread round the plate, put it in his mouth and slurped on his tea to wash it down before sitting back and pushing the plate forward.

Dolly came into the kitchen carrying a couple of old suit jackets belonging to Harry. 'Stand up,' she ordered. Boxer jumped to his feet, expecting to be ordered back to work. When he saw Dolly holding up one of Harry's jackets for him to slip his arms into, he was almost overwhelmed and, just for a second, he choked back the tears.

Dolly put the jacket on him, instinctively brushing his shoulders and pulling the back straight – just as she'd done a thousand times for Harry. Boxer was about the same build as Harry, but his belly was bigger and the jacket looked a little tight. He thought he looked a million dollars though.

'Eh, pure wool, very nice, very nice indeed,' he said to Dolly as he brushed his hands up and down the material.

Dolly's face was expressionless as she looked at Boxer wearing her dead husband's expensive clothes. 'There's a couple of shirts and two pairs of trousers as well if you want them,' she said, as if it didn't matter either way to her.

Boxer paused. 'I'll treasure them,' he said clumsily.

'I'm sorry I can't give you his best things, Boxer.'

Harry's best clothes were impossible to part with right now and were hanging in his wardrobe, all freshly washed and ironed. Dolly had even polished Harry's shoes and they too were in his wardrobe, as though he was simply away on business.

Emotions close to the surface, Dolly put the kettle on and brewed another pot of tea to regain control of herself so that she could do what she needed to do. While Boxer had been gobbling down his makeshift dinner, Dolly had been tidying the nursery. Tony Fisher had thrown the baby clothes around the small blue room and then trodden mud all over them. The cot was upside down, the tiny newborn nappies were ripped apart and the photos were smashed. There was no reason for most of the destruction; it was an act of pure evil and the thought of the Fishers taking over Harry's patch made Dolly's blood boil. As she'd stood in the nursery, she'd decided two things.

First, she was going to pack up everything in the nursery and give it to the convent this afternoon, for the underprivileged and orphaned babies and children to get some use out of. After her son was stillborn, Dolly had received great comfort from her religion. The convent doors were always open to her and she could come and go as she pleased, day or night. Some weeks, she was there every day. Her visits got fewer and fewer as her pain subsided, but by then she'd got to love the simplicity of it all in comparison to her hectic life with Harry. She'd spent hours painting and drawing and playing games with the children; all they wanted from her was love and she had so very much of that to give. And, in return, the children loved Dolly. In those initial months after losing the baby, Dolly would have fallen into a deep depression without her friends at the convent; she owed them so much and they never asked anything of her in return. So now, she'd pack up the nursery and take it all to them this afternoon when she did her weekly visit, to help the living instead of commemorating the dead. This would be closure and would allow her to move forwards unhindered. Dolly kept only one toy from her son's nursery – a small white poodle.

The second thing Dolly had decided was to implement her plan for getting the Fishers off her back . . .

Boxer sat at the kitchen table admiring his new jacket and waiting for his top-up of tea. Dolly brought the pot to the table and poured two cups. As Boxer spooned three heaps of sugar into his mug, Dolly decided he was ready to hear what she had been up all night rehearsing.

'I've got something to tell you, Boxer. It's about the ledgers, you see, I lied to you. I do know where they are.'

Boxer looked dumbstruck.

'The thing is,' Dolly continued, feigning concern for this stupid lump of a man in her kitchen. 'The thing is . . . Harry told me before he died that you're named in the ledgers along with a long list of others. It could get you into a lot of trouble – even banged up if the Old Bill gets hold of them.'

Boxer felt a chill run down his spine. Lost for words, all he could manage was to let Dolly talk.

'I worked out that Harry must have used four men in the robbery, one up front, three at the back. It's the only thing that makes sense. I know it; the coppers know it.' Dolly knew she didn't need to explain her reasoning any further for Boxer. 'Three are dead, but the fourth man is still out there somewhere. I think he's either got the ledgers or he knows where they are.' Dolly paused to take a slow sip of tea and leave Boxer's little brain to think of the right question to ask. She didn't want to tell him everything in one go, in case that might start to sound planned. Eventually, Boxer spoke.

'Who do you think this fourth man is, Dolly?'

Dolly hesitated, pretending to be thinking hard about her next sentence. 'You mustn't tell no one, Boxer. If I tell you, it's got to stay between us. You hear me? It could be very dangerous for you to know what I know.'

'I swear it. You can trust me.'

'The fourth man, the man that escaped from the robbery . . . was my Harry.'

Again, Dolly paused to allow Boxer to register what she was saying. It was incredibly important that he believed her. 'He's not dead, Boxer. I buried another member of the gang, genuinely thinking it was Harry, but I now know that it wasn't.'

'How . . . how can you know?' Boxer asked, visibly shaking.

'Because I've seen him alive. Harry's hiding from everyone right now, but he wants you back on his payroll, just like old times.'

Boxer automatically sat bolt upright, like an army private who'd just been told he's been selected for a secret mission. The fear on his face was replaced by an uncontrollably broad smile. *He's so easy to lie to*, Dolly thought, *it almost seems cruel.*

'Now this is what you've got to do. You're to keep an eye on the Fishers for him. Stay safe, though, Boxer, Harry doesn't want you taking any risks for him. You'll be his eyes and ears until he's ready to come back and take over again. You'll report to me and I'll report to Harry. No one can know he's alive, Boxer . . . you promise me?'

Boxer slapped his thigh and roared with laughter. 'I promise, Dolly! Old Harry, what a brilliant man, he bloody escaped. He played a bleedin' blinder.' He shook his head repeatedly. 'What a turn-up for the books!'

Dolly gripped his hand and Boxer focused intently on her again. 'Get it all out of your system here, Boxer, because once you leave this house, you got to keep your mouth shut. I need you to be on my side. On Harry's side.'

Boxer squeezed Dolly's hand back so hard, she nearly cried out in pain. He looked her square in the eyes and spoke with total sincerity. 'I've always been on your and Harry's side, you know that. On my life, Dolly, I won't repeat a word of this to anyone.'

'Inside jacket pocket,' Dolly whispered.

Boxer reached inside the pocket of the jacket he'd been given and pulled out an envelope.

'Two hundred from Harry. That's just for starters.'

Boxer didn't open the envelope; he didn't need to. If Dolly said there was two hundred in there, then there was. 'Back on the payroll,' he whispered.

* * *

Dolly watched Boxer swagger down the driveway. He looked full of himself as he straightened his new jacket and nodded to the detectives still parked along the road.

Back in her much cleaner and tidier lounge, Dolly slumped on her torn sofa, where she was quickly joined by Wolf. 'Hello, darlin',' she said, stroking his belly as he rolled over for her. She rested her head back and took a moment to contemplate where she had got to.

Dolly speculated that it'd be no more than two days before Boxer blurted the news that Harry was alive to someone. Especially if the tempting money in his pocket meant that he ended up off the wagon and down the local. Once the rumour was out there, the Fishers would know soon enough and that should, she hoped, keep them hyper-cautious and away from her and the other widows for fear of reprisals.

'So much still to do, my love,' she said to Wolf. She patted him, got up and went over to her writing desk.

Taking out her diary, Dolly began to make more encrypted notes. She needed to go back to the bank and check the ledgers again. She now needed a fourth person for her own robbery and she hoped that there'd be a name in the ledgers of someone she could trust completely – although it would be tricky if the fourth person was a man, she knew that much, as she'd not only have to convince them to join her but also to take orders from her. The second thing on her list was to try and find the actual man who got away from Harry's failed bank robbery. If the Fishers found him first, they'd know she lied about Harry being alive and come after her. She hoped and prayed that whoever it was had gone abroad and had no plans to return. And lastly, she had to let Shirley and Linda know what she'd said to Boxer. They needed to be right up to speed with all her plans, so they could stay alert and stay safe.

Dolly looked across at Wolf, who had bedded down into a tear in the sofa and was snuggling into the stuffing inside. There was still so much to do to make this house back into a home – but it would keep. The main thing to do right now was keep her appointment at the convent so that the watching detectives wouldn't get suspicious. She'd become very adept at losing her tail, but she knew that she must also be very careful to allow the police to follow her unhindered if she was to convince them that life was going on as normal. It made it difficult to fit everything in, but somehow the excitement of it all was giving her extra energy – she was daring to feel alive again. She turned and smiled at the photos of Harry and herself that Boxer had replaced along the mantelpiece, all in exactly the right date order. She almost felt Harry with her now and, as she shut her eyes to see him more clearly, her body ached to hold him.

She thought back to two nights before the raid, Harry had come into the bedroom and she knew intuitively that something was very wrong. She could always tell when he had done a bad business deal, or worse, when he was intending to take a big risk. He prowled round the house, in and out of rooms, sitting, getting up again, making coffee and checking his watch. Dolly was wise enough to keep quiet and not ask questions; he would tell her what was on his mind if and when he was ready.

Harry had not made love to her for months, but on that last night when he slipped into bed beside her, he'd been lustfully insistent and passionately rough with her – she hadn't minded; she adored the touch of him, the smell of him, the power of him.

Afterwards, she had held him in her arms like a baby. Then he got up and went into the spare room and she had lain there awake for hours, smiling. Even after twenty years he could make her whole body shudder inside. She was as proud of his tight muscular frame as he was. There was not an inch of fat on him. She'd take furtive looks at him when he showered or shaved, watching his muscles tense and relax.

As Dolly daydreamed, she was grateful for that last night they shared together. It was all that mattered amid the frenetic nature of her life since his death. They'd loved each other so much and, as she recalled all those times he had glanced at his beloved wristwatch, the pain flooded over her again. Harry had woken early the next morning, brought her a cup of tea and gently woken her with a kiss to her sleeping lips.

'Goodbye, sweetheart,' he'd said. 'I'll see you later.'

But there had been no 'later'. Harry never came home and the filth still refused to give her his beloved watch back.

* * *

Linda stood at the open garage doors of the mechanic's garage in the mews. She'd seen enough Italian men to know that the young kid in filthy grease and oil-covered overalls was not Carlos, Gino's mate from the pub. The kid puffed out his chest to try and impress her; her dismissive look quickly told him that she was way out of his league. 'Carlos! There's some bird here to see ya!' he shouted and then he went back to polishing a nice-looking Jaguar.

Carlos was in the small Portakabin office on the phone to Arnie Fisher, arranging the pickup of his Jag. He looked out the window but didn't recognise Linda and, placing his hand over the mouthpiece, shouted that he would be out in a minute.

Watching Carlos out of the corner of her eye, Linda liked what she saw as he ran his hand through his thick black curly hair and ruffled it up. He wore an old brown boiler suit open almost to his waist and as he turned, still talking on the phone, Linda got a full look at him. She took in every detail. He was a dish with big dark eyes, a great body and a stubbly, unshaven face. There was something very rugged and very sexy about him. Before he had even spoken to her, Linda had decided she'd have him.

When Carlos eventually came out, Linda introduced herself as Miss Linda Pirelli and, flirting outrageously, she asked him if he'd take a look at her new Capri.

'Sorry, love.' Carlos was dismissive. 'We only do company cars or regular standing customer's motors.' Brushing her aside, he got onto an inspection trolley and, lying on his back, wheeled himself under the ramped-up Jag to give it a last once-over.

Linda moved closer and squatted down, making sure her skirt was now up over her knees; she knew Carlos could see between her legs, which she parted slowly. 'Look, Carlos,' she said, 'truth is, I want to learn more about motors and how to service them so I can do me own. I'll pay you to teach me . . .'

Carlos could see her red panties as he wheeled himself out from under the car. He lay on the trolley and looked up at her. She was a bit tarty, pushy even, but there was something about her he quite liked. Before he knew what he was doing he heard himself telling her to get in the Jag while he took it for a test run. He lowered the ramp and as Linda got in the passenger seat, she grinned. He couldn't help smiling back – she was a right cheeky little cow!

Linda sat with her seat belt on, but Carlos didn't bother with his as he flung the car down the M4 at high speed. She knew he was trying to put the wind up her, but it took more than 120 miles an hour to do that, and he was clearly a good driver.

Carlos kept brushing her thigh when he changed gear, and she made no effort to move her leg. He wasn't all that tall compared to Joe, who was six foot three. Carlos, she reckoned, was about five nine, but he was a looker and seemed really nice. She also liked the faint smell of whatever cologne he had on, and as he leant towards her on a sharp bend she could smell it even more . . . yes, she would definitely try it on with this one!

Returning to the garage, Carlos found himself taking the Capri out for a road check and then teaching Linda how to do a basic service on it. He told her she'd got a good buy and it only needed a slight bit of work. There was a hole in the radiator, which he repaired there and then. He also cleaned up the spark plugs, points, air filter and rotor arm, explaining what was what and letting Linda do some of the work herself.

All the time she was at his elbow, getting covered in oil. She made him laugh because she was intent on learning as much as possible in the one hour he'd decided to give her. She even insisted on going under the ramp with him on the trolley. He couldn't quite make her out. He knew she was coming on strong, but at the same time she seemed genuinely interested in the Capri engine.

Four hours later they were still there, with the Capri's engine, as Carlos said, 'purring like a kitten'. As Carlos rubbed his hands with degreaser and wiped them on a rag, he could see Linda's legs still sticking out from beneath the Capri. She had a tidy set of pins. Her skirt was tucked into her knickers, which looked like red satin, and she wore no stockings. As she eased herself out he looked down, legs either side of her. Linda looked up, past his impressive crotch, and straight into his deep brown eyes. 'What do I owe you?' she asked.

'You mean cash or something else?' They both laughed and Carlos helped her to her feet.

This time Linda drove and it was Carlos's turn to be the passenger. As the Capri sped over the flyover towards White City, he kept his eye on the radiator temperature gauge, then as Linda changed into top gear he gave her the nod to put her foot down. The car roared forwards increasing speed rapidly – ninety-five, one hundred, one hundred and ten ... Linda flicked him a look, but he was more intent now on looking at her legs than the speedometer.

Linda wished she had made some effort to tidy the flat. While Carlos was in the bathroom, she slipped into the bedroom and cleared up her dirty washing, before shaking the duvet straight on the bed. She pulled the bedroom curtains closed then went into the small lounge and poured two large brandies. She took one to the bathroom, where Carlos was shirtless having a shave using Joe's razor. He had a gorgeous, well-defined body and Linda deliberately brushed against him as she placed the glass down on the sink. He didn't react or say anything and, feeling miffed, she walked out.

Linda downed her drink in one go then poured herself another shot. She wasn't sure what to do next, as she'd given him every 'come on' possible and, so far, he hadn't shown any signs of wanting to rip her clothes off. She heard a sound and, turning round, saw Carlos in his underpants, leaning against the frame of the lounge door holding his brandy. He was even better-looking than she had first thought. As he raised his glass and drank the brandy down, Linda could hear the bath running. God, he was certainly making himself at home! Without a word, he poured himself another brandy before heading back to the bathroom.

Linda kept Carlos waiting for a moment and then followed him. He was standing looking at some bath salts.

'Which do you like? This one or this?'

Linda shrugged. She didn't really give a shit about bath salts if she was being perfectly honest. He chose the salts he liked best, tipped them into the bath, and then moved closer to her.

'You wanna sleep with me or not?' she said petulantly. Carlos said nothing, but began to unbutton her blouse.

At last, she thought, and pulled him closer while trying to wriggle out of her skirt. God, she had the hots for him! She started to back out of the bathroom, pulling him with her, but he didn't follow. Then, without a word, he suddenly picked her up and dropped her straight in the bath, fully clothed. He laughed, then whisked off his underpants and, as he stepped into the bath with her, Linda could see a thin white line from where he must have worn bikini brief swimming trunks. He was beautiful.

* * *

DCI Resnick was on his way to the Sunshine Bread Company with Andrews and Fuller. They were following up on a lead that might mean they'd finally traced the bread truck used in the raid. Resnick was looking serious and focused now that they had something solid to work on. Gone was his self-defensive bravado and, for the first time, Fuller could see glimpses of the copper beneath the obsessed wreck of a man. But he still hated the obnoxious, fat bastard.

Fuller was driving the unmarked CID car like a maiden aunt. Resnick's impatience finally got the better of him. 'Put your bloody foot down, Fuller, for God's sake!' he shouted. 'Give it the blues and twos! We're after the biggest criminal gang in London here, not going on a fucking picnic!'

At the bread company, a uniformed PC was standing on guard next to the suspect truck. Wally Titherington from Forensics was already working on the inside of the vehicle, dusting for fingerprints, and one of his colleagues was taping the seats for fibres. Wally looked up as Resnick approached. 'Looks like he thinks he's in a Sam Peckinpah movie.'

'Right!' Resnick barked at the Sunshine Bread Company manager. 'I need an office to use as an interview room.'

The manager was clearly put out. 'How long is this disruption going on for?' he complained. 'Who exactly do you want to interview?'

'Every driver, every mechanic, every company worker and visitor using this yard, including you. Everyone who has ever come into contact with that bread truck. DC Andrews here will take everyone's fingerprints for elimination purposes.' Resnick stalked off.

Fuller stepped forwards as the manager's face started to turn bright pink. 'This is a very important case, sir, and we're grateful for your help. The sooner we get set up, the sooner we'll be out of your hair.'

* * *

Resnick looked round the ladies' cloakroom, hands on hips, and took an enormous drag of his cigarette. He tried to make light of the fact that he'd not been given an office as requested. 'If we're lucky, we'll still be here when they change out of their overalls at home time, eh, Andrews? You might even get to see your first lady.'

Andrews was keeping very quiet; the black fingerprint ink was already all over his shirt sleeves.

'Look at you!' Resnick snarled. 'How the hell do you manage to get dressed in the morning? You do know how to take fingerprints, don't you?'

'Yes, sir,' Andrews whimpered.

'I'm only checking because you sure as hell don't know how to follow an old lady walking a poodle!' Resnick stepped close to Andrews and the smell of the fat man's BO almost made him gag. 'Front desk got a call from a pensioner saying that two young hooligans had thrown burgers and milkshakes into her front garden.' Andrews squirmed. 'One more incident like that and you'll be pounding the beat in hobnails. Got it?'

'Got it, sir,' Andrews said, trying not to breathe in.

Once Resnick had walked away, Fuller gave Andrews a reassuring nod of the head. They both knew Resnick was picking on the easiest target because he was embarrassed at being given the ladies' cloakroom as an interview space.

* * *

Dolly's taxi waited while she went down to Linda's basement flat. She kept her finger on the doorbell until she saw the front bedroom curtain flick aside and Linda peer out.

Inside the bedroom, Linda's head was in an instant spin of panic at the sight of Dolly. She looked at Carlos's beautiful and sweaty body, and felt like an underage kid caught by her mum. 'You gotta keep quiet,' she whispered as she grabbed the top bedsheet and wrapped it round herself.

Dolly didn't even wait for Linda to open the front door fully before she stepped in.

'Why the hell don't you answer your phone?' Dolly demanded. 'Get dressed. I need an urgent meeting with you and Shirley at the lock-up right now.'

There was the sound of movement from the bedroom and Dolly froze and stared at the closed bedroom door. She glared at Linda in shock and anger. Shock at the thought of Linda being with another man so soon after the death of Joe, and anger at the terrifying thought that stupid, gobby, drunken Linda's pillow talk could easily include details of their upcoming robbery.

'You got someone in there?' Dolly whispered through gritted teeth.

Linda had no choice. 'He's no one, Dolly. He's a mechanic helping with the new car, that's all.'

Dolly gripped Linda's wrist hard, pulled her closer and whispered in her ear. 'Did he see me? Did he bloody see me, you stupid slut?' Dolly twisted and tightened her grip, shaking with anger. 'You got five minutes. I'll be in the taxi.' Then Dolly was gone, slamming the door behind her.

Feeling grubby and ashamed, Linda cried as she got dressed.

'What's wrong?' Carlos asked, trying to comfort her. 'Who was it?' he demanded. 'Who's frightened you? I can help.'

'I ain't frightened!' Linda screeched, pushing him away. 'And it's none of your business who it was. Just leave, I've got to go. I've got to go now.'

'You've got a boyfriend,' Carlos concluded angrily. 'You're teaching him a lesson by sleeping with me, aren't you?' The hurt look on Linda's face told him that he was wrong and he apologised as he got dressed, but it was too little, too late.

Linda, with tears in her eyes, held fifty quid out for him to take. 'Thanks for helping with the car. You can go now.'

'Linda. Linda, please. I didn't mean it. I don't want your money.' Carlos closed Linda's fingers round the money, held her gently and apologised again.

Linda looked into his eyes as she kissed him hard. 'I really do have to go. Let yourself out.' Linda was out the door before she'd finished talking.

As Carlos finished dressing, he noticed a face-down photo frame on the bedside table and picked it up. Carlos didn't recognise Joe Pirelli, but this man was clearly important to Linda. *Maybe she has got a boyfriend, or a husband*, he thought to himself. Unnerved at the thought, he replaced the photo and was on his way out when he stopped and looked down at the phone in the hallway. He picked up a pen and made a note of the phone number on the back of his hand.

He'd ask Gino a little more about Linda.

* * *

Dolly sat hunched up in the corner of the taxi, looking out of the window. She didn't speak a single word to Linda all the way to the lock-up.

Linda was in turmoil, every emotion written on her face like a petulant child who knows she's done something wrong. *What the hell is it to do with her?* Linda thought to herself. *If I want a screw, I'll bloody well have one and it's no business of Dolly's.* But at the same time, she felt incredibly guilty. Linda struggled in silence, but then realised that she actually felt an overriding feeling of what she could only describe as happiness. She really liked Carlos and, as she crossed her legs away from Dolly, she could feel that she was still wet inside from him. She glanced sideways at Dolly. *When was the last time you got your rocks off?* she wondered. It must have been at least twenty years ago. What had a stud like Harry Rawlins ever seen in Dolly? He was good-looking for an old bloke, though he could be a mean bastard at times. She decided right there and then that she wasn't going to take any more verbal insults or physical outbursts from Dolly about Carlos or about anything else. She'd give as good as she got from now on . . . she just wished she didn't feel so bloody guilty.

* * *

In the lock-up, Shirley sensed the heavy tension. Linda was unusually silent, sitting with her head bent, foot twitching and a sulky look on her face. She hadn't said a word to Dolly and Dolly was definitely giving her the silent treatment.

Shirley decided to break the ice. She was wearing one of the jumpsuits Dolly had instructed her to buy for the raid, so she paraded up and down as though she was on a catwalk, 'They were on offer.' Shirley said with a beaming smile. 'And I got us all some lovely plimsolls, really comfy for running in.'

'Oh, I been looking for some just like that,' said Linda. Dolly sniffed.

'And I got three ski masks, just like you asked.' Shirley searched among the shopping bags. 'One black, one blue and one red, so we know whose is whose. I got red for you Linda, on account of your black hair.'

'Thanks, Shirl. That'll be great for winter in the arcade. It gets bloody freezing in that booth when the door's open.'

Dolly looked from Linda to Shirley. She couldn't quite believe how stupid these two were. '*Red?!* What kind of armed robbers wear red ski masks? And that overall you've got on is far too small.'

'It fits perfect.' Shirley turned round with the black ski mask in her hand and smoothed the tight jumpsuit fabric over her slim figure.

'Overalls, I said! Big, dirty, baggy overalls. We're supposed to be men. I can see every curve, and look at your bloody ankles.'

Shirley had been told on many occasions that her ankles were one of her best features. 'What's wrong with them?' she whined, looking down at her feet.

'I can see them for a start!' Dolly barked back. 'You've even done alterations on that suit to show off your bust and put extra bloody zips everywhere. What are they for? Your lippy? I told you . . . plain black overalls, at least three to four sizes too big, as we have to pad 'em out. We've got to be wearing our own clothes underneath and be able to slip the overalls off real quick. These suits are useless, absolutely useless.'

Shirley knew she'd done wrong, just as Linda knew she'd done wrong, but whereas Linda chose to sulk defiantly, Shirley instantly tried to make amends. She held up the large black ski mask she'd bought and pulled it down over her face. 'Look, Dolly! What do you think of this? It's black and it's big enough to cover our hair.'

Dolly ripped the ski mask from Shirley's head, taking a lump of hair with it. 'The eye holes are too big and I don't want ones with a mouth hole. I can see your lipstick and your spray tan.'

Shirley looked at the floor. She knew that everything Dolly said was right, but she'd spent two days schlepping everywhere for this gear, all the way to Harlow, Windsor, even up the M1. Shirley took off the jumpsuit . . . *Twenty-five quid down the drain*, she thought. *Well, seventy-five counting all three.*

Throughout Dolly's tirade, Linda had been standing in the kitchen doorway chewing her nails. Although Shirley's shopping trip had clearly been a stupid waste of time, it was Linda who had put Dolly in a foul mood in the first place, and she did feel guilty. Not guilty enough to take any of the heat off Shirley, but even so. She decided she'd make some tea.

Seeing she'd hurt Shirley, Dolly decided to backtrack. 'If you sew up the mouth hole completely and the eye holes a little bit, it'll be fine, Shirley. Dye the other ones black and we've got ourselves the first bit of our outfit. But the jumpsuits are no good, I'm afraid. We need overalls, like I said. Once you've bought the right ones, cut the labels out and burn them so they can't be traced after we dump them.'

Shirley knew this was Dolly's way of apologising. 'What about the plimsolls?' she asked.

'Dye them black and they'll do fine.' Dolly lit a cigarette. 'Come and sit down, both of you. I didn't ask you here to talk about jump-suits and plimsolls.' As Dolly finished speaking, the kettle clicked off and Linda went to fill the teapot. 'Leave it!' Dolly bellowed.

In her rush to join Shirley and Dolly seated on the crates, Linda tripped over Wolf and kicked his backside to move him out of her way. Dolly gave her a nasty look and called Wolf over to sit next to her. She opened her bag and pulled out her notebook.

'We got problems,' Dolly started. 'I'll go through 'em one at a time . . . but most important, I've been thinking about what I read in the ledgers and I reckon Harry used four men in the raid, not three.'

'Four?' Linda repeated. She and Shirley looked confused.

'Four men and one of them got away. Leaving Joe, Terry and Harry to fend for themselves.' Linda and Shirley were riveted by what Dolly was telling them. She continued. 'This fourth man must have been called in from the outside, to drive. He must have driven the truck up front. Now there's been nothing about him in the papers, nothing at all. That means the law either haven't figured it out yet . . . which I doubt . . . or they're after him.'

'They won't be the only ones!' Linda shouted, leaping to her feet, red-faced with anger. 'The bastard!'

'Linda,' Dolly said gently, trying to calm things down again.

'No! I've got a right to speak. If he left my Joe burning to death . . . if he could have saved them and didn't, I'll kill him, Dolly, I swear I will.'

Again, Dolly tried to calm Linda. She was a hothead, after all, simply reacting in the only way she knew how.

Linda was having none of it. 'I'll kill him! You might not care about your man, Dolly Rawlins, but—'

Dolly was on her feet and at Linda so fast she didn't even get to finish her sentence. The heavy slap to the side of her face knocked her sideways.

'Don't you ever suggest I don't care!' Dolly growled. 'I saw how much you cared this afternoon, so stop with the hysterics, sit down and shut up!'

Linda slowly sat back down, holding her stinging cheek and trying to keep back the tears of grief, pain and embarrassment.

Shirley was frozen to the spot, trembling. *God, Dolly has a temper!* She'd never seen her fly off the handle like that before and could hardly believe it. And here was Dolly, sitting back smoking and checking over her notes as if nothing had happened.

From beneath her mop of black hair, Linda quietly spoke. 'Why is it I'm always in the wrong?' she asked in a trembling voice.

Dolly took a huge drag of her cigarette before replying. 'Because you're twenty-six and I'm forty-six and I'm the one paying the bills.' She looked at Shirley, who was white-faced with shock. 'Finish off making the tea, would you, Shirl?' she asked. Shirley went off to the kitchen without a word.

Dolly looked at Linda's red cheek, where her four finger marks were clearly visible. 'I'm sorry,' she said. 'I shouldn't have done that.' Linda got up and moved away from Dolly before she said something they'd all regret. Dolly didn't care about Linda's mood and continued as though her brief apology had solved all their problems. 'You know what this means, though, don't you? It means we'll have to get someone else in.'

'Not a man,' Shirley piped up from the kitchen. 'If we bring a fella in, half of London will know what we're up to.'

'Preferably not a man, no. There's no one in the ledgers I know well enough to trust, so I'll have to think on it. But we might need to put the date of the job back to give us time to find the right woman.'

'Jesus Christ,' Linda said impatiently. 'If all we need is another woman, I'll find one.'

'I'll find her,' Dolly said defiantly. There was no way anyone else was going to make a choice as important as that.

'You're the boss,' Linda sneered.

'And if you don't like it, you know what you can do! You can go back to bed with that bit of rough trade. I bet he's a right keeper and, if he's not, well, I'm sure there'll be another one along in a minute.'

Coming out of the kitchen, Shirley had no idea what Dolly meant and certainly wasn't going to ask. Linda stepped towards Dolly with furious eyes, clearly at breaking point. Shirley stepped quickly in front of her with a cup of tea, forcing Linda to stop dead. Unable to ignore the pleading in Shirley's eyes, Linda took her tea and moved away from Dolly again. Shirley sat down in between them.

'You said we had "problems" – plural,' said Shirley, waving away Dolly's horrible cigarette smoke.

'The Fisher brothers are coming on heavy and they're not going to let up. They've already started on me, ripping my place apart, and next time it'll be my face. Then they'll start on you two.' It was one thing for the widows to have a go at each other, but the Fishers were a different matter altogether. This news changed everything. Linda could walk away from Dolly if she became too much of a pain and Dolly would let her – Tony Fisher, on the other hand, would tear you apart just for turning your back on him. 'The Fishers want Harry's ledgers and they're not taking no for an answer. This fourth man, whoever he was – well I don't think he'll show his face round here again. I reckon he took off weeks ago.' Dolly stared at Linda and saw the hatred in her eyes for the coward who left her Joe to die such a slow and painful death. She spoke with total sincerity. 'We'll get him, Linda, and he'll get what's coming to him, but for the moment it's good that no one can find him.'

Linda broke the gaze first, looking down at the dirty concrete floor before Dolly could see the tears welling up in her eyes.

'We're going to pull a raid and I don't want any of us getting hurt,' Dolly went on. 'We're not big strong fellas, we're women. But we've got to start thinking like men. Boxer Davis works for the Fishers now and I'll put money on the fact that he's round there spilling the beans. And when they hear what he's got to say, they'll lay off.'

A self-satisfied smirk came over Dolly's face and, as they waited for her to speak again, Shirley was suddenly reminded of being back in the sauna and learning about the raid for the first time. Whatever Dolly said next, Shirley knew she'd be stunned by it. She was right.

'I've told Boxer that the fourth man, the one that got away, was Harry. Boxer believes that Harry's alive and when he tells the Fishers, they'll believe Harry's got the ledgers. This is the best way to protect us right now. Harry was the only person round here who could keep the Fishers in check cos of what he had on them, so we need Harry to be alive again.'

'How can you be sure Boxer will tell them?' Shirley asked.

'He'll talk. He always did, especially with a drink inside him. I gave him one of Harry's suit jackets and two hundred quid so, drunk or sober, he'll be feeling invincible.' Dolly finished her tea and handed her mug to Shirley. 'I'll be back in touch as soon as I've come up with the other member of the team.' Dolly opened her handbag, took out a bit of folded paper and handed it to Linda. 'That's a safe number for you both to call me on – it's an unlisted line at the convent I volunteer at. You can leave a message there any time and they'll contact me. Memorise it, then burn it.' Without another word, Dolly scooped up Wolf and left.

Linda looked at the phone number for about ten seconds; then handed it to Shirley. 'I've got no matches left; you'll have to eat it.'

Shirley looked at the phone number too, then was about to pop the note in her mouth when she caught the look on Linda's face.

'Joke! It's a bleedin' joke, Shirl.'

Shirley wasn't in the mood for jokes. Today had been far too stressful.

'I can't stand her sometimes,' Linda whispered.

Shirley's reply wasn't as supportive as Linda expected. 'I think the feeling's mutual.'

Linda shot Shirley a disdainful look. 'She's got no right to talk to us like we're kids. I think you did really well with those jumpsuits.'

'I didn't, Linda! They're completely wrong and you know it. Dolly was right to be angry.'

'She's no right to talk down to us or to slap me around. She's not the boss.'

'She is.' Shirley's voice was quiet, controlled and deadly serious. 'If this is really happening . . . she is the boss.'

* * *

Linda was well and truly pissed by ten o'clock, and sat in her booth at the shooting arcade in the West End red light district with a sozzled grin on her face. But no matter how drunk she got, she never gave out the wrong change. Charlie stood by the entrance door and kept looking over nervously at the booth as she took swig after swig from the vodka bottle. He worried that if the boss came in now, and saw Linda pissed and singing at the top of her voice, he'd probably get the sack as well. He sighed and smiled – if you can't beat 'em, join 'em. He threw the remains of his coffee onto the street, went over to the booth and peered through the glass at Linda. It took her a while to focus her eyes but, when she did, she gave Charlie her broadest smile.

'Charlie, my old darlin'. How are you?' Charlie held up his empty mug and flicked his eyes towards her vodka bottle. 'Bugger off,' Linda whispered through the gap where she gave people their change. 'Everyone'll want some.' Then she howled laughing. Letting her head flop forwards, she started making the odd drunken snorting noise. After a few moments, Charlie could no longer tell if she was laughing or crying. He was just about to ask if she was

OK when she flicked her head violently back again. Her eyes were hard now, and she spoke through gritted teeth.

'You know what, Charlie boy? I fucking love this place. I mean, look at it. There's underage kids with fake ID being pestered by the local paedo . . . there's a drunk kipping on the doorstep . . . there's more dealers than druggies . . . and passing trade is prossies, their pimps and their punters. I'm surrounded by the best of the best. Yeah, I'm really going places, Charlie! Cheers!' Linda emptied the remaining vodka in one swallow.

As Charlie went back to stand by the entrance door, he saw Bella O'Reilly walk in. Linda was right: the passing trade was prostitutes and their pimps or punters. Bella had brought both. She had beautiful shiny black skin, sultry looks and was dressed to kill in a skin-tight yellow satin top and tight black jeans, a matching jacket slung over one shoulder. Her high heels made her look even taller than her imposing six feet. Bella stopped in the middle of the arcade, surveying the scene, as did her pimp, who hovered a short distance behind her. Oil Head, as he was commonly known, started joking with a couple of Chinese guys while twisting his black Fedora in his hands, his gold rings glinting in the arcade's flashing lights. Charlie knew he was organising a drug deal. He'd told Oil Head before about plying his trade in the arcade, but the pimp had just laughed – a sort of grunting nasal laugh, a result of snorting too much cocaine. The problem with Oil Head was you didn't know if he was laughing with you or at you. He was a nasty bastard who liked roaring around on his Harley Davidson and all his girls were scared shitless of him, all except his number one – Bella O'Reilly.

Bella started swaggering round the machines like a seasoned rock performer working the stage, even stopping to sort out two loudmouthed youths who gave her the come-on. Whatever she said had the desired result. They both looked petrified, apologised profusely and made a hasty exit. Bella saw Linda in the booth and gave her a big smile before coming over. She didn't need to say excuse me to get past people; they nervously stepped out of her way.

'Bella!' Linda screamed from inside the booth. Bella, still walking, did a quick bump-n-grind and then stopped in front of Linda, propping herself up against the glass.

Linda and Bella knew each other from way back. Bella had always been in a class of her own: big enough to take care of herself and scared of no one. Linda, unlike Bella, had never worked for a pimp; she'd been more of a lone amateur who only gave hand or oral relief as opposed to full sex, and well before she met Joe.

'How can you stand it in here?' Bella asked.

'It's soundproof and the voddy helps,' Linda joked. 'I love your hair, Bell.' Bella's fabulous hair was now cropped close to her head, in a Grace Jones style. She wore a gold headband which, although it was cheap and sold on the market stalls, looked a million dollars on Bella and made her look like an African princess. 'What you up to these days?' Linda asked.

'Same old, same old. Three spots a night at the Z-Easy and anything I can fit in between.'

'How come you're back in this neck of the woods?'

'You know me. I was doing all right, but then I lost my temper one night and beat this geezer up. Foreign bastard he was, couldn't understand a word he was saying. His hands were everywhere, but he hadn't paid for everywhere so I told him to leave off. When he didn't I lamped him one. I pled guilty and Oil Head paid my fine.'

'So you owe him.'

'Big time. I'll pay him off then see what I fancy doing.' Bella glanced across to Oil Head, who was whispering to one of the Chinese men and pointing towards Bella. 'Looks like I might have a client.' Bella's face became serious and she moved round to the door of the booth. Linda opened it so that they could talk face to face.

'I heard about Joe and I'm really sorry. He was one of the best and you two were great together, sugar. You need me, a few quid or anything then just ask, I'm gonna move back to my old pad soon so I'll be close by and visit you more often. For now, I'm at the International.'

'Thanks, Bella. I appreciate that.'

Oil Head whistled to Bella and she held up her hand. Linda took her gently by the wrist. 'You off the hard stuff?'

Bella looked embarrassed for a moment. 'You got the wrong person, darlin', that was the old man. He did the final OD three months back.' Then she added, '. . . so I know what you're going through.' Linda knew that Bella had used heroin in the past and took her denial to mean that she was clean now. She certainly looked clean. In fact, she looked fabulous. Bella gave Linda's hand one final, comforting squeeze and then left.

Charlie appeared next to Linda. 'I could give that black chick one,' he said, scratching his balls and sneakily sniffing his pit. Linda laughed at Charlie's naivety.

'She could give you one an' all, but you wouldn't get up afterwards. You so much as look at her and she'd clip you round the ear.'

'I wouldn't dip me wick in her anyway,' Charlie said defensively. 'She'd probably give me a dose of the clap.' As he slunk away, he added, 'She looks way too much like a fella anyway.'

Linda looked across at Bella as she left with her Chinese punter. From the back, with their overcoats and short black hair, they looked incredibly similar. Linda grinned to herself as she opened the drawer in her desk and got out a new bottle of vodka.

CHAPTER 11

Arnie Fisher poured two glasses of champagne, then took both of them over to the leather sofa where Carlos was sprawled out reading a magazine. He sat close to him and put his hand on his thigh. Carlos took the glass and, laying his arm across the back of the sofa, silently invited Arnie to sit back into it. The men chinked glasses and sipped their champagne.

Arnie was looking very dapper in a new cream silk suit. He got up, admired himself in the mirror, turned and smiled at Carlos. 'Would you like one made up, too?' he asked. 'It'd really suit you.' Arnie loved to dress Carlos, like a toy doll or a dog who had no opinion of their own. Carlos didn't mind, in fact he quite enjoyed being pampered. He nodded seductively and sipped his drink.

Gloria buzzed to come through and, without waiting for an answer entered, dressed up to the nines, her huge tits bursting out of the 46 C cup. She leant on the door. 'Boxer's outside, wants a word . . . let him in, shall I?'

Arnie adored Gloria. If he had been straight, he would have had a scene with her. They got on well, he could yell and shout at her and she didn't give a toss. She was a good girl was Gloria, been with him for years, used to be a hostess downstairs, got a bit old for the racket, and went upstairs to the office. Her typing was still haywire, and she couldn't spell, but somehow she got things in order, and she looked good out there at her desk.

Gloria crossed to the champagne and helped herself to a glass before joining Arnie and admiring her figure in the mirror alongside his. She thought Carlos was a gorgeous-looking fella and didn't know how he could stand Arnie pawing at him, but then she decided that poofs were all the same – just out for what they could get. She'd no doubt let Arnie paw her as well if she got silk suits and nice motors out of it. Yes, Carlos was doing very nicely out of Arnie, especially with all the added business going his way at his garage. She wondered how long he would last, though. Usually Arnie's boys never made it beyond two months. He was a fickle bastard, but this one, this Carlos, it'd been near that already and they still seemed to be going strong. And if Carlos ever did get dumped by Arnie, well, she'd be there to comfort him.

'I'm off home now,' Gloria said, necking her drink. 'Shall I let Boxer in or what?'

Carlos stood up to leave.

'Stay. It's only Boxer Davis,' said Arnie. 'Wheel him in,' he told Gloria.

Gloria wiggled out and Boxer entered, his appearance catching Arnie off guard slightly. He'd had his hair cut, parted and flattened down on one side, which made his ears stick out, but more than that – Boxer was actually wearing a near-decent suit.

'So, what you got?' Arnie asked, lighting a cigar.

Boxer blurted it out. He'd been at the Rawlins' place and had some information, which was worth a lot of money, but it was private stuff. Boxer looked at Carlos, hoping he would leave the room.

Arnie gave Carlos the nod to get another bottle of champagne. As he left, Boxer sat down without asking. This was a surprise. Boxer never pushed his luck with either of the Fishers, but today he seemed very confident about something. Arnie let Boxer's disrespect go for now. He was intrigued to hear what the big oaf had to say.

'I got news about Harry Rawlins, Mr Fisher. I been with Dolly, gaining her trust back and, well, she confided in me.' Boxer left a dramatic pause and then dropped the bombshell. 'He's alive. Harry Rawlins is alive.'

Arnie's reaction was not what Boxer had expected. He sat at his desk, leant back, took his glasses off and suddenly started to shriek with a high-pitched laugh. Then he looked up, glaring at Boxer with icy eyes as his face turned nasty. 'Alive! She's spinning you a yarn, you stupid little prick.'

'Straight up, Mr Fisher. He wants me to work with him. Offered me a job, he did. She give me his jacket on his say-so. He wants me looking respectable for him.'

'You really are pathetic. I was at his soddin' funeral, along with the law. Who does she think she's kiddin', eh? I watched them bury him!'

'It wasn't him.'

Arnie got to his feet, making Boxer flinch. 'It was him! And you've just blown it, Boxer. You're through, you hear me! You had your chance and you fuckin' blew it. Get that rag of a suit off and go back to cleaning beer crates – it's all you're good for. And watch your step from this day forwards, speaking to me like you own the place, sitting down without being invited to. You watch your back. I'll deal with that bitch now; I'll find out if Harry bleedin' Rawlins is alive. I'll fucking well dig the bastard up if I have to!'

Boxer stood, raging at the way he was just being dismissed. Arnie was an arrogant prick who made Boxer feel dirty and useless. Well – he wasn't useless. With Harry back at his side, they'd wipe this little gay turd Fisher out. 'I'll tell you one thing, Mr Fisher,' Boxer spoke in what he hoped was a calm, threatening tone, 'Tony turned his place over and Harry didn't like that one bit.' As Boxer continued, eyes fixed on Arnie, Carlos came back into the room with a second bottle of champagne. 'Harry's furious, I'd say. Tony even done over their dead baby's nursery, so you can tell him that Harry's very, very angry with him. I'm not the one who needs to watch his back. Harry's watching my back, so I'll be fine.'

Through gritted teeth, Arnie whispered, 'Piss off.' Boxer left without another word.

Arnie's eyes were practically popping out of his head. Carlos stood in the middle of the room like a spare part, holding the champagne bottle. He could see that Arnie was ready to explode, so he put the bottle down and put his arm round Arnie's shoulders. Arnie pushed Carlos away, then quickly corrected himself. 'Not now, darlin', that's all. Not now.'

* * *

When Shirley arrived at the lock-up, Linda was sitting on one of the orange boxes looking dreadful, make-up smeared all over her face. Shirley raced across. What if Tony Fisher had been to see her and done something terrible?

'I'm fine, I'm fine,' Linda said, flapping her hands at Shirley. 'Keep the noise down a bit. My head's banging.'

'Well, what are we here for, then? You know we're not meant to call meetings, only Dolly. What's happened that was so important, Linda?'

Bella came out of the office and handed Linda a cup of coffee. Shirley stared, mouth open, not knowing what to say or where to look. 'Tea?' Bella said. Shirley couldn't think of a single thing to say. Who was this woman? Why was she here? And, most importantly, what the bloody hell had Linda told her!

'This is Bella,' Linda said, casually sipping her coffee. 'She's our number four.'

Shirley's mouth opened even wider, which just made Linda laugh. 'Don't be like that, Shirl. Bella's as good as gold and as hard as nails. She's just what we need. I know what you're thinking, but Dolly'll be fine once she's met her. And if she ain't, well bollocks. Bella's worth ten of her.' Linda nudged Bella to get her attention. 'She is loaded, mind, so, in truth, she's probably worth ten thousand of you!'

Shirley finally spoke up, 'She'll go absolutely mad, Linda, and you know it.'

'Bella's got just as much right to take Dolly's money as we have. She deserves some good luck for a change . . . and she's a widow, just like us. Dolly'll love that.'

As Shirley shook her head in disgust and disbelief, they heard Wolf yapping at the Alsatian next door and the Alsatian growling back. All three women looked towards the door, then Shirley scurried off towards the office, dragging Bella away.

'You deal with her,' Shirley snapped at Linda. 'You're in for it now.'

Linda put her head in her hands, willing her headache to go away.

Dolly raced into the lock-up, popping Wolf on the floor as she ran towards Linda. 'What's the matter?' Dolly asked, concerned 'You all right? What's happened?' When Linda lifted her head and Dolly smelt the booze, her concern turned to anger. 'You're pissed!' Dolly seethed. 'Did you call an emergency meeting, Linda, cos you ran out of vodka?'

Shirley watched from the doorway of the kitchen and office annexe. She'd never seen Dolly look so dishevelled. She wore no make-up, her hair needed washing, and she looked exhausted; her face drawn, haggard almost. For the first time ever, Shirley thought Dolly looked her age, older even than her own mum. Then again, thought Shirley, she *is* old enough to be my mum.

'I'm not pissed. I have had a couple, sure, but I'm not pissed.'

Linda was certainly pissed enough to be oblivious to Dolly's simmering rage. From where Shirley stood, she could see the veins standing up in Dolly's neck. Before anyone could speak again, Bella stepped out from behind Shirley.

Bella was a tall, impressive, commanding figure, but Dolly didn't flinch at any of that. Bella smiled and walked towards Dolly, hand outstretched. Shirley had seen Dolly when she had had a go at Linda earlier that day, but she was different now – earlier, when she slapped Linda, it was like a parent slapping a child. Now, Dolly looked even tougher and there was something almost mannish about her, as though this situation demanded something extra. When she eventually spoke, it was a growl. She flicked a look to Bella and back to Linda.

'Who the hell is she?"

Linda, empowered by the booze, introduced them. 'This is Bella,' she said.

'What's she doing here?" Dolly was desperately trying to maintain control.

'She wants in. You said we needed somebody else, so I told her and she—'

'Told her? Told her what exactly?'

Stumbling to her feet, Linda continued, 'Everything. I told her everything when she came into the arcade. Look at her, Dolly, she's perfect.'

Dolly cut Linda off. 'You in on this?" she bellowed at Shirley, who was still standing in the doorway.

'I was in bed when she called. Don't bring me into this, I'm as shocked as you are.'

'Shut up, Miss Goody Two Shoes, and let me finish!' Linda shouted at Shirley.

'Oh, you're finished all right, Linda.' Dolly had her hand on her hip and was waggling her finger in Linda's face, trying desperately to resist slapping her again. 'You can get your gear and you can get out! And you can take that black tart with you!'

'Just let me explain.'

'Explain?! Explain how you went and told the whole world about what we're up to? How many more slags you got coming down here? I want you out!!' Dolly grabbed Linda and started to push her towards the door but, this time, fuelled by the booze, Linda fought back.

'You've talked to me like shit once too often, Dolly! You treat your dog better than you do me!' As the tears came, Linda reached the point of no return and she screamed in Dolly's face. 'I bring the answer to all our problems and you throw it in my face, you stuck-up bitch.'

From nowhere, Bella pulled Linda away from Dolly and slapped her, hard. In the following silence, Dolly and Bella stood nose to nose getting the measure of each other. Then Bella spoke for the first time.

'You two want to have a cat fight, go ahead, only don't do it over me.' Bella's deep voice was calm and controlled, her eyes blazed with a silent warning. 'Look, Mrs Rawlins, anything she told me, I just forgot. It's no skin off my back. Thanks for the coffee.' Bella collected her handbag and started to walk towards the door.

Linda looked at Dolly.

'Just a minute.' Dolly's words made Bella stop and turn.

'You talking to me, Mrs Rawlins?' Bella's confidence shone as she stared at Dolly. 'Cos I got a name and it's not "tart" or "slag". My name's Bella. And I didn't come pushing my way in here, I was asked. These two might think your idea's crazy, but I don't. I know what you want to do and I wouldn't have come here if I didn't think I could be part of it.' Dolly listened intently, without breaking Bella's stare. 'How many girls out there do you think could do this? Better still, how many do you think would want to?' When there was still no word from Dolly, Bella continued towards the door. 'You can stuff your job,' she said.

'Stop. How much has she told you?' Dolly asked.

'Nothing.' Bella's tone was sarcastic now that she'd made her point. 'I've got a really bad memory. If you want to come with me, Linda, I'll walk you home.'

Linda stood between Dolly and Bella, like a small child between feuding parents. 'Please, Dolly I only did it for the best. I'm really sorry. You can't call it off, Dolly, not cos of me. Please don't let her go, Dolly, she's right, I know she is.'

'You opened your big mouth to anyone else, Linda?'

Linda shook her head. 'No. I swear I haven't.'

'What do you think, Shirley?' Dolly asked.

Shirley was surprised to be asked her opinion. She didn't know Bella and she was upset that Linda had gone behind their backs, but she still trusted her. 'She looks the part,' Shirley replied after a moment. 'And now that she knows everything, she might as well stay.'

'You married?' Dolly asked Bella.

Bella walked back towards Dolly, Linda and Shirley. 'I got no ties, Mrs Rawlins. I just do the clubs and anything else I can pick up.'

'She tell you we'd be using guns?'

'Yes.'

'You drive?'

'Yes.' Once again, Dolly and Bella stared at each other, but this time it wasn't like two Alpha females vying for position. Now there was respect in their eyes. It was Bella who finally lightened the atmosphere.

'And I play a mean tune on a harmonica.'

Dolly had to suppress a smile. Bella was a strong, powerful woman who took no shit from anyone, but she was also smart and would be a great asset to the team.

Linda and Shirley held each other as they waited for Dolly's decision.

'All right, Bella,' Dolly said finally. '. . . and the name's Dolly.'

CHAPTER 12

Forensics were able to tell DI Resnick that the rear bumper of the bread van had been modified with a heavy metal bar strong enough to ram backwards into the security wagon, and that there were still traces of the security wagon's body paint on it. This was definitely the bread van used in the botched robbery.

There had been five days of intensive police work at Sunshine Bread, during which every man and woman in the company had their prints taken and compared to those found in the bread van. It was a long, tedious procedure, but Resnick was determined.

So far, no prints taken had revealed anyone with a criminal record, and all the prints in the van belonged to company employees. But someone had to have given Rawlins the keys to the site and to the van. Someone was crooked. During the week of the robbery, the fleet manager had been told that this van was in the workshop being repaired, so Resnick started with the two mechanics. Both denied any involvement, of course, and neither claimed to recognise the photos of Harry Rawlins, Terry Miller or Joe Pirelli. One of them, Resnick insisted, had to be a liar.

'You can see it in their eyes, Fuller, and in their body language. He'll not be a criminal mastermind, he'll be a hard-up, scared little man who was slipped a couple of hundred and will have been shitting himself since the robbery went tits up.'

'Seems to me,' Fuller argued, exhausted by Resnick's 'gut instinct', 'that all he's got to do is keep his mouth shut, seeing as Rawlins and his gang are all dead and there's no one left to drop him in it.'

'There's the fourth man, Fuller. The fourth man can drop everyone in it because he's got the ledgers. No, it's one of the mechanics and I'm going to find out which one.'

* * *

Donald Franks sat in front of Resnick, twisting the oily rag in his hands. He was certainly nervous about something. Resnick had left Franks to sweat for what he judged to be the optimum length of time and was just about to start his questioning, when the phone rang.

'What?' Resnick shouted down the receiver, then his face quickly softened and his voice lowered. 'All right, Alice, thank you. Yes, I'll be back by four. I will, Alice, I will.' Resnick hung up. 'Keep a close eye on the time, Fuller,' he ordered. 'I've got to get back to the station by four.'

Within minutes of starting the interview with Franks, Resnick discovered that he wasn't nervous about being Rawlins' inside man, but about slacking off work. He and the other mechanic would clock in together and then one of them would bugger off down the pub for the day. 'Please don't tell anyone, sir,' Franks whimpered. 'The jobs always get done. There's just not enough work for two of us and we can't afford to lose our jobs as well, you see.'

'As well?' Resnick's eyes narrowed as he sensed an important lead coming his way.

'There used to be three of us, sir. Len was sacked three months back. Me and Bob're hanging on by the skin of our teeth. Please don't tell anyone.'

'Shut up whinging,' Resnick ordered. 'I don't give two hoots about you and Bob scamming your boss, but if you don't tell me all about your mate Len, I'll make damn sure your boss finds out everything.'

Franks told Resnick that Len Gulliver had been suspected of theft; Franks didn't believe it for a second, he thought it must just be the quickest way to get rid of someone. On further questioning, Resnick discovered that each mechanic had got his own set of yard keys cut in order to sneak off to the pub whenever work was light. So, if no one knew Gulliver had yard keys in the first place, it stood to reason that he could still have them now, meaning he could easily be the man who helped Rawlins steal the bread van. Resnick gave the orders to find and arrest Len Gulliver. For the first time in weeks, he actually thought they were getting somewhere. In fact, he was almost pleasant and put a tenner on Len Gulliver knowing the identity of the fourth man.

At Gulliver's house, his wife said he wasn't with her anymore, but her reluctance to let them in made Resnick think she was lying. She went on and on about the bread company treating her Len like a dog, worse than a dog in fact.

'Fifteen years he worked for them and – just like that, finished, out. They made up some rubbish about him stealing, but you don't slip someone two hundred quid to go quietly if you really think they been stealing from you, do you? Well, do you?'

Suspecting Len Gulliver had done a runner, and that she would protect him, Resnick thought it was pointless even asking where her husband was. He was about to leave when he decided to show Mrs Gulliver the suspects' photographs. Resnick was amazed when she said she recognised Joe Pirelli.

'Yes, he's been here,' she said innocently. 'He had some business with my husband. And this one –' she pointed to the photo of Rawlins – 'waited outside for him. I could see him from the kitchen window in a dark-grey Mercedes-Benz.'

Resnick felt his insides churn. It looked like Mrs Gulliver genuinely knew nothing about her husband's criminal activities. He couldn't wait to get his hands on Len Gulliver.

'And where is your husband now?' he asked.

Mrs Gulliver started to cry and pointed to the dining room.

Surprised, Resnick walked over and pushed the dining room door open.

'You're nicked, Len!' he roared, then stopped, aghast. There was a coffin on the table.

'The cancer got him in the throat,' Mrs Gulliver explained from behind him. She was in floods of tears. 'Thankfully it was over quickly and he didn't suffer long.'

* * *

They were back where they started. Once outside, Fuller couldn't stop himself. 'You're nicked, Len,' Fuller mocked. 'Gotta be a classic that . . . absolute classic.'

As they got into their car, Andrews told Resnick that Alice had been on the radio twice. Once to say a snout called 'Green Teeth' had rung for him, and the second call was to say that DCI Saunders wanted to know where he was.

'For fuck's sake!' Resnick shouted at Fuller. 'I told you to get me back to the station by four!'

'Is it something important?' Fuller asked as he started the engine, knowing full well that Resnick had arranged the meeting, not just to review the case, but to discuss his chances for promotion. Like the rest of the squad, Fuller suspected Resnick's promotional chances were, as ever, pretty low. They'd be even lower now that he'd missed his appointment. Fuller looked in the rear-view mirror and winked at Andrews.

Resnick ordered Fuller to drive to the Rawlins house so he could to speak to the officers on surveillance there. Fuller drove slowly past Dolly's house, which was in darkness with the curtains drawn. He pulled up near the unmarked surveillance car and Resnick got out. Hawkes nearly bolted through the roof when Resnick banged his window. They had nothing to report, no movement, nothing . . . apart from a furniture truck that had arrived at the Rawlins property and taken out a baby's cot and bedding along with other various nursery items. The truck had been stopped and searched up the road by a uniform patrol car, but nothing incriminating had been found.

'Take me back to the station,' Resnick ordered. 'Let's hope Green Teeth has got something more productive for me than you bunch of wasters.'

* * *

Arnie Fisher was inches away from Tony's face, talking calmly and slowly. Tony knew it was best just to listen.

'It was a simple job. You pick up twenty grand's worth of booze for twelve grand, and bring it back here. No rough stuff. No shagging the wife of the bloke you're doing a deal with. What's in your head, son?' Arnie demanded, poking Tony in the temple. 'What makes you do stupid things all the time?'

Tony wasn't fazed. 'She was a pretty little blonde with big tits who made no complaints about me touching her up.' A grin slowly spread across his face. 'Her pig-ugly husband complained though! You should have seen the fat northern prick drop. One sucker punch and he was down.'

'Then what?' Arnie asked.

Tony shrugged. 'Well, yes, I did prang the Jag on the way out of the car park, but the good news is that I pranged it on that Manc prick's Beemer. Carlos will fix the Jag, no problem. Look, Arnie,' he continued, excitement getting the better of him, 'I had the Old Bill on my tail, sirens blaring, blue lights flashing, the whole works – and I managed to lose them. No one was hurt, the booze van got back to London OK, and I got my end away – what's there to worry about?'

'The fact that the Manchester guys probably won't do business with us again,' said Arnie, beginning to lose his rag. 'And that is a worry – they're bloody good customers!'

Tony lounged back in the leather swivel chair. 'Screw the Manchester wankers! You shouldn't be worrying about small-time northern business, darlin', you should be worrying about big-time Rawlins business right here on your doorstep.'

'You think I don't know that?' Arnie barked back. 'Why did you think I sent you to Manchester? I don't need you going off the rails here, Tony. I need calm. I need tactics and brains.'

Tony leant forward, suddenly serious. 'If the law get hold of them ledgers, Arnie, you an' me go down for a fifteen stretch or more. We done three big fence jobs with that son of a bitch Rawlins and you can bet he listed every single penny we laundered.'

'You don't need to remind me!' snapped Arnie.

'Look – softly-softly's not working,' said Tony, getting to his feet. 'I'll take over from Boxer. I'll get them widows to tell us what we want.'

Arnie remained uncharacteristically silent.

'What's wrong?' asked Tony.

'Boxer did get one thing out of Dolly,' Arnie said. 'She told him Harry Rawlins is still alive.'

Tony's mouth gaped for a second, then he laughed. 'For Christ's sake, that's got to be a fuckin' joke! She identified and buried him, so don't give me that bullshit.'

Arnie was looking edgy. He sat back down behind his desk and took his glasses off. 'We don't know it's bullshit.'

Tony sighed. 'It is bullshit, bruv. You know it is. Leave it to me. I'll sort it. Don't you worry about a thing. I'll get hold of Boxer and Dolly Rawlins and get the truth out of 'em.'

'Don't do nothin' too crazy,' said Arnie. He polished his glasses nervously. 'We got a good business going, you and me. Speak to Boxer, speak to Dolly, ask a few questions. You don't rough anyone up and you don't go near the other two. We haven't heard a peep out of Pirelli or that other one, so you leave them alone.'

'Shirley,' said Tony. 'Her name's Shirley.' He was almost drooling. 'Lovely little piece.'

'That's her,' said Arnie. 'And there'll be none of that, Tony, you hear me?'

The door opened and Carlos walked in. Tony was on him like a shot.

'You knock, you ponce ... understand me? Knock before you just walk in.'

'I come to get the Jag for fixing ... again. You should drive more carefully, Tony.'

As Tony strode towards Carlos, Arnie bellowed: 'Cool it!' Tony stopped in his tracks, a few feet away from Carlos, who stared back, confident that Arnie would protect him. But one click of Arnie's fingers in the direction of the sofa and Carlos was put in his place.

Arnie moved to Tony. 'Be careful,' Arnie said quietly. There's a lot at stake.'

'Listen, petal,' said his brother, 'believe you me, Harry Rawlins is dead. We got nothin' to worry about where he's concerned. The only thing we got on our backs are the ledgers, an' if I'd had my way we'd have had 'em by now. First, I'm paying that cousin Eddie Rawlins a visit, next I'll talk to the Rawlins widow and then I'll bring that idiot Boxer back here and we can all compare notes over a nice pot of tea.'

Tony gave a cynical kissing pout to Carlos and stomped out of the room.

Carlos looked at Arnie. 'Trouble?' he asked, opening a bottle of champagne.

'Nothing for you to worry about, darlin'.' Arnie moved to stand behind Carlos, from where he could stroke his pert butt cheeks. Arnie was a little shorter than Carlos and had to raise his chin slightly in order to rest it on Carlos's broad, muscular shoulder. 'Just got a few things to tie up,' Arnie continued. 'That Rawlins, Miller and Pirelli fiasco left a few loose ends.'

Carlos recognised the name Pirelli, but said nothing as he continued to pour the champagne. Arnie, wanting to lighten the atmosphere and change the subject, nodded for Carlos to open the large, tissue-wrapped box on the sofa. Inside was a neatly folded white silk suit. Carlos held it up, smiling.

'I love it,' he said, with a beaming white smile. 'Pirelli . . .' he added, casually, 'I heard that name someplace before?'

Arnie fussed and fiddled, putting the jacket on Carlos. 'Yeah, he was a tough son of a bitch. His wife works the cash till at an arcade in Soho – real slag. But Joe, he was heavy duty.' He stepped back from Carlos, admiring the fit of the suit jacket.

Carlos thought of the photograph face down by the side of Linda's bed. 'I really like this suit, Arnie,' was all he said.

* * *

Eddie Rawlins was sitting in his dirty, dank office with his feet up on the desk. It was an old shack stuck in the middle of a car breaker's yard in Camberwell. In some areas the cars were piled three or four high. Eddie spent most of his days sitting in his office staring at them, daydreaming of the sky-blue Roller he'd buy when he made enough money. Harry had promised years ago that he would purchase an expensive top-of-the-range car crusher, which would make the business more productive. That never happened.

Eddie was on the blower to a mate with a little betting shop near Epsom; he had been given a tip for the three fifteen at Haydock, and he placed a five-pound each way bet. Although he was the careful sort when it came to gambling, Eddie would spend a hundred quid on some tart who'd have him over a 'hot fur number'. Most women he met, he reflected, as he flipped through the papers to mark a couple of other good runners, turned out to be as pony as the horses he backed.

As he chatted on the phone, Eddie heard a car draw up outside. When he saw who it was, he froze and his stomach turned over. He took his feet off the desk, put the phone down and, trying to act nonchalantly, opened the desk drawer and took out a bottle of Scotch.

'All right, Tony? Just in time for an afternoon nip. You'll join me, won't you?' Eddie bustled over to the filing cabinet to get glasses, and took a quick glance through the dust-stained window at the horrible green Ford Granada parked outside. At least Tony Fisher had come alone.

A stream of drivel flowed from Eddie's mouth. 'Business is slow here,' he babbled. 'Nobody doin' much in the breaker's trade right now. How's things with you, Tony? Nice club you and your brother run, a very nice place.' Eddie started pouring Tony a drink.

'What you know about your cousin Harry's ledgers then, Eddie?' asked Tony pleasantly.

Eddie's aim went off and he missed the glass completely. Tony Fisher was very good at his line of work; in fact, he was in many ways everything Eddie aspired to be. A hard man with bulging muscles, but well turned out in fancy clothes and well-manicured, even down to the little diamond stud in his ear. Tony sat down opposite Eddie and crossed his legs, revealing polished Gucci shoes as he brushed down his thigh with his hand. It was Arnie who had taught Tony how to look classy, although he didn't approve of the diamond earring. Tony thought it made him look sexy; he was to some women, but to others his shifty eyes let him down.

Tony Fisher never met anyone eye to eye; instead, he made a point of looking at people's foreheads when he spoke. Now he cast a slow gaze around the filthy squalid hut, knowing full well the effect he was having on Eddie. Inflicting fear always made Tony feel good.

'You know old Boxer Davis, don't you?' Tony asked, as though it was the most natural question in the world.

'Yeah,' Eddie stuttered, 'he works for you. Bit of a charity case. I haven't seen him since the funeral.'

'Well, he's been shooting his mouth off about your cousin. Telling the world that Harry Rawlins is alive and kicking. We both know that can't be true, don't we?'

'Alive?' Eddie seemed astonished. 'Harry's not alive, Tony – I mean, I'm family; he'd tell me before Boxer bloody Davis.'

Tony smiled a reassuring smile and Eddie visibly relaxed a little. Tony took out his handkerchief and leant across the table, arm stretched towards his glass of whisky. In a flash, his hand diverted from the glass and he grabbed Eddie by the hair, pulled him over the table and stuffed the handkerchief into his mouth. Hauling Eddie off the table, Tony slammed him against the wall and butted him in the face. It was over in a matter of seconds. A dazed and semi-conscious Eddie slid down the wall onto his backside. Tony squatted down, removed the handkerchief and gently wiped the blood from Eddie's busted nose. Leaning his head close, he whispered menacingly, 'Now, tell me what you know about Harry Rawlins' ledgers.'

From behind the tears, Eddie pleaded with Tony. 'I don't know anything about ledgers, Tony, I swear to God I don't.'

'But you're family,' Tony mocked. 'He'd tell you before Boxer bloody Davis and if Boxer bloody Davis knows, then it stands to reason you know.'

'I don't! On my life, I don't. Harry never told me anything. I was just bigging myself up, Tony, you know how it is. Harry had it all and I had . . . well, this shithole. Me and Harry weren't close; he didn't even like me. He told me nothing, I swear.'

Tony raised his hand to scratch his own forehead and Eddie flinched so hard he almost fell off the floor.

'Please don't hit me again!' Eddie screamed.

'Be quiet, you Jessie.' As Tony ramped up the menace, Eddie kept his hands high, protecting his face, nodding or shaking his head in response.

'Harry had it all, did he?' demanded Tony. 'Well, now I've got it all, understand? Me and my brother. And whether Harry's alive or dead makes no fucking difference to us, cos he's nothing anymore. Which clearly makes you less than nothing. Agreed?' Tony put his hand gently on the side of Eddie's face. 'So, you keep your ear to the ground . . .' Tony slammed Eddie's face hard into the fibreboard flooring '. . . and you let me know if you hear anything from Boxer Davis or if you hear anything about Harry's ledgers.' Tony tapped his hand hard on Eddie's cheek a couple of times and got up.

Eddie daren't move. He lay on the filthy floor, crying silently, eyes screwed tight shut, waiting for a boot in the face. He only opened his eyes when he heard Tony's car start up and drive away. He scrambled to his feet, holding his aching head and his smashed nose, and looked out of the window to make absolutely certain that Tony had gone. Then he picked up the phone.

* * *

In a small hovel of a flat in Portobello Road, the phone was answered by Bill Grant. Bill listened as Eddie, in a trembling, high-pitched voice, poured out everything that had just happened. Eventually, Bill couldn't take any more.

'Shut your stupid mouth, Eddie. What did you tell him?' Bill demanded.

'I told him nothing. It's all coming from Boxer Davis,' Eddie said.

'And where's he?'

Eddie paused and closed his eyes because he knew for sure that he was about to put Boxer in harm's way. Bill Grant was worse than Tony. Bill Grant was a truly hard bastard who killed people for a living in whatever way you wanted – slow, fast, he didn't care. His real skill was that he was way more subtle than Tony, which is why most of the manor had no idea he was back. Bill wasn't showy, he knew how to lay low and keep under the radar. He didn't look like much, but by God he was trouble; he had nothing and no one so he had nothing to lose – and that made him one of the most dangerous men Eddie had ever come across. Bill had just got out after a twelve stretch, but he was right back in the thick of things. Eddie opened his eyes as Bill repeated his question.

'Where's Boxer Davis?'

As he hung his head in shame, Eddie told himself that the state of Boxer's face was nowhere near as important as the state of his own.

CHAPTER 13

The three women were all busy in the lock-up. Shirley was in the corner sorting out two pairs of dark-blue overalls she'd bought, carefully cutting out the labels and dropping them in a bin so that they could be burnt later. Bella and Linda were respraying a Ford Escort van white. Both women wore face masks, as the paint spray had an acrid stink and had made Linda's eyes red-rimmed. Their own dark-blue boiler suits were now as white as the van they were spraying.

'I dunno about you, Bella, but I'm knackered. I think we done enough for now. It's got to dry out before another coat,' said Linda.

Bella nodded and continued finishing a section before she disconnected the spray and pulled off her mask. 'You reckon she's gonna turn up tonight and bring us some cash?' Bella was reluctant to ask really, but she'd given up some shifts at the club to be here; she needed to know if it was going to be worth her while.

Linda shrugged her shoulders. 'I hope so! The spray paint weren't cheap and we been here for hours now. What you reckon, Shirley?'

'I've been out shopping for all this gear and run out of funds, so I bleedin' hope so too.'

Bella sat on one of the orange boxes, pulling off her thick rubber gloves. 'You know we should talk about this, just us three. Linda, you said we're going along with Dolly for the handouts, but it doesn't feel like that anymore, does it? She could be half crazy with grief and not know what she's doing, or she could actually be planning a flaming robbery.'

'I agree,' Shirley said. 'Why waste her money on us and all the gear if she's not telling the truth?'

'If this was for real, we'd make millions . . .' Bella said. She seemed genuinely excited.

'One million,' Shirley corrected. 'Split four ways.'

Bella's sarcasm rose to the surface. 'Oh, well, let's forget it and go home, then! Who wants to do all this work for a poxy quarter of a million?' After a short pause, they all laughed. Bella continued, 'All I'm saying is this: Dolly reckons it's all planned out and all we've gotta do is actually pull it off. Personally, I look around this lock-up at what we've achieved and I'm all fired up.'

Shirley smiled shyly at Linda as she too allowed herself to contemplate the idea of actually completing the robbery, grabbing £250,000 each and never having to worry again. Now Bella had brought it out into the open, it sounded far more exciting.

Linda was, as always, the more practical voice of reason. 'If the lazy old mare was here, we could ask her straight. Truth is, she's not been around for days. We've all been playing make-believe and we're all out of cash. Now, maybe she has got it all planned and we're all going to be rich – or maybe her little breakdown is over and she's forgot to tell us. She could be sitting at home right now in her ivory tower, with a whisky in her hand and that mutt on her knee.'

'You got no faith, Linda,' Bella said, shaking her head. 'People can surprise you if you just let them.'

'Yeah? Well, I ain't been surprised by no one in a long time. I've had enough, I'm going home.'

As Linda headed for the door, Shirley tossed a match into the bin to burn the labels she'd cut from the overalls. There was a sudden whoosh as a large flame shot upward. Shirley jumped back screaming as it singed her fringe.

'Jesus Christ, Shirl!' Bella shouted. 'What did you put on them?'

'Half a bottle of turps!'

They started laughing again, but Linda held up her hand as they heard the bark of the Alsatian in the lock-up next door.

'Here she is,' said Bella. 'Here's our leader.'

Linda, closest to the door, was frozen to the spot. 'No heels. And no Wolf,' she whispered. Bella and Shirley looked round for somewhere to hide, but it was too late. The door squeaked open and a man in a Barbour coat and flat cap stepped in, Shirley let out a squeal and shot up, frightened out of her wits, Bella picked up a crowbar and Linda shouted: 'Who the effing hell are you?'

Dolly pulled off the cap. 'Glad I can pass for a bloke,' she said, looking very pleased with herself. 'Sorry about not being in contact. I still got a bleedin' squad car parked in front of me house. They been watching me day and night. Put the kettle on, Linda, I'm parched. I've been leaping over back garden fences, which isn't easy in Harry's shoes, I can tell you. They're really heavy.'

The three women stared at Dolly as she took a rucksack off her back and let Wolf out of it and onto the floor. He ran straight to the newly painted van and pissed up the wheel. 'No!' All three women shouted at once, collapsing in fits of laughter.

Dolly ignored them. They must all be very tired. She took off her jacket, lit a cigarette and started to pull out notebooks from the various pockets. Linda went to brew up some coffee, Bella went to get the chainsaw and Shirley watched her little fire burn down.

The silence was broken by Bella firing up the chainsaw and holding it aloft. It was a heavy piece of kit.

'That's great, Bella,' said Dolly, admiringly. 'When you come at them guards waving that around, they'll definitely get out of your way. No one will know you're not a fella. Shirley, those suits are coming along nicely and Linda – great job on the van.'

All three women smiled like children who'd just been praised by mum. None of them were quite sure why they were so proud – but it felt great.

With the saw making a racket they didn't hear the banging on the garage door, but little Wolf started to yap, then the Alsatian from next door started to bark again. Bella turned the chainsaw off and Dolly signalled for the girls to keep quiet. Linda moved to the hidey-hole in the floor to get out a shotgun, but Bella held her back.

'For God's sake, Linda, just stay calm,' whispered Dolly. 'Who do think you are . . . Annie Get your friggin' Gun?'

'I handle shooters all day and night at that arcade so I know what I'm doing,' Linda whispered back.

'Yeah, but they fire little pellets, not bloody cartridges filled with buckshot.'

'Shut up, the pair of you,' Shirley hissed, as the hammering began again.

Dolly was already on the move, Wolf right by her side ready to protect if needed. She flicked the lights off, then slowly opened the small door in the main gates a few inches and peered round the gap. The girls stood grouped in the inner annexe doorway, listening.

'I'm Bill Grant,' said the man outside. 'I'm a friend of Harry Rawlins. I got a lock-up further down. It is Mrs Rawlins, ain't it?'

'What do you want?' said Dolly, without confirming who she was. 'I'm very busy.'

'Can I come in?' Bill asked.

'No,' said Dolly. 'Can't open the door or my little dog'll run out.'

'That's OK,' Bill continued, 'I was just wondering, what with Harry, you know, sorry about him dying by the way, but I was wondering if you'd be selling or renting the place out? Only if you are thinking about it, I wouldn't mind first refusal.'

Dolly sniffed. 'Thank you for your condolences,' she said stiffly. 'Why don't you slip your number under the door and I'll call you when I've had time to think things over?' Shutting the door after him, she made certain that it was locked tight.

As Dolly walked slowly back to the three women, she was frowning, dragging on her ever-present cigarette. She blew out the smoke. 'Any of you ever heard of a Bill Grant?'

They looked at each other and shrugged, following Dolly back into their inner sanctum where she picked up her notebook and stubbed the cigarette out. 'We may have a problem,' she said. 'He said he was a friend of Harry's and owns the lock-up further down. He saw me coming in and wondered if everything was OK.'

'Why's that a problem?' asked Bella.

'Harry never told anyone this was one of his places, no one. And he rented it under a false name.' There was a silence as the implications sank in.

'What if the Fishers sent him?' Shirley shrieked. 'We could be in way more trouble than we bargained for!'

Linda tried to reason with her. 'Tony Fisher would never send someone else to put the frighteners on us. He likes getting stuck in.'

'But what if he thought he was going to bump into Harry? Did you think of that? Harry would scare Tony off; wouldn't he, Dolly?'

'Hang on a second,' Bella interrupted, playing catch-up. 'Why would Tony Fisher think Harry – we are talking about your Harry, right, Dolly? – why would Tony Fisher think he was alive?'

Linda and Shirley both looked at Dolly.

'Because I told Boxer that Harry survived the robbery, knowing that he'd tell the Fishers. I wanted them off our backs,' said Dolly evenly.

'Well, that ain't worked out too well if that bloke was sent by Tony,' Bella replied in her deep, authoritative voice. She didn't take her eyes off Dolly; she could almost hear her brain mulling over all the options. 'Who do you think sent him?'

Dolly lit another cigarette. 'I don't know. I'm thinking he could be the fourth man, but I'm almost certain he's not mentioned in the ledgers. I'll go to the bank again tomorrow and double check. And I'll get you all some more cash as well.'

As Dolly studied the notebooks in front of her, the others looked at each other. Linda nodded at Bella as if to say: *Go on then, ask her if we're really gonna do this*, but Bella didn't. With more cash on the way, she didn't want to rock the boat; it was the easiest money she'd made in a long time.

Dolly flicked a page on her notebook. 'Shirl – you need to get some large wads of cotton wool dressing, something like hospital issue rolls, to pad out the overalls.'

She was so tired, she couldn't help sounding a bit whiney. 'Why do I always have to do the shopping?' Shirley asked.

'Because you're so good at it, darlin',' Dolly replied quickly. 'And we need to fill the rucksacks with something heavy. Linda, you do that.'

Bella picked up one of the bricks left piled around the lock-up. 'Why don't we all work on our fitness?' she suggested.

Linda seized her opportunity. 'We could go back to that Sanctuary place and lift proper weights there.' She fancied a treat after all the hard work she'd been doing and the idea of that sauna thing really took her fancy now. She'd felt a whole lot braver since she started having regular sex again.

Dolly frowned. 'I'm not talking about pissing around with little hand bars, Linda, we'll be wearing heavy duty gear, and we got to be able to lift those rucksacks onto our back and run fast to the getaway car.'

Shirley was staring at the men's clothing Dolly was wearing. 'Are we all wearing boots now instead of the plimsolls I bought?' she asked doubtfully.

'No, the plimsolls will be fine, Shirl,' said Dolly.

'I don't mind.' Shirley cleared her throat before she dared to continue. 'Only, if we did wear boots instead, can I keep the plimsolls? Cos they go lovely with the new jumpsuit I bought. You know, the ones we ain't wearing for the robbery now.'

'Oh, they do!' Linda eagerly agreed.

Dolly could hardly believe what she was hearing. 'Can we get back to the bricks?' she snapped.

'Sorry, Dolly,' Linda said with a sycophantic smile. She was still hoping that they could go back to the health spa at some stage. 'How many bricks do you think we need in each rucksack?'

'For Chrissakes, put as many as you think a million cash split into three is gonna weigh!' Dolly was exasperated. 'Now, can you all shut up and concentrate? We only got one crack at this robbery, and everything has to be practised until it becomes second nature.'

She got out a map of a quarry on the outskirts of London and laid it on the work bench. 'Harry made notes about how he used this old quarry to rehearse jobs. It's out in the sticks and not used anymore, so it was perfect for them.' Shirley's eyes filled with tears, she put her hand to her mouth and started to cry. Linda put an arm round her.

'I'm sorry. It's nothing. Carry on, Dolly,' said Shirley, sniffing.

'No, come on, Shirl, if something's wrong, tell us,' Dolly insisted. 'We all need to be at our strongest as the job gets closer. What's upsetting you?'

'I just remembered something, is all. The week before the . . . the week before, Terry came home with his trousers and shoes covered in white dust. Do you think this is where he'd been? Practising with Joe and Harry?'

Linda and Dolly looked at each other. The quarry was exactly where Terry would have got dusty. Harry never traipsed quarry dust back to the house, of course, but he was so much more careful than Terry. Linda wiped Shirley's tears with her hanky. 'My Joe never brought white dust home with him; but you can bet your life that his blonde bitch's bed was full of it.' Linda wasn't angry as she spoke; she was phlegmatic. She had always known Joe never came straight home to her bed and she knew it was about time she said it out loud. It felt good.

'I'll find another place we can use . . .' Dolly said gently.

'No, it's fine really. I'm just being silly.'

'Shirley, we'll use somewhere else.' Dolly had made her decision. 'This is our job, not theirs. We'll use our own rehearsal place.' And with that, Dolly started to pack everything away. 'Take tomorrow off and rest up. We meet at nine a.m. the next day to go through the robbery, step by step, till we get it right. I'll call you from the safe number at the convent.' The women watched as Dolly finished packing away, with little Wolf sniffing round her boots, clearly confused by the mixture of smells from Harry and Dolly.

Dolly looked at her girls watching her and she felt a lump in her throat. She was so pleased to be with these women; these women who stood together and looked after each other so well. Yes, they bickered, but that came from caring, not from hating each other. She opened her mouth to say as much, but swallowed the words down.

'Don't forget the bricks and the rucksacks, Linda! I'll bring everything else.' And Dolly left.

Shirley sniffled and went to check that the fire in the bin was properly out. When she looked down, all she could see were ashes, no distinguishable labels. Pleased to have done something right, she said. 'It was nice of Dolly to change the venue, wasn't it?'

'It was nice, Shirl, yes,' Bella agreed. 'Course it'd be nicer if she stuck around to tidy up for once as well.' Bella collected the rucksacks, put them in a pile so that Linda wouldn't forget them and set about washing up the tea mugs.

Linda remained standing in the middle of the lock-up, staring at the door that had closed behind Dolly. 'I'd love to see what's in them ledgers.'

'I wouldn't,' said Shirley. 'I don't want to know anything I don't need to know.'

'And how do you know what you need to know, eh? What if there's not a single word written in them ledgers and Dolly's totally off her rocker? You'd need to know that, wouldn't you?'

'Not this again.' Shirley sighed as she picked up her handbag. 'I've got to go. *Dallas* is on in twenty minutes.'

Linda and Bella watched Shirley leave. Both of them had to go on to work later that night, so there was no point in them going home first.

As Linda made another cup of tea in the freshly washed mugs, she couldn't help moaning some more. Bella let her because she knew it was good for Linda to get her feelings out in the open, although it made her a pain in the arse to spend much time with. 'She treats us like right skivvies,' complained Linda. 'The name of Rawlins don't give her the right to tell us what to do all the time. If we're a team, we're a team. I mean, it doesn't feel very "teamy" when we're the ones who do all the running round.' Linda handed Bella a piping hot cup of tea. 'What do you think?'

Bella nursed her mug to warm her hands. 'We ain't no team, Linda. She's the boss and that's all there is to it. I can't pay Shirley's mortgage, or buy you a car or put enough money in my pocket to let me keep my clothes on for a month or two. Can you do that?' Linda said nothing. Bella continued, 'And I don't want to see what's in those ledgers, cos if this is for real and it all goes tits-up, I'm denying everything. The less I know, the better.'

Linda smiled; she loved Bella's honesty and clear-sightedness. She took her tea and started to pile bricks up next to the rucksacks.

Bella stayed propped against the kitchen table. There was something niggling her about Dolly, but she couldn't quite put her finger on it. She hoped Dolly was being straight with them because she really wanted to pull this job. She decided that she'd go along with everything as planned, but from now on she would be keeping a close eye on Dolly Rawlins.

* * *

Linda felt pretty knackered when she arrived at the arcade, but just as she was about to go in, she saw Carlos walking past.

'Where you off to looking that gorgeous?' she called out to him.

Carlos stopped and grinned as she ran over and kissed him.

'I'm meeting a bloke who owns a car hire business. He might want me to service his fleet. It'll be great money if I can get him to say yes.'

Carlos looked behind Linda at the arcade she'd just run out of. She was embarrassed at first; she looked like crap after a day in the garage with the girls. He was off to clinch some big business deal and she was off to stop dirty old men touching up the kids playing her arcade machines. *Sod it*, she thought. *I am who I am*. She snogged him right there in front of the whole street.

Looking Carlos up and down, Linda smiled from ear to ear. She couldn't quite believe that Carlos was all hers. Joe had been a very handsome guy, but he was a bit rough. Linda liked rough, but Carlos was something else; he had everything – he was stylish, macho, beautiful and rugged.

'You're late!' Charlie shouted from behind Linda. 'I ain't had my break yet.'

Linda's smile disappeared in an instant. 'All you do on your break is stand in the street looking at women's arses as they walk by. They'll all still be here in ten minutes, Charlie, so sod off.'

Charlie scowled at Carlos. *This must be the reason she's been so chirpy*, he thought. *This must be the geezer Linda's been getting her oats off with.* He watched as she arranged to meet Carlos the following day and kissed him goodbye, lingering and pawing all over him. Charlie had been after Linda for years and never got a look in. And Carlos looked like a right ponce, with his pale suit and his huge curly hair. Charlie pushed his way past Linda and out into the street, so she had no option but to go inside and take over the change booth.

Across the busy street, Boxer Davis was eating a bag of fish and chips. This area of Soho was alive after dark with late-night food stalls, clubs, pubs and arcades. The Fishers' club was the headline act, but there were plenty of lower-ranking venues, too; something to suit everyone. The streets were an eclectic mix of the flamboyantly stylish like Carlos, scruffy no-hopers like Charlie and general dogsbodies like Boxer. Businessmen met working girls, criminals did deals, stags and hens got pissed, people aged eighteen to eighty mixed and mingled. No one was out of place.

Boxer had seen Carlos snogging Linda and was still gawping, chip hanging out of his mouth, when Charlie passed him on his way for food. 'All right, Charlie?' Boxer said. 'Was that Joe Pirelli's missus you was talking to? Just cos I knew her old man.'

Charlie nodded and moved off. He hadn't seen Boxer in ages and didn't like him, or want to chat with him. As far as Charlie was concerned, Boxer was a drunk always looking for handouts. He glanced back at him, noting the well-cut suit he was wearing. He looked decent for a change, might be doing all right for himself – Charlie decided he might be worth acknowledging. 'See you around, Boxer . . . if you need anything, I'm working in the arcade.'

Boxer beamed and gave Charlie a wave. 'Right you are, Charlie. Right you are.'

Charlie felt a stab of jealousy and then got angry. *The day you're jealous of Boxer Davis*, he thought, *is the day you should shoot yourself.* In the chippy queue, Charlie dug about in his pocket and quickly established he could only afford a small portion of chips and a fish cake. God, he wished he could get out of this shithole! His leg was really playing him up in the colder weather and it made him limp something rotten. Even as a kid Charlie had been weak and when the polio had chosen him out of his whole school he'd been left with a gammy leg. With his coins clenched tight in his clammy fist, he put his other hand back in his pocket and took a gentle grip on his balls. He grinned, comforted, and watched the arses walk by.

CHAPTER 14

Resnick stormed through the station corridor spoiling for a fight, but no one was obliging. He wanted to smooth things over with Saunders before going to meet Green Teeth, but the station was pretty much deserted apart from the painters and decorators who had taken over the corridors, apparently with the specific aim of getting in Resnick's way. It was bedlam. Without being consulted, Resnick had been moved into a much smaller office while the main one was being painted. He'd seen the plans and knew he'd end up with a clear glass annexe. The very idea of people being able to look in at him while he prowled and thought and smoked and worked infuriated him. He was a private man who trusted very few people – the idea of sitting in a goldfish bowl for all to see made his blood boil.

'Alice!' Resnick bellowed. 'Ali—'

Alice popped her head out of a doorway. She was holding all of the files from Resnick's desk, neatly stacked in a box. On top of the box was a sandwich from the vending machine.

'Your filing cabinet's in my office, locked, I have the key. These will go in my desk drawer till your desk is moved out, and Saunders has gone home because the paint fumes gave him a headache. He'll be continuing his case review tomorrow so you'd better make yourself available. His words, not mine.' Alice nodded towards the sandwich. 'Cheese and ham. I take it you've not eaten.'

'Thank you, Alice.' Resnick took his sandwich and left to meet his snout, Green Teeth.

'How was your day?' Alice called after him.

'We found the man from the bread company who probably helped Rawlins; but I can't interview him because he'd dead.'

There was nothing Alice could say to make Resnick feel better about that, but moral support was often all he wanted. 'Well, I hope Green Teeth has some better news for you. Goodnight, sir.' She gave a sweet smile and bustled off.

* * *

Barely ten minutes later, Resnick was sitting in the back seat of the police car with his briefcase open on his lap as Fuller drove towards Regent's Park. Andrews took a covert glance over his shoulder at Resnick – the concentration on the old man's face was riveting. His eyes flicked from page to page as he speed-read his way through the reports, looking for anything that would guide him to the Rawlins' ledgers. Dolly Rawlins' surveillance notes were a particularly interesting read: hairdressers, the Sanctuary, bank, hairdressers, convent, bank, hairdressers . . .

'Andrews. Ask the surveillance team where Dolly Rawlins is right now.'

'She's in the house. They radioed through while you were in the station.'

'You seen how many times she goes to the hairdressers? No? The bank? How many times has she lost you, Fuller? Andrews?' Fuller and Andrews didn't answer. At least Andrews had the decency to look ashamed; Fuller just looked bored. 'Do you think she's playing games, Andrews, or do you think she's up to something?'

'I wouldn't know, sir.'

'No, you wouldn't, you soft—' Resnick was too tired to abuse Andrews any more today. 'Here's another one you won't know the answer to: is she very good at losing police tails, or are you all shit at tailing? Guess we'll never know, eh?'

Resnick lit up a cigarette and inhaled deeply. Fuller winced and started to open the window as the smoke wafted round the inside of the car. 'Close it,' Resnick barked. 'It's cold in the back.'

The brakes slammed on; the car came to a quick stop. Resnick's papers fell to the floor and he glared at Fuller.

'Regent's Park, as you requested . . . sir,' Fuller said, knowing how to get under Resnick's skin.

Resnick picked up the papers, stuffed them in his briefcase and opened the car door. He took one last look at his 'best men' – Fuller was staring straight ahead with a stupid grin on his face, while Andrews was yawning. *God, what a dozy pair of buggers*, he thought as he slammed the car door shut. Maybe he'd strike it lucky with Green Teeth. He certainly needed some good news today.

Resnick made his way into the park and sat on a bench, eating his sandwich, the first thing he'd had to eat all day. He gazed, mesmerised, at the branches swaying in the trees; he was so tired. He knew that Green Teeth would have watched him arrive and would come out of hiding and join him on the bench when he was ready.

True enough, once Fuller and Andrews were out of sight, Green Teeth sidled up to Resnick with all the subtlety of a caped TV villain. Like a starving dog, he sat staring at the sandwich. Resnick handed the remainder of his food over and then had to wait for Green Teeth to stop stuffing his face before he spoke.

'What's so important?' Resnick asked eventually.

'There's a rumour, Mr Resnick, spreading like the clappers,' Green Teeth mumbled, spitting crumbs all over Resnick's coat. He moved away and lit a cigarette. 'The rumour is about Harry Rawlins.'

'Well, I should bloody well hope it is.' Resnick brushed wet cheese and bread from his coat.

'If someone got hold of his ledgers it'd be like having Aladdin's bleedin' lamp . . . know what I mean?'

'Who's got them?'

'The man himself. Harry Rawlins.'

Resnick tutted. 'Have I come all this way just to hear that load of old bollocks?'

'No, he was serious,' Green Teeth insisted.

'How the bloody hell do you get hold of information like that?' Resnick barked, furious. 'You're not in Harry Rawlins' league, mate! Even if it was true, that kind of information doesn't make its way to you!'

'Boxer Davis is flashing tenners round the manor and shooting his mouth off. He's even wearing Harry's gear.'

Resnick's eyes narrowed – Boxer Davis was certainly more in Green Teeth's league. It was possible he might have heard something after all.

'Boxer worked for Harry for years, and he's telling people that he's working for him again.'

Resnick flicked his cigarette onto the grass and started to walk away.

'Hold up!' Green Teeth shouted, chasing after him and grabbing his arm.

Resnick pulled sharply away. 'I don't pay for rumours. And don't paw my coat. Look at that – you gobbed cheese on me as well! You should be paying me to fumigate my sodding clothes.'

Green Teeth sniffed and picked bread out of his teeth. Resnick handed him a fiver and headed back to the car.

* * *

As Fuller slowed down by the main gates on his third loop of the park, he spotted Resnick pissing behind a tree.

'Look at that,' Fuller said in disgust. 'How am I ever going to get promoted when I have to rely on that for a reference?'

Resnick walked towards the car, wiping his hands on the arse of his trousers and lighting another cigarette. Andrews laughed.

'Now he's going to sit his pissy backside on your nice clean seats and smoke in your face.'

But Resnick was very subdued when he got back into the car. 'Green Teeth reckons Boxer Davis is suddenly very flush. He's spreadin' it around town that he's working for . . .' He paused briefly and thought about what Green Teeth had told him. 'Ah, well – forget it. It's gotta be a load of bollocks anyway.'

'Why do you doubt the information?' Fuller asked. He was pleased that the information was bollocks, but was still desperate to know what it was so he could add it to his list of Resnick's cock-ups.

Resnick sighed. 'He's bloody rapping on about working for Harry Rawlins.'

Andrews rubbed his head. 'What? Green Teeth is working for Rawlins?'

Resnick snorted and spat his cigarette butt out the window. 'Not Green Teeth! Boxer Davis, you idiot! Apparently, Boxer's flouncing round dressed in one of Harry's expensive suits and a pair of his shoes. And he's got a few bob to throw about from somewhere.'

Still rubbing his head, Andrews raised his eyebrows and turned to look at Resnick. 'Maybe Boxer's working for Dolly? He did visit her house a couple of times.'

Resnick was stunned. 'What an idiotic suggestion,' he snapped.

Fuller frowned at Andrews. 'There's no way an old woman who spends all her time between the hairdressers and a bunch of nuns would be employing old lags like Boxer Davis.'

'Will you shut up, the pair of you! Fuller, drive down to Soho. I wanna have a look round for Boxer Davis and if he's there we'll nick him.'

'But it's almost midnight,' Fuller exclaimed.

'Then we're more likely to find him, aren't we? These old lags aren't tucked up by nine like you prissy bunch.'

Fuller and Andrews exchanged a glance; then Fuller pulled away and headed towards Soho.

* * *

Boxer returned to his run-down bedsit with his fish and chips and, for the third time, counted out the money Dolly had given him. He was tickled pink as he stacked it up in neat piles on his bed. Dolly had told him that Harry was still lying low and that he felt it best that Boxer did the same and got out of town for a couple of weeks. Dolly had given Boxer the address of a nice B & B in the countryside and said she'd drop round some more cash before he went. Harry would contact him at the B & B when the time was right. Boxer had fallen for all of this – hook, line and sinker.

Picking up a faded, unframed photograph of himself and his son from the bedside table, Boxer looked at it for a moment. The little boy was perched on his dad's shoulders, waving at the camera. Boxer rubbed his flat nose. His little fella must be about eight by now. He shook his head, annoyed with himself that he couldn't even remember his own son's age, and wondered if he should track down his ex-wife, Ruby, so he could see his beautiful little boy. She'd be proud he was still on the wagon, he thought, and his boy might even look up to him in his new suit and shiny shoes.

Boxer carefully propped the photo up against the bedside lamp; apart from missing his son he felt good, damned good. He shook his head and chuckled at the thought of his old friend and boss, Harry Rawlins, pulling the wool over everyone's eyes. He stuffed a handful of cold, soggy chips into his mouth, but they tasted awful now, so he spat them back into the paper wrapping, scrunched it up and chucked it into the already overflowing waste basket. He surveyed the battered, dirty room. 'What a shit hole . . .' he muttered, but then he brightened. Things were about to change for the better. Harry Rawlins would see that he had a decent place to move into and he'd pay him well.

'I'm on the up, my son,' Boxer said to the photo of his boy. 'I'd like to take you with me. I hope you let me try.' Easing his huge frame into a tattered and worn armchair, he closed his eyes and thought about Harry. He could see him clear as day, as if he was in the room, standing tall in front of him.

The first time Boxer met Harry Rawlins, it had been ringside at a boxing night in York Hall, Bethnal Green. Boxer had been just about to step under the ropes and into the ring when he felt a tug on his robe. Looking round, he saw a young man with a cigar clamped in his mouth.

'I'm Harry Rawlins,' he'd said. 'And there's a grand riding on you tonight, me old son, so knock him out and I'll see you right with two ton.'

The fight was over in the third round and Harry was true to his word. He was an honourable thief, thought Boxer, and that's what he always loved about him – you knew where you stood.

A loud knock on the door interrupted Boxer's trip down memory lane and his eyes sprang open. He could hear puffing and panting outside his door.

'Eh, Boxer! You in? Boxer, open up, ya hear me?'

Boxer stayed silent. It was Fran, Fran the ten-ton landlady – the huge, over made-up, foul-breathed Frances Welland. When he was on the booze and really drunk, he vaguely recalled her coming onto him and, much to his regret, he had had sex with her. He was glad that he couldn't actually remember the sex, but he could remember waking up and seeing her next to him in bed. He knew she wanted a repeat performance, but he was equally determined to ignore her.

The doorknob rattled. 'Boxer! I know you're in there. You've got a visitor – open the door!'

Boxer reluctantly hauled himself to his feet and unlocked the door. The visitor was hidden behind Fran's huge body, so Boxer couldn't see who it was until he stepped forward. Boxer's face lit up with a big smile.

'Eddie Rawlins – my old mate! Come in, come in.'

Boxer dragged Eddie inside his room and shut the door in Fran's face with a grin. He always smiled at her; he didn't want her to throw him out.

Going over to the tiny kitchen space in the corner of the bedsit, Boxer put the kettle on. 'It's great to see you, Eddie. I can't offer you much I'm afraid, but I always got tea.'

'No, no, no,' Eddie insisted. 'Let's catch up properly.' He produced a bottle of malt whisky from his coat pocket, banged it down on the table. 'Got any glasses?' he asked.

Boxer's eyes widened. The longing for alcohol was back in a split second, but he gave a strong smile, 'I'm off the hard stuff, Eddie, have been for months now. I don't mind if you have a drink, though.' Boxer passed Eddie a chipped, stained mug and they both sat at the small table beneath the window.

'Come on, Boxer. Have a small one with me . . . let's drink to Harry.'

Boxer smiled and held his hands up. Eddie must know everything, he must know Harry was alive and well and planning to take back his patch from the Fishers. 'In that case,' he said, 'I guess a small one will be OK.' He was even more excited: the old gang was getting back together.

Boxer put a second mug on the table and Eddie talked as he poured. He started by whinging about his missus and the kids, then about the car-wrecking business, all the time topping up Boxer's mug. Each time he poured Boxer a double measure, he poured himself a single and, after about half an hour, Boxer was on his way to being pissed.

Eddie waffled on so much that Boxer couldn't get a word in. He was desperate to ask about Harry, but figured that Eddie would talk about him when he was good and ready. The next time Eddie went to pour Boxer a whisky, he put his hand over his mug.

'I ain't drunk in such a long time, Eddie. It's gone straight to me head. I should stop.'

'Don't worry, Boxer, me old mate,' Eddie said kindly. 'I'll look after you.' Boxer removed his hand from his mug and Eddie emptied the bottle into it.

As Boxer took another sip, the pay phone on the landing started ringing. Boxer ignored it. 'It'll be for Fran,' he said with a drunken shrug. But the phone still rang. 'She's a lazy old lard-arse.'

But Fran had shifted her huge bulk out of her armchair and waddled her way out to the landing. 'Boxer! It's for you!' she shrieked up the stairs. Even Eddie winced.

Well pissed by now, Boxer knocked his chair over as he staggered to the door. Fran stood panting on the landing as Boxer gripped the rail for support and moved unsteadily down the stairs.

'Thought you'd gone all deaf on me,' she said as she handed him the phone.

Boxer grabbed Fran in his arms, squeezed her tightly and kissed her long and hard.

'Ooh!' she said and giggled. 'When your friend's gone I got a nice bottle of gin in my room,' she whispered in his ear, 'and an electric blanket warming up the bed . . .'

Boxer waved to Fran as she walked away, smiling stupidly and watching her huge bum with drunken lust. With his 'whisky glasses' on, she looked positively lovely.

'Who is it?' Boxer slurred into the phone. After a pause, he shouted, 'Doll! How are you?'

'You been drinking?' demanded Dolly. She had only called Boxer to ask if he was packed and ready to go to the B & B she'd recommended.

'I've had a little one, Dolly, but don't worry, everything's under control.' Boxer hiccupped. 'I'm packed and ready. 'Ere . . . guess what I saw in Soho – this'll make you laugh – I only saw Joe Pirelli's widow with an Italian lad called Carlos! She must really like the continental sort, eh? But, guess who he is, Dolly? He's only Arnie Fisher's bum-boy mechanic!' Boxer was laughing so loud he failed to hear Dolly's reply.

'Carlos *who*?' Dolly repeated in a stern voice. All she could hear was Boxer coughing and spluttering as he got his breath back, 'Boxer! Carlos who?'

Oblivious, Boxer rambled on. 'Ain't that sweet, Dol? Between that little tart and us, Arnie's lost everything and he don't even know it!' With the next belly laugh, Boxer dropped the receiver on the floor. By the time he'd risen unsteadily from picking it up, Eddie was behind him on the stairs. ''Ere, Dolly, you'll never guess who come to see me . . .' In a flash, Eddie's gloved hand slammed down on the phone and cut off the call. Boxer swayed and stumbled as he turned but Eddie caught him, holding him up.

'Come on, no time for gassing,' Eddie said with a huge smile on his face. 'I'm going to take you up West. My treat.'

Boxer didn't need to be asked twice.

* * *

Resnick and Fuller were parked outside the last known address for Boxer Davis, which he had given when arrested on a drunk and disorderly charge six months previously. Andrews came down the steps of the seedy rooming house and got in the car.

'Not here, but the landlady gave me an address in Ladbroke Grove she thinks he may be at now.'

Fuller drove off and Resnick pulled his hat over his eyes. 'Boxer Davis is a huge piece of the puzzle, you mark my words. One huge, ugly, stupid piece of the puzzle. He'll tell us everything we need to know.' Smiling to himself, Resnick closed his eyes and was snoring in seconds.

* * *

In the Sports Club, Boxer was well and truly legless, barely able to string a sentence together. He stood with Eddie at the bar, surrounded by a handful of onlookers listening to him relive his last bout, blow by blow. The walls of the club were covered with faded photos of retired boxers and wrestlers, Boxer among them. His audience knew who he was, but they also knew he was way past his prime and the fight he was currently relaying had to have been at least twenty years ago. Still, they listened; one or two even cheered and egged him on. Boxer was in his element as he charged down memory lane, flailing his arms, shadow boxing, ducking and weaving. At one point he spun round and spilt the drink of a man behind him. Apologising profusely, Boxer slung his arm round the little man's shoulders and gave him a slobbery kiss on his bald head.

The only person in the crowd not listening to Boxer was Eddie; he was watching the entrance to the bar. Then he saw what he'd been waiting for. A casually dressed man in jeans and bomber jacket appeared briefly, part-hidden in the shadows, and nodded to Eddie. Although the man's face wasn't visible, Eddie knew who it was. He nodded back and the deal was done.

One more spin and Boxer knocked into the bar, sending a tray of dirty glasses crashing to the floor. The barman had had enough, and told Eddie to get him out, using the back alley. He didn't want pissheads staggering out the front throwing up on his steps.

Eddie and the little bald man, who was still soaked in beer, burst through the exit doors and into the back alley with Boxer between them. Loud rock music thudded out from street bars, rubbish and crates of beer were stacked either side of the doors and an old tramp was busily picking his way through one of the bins.

Boxer fell to his knees as soon as the cold night air hit him. Eddie looked down the alley and saw the headlamps of a car blink once. All he had to do now was get Baldy out of the way.

'Let's get to the strip joints, eh?' Eddie said, pretending to be drunk. 'You fancy a tits 'n' arse club, Boxer? I'm paying. You too, mate . . .' Eddie turned to Baldy and patted his pockets. 'Shit, I've left me wallet on the bar. Do us a favour,' he said to Baldy. 'Nip inside and get me wallet while I get him up off the floor.' Baldy, thinking he was on to a free night of fit young women and free beer, eagerly toddled off back inside the club.

The instant Baldy was out of sight, Eddie walked off at speed in the opposite direction of the car. Boxer staggered to his feet, held onto a bin and moaned, 'Wait for me, Eddie, wait for me!'

The car tooted its horn once. Boxer turned and looked, peering down the alley to see if it was someone he knew. Suddenly the headlights came on full beam and Boxer swayed as he put his hand up to shade his eyes. Then the headlights went out, the engine roared and the car accelerated up the alley, knocking bins and rubbish into the air. Boxer, still dazzled by the bright light, couldn't see anything clearly, only hear the engine approaching fast – but his drunken brain wouldn't engage his legs. The car slammed into him, sending him spiralling into the air, up and over the car and onto the ground with a sickly thud. Bits of paper, empty bottles, rain-sodden boxes and other rubbish swirled around him as he tried to move, tried to get up, tried to get to safety.

The car screeched to a halt at the end of the alley. Looking in the rear-view mirror, the driver saw Boxer roll onto all fours. 'Tough old sod,' he muttered to himself as he slammed the car into reverse and drove over Boxer not once, but twice more, crashing his rear bumper against the alley wall in the process. As the car slowly left the alley, the damaged back lights blinked on and off.

Boxer lay among the shit and rubbish, broken and bleeding. His breathing was sharp and shallow as his lungs desperately tried to fill with air. He could see the bright lights of the street just up ahead, but no one could see him in the darkness of the alley. Partly protected from the excruciating pain by the huge amount of alcohol in his body, he managed to crawl a few feet towards the lights, before collapsing into unconsciousness among a pile of rubbish. He would have been just visible from the street if anyone had cared to look – but even if someone had caught a glimpse of an arm sticking out from behind the bins, they would have just taken him for a drunk and ignored him.

Baldy staggered out of the club and into the alley. 'Your wallet's not in—' But the alley was deserted. 'Bang goes my night,' he moaned as he went back into the club. 'I hope they get the clap.'

CHAPTER 15

Dolly was in the convent kitchen peeling potatoes for lunch. Her normal routine was to serve dinner to the children, but she'd decided to get in early today and help out. She was filled with so much energy that she had to release it somehow.

As Dolly had pulled into the grounds at around 7 a.m., it occurred to her that Bella would probably only now be getting in from her job. She worked so hard, probably for very little, and yet she was one of the strongest people Dolly had met. Linda was no doubt probably still in bed – she never listened to Dolly's advice. Now, as for Shirley . . . Dolly smiled. Shirley was starting to come round to her way of thinking.

After helping the children to make their beds, Dolly had gone to the nursery to help feed the babies. As she entered the room, she'd been stunned breathless at the sight of a baby boy lying in the cot she had donated from her own nursery. She knew that her things were here and was delighted that they were being used, but she still found it very upsetting. One of the nuns had handed Dolly a bottle of warm milk and then, without a word, left the room.

Dolly had walked slowly towards her son's cot and looked down at the unwanted child using it now. The nametag on the cot read, 'Ben'.

'Hello, Ben,' Dolly had whispered, and the baby stretched and opened his eyes at the sound of her voice. They looked at each other for a few moments, sizing each other up and deciding that they'd no doubt get on. Dolly's heart had jumped between two distinct feelings: sorrow at how anyone could not want Ben, and pride at knowing that she'd have been an amazing mum. Dolly had fed many babies at the convent since the loss of her own son, but this was the first time she'd leant down into the very cot bought by Harry all those years ago and lifted out a perfect, beautiful baby boy. He lay content in her arms and, in that moment, all of Dolly's feelings of loss connected to the past – her own and Ben's – disappeared, and she focused only on the here and now. 'I'm Dolly,' she'd said, testing the milk's temperature on her wrist, 'and I'm going to give you your breakfast.'

With the potatoes peeled, cut and boiling in a huge pan of water, Dolly fried up the mince and vegetables, thickening it with Bisto gravy granules before putting the lot into a large oven tray. She then mashed the potatoes, layered them on top of the mince and put everything into the oven to finish and crisp.

Dolly grated an entire block of cheese as she looked out of the window at the children playing in the garden. Beyond the garden fence, an unmarked police car with two bored-looking surveillance officers inside watched the convent. 'Keep watching, boys,' Dolly whispered to herself as she grated the cheese. 'Cos I'm gonna do this . . . and I'm gonna do it right under Resnick's nose.'

* * *

When Dolly finally left the convent after lunch, she drove to Knightsbridge and parked in the customer car park at Harrods. Entering the building through the main doors, she walked through various departments before stopping to try on a hat. While she turned this way and that, she looked in the mirror to see how close the officer tailing her was. She calculated she just had time to make it out of the corner door, on to the busy street and then down into the tube station before he'd be able to figure out exactly which way she went.

Once in the station, she bought a newspaper and then crossed to the ticket office and bought a return ticket to Leicester Square. She watched the reflections of people behind her in the ticket kiosk glass, but couldn't see the officer who had been following her in Harrods, although she was still wary. Any one of the sea of unknown faces could be another plain-clothes waiting to pick up her tail.

After getting off the train, Dolly zigzagged her way to the bank, changing direction numerous times along the way to be absolutely certain that she wasn't still being followed. She had stopped outside the Army and Navy Store on the Strand and done some window-shopping, but was more interested in the reflections than the goods. Once she was sure she was safe, she headed to the bank. She needed to check out the ledgers to see if Bill Grant was ever mentioned and she also needed some more money for the girls.

* * *

Shirley's mum Audrey was frozen stiff; her feet were numb and even her fur-lined boots didn't help in this weather. She stamped her feet and blew into her mitten-gloved hands. The bitter cold had made for poor trade so far today and she'd not sold a thing since ten o'clock. Audrey could murder a coffee, but didn't like to keep drinking as it made her want to pee, which meant asking 'Mushroom Features' on the next stall to take care of hers. That meant ten pence for Audrey, ten pence for him, and then she'd have a hard time explaining to the greengrocer why the takings were low against the produce sold.

She tried occupying herself with people-watching and soon spotted Tony Fisher pull up in a flash-looking motor. She knew Tony of old – his mother and her mother had worked together down Covent Garden Market, before it was all cleared out and moved to Nine Elms. Last Audrey heard, Tony's mum had a job cleaning for a big firm at the Aldwych.

She watched Tony get out the car – handsome bloke, she thought, well dressed, and the cashmere coat he had on his back must have set him back a few hundred quid. She shrugged. His poor old mother was cleaning offices and there he was, parading round like some model out of a fashion mag! She shook her head and straightened her stack of paper bags.

When she looked up again, Tony was walking directly towards her. She hid her fear and smiled at him. He nodded. *Cheeky bugger's going to demand a free apple or something most likely*, thought Audrey. Although she'd known Tony all his life, she wasn't under any illusion that this afforded her any favours; she knew his reputation. She nervously touched her woolly hat and noticed Mushroom Features flicking glances at Tony and then quickly back at her.

'You got a problem?' Tony asked him, pleasantly enough, and the squirt instantly turned his back on them. Audrey noticed that every other stall holder close by also took one look at Tony and then avoided eye contact. They knew trouble when they saw it.

'Apples look nice, Audrey,' Tony said with a beaming smile. He had been a cheeky lad when he was younger, but now there was menace to him and he was hard to read. Audrey polished and bagged an apple for him and vainly hoped that it really was all he wanted. Right now, Audrey was wishing she'd had much, much more coffee and had gone to the loo, leaving Mushroom Features to deal with Tony.

He bit into the apple and seemed pleased enough. Audrey breathed a small sigh of relief. But she knew Tony wasn't just here for one apple.

'Nice and sweet,' Tony said, 'just like your Shirley.' Audrey's smile disappeared in a split second. 'Where's she living these days?'

Audrey knew full well that the likes of Tony Fisher don't turn up out of the blue for a friendly chat; they want something, and it's usually something you don't want to give. The thought of him wanting something from Shirley sent a shiver down her spine.

'I haven't seen her since her Terry's funeral. Last she told me was she was going to Spain to do some modelling,' Audrey said unconvincingly. Shirley was suddenly very flush with cash; had her baby got herself involved with the Fishers?

Tony gripped the edge of the stall. 'I asked you where she's living.'

'She moves around a lot. Stays with friends – you know how it is.'

With one shove of his strong arm, Tony shook the stall so that the loosest fruit rolled off into the gutter that ran the length of the market.

'Please don't do that, Tony.'

'Next shove it all goes over, and what for, eh, Aud? I just want to talk to her, that's all.'

'Leave her alone, eh? She's been through so much . . .'

Tony noticed Audrey looking over his shoulder as she tailed off, before she gave a slight shake of her head.

'Hi Mum, you seen that waste of space Greg about? That duff motor he got me is playing up again and I—' As Shirley clocked Tony, the rest of her sentence stuck in her throat and the colour drained from her face.

'Hello, Shirley, how was Spain?' Tony turned slowly and stared at her forehead with a menacing smile.

Audrey quickly jumped in. 'I was just tellin' Tony you'd been in Spain doing some modelling. He was askin' where you was.'

Tony looked Shirley up and down, stopping to gawp at her tits. 'You're looking lovely, Shirl.'

'Thank you,' Shirley stuttered. She had no idea how to deal with the likes of Tony Fisher.

'I was hoping we could go for a little chat. We'll go to yours; it'll be quiet there.'

Audrey jumped in again. 'I'll give you something to take back with you,' she said, desperately trying to keep calm as she wrapped some carrots and handed them to Shirley, 'She's back with me at the moment, aren't you, Shirl? There you go, you take those back with you. We can have them with tea. I won't be far behind you. Not far behind you at all.' Audrey knew that she couldn't stop Tony from leaving the market with her daughter, but hoped beyond hope that if they went back to her house then Greg would still be there with his stupid mates.

'What do you want to talk to me about?' Shirley asked, nervously screwing the paper round the carrots till it ripped.

Tony grabbed her by the arm. 'Let's go. We can talk at your mum's.' He led Shirley towards his car, gripping her elbow so hard she was unable to resist.

Shirley glanced back at Audrey, who mouthed that she'd follow, but neither knew if she'd be able to follow quickly enough. The second Tony's car pulled out of sight, Audrey threw her money belt at Mushroom Features and ran as fast as she could towards the pub, where she hoped to get a lift back to her flat. If there was no one who could help her, she'd run the whole way, fuelled by the fear of what that bastard might do to her little girl.

* * *

Tony had to lift his feet high off the floor in Audrey's kitchen to step his way through dirty laundry and rubbish bags. The ironing board was laden with creased clothes, the kitchen table still had dirty breakfast things on it, and a week's worth of dirty dishes were stacked in the sink and all over the draining board. It was disgusting.

'You in, Greg?' Shirley shouted, but there was no reply. 'I want a word with you about that car! Come down if you're in!'

Tony took off his cashmere coat, folded it and placed it on the ironing board. 'Just us,' he whispered menacingly. He pulled two chairs out from the kitchen table, sat down in one and pointed at the other. 'Sit down with me.'

Shirley was shaking. She wasn't clever like Linda; she was scared and knew she was showing it. 'I'll make us a coffee,' she said. Anything to keep her distance from Tony.

Tony had fancied Shirley ever since he first saw her five years ago, when she was still a teenager. Why she'd married that mutton-head Terry, he'd never know. Terry had brought her down the club to a private party once; Shirley must only have been about sixteen or seventeen at the time, but she was well stacked even then, fresh-looking and ripe for the taking. Tony crossed his legs and eased his crotch. He was turning himself on thinking about what he'd like to do to her.

Shirley was shaking uncontrollably, her hand trembling as she opened the fridge door to get the milk. Tony watched her bend her lovely head and sniff at the bottle.

She made a face. 'It'll have to be black,' she said nervously as she flicked the kettle on.

Tony said nothing, just watched her. Every movement she made was sexy; the more flustered she got, the sexier she looked and the more it turned him on.

Shirley had to squeeze past him to get the coffee. As she did, he suddenly grabbed her and pulled her down onto his lap. She sat stiff-backed as he leant forward and sniffed her neck. It smelt like fresh lemons. He touched the clear fresh skin and she shivered with fear as he moved his fingers up and down. Tony began to undo her shirt buttons.

'You must know how gorgeous you are. Do you like what you do to men?'

'No,' Shirley stammered. 'I don't know . . . I don't do anything on purpose.' She tried to stop him by pushing his groping hands away but he grabbed her hard round the wrist and, with his other hand, undid another button. He let go of her wrist and was about to put his hand inside her shirt when Shirley jumped up off his knee and went for the coffee.

Tony laughed as he watched her trying to spoon out the granules, pour the boiling water and button up her shirt all at the same time. Her hands were shaking. He lit a cigarette and moved over to stand close behind her, squeezing against her body as he took the kettle out of her hands and poured the boiling water into the cup. Shirley tried to move away from him, but he placed his free arm around her waist and trapped her. 'Shall we have that chat now?' he asked.

'If you like,' Shirley said in a very small voice.

'You know anything about Harry Rawlins' ledgers?'

Shirley shook her head.

'Terry ever mention them?' Tony continued.

'Nothing, I don't know anything about them. I mean, I dunno even what they are.'

Tony drew on his cigarette and held it in his mouth, one arm still loose around her waist. The smoke stung her eyes, as it always did, but she was so terrified she hardly noticed.

Tony's arm tightened round her hip, pulling her close to his body. he pushed his groin against her backside and she could feel how excited he was by the power he had over her. He was going to rape her, she was sure. He put the kettle down and pulled her shirt forwards, roughly slipping his hand inside to cup her breast.

'Lovely,' he whispered, breathing cigarette smoke all over her.

'What do you want?' Shirley tried not to tremble but it was no good.

'All in good time,' Tony replied as he continued to fondle her. 'Very nice. Firm but soft, all at the same time.' Shirley's trembling was putting him off. 'Relax, will you? I ain't gonna hurt you. I just want to know about those ledgers, darlin', that's all.'

'I don't know—'

Before Shirley could finish, Tony had pinned her arms against her side, taken his cigarette from his mouth and held it so close to her breast she could feel the heat.

'Oh, God, no. Please don't!' Shirley screamed.

'You still doing the beauty circuits, are you? I bet they don't touch you with a barge pole if you've got the slightest blemish, do they? Sanctimonious bastards. I'd still touch every inch of you though, Shirl, don't you worry about that. Now tell me where those ledgers are.'

'I don't know, Tony, I swear I don't.'

As Tony moved the cigarette closer to her perfect skin, Shirley swiped at his hand and knocked his cigarette to the floor. 'Bitch!' he screamed, and hit her hard across the mouth with the back of his hand. She crumpled in a heap onto the floor. Her lip was cracked and a thin trickle of blood oozed out, poppy-red against her ashen skin. Tony gripped her by the hair, unzipped his trousers and began to force her head towards his crotch.

Greg had never been one for good timing, but for once he got it exactly right. The door to the kitchen swung open to reveal him in his punk leather gear and ear studs, his hair dyed pink and yellow. Behind him were his mates, Arch, with his Mohawk haircut and leopard-print T-shirt, and Fruity Tooty, who had a shaved head and thick black eye make-up, and was dressed in a full-length black leather trench coat. The three of them looked like characters out of a B-list horror movie. At first, as Tony Fisher quickly zipped up his fly, Greg thought he had caught his sister in a compromising position. He was about to walk out in embarrassment when he clocked Shirley's terrified and bleeding face. He had no option but to stand his ground. 'You all right, sis?' he asked, scared out of his wits. He knew Tony Fisher and his reputation.

Greg's mates were normally useless, but Fruity Tooty, seeing Shirley's split and bloody lip – and not knowing Tony from Adam – gallantly stepped forwards to have a go. Greg held him back, shaking his head. It would be a bad move. If he was honest, Greg wasn't even certain that all three of them could take on Tony Fisher.

Tony laughed as he picked up his cashmere coat and slipped it over his shoulders. He walked up to the boys and stood nose to nose with Fruity. 'I got a good memory for faces,' he said, and tapped him on the cheek before leaving.

Fruity and Arch had no idea what had just happened. Greg knelt next to Shirley and hugged her for the first time in years. In sheer relief, she sobbed in his skinny little arms. She was shaking and holding her top together, trying to cover herself. Greg squeezed her tighter and tighter, till she could no longer tremble.

Eventually, Shirley calmed and the tears stopped. Greg helped her up off the floor and started to walk her through to her bedroom just as their mum burst in through the front door. Audrey was sweating like a stuck pig and was as red as a beetroot; she had indeed run pretty much the whole way home. Shirley took one look at her mum and burst into tears again. Audrey stepped forward and enveloped her little girl in her arms. A split lip was nothing compared to what Tony Fisher could have done.

Audrey looked at Greg. 'Get the car sorted for your sister. Now. Go on.'

Greg, Arch and Fruity quietly left as Audrey took Shirley into the lounge and sat her down on the sofa.

'How are you involved with the Fishers, darlin'?' Audrey spoke calmly but firmly. 'I know 'em of old, see, and I know they're no good. No good at all.' Shirley shook her head and snuggled deeper into her mum's shoulder, her eyes closed and her fingers touching her split lip. 'I'm your mother, Shirley, please talk to me. I can't help if you won't tell me what's going on.'

Shirley took a deep breath and swallowed. 'He came onto me, Mum, but I don't fancy him! I pushed him away and he got angry and gave me a backhander because I wouldn't do what he wanted.'

Audrey stroked Shirley's lovely long hair. 'You sure it's nothin' else? Cos you've been flush with money lately.'

'Honest – that's all it was about. I told you the truth about the cash. I honestly found it in a suitcase of Terry's.'

Shirley had never been very good at telling lies, and Audrey knew that when her daughter repeatedly used the word 'honestly' it meant she was lying.

Shirley got up and went into the bathroom. She splashed cold water over her face, took deep breaths to calm herself and looked at her split lip in the mirror. In her reflection, Shirley saw a strength that she hadn't ever seen before; not in her eyes anyway. She'd seen it in Terry's eyes, when he used to lie to her to protect her from the truth of where he was going and what he was doing. And Shirley was now doing exactly the same for her mum.

Audrey could never know that Shirley was getting the money from Dolly Rawlins, and she could never, ever know about their plans to rob a security wagon at gunpoint. Shirley could hardly even think it; it all still sounded so absurd.

Shirley knew that she had to tell Dolly about Tony Fisher, though, and quickly. Because if he hadn't got what he wanted from her, he would be going after the others next.

* * *

Linda had been told to start at the arcade much earlier than usual because she'd been late the previous night. Charlie must have snitched to their boss – there's no way he could have known otherwise. God, she wished she could tell them both to stuff their poxy job.

When she arrived, Charlie was hovering round the entrance, staring out along the road at the ambulance and police cars parked up by the alleyway to the Sports Club.

'You should have been here earlier,' Charlie said excitedly, not taking his eyes off the commotion.

'I am 'effing early!'

'No, no, I don't mean for your shift. I mean you missed it. All the "blues and twos", you know.' Charlie had heard this expression on the telly and had no idea what it actually meant.

'Can't be arsed with other people's problems, Charlie,' Linda replied as she headed for the cash booth.

'Can you be arsed with Tony Fisher?' Linda turned and stared at Charlie's worried face. 'He popped in and asked if you was here.'

'When?' Linda asked, trying to sound as if Tony Fisher visiting her was a perfectly normal thing to happen.

'Just after you knocked off last night.'

Linda walked back to Charlie, who was now, once again, more interested in the activity up the road. Linda kept her casual tone, 'What did he say?'

'I told you, he asked if you was here.'

'And you said . . .?'

'What do you think I said? I said "no", cos you wasn't.' Linda remained silent, trying to work out what she should do. 'I'd have said you wasn't even if you was. Tony flamin' Fisher, Linda! What's going on?'

'He fancies me, Charlie. Can you blame him?' Linda walked away quickly before Charlie could ask anything else.

She sat in the cash booth, pretending to count the change into money bags, but she was making a terrible job of it. All she was really doing was making little stacks; she had no clue how much was in each. When Charlie came over and said he was going to pop up the road and take a closer look at what was going on, Linda jumped out of her skin and knocked all the coins onto the floor.

Ten minutes passed and Charlie hadn't returned; Linda suspected he'd gone for a pint. But suddenly he was running through the arcade towards her. She'd never seen him run, not with his bad leg, but now he was doing a Seb Coe and looked all flushed.

'Boxer . . . it's Boxer Davis!' Charlie was panting for breath as he pressed his face against the glass of the cash booth. 'Someone done the poor bastard in – he's like a minute steak, I've bleedin' never seen anythin' like it – blood up the walls, blood everywhere . . . They found him in the back alley of the Sports Club under some rubbish, stiff as a board, and I heard the ambulance guy tell a copper he reckoned Boxer had been there all night and all day.' Charlie was panting hard to get his breath back, the glass steaming up more and more with every exhale.

Linda just stared. As the news sank in, her body went cold and she could feel the blood drain from her face. 'Boxer? Are you sure?' Linda realised she didn't need to ask – she knew how good Charlie was with gossip.

'Course I'm sure,' Charlie said, looking up at Linda. 'He was over the road last night with his chips. I thought he must be back in the big time as he was lookin' real good, dressed in a smart suit and—' Charlie suddenly looked worried.

'What?' Linda whispered, not really wanting to know. 'And what, Charlie?'

'He was asking about you.'

'What – what was he asking?'

'Nothing really, he saw you and asked if you was Joe Pirelli's missus.'

Without another word, Linda left the booth and went to the exit doors. She stood with the rest of the gawping spectators and looked up to where the ambulance was parked on the pavement. People around her were speculating. Perhaps the dead bloke had crossed a pimp or a dealer? Shagged the wrong bloke's wife – or just been in the wrong alley at the wrong time? All bollocks. If only they knew.

Charlie appeared behind Linda. 'Why are Boxer Davis and Tony Fisher both asking after you on the same day?' he asked. 'You're not mixing with that lot, are you?'

'That lot? Don't pretend you know who "that lot" are,' Linda snapped. She was being horrible to him but, right now, she had to be horrible to someone and he was closest. 'I'm going back to work. You stand here for as long you like getting your kicks from someone else's misery. Cos as long as Boxer's lying dead just up there, you ain't the saddest bastard in the street, are you, Charlie?'

'He ain't dead . . .' Charlie mumbled as Linda stormed off. She paused and turned back.

'*What?*'

'He ain't dead. He looks like a minute steak, but he ain't dead.'

Back in the cash booth, Linda felt sick. Tony Fisher turning up at the arcade out of the blue was one thing, but Boxer showing his face on the same night asking questions about her was too much to cope with. And now he was fighting for his life in a rat-infested alley. Linda was terrified – there was no one to talk to here, no one who'd understand. All she wanted to do was get to Dolly, Bella and

Shirley and warn them about . . . what? Linda had no idea what it all meant, but she'd never felt so out of her depth in her entire life.

She sat for nearly an hour thinking it over. All she kept coming back to was Bella. Bella would know what to do. Eventually she got a grip of herself.

'Cover for me, Charlie, will ya?' Linda shouted, swinging her jacket round and head and deftly slipping her arms into the sleeves.

'No! You can't go! You only just started your shift!' he shouted after her as she barged past him.

Linda stopped. She had no intention of explaining anything to Charlie in detail, but she had to convince him to cover for her. Dolly had said right from the outset that they needed to go about their business as normal so as not to raise any alarm bells. Alarm bells were ringing in Linda's head now and she needed Charlie on her side. 'Don't be a plum, Charlie. We cover for each other all the time.'

'No, we don't,' said Charlie. 'I cover for *you* all the time. I don't need covering for cos I'm always here when I'm meant to be.' He sounded like a wounded schoolboy who'd had the piss taken by the girl he fancied.

'Look . . . I've really got to go,' said Linda. 'I can't explain why. But I'll make it up to you, honest I will.' She tried a smile.

Charlie wasn't fooled. 'If you go, I'll report you and you'll be sacked.'

'Why are you being like this?!' Linda yelled.

'Cos, apart from the minute steak up the road, I'm the saddest bastard in the street, apparently! And sad bastards do sad bastard things like drop their mates in it when they get treated like shit.'

'You know what, Charlie – sod you and sod the job!' Linda screamed. 'Cos I ain't staying.'

As she charged off down the street, Charlie looked after her and was just in time to see the ambulance doors slam shut. It crawled through the crowds, who ambled out of the way regardless of the lights and siren.

* * *

By the time Bella came off stage at the strip club, Linda was pacing the dressing room, as white as a sheet. She started talking the instant Bella walked in. 'Boxer's been beaten to within an inch of his life. He was asking about me in the arcade, so was Tony Fisher and—'

Bella, as Linda knew she would, took control. 'Calm down, Linda. I can't follow anything you're saying. Calm down and start again.'

Linda took a deep breath and did just that. Once Bella was up to speed, Linda added, 'This has to be cos of what Dolly told Boxer about Harry being alive. Don't you think?'

'Sounds like it's all getting out of hand. And it sounds like the Fishers are scared.'

'They're scared? Bleedin' 'ell, Bella, I'm shitting meself. Dolly's gonna have to sort this out. I mean if it was Tony who done over Boxer, just think what he could do to us!'

'Do we know it was Tony?' Bella asked, trying to be rational for both of them. Linda had jumped to that conclusion because he and Boxer were both in the arcade on the same night. But they had also both been asking about Linda, and that was something to worry about. Bella took time to think while she wiped the sweat from her face and got dressed. 'I'll call the convent and leave a message for Dolly to meet me here as soon as she can. You got someone who can stay with you tonight?' The wry smile that crept across Linda's face told Bella that her friend would be just fine. 'Call him and get him to pick you up from here. Do we know that Shirley's OK?'

The smile on Linda's face vanished as quickly as it had appeared. She hadn't even considered that Tony might have approached Shirley.

'Call your friend,' said Bella. 'I'll call Shirley and Dolly. Don't worry. Expend some energy. Everything will be fine.'

* * *

Dolly was sitting in her ruined armchair sipping brandy and looking through the notes she'd made from her visit to the bank earlier. Three envelopes of cash sat on the coffee table in front of her and Wolf was tucked into her hip as usual. There'd been no reference to Bill Grant in Harry's ledgers, not even a William, or a BG. It crossed Dolly's mind that the man who visited her at the lock-up could have lied about his name. She'd have to ask Boxer. If he knew anything, she'd get it out of him.

The phone rang and Dolly jumped. No one ever called this late at night. It was Sister Amelia from the convent.

'I have a message for you from Miss O'Reilly,' she said. 'It's in relation to your mutual friend, Mr Fisher. Miss O'Reilly says your presence is urgently required at her workplace.' The nun didn't seem surprised to have been used as an intermediary.

Dolly remained calm and controlled as she thanked Amelia and put the phone down. She downed her brandy and peered out of her curtains. The usual parking spot the police used was empty. She looked up and down the street but could see no parked cars that didn't belong there. In case the police had changed tactics, she decided that she would still go through the rigmarole of zig-zagging to make absolutely certain that she was not being followed.

* * *

The club where Bella worked was dark and seedy and it smelt of beer, cigarettes and fat sweaty men. No one noticed Dolly walk in because all eyes were on the stage. She stood at the back of the room, watching a girl in her early twenties performing and listening to the men tell each other what they'd like to do to her. Their crude innuendos made Dolly's stomach churn, but their drunken heckles were worse. As the girl struggled to remove her bra and stay upright in her four inch heels, they shouted at her as though she was a piece of meat. When her song ended, she left the stage to laughter and a hail of flying bottles.

The soles of Dolly's shoes stuck to the beer-soaked carpet as she tried to push towards the stage; the men, thinking she was a punter wanting a better view, wouldn't let her past. She folded her arms around her handbag and made herself as small as possible; she'd have to wait for a break in the show. The idea of touching or being touched by these men repulsed her; some of them had their hands down the front of their trousers.

When the next record began, there was a loud cheer from the men before they settled down almost to silence. Dolly strained to look over the shoulders of the crowd immediately in front of her, and eventually found a spot from where she could see the stage. Bella was already moving down the catwalk, her oiled body glistening and swaying with the grace of a panther. She was dressed in a black leather mini-skirt, a black leather bra and black leather knee-high boots, and wielded a long black leather whip, which she cracked above her head. There was a look of wildness and overpowering sensuality about her as she swayed to the music, staring arrogantly at the men. She met their eyes, every one of them, and they were totally under her spell.

Dolly was as spellbound as the rest of the audience, but for a completely different reason. *She is so strong*, Dolly thought to herself. She recognised something similar in herself: a hidden, almost masculine strength that allowed her a measure of control over people like Boxer Davis. But what Bella had went beyond that. Dolly looked around the room and could see that the men weren't speaking, or looking about, or laughing and joking – there were no disparaging comments, no jeers, no insults; they were mesmerised. In that moment, Dolly knew that Bella was exactly the right person to be their fourth man. As the men imagined Bella naked, Dolly imagined her dressed in an overall and ski-mask, wielding a shotgun instead of a whip. She smiled to herself. *Those security guards will shit themselves*, she thought.

As Bella's routine went on, Dolly was shocked to see the bra and mini-skirt come off, revealing nothing but a tiny leather G-string.

The boots stayed on and Bella stood with her legs wide open, gyrating her crotch at the front row. A great wave of howling broke out, and the men banged on the wooden stage, wolf whistling and whooping. The cheers grew louder as Bella slowly moved her head from side to side, licking her lips and curling her mouth in a snarl. Dolly clutched her handbag, transfixed. Bella seemed almost bored, detached, yet totally in control, while every man in the sordid room drooled over her sleek, toned body as if nothing and no one could touch her. *In a month or two*, Dolly promised silently, *you'll never have to do this again.*

When Bella's act was over, most of the men raced to the bar and Dolly took the opportunity to head towards the stage. As Bella picked up her discarded clothes, the Drag Queen walked on stage and was immediately greeted with boos and shrill whistles.

'Bella!' shouted Dolly over the racket.

Bella was still naked from the waist up. She stood in front of Dolly with her hands on her hips. 'We got big trouble,' she said. 'Tony Fisher is on the warpath. Last night he turned up at the arcade asking after Linda. She wasn't there, thank God, and she's at home now with some fella watching over her. I've tried to call Shirley to make sure she's OK, but there's no reply. Then there's the thing with Boxer. Do you think it's connected to the Fishers?'

Dolly had no idea where to start, so she went with the last thing she had heard. 'What thing with Boxer?'

Bella paused while she did up her bra. 'I thought you would have heard? Boxer was found in an alley last night, outside the Sports Club. He's been beaten to a pulp, apparently – properly smashed up. Dolly . . . Linda said it was awful.'

Just then, a drunk lurched into Dolly from behind. She turned and gave him a shove which made him fall through the door to the gents. She turned back to Bella. 'Boxer was supposed to leave town!' she said. 'I gave him money and told him where to stay. I can't take care of everything and I'm not responsible for what happened to him.'

Bella stared at Dolly. 'I didn't say you were, Dolly . . . but, seeing as you mentioned it, you were the one who dressed Boxer up in your old man's cast-offs, gave him money to get pissed and told him Harry was still alive, knowing full well that Boxer's incapable of keeping his mouth shut.' Even in leather underwear, Bella was a formidable opponent.

Dolly didn't respond to the criticism. Instead, she demanded, 'Who's watching over Linda?'

'She didn't say and I didn't ask, but at least she's not on her own. I've got no idea about Shirley, cos she's not answering her phone.'

'I'll keep trying Shirley. Will you be OK?' The instant the words left Dolly's mouth, she knew they were unnecessary. Bella didn't bother answering.

'I'm sure Shirley will turn up as agreed tomorrow,' Bella said. 'We can fill her in about Tony and Boxer then. But we do need to talk about it, Dolly,' she went on seriously. 'None of us like what's goin' on, and it has to be sorted before one of us gets hurt.'

Dolly liked the way that Bella shot straight from the hip. 'Listen, Bella, I'm not making light of what's happened to Boxer or of Tony Fisher sniffing round and, whether you believe it or not, my priority is the safety of you girls. All of you. We will talk about it but we also got to keep it in perspective for Linda and Shirley. They ain't like me and you. Tomorrow we need to focus on the job in hand, not be distracted by the Fishers, or an old drunk who could have just pissed off the wrong person for all we know.'

'You don't believe that for a second, Dolly Rawlins,' said Bella. 'And neither will anyone else.' But she said it with a smile.

* * *

As Dolly pushed her way out of the club her heart was pounding. She clawed through the stench of men and beer, desperate to get to the fresh air beyond. Outside, she leant against the wall and calmed herself down.

She had to hold it together. She had to hold it all together.

Bella was right about Boxer; she knew his beating must be connected to the lies she'd told him about Harry being alive. She knew it was her fault.

Although Dolly felt sorry for Boxer, she couldn't bring herself to care that much. She'd given him his chance. She wasn't heartless, she reasoned, but he was nowhere near as important to her as the widows – or the job they'd vowed to do. Nonetheless, she assured herself that when she got back home, she'd say a little prayer for Boxer Davis.

CHAPTER 16

Resnick sat in the corridor outside the Intensive Care Unit below a no-smoking sign, smoking. He'd brought an ashtray with him from the relatives' waiting room. He hadn't stayed there long; he couldn't stand being surrounded by helpless people. He needed answers, and the quiet of the empty corridor gave him time to think.

Earlier that night, Resnick had gone to Boxer's flat only to be told by his landlady that Boxer had gone out with some bloke the night before and not come back. She hadn't been able to describe the bloke or, more to the point, hadn't wanted to get involved. 'I don't want no trouble,' she kept saying.

Resnick had been about to call it a day when he got the call to say that Boxer's beaten and unconscious body had been found in a Soho alley. Rather than go to the scene of the crime, Resnick had dragged Fuller back to Boxer's flat to interview the landlady again, whether she wanted to co-operate or not.

When they arrived, they found the front door had been kicked in. Fran was lying flat on the floor like a beached whale, her face beaten black and blue, blood streaming from her nose and a deep cut to her forehead trickling blood into her eyes.

'No more! Please, no more!' she screamed as Resnick and Fuller burst in. 'I dunno where Boxer is, I swear I don't. Please don't hurt me no more.' It took her several moments to focus on Resnick's face and realise that she was safe.

'It's all right,' Resnick said as he bent over her. 'We're police. I was here earlier, remember? You're all right now. The ambulance is coming.'

Fran did remember Resnick and quickly calmed down, but she absolutely denied seeing the face of the man who had beaten the crap out of her. Resnick didn't tell her that Boxer was at death's door, he just kept repeating that she'd be OK and once she was a little calmer, he started to push her for information.

'Was the man who beat you the same man who was with Boxer last night?'

'I dunno!' wailed Fran. 'I'm so frightened . . .'

No one takes a full-on beating as severe as she had without seeing the bastard's face. He had to have been right in front of her, only inches away. But Fran wasn't going to tell them anything.

While they waited for the ambulance, Resnick and Fuller had looked round Boxer's squalid bedsit. The single bed was upturned and every item of furniture in the room had been smashed. The contents of his suitcase were strewn all over the filthy carpet, but there were a couple of pairs of balled up socks still inside: Boxer had been packing to go somewhere. Stray banknotes were scattered about the room. It was unusual for Boxer to have money and Resnick thought of the rumours he'd heard from Green Teeth. If he was right about Boxer being flush, could he possibly also have been right about Harry Rawlins being alive?

When the ambulance arrived, Resnick had been given the news that Boxer was alive but critical. Ignoring Fuller's bored expression, he ordered him to drive straight to the hospital.

Resnick had rushed straight to the ICU, where the attending doctor told him that Boxer Davis was defying all medical expectations. They now knew that it wasn't a beating, but a hit and run. Boxer had suffered horrific internal injuries and broken virtually every bone in his body. He wasn't expected to live – and, if he did, he'd never walk again.

'Listen, doc, this wasn't an ordinary hit and run,' Resnick had said. 'Both you and I know he was hit more than once before they ran. It's important that I speak to him.'

The doctor shrugged. 'You'll be lucky'.

'Well, I gotta get lucky at some point . . . it might as well be tonight,' Resnick growled.

Hours passed, but the Intensive Care Unit corridor remained empty. Although he knew Boxer wouldn't wake up, Resnick couldn't bring himself to leave. As long as Boxer Davis breathed, he would stay. Boxer was the key to it all, Resnick was sure of that. Questions swirled round his head. Why was Boxer leaving town? Was he scared? Was someone else scared and paying him to leave? Who did Boxer willingly leave his flat with the night before? One thing was clear: the man who had beaten up Fran didn't know that someone had already tried to kill Boxer, so it couldn't have been the same person who had left the flat with Boxer and led him straight into the trap. There were two men. Two men, both after Boxer for some reason. Why?

Resnick again thought back to his conversation with Green Teeth. He'd insisted that Boxer was flashing the cash and parading round in Harry Rawlins' cast-offs. He'd also implied the ledgers were being talked about as though they might be up for grabs to the highest bidder. Resnick screwed up his eyes in frustration. He felt he was so close to knowing everything, but, once again, he was about to lose the one person who could break this case wide open. First, Len Gulliver had died before he could spill the beans, and now Boxer Davis looked as if he was about to do the same. Surely it was not possible that Rawlins was alive? Even the thought made Resnick's blood boil. Nevertheless, he had to get this vital information out of poor Boxer's bastard mangled brain before the doctors decided to turn him off and clear the bed for someone else.

One packet of cigarettes and eight cups of coffee later, Resnick was still slouched in his chair with his hat over his eyes. It was 5 a.m. when he was woken by the doctor gently shaking his shoulder. He didn't have to say anything. The look on his face said Boxer was dead.

Resnick walked away, a small squat figure, head bowed, shoulders down, leaving behind him a mound of squashed coffee cups and dog ends and a faint lingering odour of BO. The doctor watched him go. It was a wonder the man was still on his feet, the number of hours he'd sat there without eating, and the amount of nicotine and caffeine he'd consumed. He hoped Resnick was off home for a nice bath and some much needed sleep, but he thought it unlikely.

* * *

Back at the station, slumped in his office and contemplating his woes, Resnick ate half a stale pork pie before tossing the rest in the bin. He opened a fresh packet of cigarettes, lit up and flipped open the surveillance reports. He was annoyed that they hadn't been filed since yesterday; he'd tear a strip off his team when they arrived for work tomorrow. Resnick wasn't going to let any messy paperwork let him down. His team was under instructions to scour the streets for information on the hit and run, which meant no weekend leave for anyone. He knew this wouldn't go down well, but he was including himself in the extra legwork, so he didn't give a shit. If he didn't give the Super something soon, he'd be taken off the case, and that would mean no more chances at promotion. His case needed to be beyond reproach – especially as he'd missed his review with Saunders.

He burped, tasted the stale pork pie in his mouth and dragged heavily on his cigarette. Tapping the desk with a pencil, he acknowledged that the only tangible witness he now had to work on was Boxer's landlady, Fran. But she was so scared he doubted she would ever tell or even describe who had been responsible for assaulting her. He had to get tougher with her. Boxer was dead; this was now a murder inquiry. Being frightened wasn't a good enough excuse. He'd get her down the Yard as soon as she was released from hospital and make her go over every mugshot of every known associate of the Fishers or of Harry Rawlins until she came up with the man who beat her up and scarred her face for life.

Opening a bottle of Scotch, Resnick poured a large measure into a dirty coffee mug on his desk and almost swigged a bit of green mould floating in it. He winced as he tried to pick it out, mulling the details of the case over again and again. He kept returning to the identity of the fourth man, the man who had walked safely away from the armed robbery and the exploding Ford Escort van. Eventually, he gave up chasing the mould round his Scotch, picked up another slightly cleaner mug and poured another measure. As he drank he got up and stared at the row of photographs stuck up along his office wall; all known associates of Harry Rawlins.

'One of you is my fourth man,' he mumbled to himself. 'Was that why Boxer was silenced, because he knew who you were?' *Dear God, it couldn't possibly be Harry Rawlins?*

Resnick was confused by the cash strewn all over Boxer's bedsit. Boxer had been telling people that he was back on Harry Rawlins' payroll, which would explain why he had money, but why did the thug who turned his place over and half-killed Fran just leave the cash lying around? He can't have been interested in the money; he was after something very specific. So, did he think Boxer had the ledgers?

Another interesting detail Resnick had noted was that whoever had taken Boxer out on the night he was murdered, had washed and wiped clean one chipped mug; the one he had used, no doubt. It had been the only clean thing in the whole place. So, this mystery person was someone with whom Boxer was happy to have a drink and go out on the town. 'Careful bastards,' Resnick whispered to himself, 'are careful for a reason.' He moved along the wall to the mugshots of the three dead robbers and stared at the image of Harry Rawlins, the most careful bastard he'd ever known. 'Was it you, Rawlins?'

Resnick doubted Rawlins was Boxer's mystery drinking companion, or the frenzied attacker of Fat Fran or the hit and run driver. If he really was alive, he wouldn't be out in the open like that. But he might pay someone else to be . . . Boxer's killing bore all the hallmarks of a professional, and Rawlins knew plenty of them.

Picking up three darts from his desk, Resnick took aim with one and threw it at the wall. It bounced off and he had to jump out the way as it flew back towards him. He picked it up again and threw it harder. This time it stuck with a thud in the wall just above Terry Miller's photo. He smiled, poured another drink and swigged it back in one go.

* * *

In early for work, Fuller saw the light on in Resnick's office. With no one else around, this was his opportunity to vent his frustration at all weekend leave being cancelled. He'd already arranged to go out with his wife and he was damned if he was going to miss out just because Resnick was trying to save his already ruined career. As Fuller marched to Resnick's office, he tried to control his breathing; he would start by asking Resnick nicely to keep the weekend clear for him.

Fuller knocked and at Resnick's barked 'Enter!' stepped into the untidy office. Resnick was sitting staring at the three photos on the wall aiming another dart. He threw it across Fuller's path instead.

'Unless you've got something positive to say, don't bother opening your mouth,' growled Resnick.

'It's about the weekend leave, sir. I've actually got plans.'

Resnick flapped a hand at Fuller. 'Don't we all, Fuller.'

'I've done forty-eight hours on the trot!' Fuller was tired of being treated like a dogsbody.

'We've all been working hard,' said Resnick, 'but we're close to the payoff.'

'Are we really?' Fuller said sarcastically. This was a dead-in-the-water case.

'Look,' Resnick said, ignoring Fuller's tone. 'Rawlins used four men in that raid, right? Now we know where those three men are –' he pointed to the mugshots of Rawlins, Miller and Pirelli – 'but as for the fourth man's identity, we've got bugger all on him . . . until last night.' Resnick paced up and down as he recapped. 'The rumour is that Boxer was on the up, and Green Teeth thought he had the ledgers, or he knew who did. Then he ends up in an alley, lured to his death by someone he knew – a proper professional job it was, too. Twenty-four hours later we still haven't had any dabs off those mugs in his place and the landlady's too terrified to talk. But she's all we got, Fuller. So, first thing tomorrow, I want her in here and I want to know who gave her that thrashing.'

Even with his stupid glazed expression, Resnick knew Fuller was listening. 'You think it was the fourth man,' Fuller said slowly.

'Now you're getting it, son.' Resnick almost beamed. 'Now you are getting it.' He sat back down behind his desk, picked up a dart, took aim and hit Harry Rawlins right in the forehead.

Fuller stood for a moment, looking at the dart sticking out of the wall, looked to Resnick, then back to the dart. He shifted his weight. The fat man had probably got a point, but there was no way he'd say as much.

'You going for a few jars? Reckon we deserve it.' This was Resnick's attempt at being nice. It didn't mean he was going to buy them, of course. The only person he'd ever bought a pint for was Alice . . . and she'd asked for a gin and tonic. She'd drunk it nonetheless so as not to offend him.

Fuller turned to go. 'It's six a.m. . . . sir,' he said.

'Oi!' Resnick shouted. 'Being tired is no excuse for being a bad copper. Tell the rest of them when they come in to do their surveillance sheets and get this file up to date.'

Fuller sighed and took a deep breath. 'DCI Saunders removed the surveillance on the Rawlins house.' He watched Resnick's face as it slowly went crimson from the neck up. 'It was one of the things he was going to discuss with you during your meeting. The meeting you missed.'

'It starts again!' hissed Resnick, 'You hear me, Fuller? It starts again right now.'

Fuller nodded, too tired and too pissed off with this ridiculous case to argue. He left Resnick's office, closing the door behind him.

As Resnick sat alone, there was much that bothered him about the conversation he'd just had with Fuller. It wasn't just that he'd been up all night. What really got his goat was that he couldn't remember the last time he'd heard the words: 'Coming for a snifter, guv?' Before his suspension over the newspaper fit-up, no one ever left the station without giving him a yell. Now, nobody gave a toss about him, and it would only get worse when he moved into the new glass office annexe, where everyone could look at him. And how the bloody hell could Saunders cancel surveillance on *his* case, and not one of his officers give him the heads up?

Resnick suddenly felt terribly lonely. His marriage was stale and empty. His wife hardly even spoke to him never mind had sex with him – not that he'd want her to. For months, he'd been using the box room to sleep in because of coming in so late and going out so early – or at least that was the excuse. In truth, the idea of lying next to a woman who disliked him was too much to deal with; he hid in the box room because it was easier.

As he walked slowly to his office door, the exhaustion finally hit him. Glancing at the faces of the three dead men one last time, he headed to the local cafe for a solitary breakfast.

CHAPTER 17

The motorbike's wheels tore up the sandy gravel path, leaving deep tracks and wheels as the rider spun and slid, enjoying the thrill of being able to let loose and really test what this machine could do. As the bike came to a skidding halt, it sent a tidal wave of sand and pebbles spraying up against the cliff face.

The beach below was beautiful. Miles and miles of nothing much – just what the doctor ordered. Bella took her helmet off and sat on Oil Head's bike, admiring the view. Oil Head had recently been put away for six months for dealing drugs and he'd asked Bella to run his bike out every now and then so it didn't lie idle. He'd meant her just to start the engine every three or four weeks but – what the hell! It was a fabulous bike and because he was behind on the payments, Bella knew it'd be repossessed before he got out of prison. She might as well get the most from it before the repo men turned up, flexing their muscles.

Cruising down clear early morning roads in her black leather motorcycle gear, Bella had opened the throttle and bent low over the handlebars . . . even though she had been riding motorbikes for years, this was her first solo ton. She had felt exhilarated, speeding through the country lanes like a TT racer.

Bella was the first to arrive at Birling Gap. The beach was deserted. She heaved the bike back on its stand and walked to the edge of the cove. The tide was out. She smiled; Dolly would have factored in the tide patterns. Dolly thought of everything. Bella made her way down the small wooden-stepped path onto the main beach. A couple of old boats lay rotting on their side, and, about twenty yards up ahead, was an old rusting Morris Minor with no wheels, the seats torn and covered in seaweed. Again, Bella smiled, this time at the thought of some stupid tourists parking on the beach for a lovely picnic before being stranded by the incoming tide. They would have been forced to go up the way she had just come down. The kids round here could strip a car in thirty minutes, she thought.

As she walked up and down the beach, inhaling the fresh air, Bella sized up their training ground. She was glad Linda wasn't there yet; it gave her time to focus and prepare the area without being interrupted by Linda going on about her shagathon or about Tony Fisher or about how much of a nag Dolly was. She began collecting driftwood to mark out the run they would have to make with the money on their backs. Bella wanted to do this properly, without interruption.

By the time Linda arrived, the run from the security wagon to the getaway car was all marked out in the sand. Bella looked up to the gravel track as the Capri braked sharply, pebbles flying up as it skidded to a stop. She waved to Linda, who began unloading sacks and blankets from the boot to carry down the steps.

When she reached the beach, Linda threw the armful of goods onto the sand. She was already moaning. 'What's she picked this place for, I don't know. She must be barmy! How're we gonna rehearse the raid here?'

The fresh wind had put some colour into Linda's ashen face and was blowing her dark curly hair all over the place. Linda had an odd face with a hawk nose, high cheekbones and dark, lively eyes. She could veer from downright plain-looking to an angular beauty. *With her big gob shut*, thought Bella, *she is quite beautiful.*

'I spoke to Dolly,' Bella said, ignoring Linda's complaints. 'She's up to speed about Tony Fisher and Boxer Davis. I said we need to talk about it first thing today, before we get stuck into rehearsals.'

'You heard from Shirl?' Linda asked. She seemed genuinely concerned.

'Dolly picked up on that while I finished my shift at the club. Shirley will be fine.' Bella's glib reassurance was exactly what Linda needed. She'd been unable to focus on Carlos at all last night for worrying and they'd only shagged once in the end; not their usual standards at all. Carlos had been very understanding and had settled for cuddling instead. It was a shame about poor old Boxer being beaten up, but at least they needn't worry about him anymore. But Tony Fisher – he was still a big worry.

''Ere, I had a brain wave!' Suddenly cheerful, Linda ran to the pile of stuff she'd brought down from the boot of her car. She came back to Bella with the rucksacks, three pillowcases, two plastic buckets shaped like a castle and two spades. 'I thought – why lug bricks from the lock-up when we got what we need right here?' Linda filled a pillowcase with sand and put that into the rucksack. 'Not just a pretty face, am I, eh, Bel?' Linda picked up a blanket and laid it out at one end of the track Bella had marked out in the sand with driftwood. She scooped sand onto each corner of the blanket to hold it in place.

'What's that meant to be?' Bella asked.

'That's the security van! And later, it'll be for our picnic. Two birds with one stone, see.' Bella loved this childlike side to Linda; she was a real laugh when she wanted to be.

Up on the gravel track, Shirley's car pulled to a slow and steady stop. No gravel was flung up from the tyres the way Shirley drove. Bella and Linda watched as she carefully picked her way down the uneven wooden steps to the beach. She was carrying her stuff in high street shopping bags and wearing one of the very feminine jumpsuits that Dolly had said were no good. She looked like she'd just come from Kensington High Street.

'I must ask her where she got that jumpsuit from. I reckon it'd suit me,' Linda mocked.

Bella looked Linda up and down. She was wearing ripped jeans, dirty plimsolls and a huge jumper that must once have belonged to Joe. 'Well – you look like a scarecrow in that gear,' Bella commented with a smile.

'I'm dressed for the occasion, I'll have you know,' said Linda. 'This is my "rehearsing for a hare-brained robbery" outfit.'

As Shirley got to the bottom of the steps and tiptoed through the sand so as not to get any in her still-pristine plimsolls, their smiles faded. The split to Shirley's lower lip and the surrounding bruise was visible from ten feet away. They raced forwards.

'Tony bleedin' Fisher,' Shirley said.

Bella and Linda took the shopping bags and dumped them on the bonnet of the old Morris Minor.

'I wish I'd brought a heavier jacket,' Shirley said. 'I think it's going to rain.'

'Forget that!' Bella snapped. 'What happened?'

Shirley's eyes filled with tears and she fought to keep them back. 'Please, Bella. I only want to say it once, so let's wait for Dolly.' She walked away to stand at the shore edge, looking out to sea. Taking her lead, Bella and Linda left her alone and continued to get the beach set up for their rehearsal.

* * *

By the time Dolly arrived in her Mercedes, the beach was ready and the rain had started belting down. Dolly stood at the top of the cove and looked down at the outline of the fifty-yard run Bella had marked out with driftwood; it was like looking at the drawing in Harry's ledgers. The picnic blanket represented the security wagon, and several abandoned pallets had been laid out in front of it to represent the 'blocking van', with the Morris behind it representing their Transit van. Three full rucksacks sat on top of the Morris's bonnet. At the far end of the run more pallets signified their get-away car. Linda and Shirley were seated inside the Morris sheltering from the rain, and Dolly could see enough of Shirley to know that she was wearing that bloody catwalk jumpsuit. She could hear the pair of them laughing and giggling, while Bella wandered round the wet sand collecting more driftwood.

They were worryingly close to the date of the robbery and Dolly was overwhelmed with worry. Linda had yet to find a suitable large vehicle to be used to stop the security wagon and Dolly was yet to get the actual route plan and times off Harry's inside man. As the girls' laughter echoed round the cove, Dolly wondered if she was the only one taking this seriously. Were the others just using her as a cash cow to replenish their wardrobes, get them freebies at health spas and pay for the upkeep of their vodka stash?

In a bad mood now, she made her way slowly down to the beach. The picnic hamper she'd brought was heavy so it was slow going; she was also carrying an umbrella and Wolf kept getting under her feet. Linda watched her make her way towards them and shook her head with annoyance. Again, they had done all the hard work – and here she was arriving like the Queen Mother on a day out at Sandringham.

'Bella!' Linda shouted and nodded towards Dolly. Bella turned and waved a large lump of driftwood. From where Dolly stood, it looked uncannily like a sawn-off shotgun.

Dolly gestured to Linda to come and join her.

'Yes, ma'am,' Linda mocked as she clambered out of the Morris. 'On my way, ma'am.' She glanced back at Shirley and winked. 'Wolf's probably done a shit and she wants me to pick it up.' Shirley gave a wan smile.

As Linda plodded over towards Dolly, she suddenly felt miserable. Her hair was dripping wet and Joe's jumper was now twice as big and heavy as it had been when she put it on this morning. She was waterlogged, unlike Dolly, who was as immaculate as ever in her matching raincoat and wellies. She looked Dolly in the eye.

'Bella told you about poor old Boxer getting done over,' she said petulantly.

Dolly nodded, handed the picnic blanket to Linda, and kept on the move. Linda followed close behind her.

'What you gonna do about it, Dolly? Tony Fisher's a nutcase and—'

Dolly suddenly turned and stopped right in front of Linda. 'That bloke I found you in bed with the other day, the mechanic, was he the one with you last night?'

Linda shook her head. She felt a twinge of guilt for lying to Dolly, but what bleedin' business was it of hers anyway?

'You're still seeing him, aren't you?' Dolly pushed.

Linda shook her head, but now Dolly stepped closer.

'You worry me, Linda. You drink too much and when you do, you say all kinds of things to all kinds of people.' Dolly was referring to the night Linda had spilled the beans to Bella in the arcade. 'I need to be sure there's no pillow talk going on between you and some random fella off the streets.' Dolly knew full well that Carlos wasn't random at all; she knew from her short conversation with Boxer that Carlos was Arnie's bum boy.

'Oh, believe me, we didn't do no talking,' Linda quipped, trying to make light of things.

Dolly's stony glare told Linda that she wasn't in the mood.

'Look, Dolly, he was a one-night stand; there was nothing in it. I've not seen him since, just like you told me, I've kept meself to meself, all right? There's no one.'

Dolly looked at Linda hard, trying to detect if she was lying, but Linda held her gaze. Dolly toyed with the idea of telling Linda exactly who Carlos was, and telling her that she knew Linda was with Carlos on the night Tony went on his rampage – but that would ruin the day's plans. No, Dolly needed to focus today. She walked round Linda and headed for Bella. Linda followed close behind, unable to zip her mouth.

'Don't change the subject from what I asked you,' she whined. 'What you gonna do about the Fishers? Old Boxer must have run straight to 'em, just like you said – only now look where he is!'

'He was a fool, Linda. And fools don't know what's good for 'em.'

Linda dropped the hamper on the picnic blanket and continued after Dolly.

Realising that all three women needed reassurance, Dolly went on, loud enough for them all to hear: 'I never meant for anything to happen to him and we don't know it was the Fishers who got to him. It could have been an accident; he was pissed as a fart when I spoke to him earlier in the evening. I'm well aware of the problems we got, but we still got a job to do here today. And it ain't my job to keep Boxer safe. It's my job to keep you lot safe.'

Linda clenched her teeth, making the muscles in her cheeks visibly jump. 'Well, you ain't doing a very good job of that either.' She looked at Shirley.

Shirley had her head down, trying to hide her split lip, but Dolly had seen it and the look on her face made Linda smirk in triumph. After a pause that seemed to last an age, Dolly went over to Shirley and lifted her chin with her hand.

'What happened to your lip, darlin'?' she asked softly.

Shirley hesitated. 'It's nothing.' She looked down again.

Dolly repeated the question.

Tears welled up in Shirley's eyes. 'Tony Fisher grabbed me off the street and took me to my mum's place. He said he wanted to know about your Harry's ledgers. I was terrified and told him I didn't know nothing. He threatened to burn me with a cigarette and kept insisting that I must know. I kept on saying, "I don't! I don't know anything!" Then he got angry and punched me in the mouth. Oh, God, his hands were all over me, inside my clothes and . . .' As Shirley let it all out she threw herself into Dolly's arms, sobbing. Nobody said a word. It was Dolly who broke the silence.

'Did he . . . darlin', what did he do?'

Shirley regained control of herself. 'Greg showed up with his two mates. Tony would have raped me, I know he would. He said as much. But I didn't tell him nothing about us, Dolly. I didn't tell him about Harry's ledgers or about what we're doing. I swear I didn't.'

Dolly got out a hanky and wiped the tears from Shirley's eyes. 'I know you didn't, love,' she said. 'Don't worry about that. I'm so sorry for what that bastard did to you and believe me, he'll get what's coming to him.' Dolly glanced at Bella and Linda. 'We keep this between us, OK? No police, no repercussions. We're all going to be just fine.'

Dolly picked up one of the rucksacks from the back seat of the Morris. 'Too heavy – take some sand out. We're carrying bank notes, not gold bullion.' The conversation was closed.

Linda couldn't believe how quickly Dolly had glossed over Shirley's near-rape, but Shirley jumped out of the Morris and started tipping some of the sand back out.

'About a quarter, I reckon, love, that should do it,' Dolly advised.

Shirley smiled at Dolly and Linda understood that focusing on the practical was exactly what Shirley needed. Bella also saw this, but she realised that Dolly was hiding something – and that something was fear. Dolly was worried. She decided to say nothing: she, too, would focus on the practical.

'We thought we'd use the Morris as our tailing van,' Bella said. 'So we can practise getting in and out. It's not ideal, but it's better than a picnic blanket. And I can cut it up later, get used to using the chainsaw.'

'Good idea,' Dolly said. 'The chainsaw and the sledgehammer are both in the boot of the Merc. I couldn't carry everything in one go.'

'Don't worry about them, Doll,' Linda said sarcastically. 'We're only rehearsing for an armed robbery. Who needs a chainsaw and sledgehammer, when you brought pork pie and sarnies?'

'And who needs a blocking van, when you brought a picnic blanket?' Dolly snapped back. 'At least I've got a chainsaw and sledgehammer, Linda, you got the van yet? I've already asked you a number of times to sort it, so pull your finger out and get it done.

We need to know what size it is so we can reinforce the rear bumper with a steel bar.'

Linda was fuming inside, but a touch on the arm from Bella made her bite her tongue. She took a couple of deep breaths and then replied. 'I know exactly what I'm looking for. I got a couple of possibles lined up, but want to give it another week.' She spoke in a slow, controlled voice. 'You'll have your van soon enough.'

As Dolly headed off to walk through the fifty-yard run with Bella, Linda said under her breath to Shirley, 'I ain't risking jail for nicking a crappy old van just cos she's got some ridiculous fantasy about an armed robbery.'

Shirley touched her split lip. It stung every time she spoke and opened up every time she smiled. 'I hope it's not a fantasy, Linda,' Shirley said gravely. 'I want better than this.'

Bella and Dolly marched to the far end of the fifty-yard run, using long strides to make certain the distance was correct.

'That feels about right,' Dolly said. As she started the walk back, Bella stayed still. Dolly turned.

'What's worrying you?'

'Feels real.'

'It is real,' said Dolly. 'Always was.'

'For you,' Bella said. 'I wasn't so sure. I didn't even know who you were, Dolly Rawlins. You could have been some eccentric old woman grieving for her dead husband for all I knew. Keeping him alive by recreating what should have been his finest hour.' Bella caught up with Dolly. 'But you got me now. I've bought in, I'm going to give you a hundred per cent and we're actually going to steal a million pounds.' Bella stared deep into Dolly's eyes and gave her a smile of absolute respect. Dolly had a lot on her shoulders and Bella wanted her to know that she was there to help.

Dolly's expression remained impassive. She gave a little nod of understanding, turned and walked back to the others. 'Less of the "old",' she said over her shoulder.

Back with Linda and Shirley, Dolly got down to business.

'Let's get cracking. Linda, you'll be driving the van behind the security wagon with me and Shirley in the back. The clapped-out Morris is our van for today, so just mime it through for timings.'

Linda snorted, and looked at the rusty wreck of a car. 'Well, I wasn't thinkin' of racin' it up and down the effin' beach.'

'Bella, you'll be driving the blocking van up front. The one that Linda is hopefully gonna pull her finger out and get—'

Linda interrupted, 'All right, you made your point. No need to hark on about it.'

'You two –' Dolly ordered Bella and Linda – 'go and get the chainsaw and sledgehammer. Let's see how ready we are.'

Once all the equipment was assembled and everyone was back on the beach, Dolly gathered them round for further instructions. Shirley was shaking her legs, warming up the muscles; Linda, in contrast, was perched on the bonnet of the Morris. Dolly addressed Linda first.

'We'll practise getting out of the car and starting up the chainsaw first of all, and trying it out on the side of the wreck—'

Before Dolly could finish, Linda butted in. 'Bella's doin' the saw, Dolly. That's Bella's job. You just said I was drivin' the van.'

Dolly tapped the wet sand with her welly and shook her head. 'I've changed me mind,' she said. 'Bella drives the front van and I'll drive the van behind.'

'But that's bloody stupid,' Linda persisted. 'Bella's the only one of us so far that's been able to handle the saw. I can hardly lift it . . . And I thought you was in the front truck doin' the blockin'?'

Dolly sighed, clenching and unclenching her hands. 'I've changed me mind!' she repeated aggressively. 'Once the security wagon has gone into the back of the front vehicle, Bella has to get out of the blocking van and hold the guards at bay with the shotgun while we load the cash. She'll also have to be the last to leave. Unless I say different, that's the position she takes. Right?'

'Fine by me,' Bella said impatiently, wanting to get on with it.

The rain had stopped now, and Dolly took her coat off to reveal a pink Dance Centre tracksuit. Linda and Shirley bowed their heads to hide their giggles. She looked like a hideous pair of velour curtains. Linda imagined her at the Sanctuary, bouncing about in an aerobics class, sweating like a fat fluffy pink pig. Oblivious, Dolly took a stopwatch out of her pocket and handed it to Bella, then folded her coat neatly and placed it on the picnic blanket.

Following Dolly's lead, Shirley and Linda each put a heavy rucksack on their backs. Linda tried to lift the chainsaw, but the weight of it was clearly too much for her. 'This is a bloody waste of time,' she muttered. 'It's obvious that Bella should be the one carrying the saw!'

Shirley tightened the shoulder straps on her rucksack to stop it bouncing as she ran. 'Why don't we just do what Dolly says and start rehearsing? We don't know anything for sure yet.'

Bella winked at Linda and settled down on the picnic blanket to watch them run through the initial stages of the operation.

Dolly sat in the driver's seat of the Morris, with Shirley and a stony-faced Linda in the back seat. Linda had the chainsaw on her knee, complaining about its weight.

'OK,' Dolly explained, 'we've got four minutes from start to finish. Let's just try timing getting out and starting the chainsaw. Ready, Bella?'

Bella gave them the thumbs up.

'Three, two, one . . . GO!' Dolly leapt out of the driver's seat, raced to the back of the Morris and pointed Bella's driftwood shotgun out into the distance behind them. Shirley scrambled out of the back seat and stood by the edge of the picnic blanket, pointing her driftwood shotgun in the direction of the security guards. And Linda . . . Linda was still stuck in the back seat of the Morris, smashing the chainsaw against the door frame like a dog trying to get through a door with a long stick in its mouth.

'It's too long to get out of the fucking door!' Linda screamed in sheer frustration.

'Well, you got it in there, you must be able to get it out!' Dolly shouted back.

Eventually Linda manoeuvred the chainsaw into the other seat, and flung herself out, dragging the saw after her. She gripped the start cord, pulled it much harder than required, let go of the wrong bit and dropped the saw on her foot. 'Bollocks to this, I'm not doing it!' Linda shouted as she hopped around. She threw her rucksack down onto the sand, and refused to budge. As though the raid was for real, Dolly ran back to Linda, picked up the chainsaw, started it and shoved the end into one of the Morris' door panels.

Shirley was in awe of Dolly's complete determination not to be beaten. Linda hoped the old cow would drop the saw and cut her own leg off. Meanwhile, Bella sat patiently on the picnic rug, timing everything. The noise of the chainsaw on metal was horrific. *It will scare the living shit out of the guards when they hear that from inside their security wagon*, Bella thought. By the time they glimpsed the four masked 'men', they'd be putty in their hands.

It took fifteen minutes for Dolly to cut through the side of the car. It wasn't so much that the saw blade was blunt, but that she simply didn't have enough strength to push it down into the metal. Linda sat on the edge of the blanket, next to the pillowcases full of sand, feeling guilty as she watched the sweat drip from Dolly's forehead.

Once Dolly had cut a segment out of the car's door, she raced to the blanket and picked up one of the sandbags. Automatically, Linda leapt to her feet and Dolly stuffed the sandbag into her rucksack. 'Ready to reset, Bella,' called Dolly, breathing heavily. Bella got to her feet as Linda put one sandbag into Dolly's rucksack and another into Shirley's.

Linda spoke as she moved. 'Why are we still timing this shambles? The coppers would have shown up, nipped for a tea break, come back and nicked us all before we even got a sniff of the cash.'

'GO!' Dolly screamed and led the way down the fifty-yard run. In no time at all, Shirley and Linda had overtaken her and were having their own race, while Bella effortlessly jogged along by their sides.

At the end of the run, the three younger women waited for Dolly as she came coughing and spluttering across the line and fell to her knees on the pallets. 'Again,' Dolly said, sounding as if she was about to be sick.

'No,' Bella said taking control of the situation. 'Let's get a cup of tea. We'll go again in twenty.'

Dolly scrambled to her feet. 'We'll go again now!' she screamed.

Bella stood her ground. Bent under the weight of the rucksack, Dolly looked even smaller compared to the elegant height of Bella. 'We now know the order of events and we know we can do it,' Bella said calmly. 'But that took twenty minutes longer than it should have done. If we go again now, we'll achieve nothing. So, let's have a cup of tea, get your breath back and we'll go again in twenty.'

For a moment, no one spoke. The four women walked slowly back along the beach between the neatly laid out pieces of driftwood towards the Morris, the picnic blanket and the waiting hamper.

'I meant to ask, Shirley . . .' Linda said, breaking the tense silence. 'Where did you get that lovely jumpsuit?'

CHAPTER 18

Terry Miller had been at the disused quarry for two hours setting up the vehicles. Jimmy Nunn, an ex-racing driver, was an old mate of Terry's and was going through a bit of a hard time, having, ironically, been banned for dangerous driving. Married and on the dole, Jimmy desperately needed a job and Terry thought he might be their perfect fourth man – not that he'd dream of making that sort of decision without Harry Rawlins' approval.

Terry had taken Jimmy to meet Harry in a pub three months previously, although Jimmy had had no idea what for. Harry liked to take his time to size up new boys before working with them, or telling them what he was up to. That day at the quarry, Harry was there to watch Jimmy at work. If he liked what he saw then he'd tell him what the job was and put him on the team as a driver. Jimmy was a good-looking fella, about thirty-three, six feet, with a big frame. With no criminal record other than petty driving offences, he'd never had his fingerprints taken. He had been on a couple of bank robberies as a driver before, so came with good references, but his reputation for not bottling it had more to do with the risks he'd taken when he was a racing driver.

Jimmy was testing the engine of the bread truck that Len Gulliver had nicked for Joe Pirelli from the Sunshine Bread Company. It was a good, square-shaped vehicle with double doors at the back. Joe had attached a heavy metal bar under the rear bumper, strong enough to take the impact when the security wagon rammed into the back of it, and had fitted a cross harness to protect the driver from the impact. Jimmy put his foot down and did a circuit of the quarry. It didn't sound too good, but it would by the time he had finished with it. Once back with Harry and Terry, Jimmy jumped straight out of the van, yanked the bonnet up and leant into the engine to fine-tune it. Harry was impressed.

While all this was going on, Joe Pirelli was in the woods that ran along the side of the old quarry, test firing his sawn-off shotguns by taking a few pot shots at woodpigeons and the odd pheasant. Joe was a professional and fanatical about his 'irons', regularly cleaning and greasing them down with oil. For the past three years, Joe and Terry had worked together closely and Terry respected his self-assurance and nerves of steel. Joe also had a quick temper and could be violent, but Terry and the others always knew how far they could push him. If you saw his dark eyes give a strange jerky flick, that was the warning . . . then Joe Pirelli was lethal. Although they shared a mutual respect, they weren't close friends and never socialised together outside of work. One of the Boss's rules. And if you worked for Harry, you did as he said without question; that was the way it was and the way it had to be for everyone's safety.

Joe walked back up the quarry. In one hand he carried his 'irons' in a long black wooden case lined with red felt; in the other he carried a dead pheasant. Terry watched as Joe went over to his Lancia and placed the gun case and bird in the boot. Joe was tall, six-three, maybe more, with dark Italian looks, and he was obsessed with physical fitness. He was lean, with a chiselled face, and those odd-coloured eyes – hazel, maybe? He was a tough man, and Terry was glad they were on the same side.

Terry signalled to Joe and the two men checked their watches before checking out the dummy security van. Harry Rawlins liked everything to be ready before his arrival, and Joe and Terry carefully went over every detail: the money sacks were weighted; the vehicles' positions exactly measured to reflect where they'd be for the raid itself. After the rehearsal, it would be their job to clean the cars and bread truck and take them back to the lock-up.

The bread truck now sounded as if its engine was running smoothly. Jimmy got out of the driving seat and gave the thumbs up to Joe and Terry over by the dummy van. They made him nervous – well, Joe scared him more than Terry. He didn't know exactly what the job was yet, and he was aware he was still on trial, but he admired Harry Rawlins and wanted to be in on his team.

Harry's silver Merc was so quiet it seemed to float over the gravel road. No one heard it arriving, but as soon as Terry and Joe saw it pull up and Harry get out they almost stood to attention, like troops about to be inspected by their commanding officer. With his fawn cashmere coat hanging over his shoulders, his immaculately tailored navy suit, his black briefcase and his dark glasses, Harry Rawlins looked more like a city banker than a man about to rehearse a security raid. He went over to Joe and Terry.

'He's got the bread van purring like a kitten. It'll be no bother now,' said Terry.

Harry looked over at the BMW getaway car and nodded at Jimmy.

This was Jimmy's big chance. He ran to the BMW, jumped in, started her up and, with a screeching smoking wheel spin, accelerated round the quarry at an incredible speed, sweating as the car screamed up and down. Speeding past the three men, he pulled on the handbrake, did a one-eighty turn and accelerated away again. In his rear-view mirror, he saw Terry grinning and give him the thumbs up.

Harry went back to his car and took his coat off, methodically changing his clothes, folding each garment up and placing it on the back seat. Any other man would have looked fairly ridiculous standing there half undressed, but there was something neat and organised about the way he changed into his tracksuit.

'We'll try the explosives,' Harry said, bending down to tie up his plimsolls.

Terry took a small sampler over to the dummy security wagon, stuck the explosives to the side of it and lit the short fuse. He stepped round the side of the van, out of the way – and BOOM. *it was over and done within a matter of seconds, leaving a nice round hole the size of a fist in the side of the vehicle. Terry walked back, grinning.*

'When I use the proper amount,' he said, 'it'll leave a hole big enough to get me granny through, and she's a big old trout, Harry.'

Harry went over the instructions with the team, quietly but with precision and attention to detail. When he finished, each man put a rucksack on and Joe got the shotguns, Harry handed Jimmy the stopwatch to time the run through.

'The whole raid has to take less than four minutes from start to finish,' he said.

All three vans were in position. The bread truck was up front, the fake security wagon was in the middle and the van Terry had driven there was at the back. The convoy was set up as though the security wagon was now trapped in the Strand underpass. Jimmy was standing next to the bread truck so he could see Harry's signal to start the stopwatch, Harry was in the driver's seat of the rear van, with Joe and Terry in the back.

'He don't look like he's got it in him,' Joe said, pointing at Jimmy.

'He has, Joe. I promise he has,' Terry said.

'When you're nervous, the old trigger finger gets shaky and suddenly – bang! We're all looking at life for murder.'

'That's why we're here today,' Harry interrupted. 'He's up there counting the seconds till I give the order. Is he winding himself up into a useless frenzy or is he as cool as ice? We'll soon find out.' Harry raised his hand and Jimmy raised the stopwatch in acknowledgement.

When Harry's hand came down, Jimmy started the stopwatch and the men moved like lightning. Joe leapt out of the van and stood with his shotgun held towards the imaginary traffic behind. Terry slammed the explosives onto the side of the fake security wagon and Harry climbed onto its bonnet, pointing his shotgun at the imaginary security driver and passenger. 'Get out of the wagon!' he screamed, his deep voice echoing round the quarry. The intention was that the two guards in the cab would get out and be forced to lie on the ground in front of Joe.

BOOM! A large Harry-sized hole was blown in the side of the fake security wagon; Harry crawled in, followed by Terry. Harry quickly loaded Terry's haversack with accurately weighted bags before shouting 'Go!' Terry and Joe then switched places, Terry pointing the shotgun at the non-existent traffic and the imaginary guards while Joe's haversack was filled. Joe then filled Harry's haversack and all three men raced towards the getaway car parked exactly fifty yards away.

It was a slick operation and, as Jimmy watched them run, he couldn't wait to learn more about the job.

* * *

Dolly sipped tea from the lid of her thermos, listening to Linda and Shirley argue over the last chicken sandwich. Shirley felt that the two slices of pork pie Linda ate meant that the sandwich should really be hers; but Linda argued that you can't legitimately compare a pie to a sandwich. While they bickered, Bella grabbed it and ate it herself.

'Shut your gobs,' she said.

Dolly, who'd eaten nothing, got to her feet. She handed a 'shotgun' stick to Shirley and kept the other for herself. 'Let's do just the run; see how long it takes.' Bella jumped up and ran off to the far end of the beach with her stopwatch. When Linda stood up, she was clearly in some pain from where she'd dropped the chainsaw on her foot.

'I don't think I can do it, Dolly,' she whimpered.

'Is that what you're gonna say if something happens on the day?' Dolly asked. 'Or are you gonna run for your life anyway?'

Linda shut up and the three of them stood, rucksacks on their backs, ready for the cue from Bella.

From fifty yards away, Bella thought they looked like a right old mishmash of mums doing the parents' egg and spoon race at sports day. Dolly in her bright-pink tracksuit, Shirley in her catwalk-style jumpsuit and Linda looking like a tramp. She shook her head. 'Ready!' she shouted. Dolly gave her the thumbs up. 'One, two, three. GO!'

No matter how many times they did the run, Dolly always lagged behind. She didn't have the energy or the fitness level of the other three, and began puffing and gasping for breath after the first twenty yards. Every time they made it to the finishing line, she paused, clasped her side, heaved for breath and asked what time they had done. It was obvious she'd never be able to complete the run in the required time. But Dolly wouldn't give up: time and time again she turned and walked back up the beach to the old Morris. After the fourth time, Linda felt that she had to say something.

'This is ridiculous, Dolly. I can do it, Shirley can do it – so what's the point in all three of us running up and down time and time again just because you can't do it? *You're* the only one holding us up. Take a rest and then try it again on your own.'

Dolly walked away, hands on hips, head down. She was pushing herself to breaking point, but she refused to give in. Reaching the rusty Morris, Dolly held up her hand, indicating to Bella that she was ready to go again.

Bella crossed her fingers. 'Come on, Dolly. You can do it,' she whispered. Dolly dropped her hand and started to run.

This time she was on target for the time limit, but it was awful to watch the veins standing out on her neck, her arms flailing at her sides. Just a few yards before the finishing line, her body caved in. Her legs started to buckle under her as she forced herself on. She flung herself towards the finishing line then collapsed in a heap, her breath forced out in noisy, heaving, rasping sighs. On her hands and knees in the sand, she just managed to wheeze, 'Get this off me, Bella!'

Bella quickly lifted the heavy rucksack from Dolly's back. Linda smirked and shook her head smugly. Shirley looked daggers at her, and knelt beside Dolly.

'It's no good, Dolly,' she whispered. 'You can't make the run.'

Gradually, Dolly's breathing slowed and settled. She gave one final heavy sigh and got herself to her feet. She picked up the rucksack and handed it to Bella, who gave Dolly the stopwatch. Bella stripped off her bike leathers to reveal a pair of running shorts underneath. Heaving one rucksack on her back, she took Shirley's rucksack in her hand and strolled off down the beach.

'Just watch her go,' Linda bragged. 'She used to run for her school.'

Shirley could have hit her; sometimes Linda was really evil. Dolly said nothing as she watched how effortlessly Bella walked with the weight on her back.

Back at the Morris, Bella emptied Shirley's rucksacks of sandbags onto the picnic blanket; she'd need these when Dolly was timing her. Picking up the chainsaw, she tested the engine, starting and restarting it. Satisfied Linda hadn't damaged it, she got into the wrecked Morris Minor, rucksack on her back and chainsaw in her hand.

The second Bella jumped out of the car, Dolly started the stopwatch.

They watched in silence as Bella started the saw with one pull of the cord and cut a hole in the car door large enough for a shotgun to be pushed through. Bella then ran to the picnic blanket and lifted the sandbags, pacing the time it would take for her to fill Linda's rucksack, then Shirley's. She was like a machine. When Bella set off down the beach, Linda couldn't control her excitement any longer. She began jumping up and down, waving her arms in the air.

'Go, girl! GO! GO! GO!' Linda screamed.

Dolly's eyes flickered between Bella and the stopwatch. Bella ran towards them in long easy strides, as if the weight on her back had no effect at all.

Dolly didn't have to give the actual time because it was obvious Bella was by far the quickest. While Shirley and Linda hugged Bella, Dolly walked back up the beach towards the Morris alone.

'Let's do the whole thing now,' she called back to them, and whistled to Wolf, who was rolling in a dead seagull.

* * *

They spent another hour running through the plan before calling it a day. While Dolly packed up the picnic hamper, Bella and Linda carried the chainsaw and rucksacks back up to the boot of her Merc. Shirley emptied the sand from the pillowcases and watched Dolly from the corner of her eye. Dolly's lips were pursed tight and she seemed still to be seething at her own inability to keep up with the rest of them. Shirley had tried a big, consoling smile, but her split lip opened up again and anyway, Dolly had just ignored her. She was a tough old bird. Her own weakness in the face of Tony Fisher's assault was playing on Shirley's mind. *I was pathetic*, she thought angrily. *But I won't be anymore . . .*

The final rehearsal run had been the slickest yet and well under time. Dolly's decision to reorder the roles, with her now driving the blocking van up front, Bella back on the chainsaw and Linda driving the transit van behind, turned out to be absolutely the right thing to do and played to everyone's strengths. They'd finished the day on a high, tired, filthy, achy, but invigorated. For the first time it seemed real, very real. As Shirley cleared the beach of their debris, she picked up one of the driftwood shotguns and smiled. Checking Dolly's back was turned, she held the 'gun' in position one last time before throwing it into the dunes.

Dolly hadn't cared about the decision she'd had to make about driving the lead van, but she did mind failing in front of her girls. They looked to her for guidance, for stability and for leadership and she had to maintain that role; there was no way they could think she was weak in any way.

Linda and Bella were almost at the bottom of the steps by the time Shirley and Dolly were packed up and ready to go. As Dolly looked at her three girls, she spotted the not-so-subtle sideways glance that Linda gave the others. While they no longer seemed to doubt that *they* could do this, by the way they looked at her, Dolly could see that it was her they doubted now.

She picked up the sledgehammer. 'I never practised my bit, did I?' she said cheerfully. Standing a couple of feet from the Morris, legs apart, hands firmly gripping the handle, Dolly swung the hammer. The veins stood out on her neck and she let rip; not exactly a scream, but a weird guttural roar right from her belly. She let the hammer go and it flew through the air before smashing through the Morris's windscreen, shattering it into a thousand pieces. Beads of glass flew backwards, sprinkling over the back seats. For a second or two, the inside of the car looked like a snow-globe and it was almost beautiful to watch.

As the sledgehammer landed on the back seat, the three women gasped in shock.

'Oh, my God!' Linda spoke for all of them. 'It's like the first time you hear your mum say "fuck"!'

Dolly looked at them with an impish grin. 'I know my strengths. And I know yours,' she said. She turned serious. 'We've got this, girls. We've bloody well got this.' And then she said something that brought a lump to even Linda's throat:

'I won't let you down.'

Now, Dolly saw no doubt in their eyes at all; only respect. They knew she could lead and she knew they'd follow.

* * *

By Harry's third run, it was clear that he was holding them up. He simply wasn't fast enough and, no matter how many times he tried, he wasn't getting any faster.

No one said a single word as Harry thought through his options. His face was tight with anger and his jaw muscles twitched erratically. His anger was directed at himself, they could all see that, so they respectfully gave him the time and space he needed. Eventually, Harry handed his rucksack to Jimmy.

'Lemme see you run, kid,' he said.

As the sweat trickled down Harry's bright-red face, Jimmy completed the run in a spectacularly fast time. In Harry's younger days that run would have been a piece of cake, but he was smart enough to know where his team's strengths lay – and his wasn't running; not anymore.

'Back to your start positions,' Harry ordered. 'I'm gonna time the whole thing.'

As he watched Terry, Joe and Jimmy walk back towards the follow van, Harry was hurting, inside and out. He'd always led from the front and to have to relinquish that position was heart-breaking.

Joe and Terry clambered into the back of the follow van while Jimmy lagged behind. He was tapping his watch.

'What's the problem?' Harry asked.

'Nothing.' Jimmy didn't want to look stupid or cause trouble. 'It's just my watch. Overwound it, I expect.'

Harry took his gold Rolex off and handed it to Jimmy. 'Here,' he said. 'Have this. I'll be buying myself the latest model when this is all over.' He climbed into the driver's seat of the bread truck.

As Jimmy took up his new position in the driver's seat of the follow van, he admired Harry's gold Rolex with its diamond-encrusted face. It was the most beautiful watch he'd ever seen. He vowed never to take it off.

CHAPTER 19

Fuller's weekend had been spent at the Yard, showing Boxer Davis's landlady, Fat Fran, hundreds and hundreds of mugshots. She said she'd do her best to help him, but Fuller wondered if she was just stringing him along for the free food and all the hot and cold drinks she kept asking for. Sometimes she'd point at a face and say, 'I think, but I'm not sure, but it could be him . . . let me have another cup of tea and some biscuits while I think about it.' Fuller would then run a computer check on the individual she'd selected, only to discover they were serving time in prison, or that they were dead. But Fuller had to keep going with her because she was their only lead now. Each time she mentioned a lag by name, it got his hopes up, but most of them turned out to be ex-lovers and one even turned out to be her husband. *Bloody hell*, Fuller thought to himself sourly, *she's had a lot of fellas for a woman of her size and odour.* As for the man who attacked her, Fran finally admitted that she simply couldn't remember what he looked like.

Andrews had spent the morning with Forensics. He'd asked them to check out a stolen vehicle found abandoned in a side street off Shaftesbury Avenue. The car had blood on the undercarriage, which came from the same blood group as Boxer's. There was damage to both the rear and front bumpers, and a headlight was broken: similar glass had been found in the alleyway where Boxer was discovered. It hadn't taken the forensic team long to confirm that the fibres snagged on the broken headlight matched the suit that Boxer had been wearing, and they were also able to match the glass left at the scene with the stolen car. A positive result, but it led nowhere: the car had no suspect fingerprints in it, and the leather glove marks suggested Boxer's killer had a criminal record and didn't want to be caught. It was yet another dead end.

Fuller hammered each key down as he made his methodical notes, wishing it was Resnick's head. There had been a big jewellery raid in Mayfair the night before and the whole station was buzzing about it. By rights, Fuller should have been assigned to it, but he was stuck on the Rawlins case. So, instead of tracking down proper criminals – ones who were actually alive – he'd spent his time waiting on Fat Fran and getting nothing in return. He was sick and tired of being Resnick's whipping boy – and the other CID officers was pissing him off, too. They knew how much Fuller hated Resnick, and kept joking about how inseparable the two of them were, and how Fuller was putting on weight and starting to smell like an ashtray as he slowly morphed into his 'boss'. Smarting with resentment, Fuller finished typing and angrily yanked his report from the typewriter, tearing it down the middle in his haste. He looked up at the ceiling, calmed himself and started again.

When Andrews came in, he too was angry. The chief had hauled him over the coals for requesting forensic priority on the stolen car used in the hit and run on Boxer Davis over the Mayfair job. Andrews had had to stand there like a wet lettuce while he took the bollocking that should have been given to Resnick. Now he paced up and down the room, watching Fuller hit the typewriter keys with such force it was moving across the desk.

''Ere Fuller, how's your mate Resnick?' Detective Sergeant Hawkes popped his head round the door with a big grin on his face.

'Fuck off,' said Fuller.

'With pleasure,' said Hawkes. 'I'm off the case, and so's Richmond, and we're on the Mayfair job. No more wasting time doing surveillance on the Rawlins woman for us.'

'How come you got moved and I didn't?" Fuller was seething.

'I think the DCI's keeping all rejects in the one team so as not to infect the rest of the station,' Hawkes mocked.

Fuller was livid. He thought of asking the chief if he could get on the Mayfair job, but then he figured the chief would have already asked if he'd wanted him. God, what if Resnick's incompetence really was rubbing off on him? He glared at Hawkes.

'Resnick know about this?' Fuller asked.

'No idea. I've not seen him and I don't care. It's the DCI's decision,' Hawkes said cheerfully, shutting the door and leaving Fuller to stew in his own juices.

Five minutes later, Alice walked in. She was about to be transferred to Criminal Records and was relieved in a way: the stress levels would be much lower.

'You're moving back to your office today,' she reminded Fuller and Andrews. 'The decorators have done a lovely job. It's all nice and fresh with brand-new equipment.' Her voice was a cross between a kindly mum and a strict headmistress.

Fuller had already had most of his desk and files packed and moved. Andrews had slipped out to the canteen before he could be commandeered into moving any office equipment.

'DCI Resnick in yet?' Fuller asked Alice, as he carefully pulled his report from the typewriter and picked up the last bits of paperwork from his desk.

'No, and I'm furious that he hasn't done a thing about clearing his office! I gave him boxes to put things in but he's not even managed that.' Although she was a group secretary for the CID senior officers, Resnick behaved as if she worked for him, and him alone.

'Alice,' Fuller said kindly. 'What did you expect?'

Alice looked sharply at Fuller. She hated the lack of respect for Resnick, although she knew exactly what Fuller meant. Resnick was bone idle when it came to practical things; he knew that if he left something for long enough, Alice would do it for him. She'd once caught him laughing about it with one of his colleagues. 'Why have a dog and bark yourself?' he'd said, which had hurt her deeply, although she knew he didn't really mean it. Resnick was lazy because she liked looking after him, not the other way round. She still defended him. 'Well, he's very busy, Detective Sergeant Fuller. He has no time for menial tasks.'

Fuller smiled at Alice as he left with his last box of property. 'He's lucky to have you, Alice. And I'm sorry that I can't say the same for you.'

'Do you know when you might expect him?' Alice shouted after Fuller.

'Don't know! Don't care!' Fuller shouted back.

Alice went along the empty corridor and stood outside the cracked, Sellotape-covered door to Resnick's office. She rattled the handle. It was, as usual, locked. The silence was shattered as the swing doors at the end of the hall banged open and Resnick appeared. As he passed the new office, he bellowed for Fuller and Andrews, and was about to bellow for Alice when he saw her waiting for him.

'Morning, flower,' he said, unlocking his office door and bursting into one of his coughing fits.

Resnick's office was as shambolic as ever; he'd made no effort even to begin boxing things up. He flung his dog-eared, chewed briefcase onto his desk and picked up the phone.

'It's been cut off, sir,' said Alice patiently. 'The decorators are starting in here today and you're supposed to have moved upstairs into the new annexe office.'

Resnick banged the phone down. 'Why didn't you tell me?!"

Alice had in fact told him five times, but she didn't say so.

He handed his office keys to her. 'Don't let anything out of your sight,' he said, earnestly looking her straight in the eyes. He trusted her as he trusted no one else.

'Of course,' she replied equally gravely. And he was gone.

Alice stood amid the horrible mess that was Resnick's professional life. If it had been anyone else's office, she'd have delegated it to the typing pool. But not Resnick's. He'd given her the keys to his sanctuary and she wasn't going to let a single scrap of paper out of her sight. She sighed heavily. *Why do I always let you do this to me?* she thought. Resnick barged in and out of her life every day like a tornado, and every night she'd pick up whatever he left in his wake. He never listened to a thing she said, unless it was an answer to one of his questions, and she couldn't recall how many times on leaving the office, he'd shouted: 'Give my regards to your dad! Slip him a hot toddy – that'll cure anything.' Even though she'd told him a thousand times that her father was dead.

But Alice knew exactly why she ran round after Resnick, and why she would do anything for him. She'd loved him for fifteen years.

CHAPTER 20

Linda sat in her arcade booth, biting her nails. The throbbing music had given her a headache. She was thinking about the meeting they'd all had at the arches lock-up after the beach rehearsal. And she didn't like how it had turned out.

They had all been on a high after the successful practice runs, but the meeting had turned sour. It had started when Bella had asked Dolly where she was going to stash the money after the raid.

'I'm not telling you,' Dolly had replied, quite matter of fact. 'What you don't know, you can't tell. It's as simple as that. It'll be safe. That's all you need to be sure of.'

'Don't you trust us?' Linda had said, instantly defensive.

'If you don't like it, Linda, you know where the door is.'

The three of them had stood in disgruntled silence as Dolly had handed them another checklist. After the raid, each girl was to travel to Heathrow airport separately for flights to Rio. Exact times and dates would be confirmed once Dolly had met the security contact, but for now they each had instructions on how to travel to the airport and how to behave during their journey. Lastly, Dolly gave them each an envelope full of money to pay for their hotel bills.

Shirley's face was beaming. She was both excited and frightened by what was happening. 'Where you going before Rio, Dolly?'

'Nowhere,' Dolly had said curtly. 'I got to find the right time to stash the money and then settle my Wolf into kennels. If we all disappear at the same time, people might ask questions. I'll be bringing out a considerable amount of cash for us to stay in Rio. Enough for at least two months. The longer we're away the safer it'll be for all of us.'

Linda opened her mouth to ask Dolly the question that was on everyone's mind, but Bella interrupted. She didn't want this to escalate into a slanging match. 'And the bulk of the cash . . . only you'll know where that's stashed?' she asked politely.

Dolly had seen that the girls needed reassurance that she knew what she was doing, and why. 'We work the way Harry did. None of his team ever knew where the money was stashed and he never ripped any of them off. They trusted him with their . . .' Dolly had looked down at the ground, not wanting to meet Linda or Shirley's eyes and regretting her choice of words. 'They trusted him,' she amended. 'They were good men, but Harry knew they'd be tempted to go out and start blowing the money right away. That attracts attention from others . . . especially the Old Bill.' She paused. 'Now look, I ain't gonna pull a fast one and disappear with the money.'

'What if something happens to you? What if you get caught or hit by a bus?' Bella was still worried.

Linda, who was bursting to know everything, had chipped in. 'We'd be stranded in Rio with nothing, that's what. We need to know it all, Dolly.'

Dolly had been hurt more than angry: hurt because they still didn't trust her. She turned on all three of them.

'Right now,' she said through clenched teeth, holding her index finger and thumb an inch apart, 'right now, I'm that close to calling it off and walking out of here. You can pay back every penny I've given you. You're all standing there holding more cash than you've ever seen in one place. How dare you question me! And if you think you can pull the job off on your own, then go ahead. Go ahead without me and see how far you get! I'm sick of being questioned. You make a choice right now, all of you. You want to pack it in? You want to do it on your own? Tell me now! Tell me right now!'

Although Shirley had said nothing to anger Dolly, she hung her head guiltily – she'd *thought* enough bad things about Dolly. Linda was less bothered by Dolly's ranting, but she knew that without the ledgers and the security contact, there was no way they could do the job on their own.

In the end, Bella had been the sensible mediator. 'We don't need to know where the money's being stashed, Dolly. We trust you. We have to.'

Dolly shrugged. It was a backhanded compliment from Bella, but it would do for now. Picking up Wolf, she left before she said something she might regret.

As the door closed behind her, Bella had turned to Linda and Shirley. 'I didn't lose a husband like you two did in her precious Harry's raid, but you need to know this . . . if she tries anything on, I'll kill her. My life's on the line here because I believe what she's promising. I ain't never had this much to lose before. And if anyone takes it from me, they'll be sorry. Very sorry.'

Shirley had looked shocked; she knew Bella wasn't kidding. Linda had chewed her last nail down to the quick, making it bleed. Like Bella, she still couldn't bring herself to trust Dolly completely. They'd have flown halfway round the world, and Dolly would be the only one who had access to all the money from the robbery. And they wouldn't even know how much they'd got away with!

Now, after several hours in her arcade booth mulling over what had happened in the lock-up, Linda was very angry. She poured another vodka into her coffee, and slugged it down. She hated feeling controlled by Dolly; she hated being treated like a child; and she hated not being her own boss anymore. When she thought about all that, was the idea that she, Bella and Shirley could do the job themselves such an impossibility?

* * *

Shirley looked at herself in the long mirror and smiled. She was pleased. The new face pack she'd tried out had done wonders for her skin, which now had a fresh glow. She began cutting and filing her nails. The rehearsal at the beach had been murder on them. Just as she began to relax, the doorbell rang. Shirley nearly shot out of her silk nightie.

Her heart began thumping. What if Tony Fisher was standing on her doorstep? She was on her own! He could break the door down, he could beat and rape her this time, even kill her. Shirley looked at the clock; it was one fifteen in the morning. Terrified, she didn't move or make a sound.

On the landing, Linda kept her finger on the doorbell. She'd seen from the street that Shirley's bedroom light was on. She giggled. It would be a laugh if she'd actually caught Miss Goody Two Shoes with her leg over a bloke!

The doorbell continued to ring. *It couldn't be Tony Fisher*, Shirley reasoned. He'd have kicked the door in by now, or at least screamed at her to open it. She tiptoed to the door and asked in a trembling voice: 'Who is it?'

Linda was oblivious to the hour and Shirley's nerves. 'It's me, you stupid cow! Open up.'

Linda waited impatiently as Shirley undid the numerous locks on the door. It sounded like Fort Knox: bolts, chains, a double or even a triple lock . . . Linda couldn't tell how many. When the door eventually opened, she could see the look of relief on Shirley's face.

'Bloody hell, Linda, you gave me the fright of my life. What do you want?'

'I just wanted to talk to you about Dolly,' said Linda, swaying a bit from the vodka.

She walked into the lounge, leaving Shirley to re-bolt and lock the front door. She was taken aback. Shirley's flat was like something out of an interior design magazine: soft pale colours everywhere, big thick rugs, classy furniture and a lovely stripped-pine dresser. Linda felt jealous. It must have cost a fortune decorating and furnishing the place: Terry must have made a lot of money doing jobs with her Joe and Harry Rawlins. Joe must have got the same cut as Terry, of course, so why had he spent so little of it on her or their place? It wasn't that Joe hadn't been generous with Linda, it was that he'd been a bloody charity to his own family; finding them places to live, flying them over from Italy, paying their rent and giving them handouts all the time. It was also true, Linda acknowledged, that Joe had thrown his money away down the clubs, gambling and buying drinks for all and sundry. And then there were the blonde bimbos she knew he played around with . . . Linda found herself getting edgy, and angry, as she watched Shirley in her expensive silk nightie fiddle with the central heating dial. None of it was Shirley's fault, but Linda wasn't in the mood to be reasonable.

'What about a drink then?' Linda asked.

Shirley could tell Linda had already been drinking. *Vodka, probably*, she thought. The pie-eyed 'grumpy ferret' look on her face gave her away. She didn't have vodka, so she poured Linda a large brandy in one of her best cut-crystal glasses and handed it over.

Linda noted the glass, but didn't say anything as she swirled the brandy round and round, looking as if she knew what she was doing. She sat on the floor on the thick white rug and leant against the Heal's three-seater sofa. Taking a swig of the brandy, she got straight to the point. 'You think Dolly's been straight with us, then, or what?'

Shirley stayed near the fireplace. She was tired and she was sick of Linda's suspicious mind. 'Of course I think she's being straight,' she said sternly.

'Me and Bella been talkin'—' Linda began.

'And drinking,' Shirley interrupted.

'Just shut up a minute, will ya? This rumour Dolly started spreadin' about her old man being alive . . . and this fourth man, the one that got away. We was thinking, well, what if both them things are true? What if Harry Rawlins is alive and what if he's the one that got away and left *our* fellas to burn to death?'

'Don't be so bloody stupid!' Shirley snapped. This had to be the most ridiculous thing Linda had said to date.

'What if we're being shipped off to Rio, not knowing where the money is, not knowing where Dolly is? What if this fourth man is still around here, hiding locally, and what if he swans in and takes the lot? What if it's Harry, and Dolly's in on it? She loves the man to death, Shirl. She'd do anything for him.'

Shirley tensed up, cheeks flushing. She clenched her hands for control. She'd never heard such ungrateful, spiteful nonsense in all her life. Linda was now up on her feet, bending over, prodding Shirley with her chewed finger. Shirley pushed Linda away from her and stood tall, hands on hips. She didn't shout. Her voice was calm, but she let Linda have it.

'You think that woman's grief wasn't real? You think that day in the sauna when she came to us with this plan was all part of some bigger picture that doesn't actually involve us? Harry's dead! Just like your Joe's dead and my Terry's dead. Don't you dare expect me to believe that her grief ain't as real as mine. Just because you've bounced back, don't mean we have!'

'All right, keep your wig on! So, it might not be Harry who walked away – but she could still be having us all on. Why won't she tell us where she's stashing the cash, eh?'

'She's explained that!' Shirley's eyes were wide, her face tight and serious. 'If you've got something to say to Dolly, Linda, say it to her face. You and Bella can think what you like, but I won't believe she's playing a double game. She didn't want to drive the lead truck, but she is. It's the most dangerous position and she took it because it's the right thing to do for all of us.'

Linda tried her best to stand her ground. 'Me and Bella—'

Shirley shrieked her frustration. '"Me and Bella! *Me and Bella!*" You brought Bella in and now you both want to stir up trouble and expect me to take sides with you. Well, I won't. Dolly hasn't let us down yet, and I for one don't believe she will. Not on purpose.'

'I'm sorry, all right. I'm sorry,' Linda said, backtracking.

But Shirley wasn't about to let her get away with it that easily. 'No, it isn't all right. You come here in the middle of the night trying to start a mutiny when Dolly's done nothing but look after us. You've never had it so good, Linda! And you didn't have Tony Fisher onto you. You didn't have that bastard trying to burn your tits off! You frighten me, Linda, you understand? You frighten me.'

Linda knew she shouldn't have come. She reached out for the bottle of brandy to settle her nerves.

'I think you've had enough. You should go,' Shirley said, and snatched the bottle away.

Deflated, hands stuck into her jeans pockets, Linda stood head down like a naughty schoolgirl. Shirley sighed, unscrewed the bottle cap and poured her a small measure. Linda carried the glass over to the sideboard and looked at the row of photographs displayed neatly on it. She sipped her drink and pointed at one.

'That your mum?' Linda asked.

Shirley wasn't remotely in the mood for small talk, but this seemed to be Linda's attempt at an apology, so she went with it. 'That's me brother and that's me dad,' she said.

With her back to Shirley, silent tears rolled down Linda's cheeks. Shirley couldn't tell Linda was crying until she spoke.

'My dad walked out when I was three,' Linda said. 'Then me mum dumped me in an orphanage and never came back. I don't remember her now – not even what she looked like.' She polished off the remainder of the brandy. 'Nice family,' she said. 'You're lucky, Shirl.' Suddenly back to her usual grinning self, Linda asked: 'You got a fella?'

'Course not,' Shirley replied, hoping that Linda wasn't now going to get all slutty and inappropriate like she usually did when she was drunk. But Linda stayed quite ladylike.

'I've got a fella,' she said. 'I'm not supposed to be seeing him – Dolly don't approve. But I like him, Shirl, I really do. He's gentle. And he's got prospects, better prospects than Joe ever had. He's got his own garage. He wants to be a racing driver,' she added proudly.

'Oh, my God.' Shirley's eyes suddenly widened as if she'd seen a ghost. Falling to her knees, she flung open the bottom door of the sideboard, pulled out a photo album and started frantically flicking through it. 'It's got to be him!' she kept saying. 'It's got to be him! There!' She'd found what she was looking for. Grabbing Linda by the arm, she dragged her down to the floor next to her, pointing at a snapshot of Terry with his arm round a man in white mechanics' overalls.

'That's Jimmy Nunn!' she said excitedly. 'He was a racing driver. I reckon he could have been the fourth man, Linda! Terry could have brought him in to the team. That's why he's not mentioned in any of Harry's ledgers – that's why Dolly can't find out who he is . . . he was new.'

'How can you be sure?'

'I remember Terry going on about him. How good he was, how no one could catch him. I think he must have driven the lead truck. It makes sense. Why else can't we find him? He was *new*.'

Suddenly sober, Linda took the photo from the album. 'Don't say anything to Dolly,' she said. 'Not till we're sure. I want to find him, Shirl, please let me find him and then we'll tell Dolly.'

'How you going to find him?' Shirley wasn't at all convinced, but Linda seemed desperate.

'Please, Shirl,' Linda begged again. 'Let me do this. I'll do it right, I promise.'

Shirley nodded reluctantly and Linda was out the front door like a shot. Jimmy Nunn . . . she was determined to find the bastard who'd left their men to die. But, more than that, she was determined to prove to Dolly that she had a brain in her head and that she was part of the team.

* * *

Detective Chief Inspector Saunders' face was expressionless as he listened to Fuller complaining. Occasionally Saunders would look up from the file Fuller had given him, give Fuller a quick nod as though he was still listening, and continue to read.

Fuller was in full flow, keen to get it all off his chest. 'I don't want it to seem as though I'm telling tales out of school, sir, but you should know how DI Resnick's handling this case. And it seems to me, sir, that the Mayfair case needs more officers and I could do some real good there. Instead, I'm sitting outside a dead man's house and following his wife to the hairdressers or to the convent or when she's taking her dog walkies. With respect, sir, it's a waste of resources. And at the weekend . . . well, it's costing the service overtime, there's still nothing to show for it, and it's impacting on team morale.'

As Fuller continued venting his spleen, Saunders wandered to his office door and opened it. Fuller instantly fell silent.

'You don't have to like him,' said Saunders, 'but you do have to work with him.'

Fuller stood and reached across Saunders' desk to retrieve the file he'd brought with him.

'I'll keep that,' Saunders said.

Saunders closed his door behind Fuller and took a deep breath. Fuller was a good, hard-working officer, but he was no team player. And he would have been surprised by how highly Resnick rated him. 'He's a prissy little ponce who thinks he's better than everyone else,' Resnick had told Saunders, 'and he gets my back right up when he acts like the leg-work's beneath him, because he's a smart kid. And he's so anally retentive that not much gets past him. He needs to start listening to his gut more, but he'll get there. And he might just be right about being better than the rest of the team.'

Fuller puts himself and his career above anything else, which was something that Resnick has never done, Saunders reflected. Resnick was a pain in the arse, but that's because he was like a dog with a bone when he got an idea in his head. And he was right more times than he was wrong. Like most of the station, Saunders thought Resnick was letting his emotions rule in his pursuit of Harry Rawlins, but then, he'd been framed, so no one could really blame him. It was Resnick's blinkered attitude that would finally see him pensioned off; Saunders just needed to give him a little more rope to hang himself with. And the file Fuller had just given him was exactly the rope he was looking for.

After a suitable interval, Saunders followed Fuller to the new offices to have a chat with Resnick. In the lovely new annexe, Resnick's new desk was completely empty. Saunders retraced his steps to Resnick's old office and found Alice filling a cardboard box with files.

Alice froze. 'DI Resnick was packing as requested, sir, but then I sidetracked him, I'm afraid, so he got a little behind.' She was a convincing liar. 'I said I'd finish packing for him, seeing as it's really my fault he's behind schedule.'

Saunders gave Alice a gentle smile. He truly admired her loyalty and had always thought that she would have made an exceptional officer. He picked up one of the files from a packed box. It was incomplete and months old. Next, he looked at Resnick's desk diary: page after page was blank, with no indication of his whereabouts. Saunders' face flushed at Resnick's total lack of respect for the rules and regulations of basic policing.

'When DI Resnick comes in,' Saunders said crisply, 'tell him I want to speak with him in my office. Without fail. And no excuses this time, Alice.'

CHAPTER 21

Linda was feeling pleased with herself. After a phone call to Brands Hatch racing circuit and a bit of flirting and digging around, she'd managed to find out where Jimmy Nunn lived. And it turned out that no one had seen him for a while: the mechanic she'd spoken to had said he'd be grateful if she'd jog Jimmy's memory about the fifty quid he owed him. *I bet he's a right charmer*, she thought, recalling the way her Joe used to charm small 'loans' off dozens of people so he could take her away for a posh weekend.

Now, Linda sat in a Greek cafe in Old Compton Street, looking out of the window waiting for Dolly. When Linda had called Dolly at the convent, the Mother Superior had been sitting just yards away and Dolly had been in no position to question why Linda was asking for a meeting just for the two of them, and out in the open. *Dolly will be dying to know what on earth was so important*, thought Linda, smiling to herself. For a change, Linda was looking forward to seeing her. She was the one with something to offer; she was the one who should be listened to, just like when she brought Bella into the team. She felt powerful.

As Dolly's Merc pulled up opposite, Linda waved to the cafe owner for two more coffees. She watched Dolly, Wolf tucked under her arm, pop some coins in the parking meter and stare across the road at the little cafe. *Just come in, you snooty old cow, it'll be worth the trip!*

Dolly sat down opposite Linda, stony-faced. She couldn't stand the heavy smell of cooking fat and fried food, hated the way the smell of these greasy spoon cafes lingered on your clothes. The Greek owner carried the coffee over, spilling some into the saucers, and wiped his hands on his filthy, food-stained apron. The Demis

Roussos hit 'Forever and Ever' started up on the jukebox; the record was scratched and sounded tinny over the cheap speakers.

Dolly looked at the dirty rim of her small espresso cup with distaste and waited for Linda to start talking.

'Do you know Jimmy Nunn?' Linda asked, knowing this was unlikely.

'Never heard of him,' Dolly replied.

Linda decided she'd better get to the point pretty quick. 'I think he was the fourth man. The one who did the disappearing act on our fellas.'

Dolly said nothing. She waited for Linda to speak again.

Linda slid a folded piece of paper wrapped around the photo of Jimmy Nunn she'd taken from Shirley's photo album across the table to Dolly, like a spy delivering a secret message. 'He's an ex-racing driver friend of Terry's. That's his address. Thought you might want to suss him out, seeing as you're the boss. Then I think we should all have a meet, don't you?'

'I'll say when we have a meet,' said Dolly. 'And this one being in public might not be doing us any favours, Linda.'

'You're a dab hand at losing the filth by now, ain't ya?' Linda said.

Dolly ignored her. She read Jimmy Nunn's address, glanced at the photo, and then put them in her coat pocket.

Linda continued. 'I didn't knock on his door or speak with neighbours. I just parked up and watched for a bit, but I never seen him come or go. I bet your life he's the fourth man you're looking for, Dolly. Bet you he's the bastard who left our men for dead.' She sat back and waited for Dolly to say something . . . something like, 'well done' or 'good work'.

'Waiter!' Dolly summoned the cafe owner over. 'I'd like some biscuits, please.' When they arrived, she leant down and started feeding them to Wolf.

Fuck, thought Linda. Had that blabbermouth Shirley already told Dolly about Jimmy Nunn because of his connection to Terry?

Dolly broke off another piece of biscuit, fed it to the little rat and then looked at Linda.

'You're not the only one who's been playing detective,' Dolly said. 'Why did you lie to me?'

In that split second, the power dynamic flipped right back. Linda could feel the sweat building on the palms of her hands. 'I ain't lied, Dolly,' she said. 'Me and Shirl found Jimmy Nunn's picture in an old album and—'

'Not about Jimmy Nunn,' interrupted Dolly. 'I'll deal with that from now on. I'm talking about your new boyfriend. Carlos, isn't it?'

Linda was taken totally by surprise. She could feel the warmth rising in her cheeks as her face flushed red.

'You haven't told him anything about us, have you? About what we're doing?' Dolly demanded.

'He's not a boyfriend, Dolly. He's just that mechanic I had a bit of a thing with after I bought the car,' Linda said. 'That weren't nothing.'

Dolly's stare burnt into Linda's soul, a strange mix of anger and disappointment. 'You stood on that beach, looked me right in the eye and told me you were seeing no one.'

'It was none of your business,' Linda bit back, lighting a cigarette. As she sucked hard on the fag, she wished she'd never bothered calling Dolly at all. Why the hell was she more bothered about Carlos than Jimmy Nunn?

'Why do you think I asked about him?' Dolly said. 'You think I want to know about your dirty sex life, or do you think maybe I'm trying to protect you? Protect all of us.'

The smile slipped from Linda's face. She knew she was about to be put in her place and, once again, she hadn't seen it coming. She stared at Dolly, waiting for the big hit.

'Carlos works for Arnie Fisher,' Dolly said. 'Your lover boy, Linda, is a little queen; a poof hopping from your bed straight into Arnie's. Apart from servicing Arnie Fisher as his bum boy, Carlos also services all of his dodgy motors. He's as bent as they come . . . in more ways than one.'

Linda was numbed into silence. The name Arnie Fisher rang round her head. The thought that he was having sex with Carlos made her feel physically sick. Her mouth dried up and she didn't notice her burning cigarette dropping ash on the table. Dolly fed another piece of biscuit to Wolf, giving Linda time to absorb what she'd just said.

Eventually, Linda's brain caught up. She attempted a smile and drew on her cigarette. 'I don't believe a word you're saying.' But although she hated Dolly sometimes, Linda knew that she'd never lied. Ever.

'Boxer Davies told me,' said Dolly. 'Before someone made mincemeat out of him. So when I asked you about Carlos at the beach and you said you weren't seeing him anymore, I knew you were lying. I chose not to say anything cos we had a heavy day ahead and I thought you might wise up of your own accord . . . but no. You just race from one stupid decision to another, don't you?' The short pause Dolly left before continuing was excruciating for Linda. 'What car were you sitting in when you were outside Jimmy Nunn's flat?' Dolly was going in for the kill. Tears welled up in Linda's eyes. 'Were you sitting in your own car by any chance? The car Carlos helped you repair? The car he's seen parked outside your flat, and outside your place of work, *and* outside this cafe that you called me to so the whole world can see us together? Was it *that* car, Linda?'

Linda wanted the ground to open up and swallow her whole. But still Dolly didn't let up, even as the tears rolled down Linda's face.

'You've been a stupid little tart, but it stops right now, you hear me? I'm the boss for a bloody good reason. Now, before I tell you what you're going to do next, I'm going to ask you a question. I've already asked it once and this time you'll answer. Did you tell Carlos anything about what we're up to?'

'I swear I haven't. Not a word. On my life, Dolly . . .' And Dolly knew this was true.

'You're going to get rid of him, Linda,' Dolly said.

For a second, Linda thought Dolly looked and sounded like a mafia boss ordering a hit. 'How do you mean?' she asked in a pathetic, croaky voice.

Dolly wanted to get hold of her by the scruff of the neck and knock some sense into her. 'Well, I ain't on about concrete boots, if that's what's going through your stupid brain. He's the Fishers' wheels man, right? He must have a garage full of hot cars.'

Linda's mouth dropped open. 'You want me to shop him to the Old Bill?'

'One phone call, Linda. Get them to raid his place. Today.' Dolly stood up and tucked Wolf under her arm. 'And don't you ever lie to me again.' Dolly turned and started to walk away, but paused and looked back at Linda, sitting with her head down, staring at the cigarette ash floating in the cold espresso in front of her. She looked totally defeated. Dolly still didn't feel sorry for Linda, but she did need her to get her act together and get rid of Carlos. 'Thanks for Jimmy Nunn's address,' she said. 'I'll look into it.'

Linda sat alone at the table. On the other side of the cafe, the Greek and three swarthy builders were eyeing her up. She felt disgusting. Stupid and disgusting. It had taken less than five minutes for Dolly to turn one of Linda's proudest moments into one of her most shameful. She fucking *hated* Dolly Rawlins! She was a horrible, horrible woman. Horrible for not having a heart, and for crushing Linda's in one conversation. *She hadn't needed to use terms like 'bum boy'*, Linda thought; *she did it because she was a sad, old, hateful witch of a woman.*

Her right hand found the gold necklace and the pendant of Sagittarius the archer that Carlos had given her. He'd made her close her eyes as he slipped it over her head, kissed her gently and settled it into the hollow of her neck. She loved it. She loved him.

They'd made love, standing, watching each other in the mirror. In the morning, Carlos had left before she woke, leaving a note saying he'd see her after work. But now all she could see in her mind's eye was Carlos kissing Arnie with those same luscious Italian lips.

That bitch, that twisted bitch! The pain Linda felt was unbearable. She tried to expunge the image of Arnie and Carlos from her head but she couldn't. She twisted the necklace until the gold chain snapped. A small trickle of blood ran down her neck where the archer's bow had cut her skin, and she wept.

CHAPTER 22

Dolly checked the address Linda had given her. She was parked in a street of squalid, run-down houses. She spotted a kid gliding down the pavement on a skateboard and, lowering the window, yelled at him to come over.

'D'you know who lives at number thirty-nine?' she asked.

The kid looked over to the house then back to Dolly. He shook his head.

'Don't have a clue, missus. Why you askin'?'

Dolly got out of her Merc. 'I'm visiting an old friend.'

'Then you should know more about them than me, shouldn't ya?' the kid replied with a cheeky grin on his face.

Dolly looked around. The Merc was a big prize in a street like this. 'Look after my motor and I'll give you three quid,' she said to the kid.

The boy's eyes lit up. 'I'll do it for a fiver,' he said.

Dolly smiled. She liked this kid. They shook hands and Dolly headed towards Jimmy Nunn's place.

The house had been split into four flats and the front door was on the latch. It was even worse on the inside than she imagined: the hallway full of flyers, black plastic rubbish bags, broken milk bottles, free newspapers and used takeaway cartons. The hall light switch didn't work and she saw there was no bulb in the dangling light socket. Using her lighter to help her see her way, she moved on up the stairs. By the time she'd reached the second landing, the smell wasn't so bad. She stopped, held her lighter near the door and saw the number four. As she knocked a baby began to howl. She waited, knocked again and the baby howled louder.

'Who is it?'

Dolly knocked again.

The door inched open and a young woman peered through the gap. 'I ain't interested in buying nothing.'

She started to close the door, but Dolly was faster.

'Mind if I have a chat, love? That's all I want,' Dolly asked, pushing past her into a small, cheaply furnished room. She lit a cigarette. The young girl's perfume was cloying. 'I'm looking for Jimmy Nunn. Is he in?'

The girl said nothing; she clearly had no clue who Dolly was.

'I'm Mrs Harry Rawlins,' said Dolly, blowing smoke through tight lips. 'Your husband worked for mine. And your name is . . .?'

'Trudie,' said the girl reluctantly. The name of Harry Rawlins had certainly meant something to her. 'I ain't seen Jimmy in months. Said he had some business, walked out and I ain't seen him since.'

Dolly was taking in every inch of the room: the baby clothes on the heater, the untidy, shoddy furniture, but most of all, Trudie. The girl was beautiful in a cheap, tarty way: good figure, sexy, lovely blonde hair, heavy pouting mouth and big, innocent, wide eyes. She'd be easy to get information from, thought Dolly. All she had to do was be nice. She offered Trudie one of her cigarettes, but she shook her head.

'I don't smoke,' she said.

So the overflowing ashtray on the armchair next to Trudie had been filled by someone else. *The sex bomb might not smoke*, Dolly thought to herself, *but someone else here does* . . . As Trudie stood with her baby in her arms, Dolly stood with Wolf in hers. Putting Wolf down, Dolly sat carefully on Trudie's scraggy sofa and lit herself another cigarette. Wolf jumped up on the armchair, sniffing and scrabbling about down the side of the seat cushion. In his frenzy, he knocked the ashtray onto the floor.

'Get down!' Dolly scolded and he did as he was told, sitting by her feet, wagging his tail. She made no effort to pick up the ashtray or the scattered dog ends. It wouldn't have made any real difference to the state of the room. She got the photograph out of her handbag. 'Is this Jimmy?'

Trudie looked at the photo of Jimmy and Terry standing together and nodded. 'He owes you money, does he?'

Dolly stood up, brushing down her skirt, and handed Trudie a phone number on a piece of paper. 'If he should put in an appearance, tell him I'd like to talk to him. He can get me on this number. It's Mrs Rawlins,' she repeated.

'I got your name,' Trudie said.

What a naive and stupid girl, thought Dolly. *Especially to get herself lumbered with a kid.* A constantly whinging kid. The smell of Trudie's cheap heavy perfume hit her again. Perhaps that was what was making the baby cry? He was actually a sweet little thing, about six months old. Dolly patted his cheek lightly and Trudie, looking nervous, took a step back. As Dolly opened her handbag and took out five crisp ten-pound notes, Wolf jumped back up onto the armchair and started digging at the cushion again. Dolly ignored him.

'This is for the kid,' she told Trudie, handing her the fifty quid. 'And when Jimmy makes contact with me, you'll get a lot more.'

Trudie looked at Wolf digging at her armchair.

'Wolf!' Dolly shouted. 'Get down!' She scooped him up in her arms. As she did so she noticed something glinting, stuck in the crevice between the cushion seat and arm of the chair. 'I am sorry . . .' she said, pretending to ruffle the cushion. With her back to Trudie, she pulled out a gold Dunhill lighter, exactly like the one she'd bought all those years ago for—

Trudie's voice seemed to come from somewhere a long way away. 'If that's your motor down there, Mrs Rawlins, you'd better go and see to it.'

Dolly quickly dropped the lighter back down the side of the cushion. She desperately wanted to turn it over and see if the initials 'HR' were engraved on the back. But Trudie's voice came again . . .

'There's loads of kids round it. It looks like you lost a wing mirror already.'

But Dolly had already gone. She didn't look back for fear of what she might see.

* * *

Trudie watched from the window as Dolly ran across the road and clipped the ear of one of the kids standing by her car. Trudie grinned. 'Tough old bird, ain't she?' she said. The kitchen door opened a crack. 'You'll never guess what, love – she gave me fifty quid for our kid.'

CHAPTER 23

Linda was back in her arcade booth, clutching the necklace Carlos had given her. She'd fixed it – she thought Carlos would notice if she suddenly stopped wearing it. Dolly's words went round and round her head. She still couldn't make it make sense; she still couldn't believe Carlos swung both ways, not the way he held her in his arms and made love to her. She looked up and her heart lurched. Carlos was striding towards her with a big smile. He was wearing a smart cream suit – silk by the look of it – and very expensive. Unable to look him in the eye, Linda began frantically re-counting change.

'What d'you think?' he asked, standing by the booth window, heavy cologne permeating the air around her.

Linda slowly raised her head. Carlos was pointing at his suit and smiling, his dark handsome face freshly shaved. She loved his beautiful dark eyes, but she couldn't hold his gaze. Not now. She looked away. 'You goin' some place nice all dressed up like a dog's dinner?' Her voice was shaky.

'Meeting some people for a business dinner,' he said airily. 'Open the booth so I can give you a cuddle.'

Linda fumbled as she unlocked the door. Carlos put his hands round her waist, pulled her close and kissed her. She was tense and he could feel it.

'I got to get on.' She pulled away. Carlos held her, touched the pendant on her neck and a shiver ran through her.

'Looks good on ya and makes me proud you wear it. Maybe I can see you after my business dinner?'

'I'm on lates. I'll be tired.'

Carlos leant over, put out his hand and tilted her head towards him. 'Something the matter? You seem a bit cold?'

Linda pulled her head away and began to twist the pendant nervously. 'Nah. It's just that I'm working till late. I'm so tired I just want to go home to bed and sleep.'

Carlos stepped back and looked at her, but she wouldn't look him in the eye. He gave a slight shrug, and after a few seconds of silence, said, 'Suit yourself.' Turning sharply, he walked towards the exit.

'Twelve,' Linda blurted out. 'I'll be finished at twelve.' She didn't know what made her say it.

Carlos turned with a smile and a wink. 'Back later!'

Linda waited a few seconds, biting her nails, and then yelled for Charlie. 'Here,' she said, handing him the booth key once he'd ambled over. 'I'll be back in a minute.' Before Charlie could ask where she was going, Linda was out the door.

The white suit made Carlos easy to follow. Linda kept her distance on the opposite side of the street, and paused by shop doorways in case he turned around. She watched as he stopped and looked at his reflection in a shop window, patting his hair and straightening his tie before continuing down Wardour Street and entering a small French bistro.

The bistro had a mid-line red curtain across it. Standing on tiptoes, Linda could just see Carlos being led across the restaurant by a waiter. A blonde woman smiled and waved at him. Well, if he was doing the dirty on her, at least it was with a woman . . . But it was the waiter, not Carlos, that the blonde was waving at.

Carlos was ushered to a booth at the back of the restaurant, where he stood chatting to someone. Linda couldn't see who it was, but she did see a hand reach out and squeeze Carlos's backside. Then whoever it was leant forward and kissed Carlos on the cheek. For a fraction of a second Linda saw the other man's face clearly. It was enough. It was true. *Dear God*, it was true. Arnie Fisher and Carlos were lovers.

Linda's head was spinning as she ran across Wardour Street without looking, causing a car to swerve and almost crash into a bus stop. She ran towards a telephone kiosk, went inside and scrabbled through her jeans pockets for some change before she remembered that 999 calls were free.

* * *

Later that night, Linda had sex with Carlos. She hadn't wanted to, but she had to make him think nothing was wrong. Afterwards, when she was satisfied he was asleep, she slid out of bed and paced round the room before sitting at her dressing table.

Carlos had only pretended to be asleep. He opened his eyes a fraction and watched her beautiful naked body as she sat staring at herself in the dressing table mirror, his pendant hanging between her breasts. She frowned, picked up a piece of cotton wool, squeezed some make-up remover on it and wiped her face. *Something's the matter with her*, he thought. She'd been edgy at the arcade and the sex was not as wild and passionate as usual. As she got up from the dressing table and climbed back into bed, Carlos pretended to stir. Slipping his arm round her, he stroked her gently, rolled on top of her and they had sex again. After he finished, Linda turned away from him.

'What's wrong?' whispered Carlos.

'Nothing,' said Linda. 'I'm just exhausted.'

Carlos squeezed her again and kissed the back of her neck. He had never told her he loved her, but he wanted to tell her now. He leant up on his elbow and whispered her name, but she had fallen asleep. Gently, he moved a strand of hair from her face before turning over and going to sleep himself.

In the dark, Linda opened her eyes and stared at the curtains. She felt as if her heart was turning to stone. Could that arrogant cow Dolly be wrong? Maybe Carlos was stringing Arnie Fisher along for cash and didn't actually sleep with him at all? But Linda knew she was just clutching at straws.

* * *

Carlos was up and dressed before Linda. He knelt on the bed and shook her awake. 'Sorry. I'm late for work. I don't suppose I could cadge a lift?' Relieved that was all he wanted, Linda got up.

She drove in silence, Carlos's silk suit was crumpled, his tie flung on the dashboard and the overnight growth of stubble on his chin gave his face a swarthy look. He turned on the radio and rested his arm along the back of her seat. Linda felt pangs of guilt as she arrived at the top end of the U-shaped mews.

'Drop me here,' said Carlos. He got out and leant back in the door across the passenger seat and kissed her on the cheek. 'You OK?' he asked as he cupped her chin in his hand.

Linda nodded and then he was gone, whistling as he walked down the mews with his hands stuck in his pockets. Suddenly she noticed his tie on the dashboard. Leaving the engine running, she got out and chased after him. She didn't want any evidence of him anywhere near her if he was going to be nicked.

Inside the garage, Johnny, the young apprentice, sat handcuffed between two uniformed officers while three detectives looked through the books and filing cabinets. As they heard Carlos's whistle and his footsteps approaching, the officers tensed up and got themselves into position. Outside, Carlos fished in his pocket for the door keys . . .

'IT'S THE LAW, CARLOS!' Johnny shouted.

'Go, go go!" one of the officers in the garage shouted down the radio to his colleagues parked round the corner. In a split second, Carlos had turned and was racing towards the blind exit at the other end of the mews. The unmarked police car skidded round the corner, accelerating past Linda, who dropped the tie and ran back to her car.

Slamming the driver's door shut, she screeched off down the road, not really knowing which way she was going. She drove straight to the top of the road and made a left, but just as she was about to make the next turn she heard a loud thud, a scream and a screech of brakes.

Up ahead of her was the other entrance to the mews. Pulling over, she saw a red Post Office van halfway up the pavement, crashed into a lamp post. As she watched, the driver stumbled out of the van holding his head, blood dripping from a cut over his right eye.

Still in shock, Linda edged closer, gasping for breath. There was no sign of Carlos. Craning round the unmarked police car in the middle of the road, she saw a group of uniform officers clustered around the Post Office van. One was talking on a police radio.

She knew she should drive off in the opposite direction, but she was desperate to know if Carlos had got away. As she drove slowly past the van, an officer stepped out and waved at her to move on. Then she saw Carlos.

Jammed between the Post Office van and the lamp post, his white suit was covered in blood. His face was contorted in pain, his eyes were open, blood was running from his mouth and a deep pool, as red as the Post Office van, lay on the pavement around his feet. The officer on the radio shook his head, while another laid an empty post office sack over Carlos's upper body. As Linda stared, Carlos's beautiful white suit got redder and redder.

* * *

The hammering on the front door was so loud and so sustained that Bella thought she was being busted. As she got closer, she could hear Linda sobbing outside, shouting and screaming to be let in. When she opened the door, Linda fell into her arms.

'I've killed him! Bella, I've killed him! You've got to help me. *Please*. Oh God help me, I killed him!'

Linda began to heave as though she was going to vomit and Bella rushed her to the bathroom sink.

'OK,' she said. 'Calm down. What's happened?"

'He was covered in blood,' Linda sobbed hysterically. 'It's not OK, Bella! I've killed him!'

Bella slammed her hand over Linda's mouth. 'Stop it!' she demanded. 'Before the whole block comes knocking.'

Linda slumped to the floor at the side of the bath and sobbed.

Ushering her into the bedroom, Bella poured her a glass of whisky and held it steady while Linda knocked it back. Bella poured her another one, and sat down beside her on her the bed. 'Tell me what happened,' Bella asked again.

As Linda spoke, she twisted the Sagittarius pendant round and round between her fingers. 'He's dead, Bella. He's dead.'

'Yeah, I got that bit. Who's dead?'

'She *said* I had to do it. She said I had to phone the police and tell them about his garage and his dodgy cars.' Linda suddenly yanked the chain from her neck and threw it across Bella's bedroom. 'That bitch!' she screamed. Bella stroked her back and waited. 'She said the most terrible things about him, Bella. But I didn't know – I swear I didn't. I was with him all last night . . . just looking at him, at his beautiful face and his beautiful body and I couldn't believe what she said was true. How could it be when he's lying there with me? I was so sure she was wrong . . . but it was too late. I'd already rung. I'd already told them about him and I couldn't take none of it back. They were waiting for him when he got to work this morning. He ran and . . .' Linda put her head in her hands. Through the tears, she carried on, desperate to tell Bella everything. 'The van hit him and he was dead in the road and there was blood everywhere!'

'It was an accident, then,' Bella said.

'It was my fault!' Linda shouted, jumping up from the bed. She was exhausted from all the crying and the guilt and the grief. 'I hate Dolly's guts.' Linda spoke with a venom Bella had never heard before.

'I know.' Bella stood and walked across to Linda. She stood close, held her arms out and let Linda fall into them. Bella squeezed her tight, nursing her like a loving mother comforting a small child. Linda rested her head on Bella's shoulder and stared into the distance.

'She's an evil cow, Bella. She's cruel and heartless. She made me feel so small and stupid and she made me hate him. I hate her so much. She'd better watch her back.'

CHAPTER 24

Dolly was waiting in her Mercedes in the car park of the Little Chef, just off the A23 road to Brighton. Wolf was asleep on the passenger seat. She'd parked at the far end, but she still had a clear view of the entrance and car park. She was becoming impatient; she'd been there for over half an hour, and he was late. Nervously tapping the briefcase on her lap, she looked around, feeling edgy. Was he was going to turn up at all?

To keep herself occupied, she got out her notebook and flipped through it, going over the last details of the robbery and things yet to be done. She sighed. Linda still hadn't got a suitable van to act as the front blocking vehicle. Dolly understood that Linda must be under considerable stress after what she'd told her about Carlos, but she was smart enough to know when something was serious. And Carlos being in Arnie's pocket and his bed was very serious. Dolly could never be one hundred per cent sure of any of her girls but she had to trust Linda now. She wondered whether Linda had had the sense to disguise her voice when she called the police to grass on Carlos . . .

Suddenly, she slammed her fist on the briefcase, jolting Wolf awake. 'Where the hell are you?' she shouted. 'Come on, you bastard. You'd never have kept Harry waiting like this.' The problem with this meeting was that if it didn't happen, the job was off – simple as that. She'd called Brian Marshall and said she worked for Harry Rawlins. Although he was dead, she was collecting debts owed on behalf of his family. Marshall had sounded doubtful on the phone, but had reluctantly agreed to meet, although he could just as easily have decided to run and Dolly would have had no idea how to track him down.

As she sat there, wondering how on earth she would tell the others, a Rover entered the car park and stopped on the other side. Dolly waited to make sure that the car, whoever it was, was alone and hadn't been followed, ever wary of a trap.

Brian Marshall had already drunk half a flask of brandy by the time he pulled up, but was still shaking as he looked around: he had no idea what to expect, or who the contact was. Fortunately for Dolly, he'd decided that failure to turn up would be disastrous for him. His hand reached to his pocket for the flask of brandy, and took another swig. He felt disgusted with himself.

Brian Marshall's drinking went hand in glove with his gambling and, ten years ago, he had drifted from the legitimate casinos into Arnie Fisher's club, where the higher stakes attracted him. It was there he'd met Harry Rawlins. Harry was charming, always friendly and seemed interested in how Brian was and what he was doing for work. During one drunken conversation, Brian revealed that he was married to the sister of the owner of Samson's, one of the country's biggest security firms. From this point forwards, Brian was in big trouble – not that he'd been aware of it . . .

Rawlins had continued to act like Brian's friend, lending him money, encouraging him to gamble beyond his means. Brian had no idea how dangerous Harry was; until the night he had drunkenly allowed Harry Rawlins to pick up a seven-thousand-pound gambling marker to Arnie Fisher. Then Brian had belonged to Harry.

Rawlins waited patiently. It wasn't until nearly a year later that he demanded Marshall pay off the debt – money he knew Marshall didn't have. In return for cancelling the debt, and a seven-thousand-pound cash gift on top, all Rawlins wanted was to be told the different routes Samson's security wagons took when delivering large sums of cash. They regularly changed the routes as a security measure, and often at short notice. Rawlins promised to leave Marshall alone for good if he helped on this one job.

Terrified and under pressure, Marshall had had no option. He'd hoped against hope that Rawlins would be as good as his word and would leave him alone once the job was done. When he'd read of the botched robbery and Rawlins' death, he had heaved a sigh of relief – but then he'd had the phone call . . . Scared that the meeting with this mysterious woman was about something much more sinister than the debt, Brian checked the envelope he'd tucked down the side of his seat. He'd come prepared. The passenger door opened, making him jump. A woman wearing dark glasses and carrying a briefcase got into his car.

Dolly could smell the booze straight away. She looked in disgust at Marshall's red face, blotched from years of alcohol abuse. The collar of his pin-striped suit was covered in dandruff.

'I'm not here for the seven thousand,' she said, looking straight ahead.

Marshall closed his eyes. If she didn't want the cash, then she wanted something much worse. 'I knew it would happen again,' Marshall whimpered. 'It's my brother-in-law's security firm. This'll break him!'

Dolly maintained her composure. Marshall was clearly terrified of her and she had to keep it that way to get what she wanted. She noted the child's seat in the back of the car. *Mr Marshall will do as he's asked*, she thought.

'There's ten grand here,' she said, flipping open the briefcase on her lap. Marshall's eyes widened at the rows and rows of banknotes. She snapped the case shut again. 'That's more than you were offered last time.'

'I was promised that last time was the last time,' Marshall whined. 'Rawlins gave me his word! He said he'd let me off the hook and—'

'Rawlins is dead.' As the words left Dolly's mouth, her heart jolted, but she couldn't let Marshall see how much those words hurt her. 'Even though three men died, you still got paid seven grand. And Harry Rawlins picked up your marker.'

'You said you weren't here for the seven thousand!'

'If you keep to your side of the bargain, I'm not. If you don't keep to your side of the bargain—'

'Bollocks!' interrupted Marshall. He looked at the hard bitch of a woman sitting next to him. He didn't know who she was or who she worked for, but he disliked her intensely. He could feel the brandy giving him confidence. 'I'm broke, so you can demand money all you like; I don't have it to give. And I can't get the delivery routes again because my brother-in-law's upped his security. So – what can you do?'

Dolly stared at Brian, unblinking. 'If you don't keep to your side of the bargain,' she continued as if Marshall hadn't interrupted at all, 'the debt gets sold back to the Fisher brothers. You do know the Fisher brothers, don't you, Mr Marshall?'

Instantly, the boldness instilled by the brandy ebbed away and the blood drained from Marshall's face. He didn't know the Fishers personally, but their reputation was enough.

Dolly continued, 'Give me the route, your seven-grand debt goes away and, when the job's done, you get this ten grand in cash. You should be glad I'm giving you this opportunity. The Fishers won't be so kind.' She opened the passenger door and got out, taking the briefcase with her, glancing very obviously at the baby seat as she slammed the door.

Marshall's mouth trembled as he squeezed the leather steering wheel. Dolly walked away, her stride was even and controlled: she didn't give a damn about him or his family. He found his hand on the car key in the ignition. It would be easy to knock the bitch down, steal the briefcase and disappear for good. The thought was fleeting – Marshall was a coward.

Taking the brandy flask from his pocket again, he drank it down, thinking of his wife and kids. The tears welled up and the pressure in his head was almost painful. Then he heard that voice inside, the one that spoke every time he took a drink. Everything was all right, his brother-in-law was insured, he was the family drunk, the charity case. No one would expect anything less even if they did find out. And he desperately needed that money! Ten thousand pounds . . . He could pay off all his debts with it; maybe even start up his own business.

As Dolly got back to her Merc, her heart was beating so fast she thought she was going to faint. God knows how she had walked so calmly across the endless car park, but she couldn't let Marshall see how worried she was. 'Stay upright, Dolly,' she mumbled to herself. 'Stay upright.' As she got to her car, she put the suitcase on the roof and leant her back against the door. From where Marshall was parked, it would look as though she was relaxed, waiting for his decision. In reality, she was leaning against her car to stop herself from falling over. Little Wolf watched Dolly from the passenger seat, probably wondering why she wasn't getting back in beside him.

On the other side of the car park, Marshall didn't move. *Come on*, Dolly thought. *Come on.* Had she been too threatening? Not threatening enough? What if he called her bluff and drove away? Perhaps it would have been better to cajole Marshall, be nicer to him, lie to him, tell him that Harry respected him. *Come on, Marshall, come on!*

The Rover's engine started up. Dolly held her breath; the direction Marshall took would decide her future. He pulled out of his parking space and headed for Dolly. Breathing a huge sigh of relief, she composed herself. The Rover pulled up neatly beside her and Marshall handed Dolly the envelope he'd brought with him.

'The routes, dates and times for the next month are all in there, but I want the briefcase with cash up front now and your assurance the gambling marker is over and done with.'

Dolly took the envelope and handed Marshall the case. 'Be assured, Mr Marshall, if the details in the envelope are correct and if the police remain unaware of the plans, then the Fishers' marker will stay with me and you'll be in the clear. You have my word.'

Once Marshall was out of sight, Dolly climbed into her car and succumbed to a buzzing sense of excitement. She had the plans! She planted a massive kiss on Wolf's little head. He stood with his feet on her chest and listened as she told him, 'Daddy would be proud of us, darling. So proud. And the girls will be so excited! It's all coming together, Wolfie. It's all coming together, just as Harry planned.' The words stuck in Dolly's throat. It was not just as Harry planned at all. Very, very far from how Harry had planned.

She hugged Wolf tight and took a moment to recollect just how Harry's plans had gone so terribly wrong. She had the strength and the motivation now to finish what he'd started. Then she cleared her mind of all bad thoughts and filled it with thoughts of her girls. They were so close to the finish line . . . Yes, Linda still had to get the blocking truck and they still had to get used to the guns, and the padded overalls, and the chainsaw, and now they would have to learn the exact route on the day of the big run – but they'd come so far from those weak, crying, grieving widows who had met in the sauna all those months ago. Now, they were a team. Dolly smiled. Regardless of their faults and their moods and their inexperience, they were a team. Her team. And nothing and no one was going to stop them now.

CHAPTER 25

Resnick and Andrews had been waiting outside Fat Fran's house in an unmarked car since nine o'clock. It was now 10.15, and although the heater was on it was still cold. The car was full of cigarette smoke, Andrews was red in the face and could hardly breathe; no sooner had he opened the window to let some fresh air in than Resnick barked at him to close it again. Andrews hated working alone with Resnick. At least when Fuller was there, he had some support. Alone, he was open to all kinds of abuse from Resnick if the mood took him. The station was in some chaos after the Mayfair heist and the botched raid on Carlos's garage and the chase that had led to his death. With so many officers writing up notes, processing evidence and doing door-to-door, someone from Resnick's team had to stay desk-bound and help with all the extra paperwork. Andrews imagined Fuller sitting with his feet up in a warm, smoke-free office, sipping on a cup of tea.

'Sir!' Andrews pointed out of the car window. Fat Fran was heaving her bulk down the road. Every ten yards, she paused to put her shopping down and get her breath back before waddling on again at a snail's pace. As she got nearer, they could both hear the chinking of the bottles in her carrier bags.

'Stone the crows,' Resnick said. Fran's heaving bosom almost fell out of her blouse as she bent to pull her sagging tights back up into position round her crotch. 'Close your eyes, Andrews. That's no sight for an innocent like you.'

Andrews spoke without thinking. 'I have seen breasts before, sir.'

'Not like them you haven't.' Resnick opened the car door, flicking his cigarette butt into the road before heading after Fat Fran.

They followed her as she turned into the scruffy overgrown path, the already open gate hanging by one rusty hinge. Leaning against the front door, she took out her key.

'Oi!' Fran jerked her head round at Resnick's voice, loud behind her. 'We need another word with you, Fran.'

* * *

The stench in Fat Fran's flat was overpowering: cats, stale beer, food and body odour. The living room was dusty and dark; the heavy moth-eaten curtains looked as if they hadn't been opened in years. Resnick helped her off with her coat, while Andrews picked up the bottles of booze from the floor and put them by the door to the adjoining dining area.

'Sit yourself down, love. How are you feeling?' said Resnick. He didn't give a damn how Fran was feeling, but he did want her to co-operate. He folded her coat neatly, placed it on the back of a dining chair, then sat on a pouffe in front of the low easy-chair she was now slumped in.

Fran still had bruising over her right eye, although it was now a yellowy-purple colour rather than the deep blue and black of a few days ago. Plasters covered the cuts, which made her face look even worse than before, and one side of her head had been shaved at the hospital so they could stitch the wound.

Andrews glanced at his watch. Whenever Resnick did his 'good cop' routine, the attending officer always timed it. Whoever witnessed him last more than sixty seconds would win a tenner off the others.

'Now then, love, isn't it about time you told us who did this to you so we can lock 'em up and keep you nice and safe?' Resnick asked gently.

Fran smiled and patted Resnick's hand. 'You're a lovely man,' she said. Her cold and clammy sausage fingers tickled the back of his hand and he desperately wanted to pull away. 'I wish I could tell you, my love,' she went on, 'but I just can't remember. I ain't lying to you. I've had a bump to the head. I can't picture the fella at all. I think I blocked it, you know. Trauma does that, the doctor said so. It blocks things you don't want to remember.'

'Your little trauma doesn't do that, Fran, money does. Where d'ya get the money for all that booze?'

Andrews stopped timing Resnick. Fifteen seconds!

'I do run a business, you know. I can earn money!' Fran insisted.

'What you going to do if he comes back, eh? Pour him a whisky?'

'He won't come back!' Fran howled in fear. 'Why would he?'

Resnick had Fran on the back foot. 'Well, you did come to the station of your own free will, my dear . . . and we're here now, ain't we? What if he's watching you?' The fear in Fran's eyes grew as Resnick continued. 'He doesn't seem the tolerant type, and if he thinks you're telling us stuff, he might just visit you again. But tell us who he is, and we'll take him off the streets and put him behind bars. Then you can sit in your lovely little flat and get pissed, safe in the knowledge that he's not going to be knocking on your door any time soon.'

By the time Resnick had finished, Fran was blubbing awful, childlike sobs, her belly bouncing up and down as she squeezed the air from her lungs in short, sharp bursts. Andrews felt so sorry for her that he took out his handkerchief and handed it to her. As she loudly blew her nose, Resnick stood up sharply, knocking the pouffe over.

'Take her in for obstructing the police,' Resnick instructed Andrews. 'Come on, love, get to your feet. I've had enough of you lying to me.'

Fran wailed and held her hand out to Andrews who, without thinking, took hold of it. 'Ooh, don't take me in! I've told you everything I know. I can't remember no more, honest I can't.'

Andrews pulled his hand away from hers and tried to get her to her feet. It was like trying to lift a dead weight.

'Please don't take me in,' she wailed. 'I wish Boxer was here – he'd look after me. Where's Boxer? I want Boxer!'

'Boxer's dead,' Resnick spat. 'Killed by whoever it was who beat you nearly half to death. If you care for Boxer, you'll tell me who did this to you!'

Fran's wailing went up an octave. Andrews backed off to save his ear drums. Resnick had the decency to pause and let the woman grieve for a moment. Once she'd wailed long enough, he crouched back down in front of her.

'Now you listen to me, Fran,' Resnick said firmly. 'If you've been paid to keep your mouth shut, me and you are going to fall out big time.'

'I ain't—'

'Shut up and listen, because I'm running out of patience with you! I know you've been hurt, but others have been hurt worse.' Resnick leapt up, grabbed one of the shopping bags of booze, held it up and leant in close. 'Who gave you the money for all this? I know you don't earn enough renting rooms in this fleapit. Who? Come on, Fran, who?' As Resnick waved the heavy bag in the air, one of the handles snapped, sending the bottles crashing to the floor. Brown frothy beer flowed across the carpet. Fran lurched forwards with another howl.

'Aargh, me beer! Me beer!' Fran buried her face in her hands and wept again.

Resnick was now very red in the face, frustrated at not being able to break Fran. 'You tell me who attacked you and who gave you the hush money—'

'I don't know! I don't know! I told you a thousand times. This nice man come and asked to see Boxer and I showed him upstairs. The other one come later . . . the one that hit me. I didn't know either of them. I swear I didn't. I can't remember nothing else.'

'Try!' Resnick barked.

'I was so tired. I said to this woman—'

Resnick interrupted. 'What woman?'

'The one that rang. I said, "He's gone out", I said.'

'Just a minute!' Resnick focused in on this new detail. 'A woman phoned for Boxer?'

'Yes, I just told you.'

Andrews watched as Resnick's tone changed again. 'When, Fran?' He was willing her onwards. 'When did she call?'

'She called twice. First time she spoke to Boxer.' Fran put her head in her hands again. She was flagging, getting tired and confused.

'And the second time?' Resnick paused for Fran to think, then gently prompted her. 'Listen, love, this is really important. What were you doing when she called the second time?'

'Watching telly.'

'What was on?'

Fran looked up at Resnick. '*Coronation Street*.'

'Good girl. So, the woman called during *Coronation Street*. What did she say?'

'She said she'd been cut off the first time. But, well, now Boxer was out with the first man, the nice man, so she just hung up on me. Oh, God, Boxer!' Fran whispered almost to herself. 'I ain't never gonna see my Boxer again.'

'Help me find who killed him, Fran,' urged Resnick. 'If you ever felt anything for Boxer, help me!'

Fran gripped Resnick's forearm. 'He came to the hospital,' she whispered. 'God help me, he came to the hospital and said he'd kill me if I tell you.'

I'll fucking kill you if you don't *tell me*, thought Resnick. What he actually said was, 'I'll protect you.'

'He was tall with dark hair. Piercing eyes that was cold as ice. He weren't no thug, Mr Resnick, he was a gent. A cold, callous, bastard gent!'

Resnick caught his breath. He pulled an A4 picture from his inside jacket pocket and showed it to Fran. 'This man?'

Fran pushed the picture away so her eyes could focus properly on it and, when she did, Andrews saw that it was the image of Harry

Rawlins from Resnick's office wall, complete with dart hole in the forehead. Resnick was sweating, his face beetroot red.

'That ain't him,' Fran said.

'Look at it properly. Look at it!' Resnick shouted, waving the image of Harry Rawlins in Fran's face. 'It was him, wasn't it?"

'No.'

'Yes. This is him! Harry Rawlins is the man that beat you senseless. Tell me, tell me – I know it was him!'

Just as Andrews was working up the courage to step in, his radio crackled.

'Get out! How can she concentrate?' bellowed Resnick. Andrews reluctantly left.

When Andrews came back from answering the radio call, Resnick was still shaking the photo of Harry Rawlins in Fran's face and shouting the same question over and over.

'Was it him? Was it him?'

Andrews toyed with the idea of radioing Fuller and getting him to come and talk the old man down, but then he'd be the station joke for not being able to cope with a raving lunatic pensioner. Anyone could see that Fran's description of her attacker was a fit for Rawlins, but it was also similar to half of London, so why Resnick seemed convinced that a dead man had come back to life and beaten the shit out of Fat Fran, he wasn't at all sure. Andrews put his hand on Resnick's shoulder.

'Sir, there's been an important development just radioed through—'

'Shut up, Andrews!' Resnick growled, shaking Andrews' hand away. 'Fran's just about to confirm that she was assaulted by Harry Rawlins, aren't you, Fran?'

Fran looked up at Resnick, her face terrified at the possible repercussions of what she was about to reveal. 'No, Mr Resnick. It wasn't Harry Rawlins. It was . . . it was Tony Fisher.'

* * *

As they drove back to the Yard in silence, Andrews stole sidelong glances at Resnick, wondering if he should report his strange behaviour to the DCI. Resnick looked drained and beaten, like he'd given up altogether. He didn't even smoke and he always smoked in the car. As they turned the final corner towards the station, Andrews braved talking.

'The call, sir. It was from Fuller. The kid killed by the Post Office van this morning was Carlos Moreno. He's the Fisher brothers' wheel man.'

Resnick didn't acknowledge that he'd heard anything Andrews had said. He just stared out of the window.

CHAPTER 26

Fuller was pleased with his morning's work – he'd got so much done without Resnick breathing down his neck. He grinned as he contemplated what sort of morning Andrews might have had. He bet it had been horrible.

Fuller had a full report prepared for Resnick detailing every piece of incriminating evidence found in Carlos's car yard. It looked as if they could, at long last, pin something on the Fisher brothers. One of the cars recovered was a brown Jag with frontal damage and false plates in the boot. A subsequent check on the false plates revealed a brown Jag had recently been involved in a job in Manchester, chased and lost by police. Fuller had the vehicle checked for prints and was beaming when he was told both the Fisher brothers and Carlos's prints were found inside and outside the car, but the false plates were clean. This was real police work; this wasn't chasing ghosts and Fuller felt good. The Fishers were alive and well and about to be arrested.

Fuller had already spoken with DCI Saunders and told him about the death of Carlos and the good news about the Fishers' prints being on the Jag. He was still agitating to be moved to the Mayfair robbery team, and hoped this would help his chances. Saunders had congratulated Fuller on a great morning of hard work, but moved on, once again, to the subject of bloody George Resnick.

'Where's your boss?' Saunders had asked. 'Chasing wild geese again, is he?'

'Couldn't say, sir,' said Fuller.

'As soon as they're back,' Saunders ordered, ignoring him, 'I want to see Resnick and Andrews, separately, in my office. Do *not* let that man leave without seeing me.'

Fuller had returned to the main office with a smug smile on his face. He knew where Resnick was and he knew that Resnick had been bullying Fat Fran into saying that she'd been assaulted by a dead man, because Andrews had told him over the radio. Fuller hoped that Andrews had the balls to drop Resnick right in it.

Now, Fuller looked up when Resnick and Andrews walked back into the office. *This is it*, he thought. *This is the day Resnick gets his papers.* Fuller couldn't help the smirk and Resnick saw it.

'What you lookin' so bloody happy about?'

'I've identified the Fishers' wheels' man, sir. Didn't Andrews tell you?'

Resnick shrugged, uninterested. 'Big deal. I got Fat Fran to admit that it was Tony Fisher that gave her a pasting.'

Fuller was taken aback. Andrews raised his eyebrows and shook his head.

'She's that scared,' Andrews chipped in, 'she'll never give evidence against him. You could nick Tony Fisher, but we all know he'll never admit it and, without her statement, why bother? He'd walk the same day, then be free to go back and give the poor woman another beating, or worse . . . kill her.'

Resnick was lost for words; he'd never heard Andrews say so much in one go. Fuller offered:

'So, if we could put Tony Fisher away on another charge, she might feel safer and open up then?'

'You're referring to your sterling police work with regards to the raid on Carlos's car yard, no doubt?' Resnick said with a sneer. 'Where's this evidence that's going to rid London of the Fishers then?'

'On your desk, sir,' Fuller replied, pointing. If his report was good enough for Saunders, it was definitely good enough for Resnick. As Resnick picked it up, Fuller added, 'Oh, yes – Andrews, Saunders wants to see you.'

'What for?' demanded Resnick.

'No idea,' said Fuller. Andrews shrugged and left the room.

Resnick walked into his new glass annexe office, turned and walked straight out again. 'I asked for bloody blinds so I wouldn't have to look at your ugly mugs all day. Where are they?' He barked. 'Get onto Alice – she's the only way to get things done round here.'

While Fuller went off to track Alice down, Resnick sat in his 'goldfish bowl' annexe, opened the Carlos Moreno file and began to read, picking his nose all the while. When Fuller came back five minutes later. Resnick tapped on the glass, smiled and beckoned him into his office.

'Interesting report, Fuller, very detailed and thorough,' Resnick said as he sat down and placed the report on his desk.

'Thank you, sir,' Fuller replied. 'As you can see, I have uncovered evidence that could put the Fishers away for car ringing and potentially link them to an illegal booze racket in Manchester. That then gives you a fighting chance of persuading the Fran woman to make a statement against Tony Fisher for the assault. If he's already behind bars, she's got nothing to be scared of.'

Resnick looked up at him and shook his head. He tapped the report. 'This is a bloody cock-up! The Jag had its real plates on it when you recovered it and it's registered to the Fishers' club, so their prints on the motor are worthless.'

Fuller looked embarrassed. 'Well, the false plates were in the boot . . . and they tie up with a brown Jag used on the Manchester job.'

'So fucking what? The Fishers have an expensive lawyer who will crucify your case. In letting Carlos Moreno do a runner and get squashed to death by a Post Office van, you've given them a perfect alibi. If I need to spell it out, Fuller, you're thicker than I thought. The Fishers can pin everything on Carlos and walk away.'

Fuller felt totally deflated. Resnick was right. The Jag was in for a service, so all the Fishers had to say was that Carlos must have taken the Jag to Manchester for the illegal booze racket. With Carlos dead, there was no one to argue with anything the Fishers might claim.

Humiliated, Fuller turned to leave.

'Wait,' Resnick said, opening the file again. 'Your report says the tip-off about the Moreno garage was anonymous and made by a woman.' Fuller nodded. 'An unknown woman also rang Boxer Davis at his bedsit the night he was killed.' Resnick clicked his fingers at Fuller. 'Have a look in that box of my stuff down there for the phone tap reports on calls made.'

Fuller searched through the box of files Alice had packed for the move. He found the phone tap report file and handed it over.

As Resnick flicked through the pages and pages of calls made in and out of Dolly Rawlins' house, Fuller spotted Andrews coming out of Saunders' office. He looked depressed. Fuller cheered up. It was all coming to a head. All of Resnick's short cuts, unprofessionalism and sidestepping of red tape, his crazed obsession with the Rawlins case, was coming out into the open and would see the end of him. Andrews would have just told Saunders about the picture of Harry Rawlins Resnick carried in his pocket at all times. Saunders would see him for the obsessed weirdo he was.

Andrews knocked on Resnick's open door. 'DCI Saunders would like to see you, sir.'

Resnick ignored him and continued to run his finger down the numbers called, checking to see if Boxer's number or if the anonymous call to the police station on the night Carlos died was on there. At the bottom of the third page, the list of numbers suddenly stopped: no more recordings, no more notes, no more information. Resnick shot to his feet, knocking his chair over and slammed the file shut.

'Well, I hope Saunders will be telling me what the bloody hell's going on, because it seems he's been keepin' me in the dark and I won't have it! First he stops the surveillance and then he stops the bleedin' phone tap! What's the point in me being here?' He stormed off towards his boss's office.

Andrews still had a faced like a slapped arse.

'So, what did you say to Saunders?' Fuller asked.

Andrews sighed and dug his hands into his pockets. 'He did all the talking.'

This was disappointing. Fuller had hoped Andrews would have been spilling the beans on Resnick's lunatic moment with Fat Fran.

'Resnick gave me a lousy work report,' Andrews continued. 'And Saunders said I'd failed to make the grade, so I'm back on division and routine crime as of next month. I can't believe it! I've always worked as hard as anyone else, done as I was told and never let Resnick down.'

Fuller suspected Andrews was for the chop; he felt sorry for him and said as much, but the fact was that, although he was a nice bloke, armed robbery investigations were out of his league. Working on division, investigating thefts and criminal damage would be more his forte. 'Don't worry. This job's a roller coaster,' Fuller said as he walked away. Then he whispered to himself: 'I'm on my way up and you're on your way down.'

When the explosion went off in Saunders' office, the whole annexe heard the boom of Resnick's voice as he shouted at the top of his voice. All eyes looked over to the DCI's office, where Resnick could be seen through the glass partition, red-faced with anger and thumping his fist on Saunders' desk. Turning his head, Resnick saw Fuller, Andrews and others looking at him. He flung open the DCI's office door and stepped into the corridor.

'You all havin' a bloody good gander and gettin' an earful, are you? WELL, ARE YOU?'

Everyone in the annexe suddenly pretended to be busy: there was a general rushing about and gathering up of papers, the typists typing frantically and officers picking up phones to make suddenly urgent calls. Except Fuller – Fuller stared Resnick down square for at least five seconds before looking away.

'You know what?' Andrews said, as he watched Fuller gloating. 'You're a bigger bastard than he is. He doesn't make a conscious decision to be a shit; you do.'

Back in Saunders' office, Resnick stood with both fists on the DCI's desk as he leant forward and glared at him. Saunders looked down at his memo pad and tapped it with the point of his sharpened pencil.

'I withdrew the phone tap on the Rawlins woman when I found out about it a few days ago. For one, you had not sought mine or any other senior officer's approval, which means it was illegal, not to mention the cost of having an officer monitor and write down the number of all the calls in and out, day and night. And I withdrew the surveillance for pretty much the same reason. I couldn't justify two officers sitting outside the Rawlins house with Boxer Davis's killer on the loose.'

'Why didn't you tell me you pulled the tap?' Resnick said, trying to regain his composure. 'It could have been Dolly Rawlins that phoned Boxer Davis and who grassed up Carlos Moreno. It was a woman, sir. A woman who called to speak to Boxer Davis twice on the night he died. You should have told me.'

Saunders sat back in disbelief. 'I should have told you? George – have you any idea how many times I have gone looking for you, only to find you were out God knows where? I left a copy of this memo on your desk. If you failed to read it that's not my problem.'

'I'm so close, sir.'

'Close to what, exactly?' Saunders asked.

Resnick sucked in his breath, trying to keep control of his temper. He'd already blown his top once; he knew he could only go so far with Saunders before he bit back. They'd been friends for so long . . .

Saunders placed the pencil down, leant forwards and stuck the knife in. 'The Rawlins case is closed, George. You and your men are to assist on the Mayfair robbery. They have a few good leads and need more troops.'

'Oh, no, no, no, please, just two more weeks. I'll have something within two weeks,' Resnick pleaded, sharing everything he had with his old friend. 'We know there was a fourth man and I'm *this* close to finding him. When I do, I solve four cases in one go. He's connected to them all, I know he is. Rawlins is connected to them all. It stands to reason that the fourth man is as well.'

'Who do you think it is?' Saunders enquired.

'I'm close. Give me time. A little more time, that's all. The fourth man and this woman who's been calling people . . . they're the key.'

'I thought Fran was the key? Last week, Boxer Davis was the key. The week before, Len Gulliver was the key.' Saunders shook his head. He'd heard enough; he wasn't going to back down. 'I'm acting on orders that come from higher up, George. Your case is closed.'

'You're giving up on me!' Resnick snapped.

Saunders snapped his pencil in two. He spoke through gritted teeth. 'How dare you? How bloody dare you? You were given the Rawlins case on my recommendation. Not one senior officer bar me thought you were up to it, but I fought your corner and got you the case. The case you've wanted to close for your entire career. But all you've found, George, are dead ends. No useful leads or evidence. My hands are tied.'

Resnick bowed his head in a mixture of shame and despair; he knew the system well enough to understand where Saunders was coming from, but he still hated it.

'I know what that bastard Harry Rawlins did to you,' Saunders continued, 'but now you're carrying a personal grievance too far. Give it up, George, and move on for your—'

Resnick interrupted him. 'What personal grievance?'

'You know exactly what I mean.'

Resnick leant over the desk and slammed his fist down again. 'The man's a bloody villain and—'

'The man's dead!' Saunders shouted, shocking Resnick into silence. 'Andrews told me what happened with Fran. He told me about the photograph of Harry Rawlins. You were wrong, because she admitted it was Tony Fisher who assaulted her. I hate to say it, George, but you're becoming obsessed and need to face facts – Rawlins is dead and buried.'

Resnick opened his mouth, but Saunders held up his hand to stop him. 'If you don't want to move to the Mayfair robbery, might I suggest you take time off? The chief superintendent will approve your leave.'

Resnick stared at Saunders. 'Sounds as if you know that for sure. You've already asked him, haven't you?' He held Saunders' gaze. 'I expect he's already approved my transfer if I want that as well, has he?'

'He approved your transfer months ago, George. I've been fighting to keep you here, on the case you want, doing the job I know you were excellent at.'

'Were?' This single word from Saunders cut like a knife. 'Then I expect it's pointless me asking if the super's read my application for promotion?'

Saunders chose to ignore Resnick's last question. He waffled on about what a good officer George was and how he was sure this time he would get the promotion, perhaps to a quieter station where he could serve out his time. He said he knew that, by rights, George should be sitting where he was.

'Then why aren't I?' Resnick snapped.

'Because of the bloody Rawlins case, George! This personal—'

'It's not personal! He's just a villain.'

'A dead villain,' Saunders said, hammering this home one more time.

'Dead or not, he's responsible for dozens of unsolved robberies and I'm *this* close to solving all of them,' Resnick repeated. But he'd heard enough. He hated being patronised. He stood up and stabbed his finger at Saunders. 'You are too right, sonny. I should have been sitting where you are long ago. You, me and everyone in this bloody place knows I'm not because of Harry Rawlins. It was personal, you're right – how could it not be? But it's not anymore. Now, it's about good solid police work. I want his ledgers, I want the fourth man and I want the woman on the phone. Because that's how we clean up London! And, just so you know, *sir*, people with their ear to the ground, people in the know, don't think Rawlins is dead at all.'

Resnick took a deep and rasping breath, taking in oxygen to calm himself down. Reaching into his pocket, he pulled out his warrant card and threw it down on Saunders' desk. 'You can stuff my promotion application and I resign from the Met.'

Saunders sighed and stood up. This wasn't what he wanted, but Resnick had overstepped the mark and Saunders had had enough of trying to appease him. 'I think you had better take your resignation up with the chief super.'

'I'm taking it up with you! People in the know . . . you remember that: Boxer, Green Teeth, me. The Fishers – they're running scared from someone bigger and nastier than them! You mark my words; you haven't heard the last of Harry Rawlins. He's out there somewhere, alive and well . . . I know it. And it won't be me he comes back to haunt, it'll be you!'

Saunders was now convinced that George was losing it. 'Please, George, just go home and rest. Don't make any rash decisions here and now.'

'My resignation will be on your desk first thing in the morning. That's what you've wanted all along, isn't it? Well, I hope yours and everybody else's heads bloody well roll when you all see I was right.' Resnick stormed out of the office.

* * *

Resnick was on the ground floor heading towards the main exit when he stopped to have a coughing fit. He could hardly catch his breath, his heart was hammering so rapidly he thought it was going to leap out of his chest. As he leant against the wall, waiting for the heart attack he was sure was coming, he saw Alice walking towards him. Her pace quickened when she saw the state he was in.

'Deep breaths sir, long deep breaths.' Resnick knew what to do when he got like this, but Alice's gentle reminder was still soothing. Especially now. She gave him time to get his breathing back to normal then asked if she should fetch a glass of water.

'No, I'll be fine,' Resnick said. 'But I need you to do me a favour, Alice, love. I want you to write a letter.'

'I can't . . .' Alice began, trying to tell him she wasn't working for his department anymore.

One more rule broken wasn't going to harm either him or Alice now. 'No,' said Resnick. 'I really need you to do this for me, Alice, please. It's my letter of resignation.'

'Oh, sir.' Alice didn't know what else to say.

'They took the case off me, so I quit.' Resnick looked so wretched, his head bent as he quietly told her exactly what he wanted written.

Alice wasn't listening; she never did when he dictated letters. She usually just wrote what she knew he would have said if he'd had the time to think straight. She'd do the same now. She imagined herself saying, 'I'll quit with you, George. We're both meant for better things.' The very idea of actually calling him 'George' brought a lump to her throat and she hoped she didn't have to say anything before it went away. He'd always been such a grouch, but he was *her* grouch. He was her grumpy, brilliant, disgusting, dedicated policeman, and no one knew how to handle him except her.

Once he'd finished, Resnick looked up at Alice. 'When you do the whip round for the retirement pressie, no teasmade, all right?'

Alice tried to smile but she just wanted to cry.

Resnick leant forward and kissed her lightly on the cheek. 'Thanks for everything, Alice. And thanks for putting up with me.'

As she watched Resnick walk away, with his manky old coat flapping and his moth-eaten briefcase in his hand, she finally broke down. She'd be the first to admit that her feelings for such an outwardly unlikeable man were hard to comprehend. But Alice knew where she stood with Resnick, she knew her role, she knew she empowered him to be the best officer he could be by covering his back, listening to him moan, reassuring him when he had self-doubt and protecting him from . . . well, himself mainly. And she'd failed him. He gave her life purpose and that was more than any other man had ever done. Resnick had no idea how much she loved him – and now he never would.

CHAPTER 27

Bella took off the paint mask and stepped back to breathe in some air. Beads of sweat trickled down her forehead and cheeks. She surveyed the Ford Escort van that was to be their getaway vehicle with pride; she'd never sprayed a vehicle before, but she'd spray-tanned plenty of strippers backstage at the Z-Easy club, and it was pretty much the same.

When Dolly had bought the van – under a false name and in cash – two weeks ago, it was red. Now it was a gleaming white. The engine had been a bit knackered, but Linda had got to work and it had a lot more poke under the bonnet than before. Linda had learnt a lot about engines from Carlos during the few weeks she knew him, the most important being how to 'feel' the engine. He'd said she could read manuals if she wanted to, but they didn't replace intuition. That might have worked for him, but she'd read the manuals too – especially for the vehicles in Dolly's lock-up. If they broke down, they went to jail. Simple as that.

Bella wandered across to Shirley, who was humming to herself as she busily painted magnetic signs for the sides of the getaway van. 'The van's ready when you are.'

Shirley looked up. 'Do you think these are OK, Bella?' She cared what Bella thought.

Bella nodded. 'Very professional. It'll look like a genuine GLC van when these and the false plates are on.'

On the far side of the lock-up, Linda was sitting on a crate, cleaning the sawn-off shotguns. Her face was ashen, her mouth a thin tight line, and she kept flicking looks towards the exit. She was waiting for Dolly.

'Is everything OK, Linda?' Bella asked, worried she was going to blow her top when Dolly arrived. It was early evening now and

Bella had been watching Linda all day. At one point she'd tried to persuade her to go home, but Linda had refused. She'd sat in the lock-up, biding her time like a taut wire ready to snap. Now, Bella leant in and whispered in Linda's ear.

'I know you're hurting about Carlos, but losing it with Dolly ain't gonna bring him back. Wait until the job's done and, once you got your cut, you can call her what you want. You can even slap her about if it makes you feel better. Do ya hear me, Linda?'

'It's hard, Bella,' said Linda. 'It's like she's ripped the soul out of me . . . but I'll do me best to keep me mouth shut. I don't want to ruin it for you and Shirl.'

Bella patted her shoulder and went to put the false plates on the van.

Ten minutes later, Dolly breezed in and plonked a bag of shopping on the floor. She was still on a high and eager to tell the girls about her morning. 'I've got us the final route and times for security van,' she said with a beaming smile.

Shirley and Bella went over and congratulated her. Dolly waved her hand to Linda to join the group, and then cleared a space on the table, laid out the route map Brian Marshall had given her and lit up a cigarette. Bella wanted to ask how she had got the route map, but if Dolly wanted them to know, she'd tell them.

'OK, so I've spent the afternoon driving this route,' Dolly started. 'I done it about six or seven times. To do timings, and find the best position for the blocking van to be parked up before we head into the underpass, that sort of thing.' Dolly quickly flicked through the other papers given to her by Marshall. 'We've got the exact date and time now . . . it's two weeks ahead of schedule.'

'How come?' Linda asked, just to be awkward.

'Because that date and time gives us the best balance between cash haul and the opportunity to pull the job quickly and successfully. We've got to account for rush hours, road works, school holidays, all that sort of thing. I got it under control, Linda, don't you worry.'

As usual, Dolly's patronising tone got right up Linda's nose, but she bit her tongue as Dolly continued.

'Memorise the route and then we'll burn it. Drive it as many times as you think you need to, so you learn all the tricky parts, the lights, the roundabouts, the zebra crossings, anywhere things could go wrong.'

As a train rumbled by overhead, the big dog in the lock-up next door barked. Wolf started yapping. Linda felt the tide of anger rise.

'I also marked on the map where the getaway car will be parked, so learn that as well. Drive it from the pick-up point to the car park, where your own motors will be parked, ready to get you to the airport. Time everything down to the last second. Drive it again and again till you can do it blindfolded. You lot got your holiday stories sorted?' Dolly asked.

They were all prepared; their plans had to be above suspicion. Linda was either to leave the arcade or get herself sacked, and Bella was to quit her job at the strip club. No one must suspect they had any contact with each other. Shirley was uncomfortable lying to her mum, but she'd do it. She had to.

'Right, here are your tickets to Rio. You got your passports? 'There's two flights that day, so I've booked Bella and Linda onto the first one. Shirl, you'll fly later the same day. Keep away from each other till you land,' Dolly continued. 'Learn your flight times and numbers, and your weight allowance. We can't have anyone being stopped for something stupid like their suitcase being too heavy!' Dolly laughed and Bella and Shirley were polite enough to giggle, albeit a little late. Dolly seemed perkier than usual as she ticked off everything she'd covered in her precious notebook. 'Right,' she said with a buoyant tone to her voice. 'Let's see what you been up to.'

She was pleased with the work they'd done. The paint job and signs on the van were very good, and the set of number plates were a copy of ones they'd seen on a white Ford van on their trip to the beach near Brighton. Bella demonstrated how fast the signs could be peeled off and the van's false plates changed back to the originals.

Dolly walked over to Linda, who was checking the spark plugs on the van. 'You sorted the lead truck, yet? You're going to have to nick it earlier now.'

Linda couldn't look Dolly in the face. 'I got a big Leyland laundry van lined up,' she said offhandedly. 'It'll be perfect and a doddle to nick.'

'How big's "big"? Will it fit in here or do we need somewhere else to stash it?'

Before Linda could snap back, Shirley butted in. 'Mum's block of flats. She's got a parking bay underneath. You can dump the van there, no problem. Market vans come and go all the time so it won't look out of place or nothing.'

Dolly remained focused on Linda. 'Can you get it this week?'

'I can get it whenever,' Linda said curtly, straining to hold back her temper. She walked away from Dolly.

'We need it quick, Linda!' Dolly raised her voice as she followed Linda to the other side of the lock-up. 'We got to change the number plates and reinforce the rear bumper with a metal bar . . . you sure a laundry van can withstand a heavy security truck crashing into the back of it?'

Linda ignored her and picked up one of the sawn-off shotguns on top of the tool trolley. She would have liked to turn it on Dolly and blast her right there and then.

'What's up with Linda?' Dolly asked Bella.

Bella shrugged and busied herself wiping the false plates with a rag to remove all prints. Dolly suspected Bella did know what the matter was. She looked over at Linda. Wolf was sniffing around Linda's feet, and the next second Linda kicked the little dog, causing him to yelp in pain. Dolly had had enough.

'Don't you ever kick him again!' Dolly shouted, striding over to Linda and pointing her finger straight in her face.

'Well keep the mangy thing away from me,' Linda replied.

'Come on – out with it. What's the matter with you?'

Linda kept her head down. 'Nothing,' she muttered,

'Is this about me asking you to get rid of your mechanic?'

Linda looked at Dolly. 'I did as you asked. He won't be a problem no more.'

'Good,' Dolly replied coldly. 'He suss anything?'

'Wouldn't matter if he did. He's dead.'

Dolly was stunned into silence. For a moment, she wondered if Linda was trying to make her feel as guilty as possible, but the look of anger and sorrow in Linda's eyes showed she was deadly serious. 'I'm so sorry, Linda. What happened?'

'I saw it, Dolly. I saw the whole thing. Do you want the details or will "he's dead" be enough for you?'

'I'm sorry, Linda, I truly am. You should have told me as soon as it happened.'

'Why? What would you have done to make me feel better about making me kill my boyfriend? Cos that's what happened, Dolly. You said to grass him up, the police raided his place, and he ran . . . straight under a van.' Linda walked away before she did something she'd regret.

As Dolly started to follow Linda, Bella stopped her.

'She turned up at my flat in a right state,' Bella said under her breath. 'She saw him under the wheels of the van lying in a pool of his own blood, so you give her this one, OK? Let her be mad with you. Let her take it out on you. Let her blame you, because the only other person she can blame is herself. You can take it – she can't.

You want this robbery to go ahead? You take this one on the chin.' Bella went into the office, where Linda was shakily trying to make herself a cup of tea.

As Dolly watched, Bella put her arms around Linda's shoulders and gave her a hug. She wished she could do the same. She wished she could tell her again how sorry she was. But Dolly knew that Linda would never see her as a friend like Bella; all she could do was provide Linda with enough money to live the life she wanted. Dolly mentally revised her plan for the day. She had been eager to get the girls into a run-through, but she thought she'd give Linda some time to drink her tea.

While she waited, she picked up one of the shotguns and tried to cock it but her finger slipped and got nipped between the firing pin and hammer. She stifled a scream, but couldn't help letting out a little screech: 'Ow! For fuck's—'

From the office, Linda snorted in derision. Dolly looked round, annoyed, but after a warning glance from Bella, let it slide. She freed her finger, shaking it up and down till the pain subsided. A large blood blister was already forming. Right – that was it!

'OK – let's get our overalls and masks on and have a rehearsal!' Dolly shouted. This time she wanted to practise unlocking the body harness, picking up the shotgun and sledgehammer, Bella with the chainsaw, Linda with a shotgun and then Bella with the shotgun. 'Everything has to repeated till it's second nature,' Dolly said. 'I don't want nothing bad to happen to any of us.' She tried not to catch Linda's eye.

They moved out of the annexe into the large, filthy main garage. An old furniture truck, minus wheels and one door, would act as the lead truck for the rehearsal. Shirley had already placed the harness over the driver's seat and unbuckled it. This was where Dolly would be sitting, all strapped in, at the moment she slammed the brakes on, forcing the security wagon to slam into the back of her. The harness had to be strong enough to keep Dolly in her seat during the impact, and simple enough to unbuckle the very next moment. They had to get this right. Dolly's actions would start the robbery. If she couldn't get herself free, they'd all be sitting ducks.

Dolly put the sledgehammer in the back of the van, right by the rear doors. Her shotgun dangled from her waist on a makeshift belt. She then got in the driver's seat and buckled herself into the harness. Shirley watched every move, making sure the straps weren't twisted, too tight or too slack.

'As soon as Linda gets the laundry van, I'll move the harness into that and you can practise for real,' Shirley said.

Dolly threw herself back and forth in her seat. The harness held fast. She gave Shirley the thumbs up.

'Right,' said Dolly. 'I'm in the lead van – Linda's laundry truck – all strapped in, shotgun by my side, sledgehammer by the rear doors. The security wagon's behind me and you lot are in the van behind the security wagon. Bella, you'll have your chainsaw and shotgun, Shirley, you'll have your shotgun, Linda, you'll be driving.' Dolly looked at the girls, standing by the side door of her van, listening. 'Go and stand by the back doors of this van for now. We'll do everything from the stop to the moment I burst the back doors open.'

Shirley, Linda, and Bella lined up at the back doors of the furniture van. 'Ready?' Dolly shouted.

'Ready,' Bella shouted back. 'I'm timing you.'

'At the twenty-yard marker, I slam the brakes on, the security wagon rams into the back of me, I drive forwards, then ram backwards, and now the security wagon's trapped between my van and yours.'

Shirley, overexcited, piped up, 'I run up to the security wagon and cut their aerial off so they can't radio for help.'

'Shut up, Shirley!' Bella whispered. 'You don't do that yet – Dolly hasn't finished her bit . . .'

Dolly continued, oblivious to Bella and Shirley, 'I undo my harness . . .'

There was a sudden silence. The girls glanced at each other. They closed in on the back doors of the van, and all they could hear was Dolly mumbling 'fucking thing!' Bella stopped the stopwatch and they all waited.

Shirley asked, 'Need a hand with the harn—?'

'NO!'

They heard the harness buckle drop to the floor. Bella started the stopwatch again.

Dolly shouted, 'I undo my harness, move to the back doors and . . .' with one huge kick from inside, the back doors of the van flung open to reveal Dolly standing there, legs wide apart like a bloke, swinging the sledgehammer above her head. One of the van doors smacked Shirley on the shoulder, sending her flying, and the sledgehammer was so heavy that it toppled Dolly over backwards.

Bella stopped the stopwatch again. 'Don't swing it overarm,' she said, 'you swing it underarm, just like at the beach.'

Dolly clambered to her feet. 'Again. From the top.'

The three women stood by the back doors of the van listening to Dolly shouting her routine again. This time, as Dolly kicked the back doors open, she swung the sledgehammer underarm, letting go of it at the end of the swing, sending it flying across the garage and forcing them to dive out of its way. She then swung the shotgun up to her hip, pointed it at the imaginary security wagon and yelled: 'Stay where you are!'

From where she'd landed on the floor, Bella shouted, 'Bleedin' hell, Dolly! You didn't say you was going to let go of the sledgehammer!'

'I'm throwing it through the windscreen of the security wagon! Course I'm going to let go of it.'

'I meant *now*!' Bella got to her feet and then helped Linda and Shirley up.

Dolly looked down from the van at them. 'How does it look?' she asked.

'Well,' Linda replied, 'it'll look a whole lot more convincing if you take the safety catch off the shotgun.'

'Oh, for fuck's sake!' Dolly cursed as she looked at the shotgun. 'I get my finger caught every time. You'll have to help me, Linda.'

Without thinking, Linda stepped forwards and talked Dolly through how to remove the safety catch. Bella watched Linda teaching Dolly, with patience and kindness; they could get on when it really mattered. Suddenly she realised *what* she was actually watching – a shooting arcade worker teaching a convent volunteer how to work a shotgun . . . She shook her head, put her hand to her mouth and sniggered. Sometimes it was hard to believe what they were doing.

Once Dolly had got the hang of the shotgun's safety catch, Linda returned to stand by Bella and Shirley. 'Right, let's hear what you're going to say,' she said.

Dolly swung the shotgun up onto her hip and shouted, 'Don't move! Guard in the back, show your face at the hatch!'

Three blank faces stared up at Dolly. 'Is that what you're going to say?' Shirley asked.

'Well, what do you want me to say? "Stick 'em up, this is a raid"?'

'Come on, you lot, sort it out. I got to go to work,' Bella said, resetting the stopwatch.

Linda stepped forwards again to help. 'It's not *what* you're saying that's the issue, it's your voice. You sound like bleedin' Bambi! Apart from pissing themselves laughing, the security guards will know it's a woman's voice and the cops will be straight onto us.'

'Can you lower your pitch?' Shirley suggested. 'There was a singing round in a beauty competition I entered once and I had to learn how to sing a semi-tone lower than I normally—'

'DON'T MOVE!' Dolly bellowed.

Bella shook her head. 'That's still Bambi, just louder. Stick something in your mouth and try again.'

Shirley handed Dolly a white hanky with a red 'S' embroidered in the corner. Dolly stuffed it into her mouth and this time when she shouted, the words were completely inaudible and she nearly choked herself.

'Forget it for tonight,' Dolly said, spitting the hanky out onto the floor. 'Bella's got to go anyway.'

As Bella slipped into her motorbike leathers, they all chatted about Carlos. Dolly watched – three friends gossiping, reassuring, getting on like a house on fire. For a moment, she felt a twinge of jealousy, but she knew she had to keep her distance.

Dolly dished out her final orders for the night. 'Right, listen, you lot. It's all coming together now, so let's keep well away from each other as much as possible, right? I know you can only talk to each other about certain things, but it'll have to wait till you're all in Rio together.'

'We,' Bella corrected. 'Till *we're* all in Rio together.'

'Don't start that again,' Dolly said, picking up her tweed coat and handbag.

Bella continued regardless. 'It's the only bit of the plan I still got a problem with, Dolly. But it's easy fixed.'

Dolly flung her handbag down. 'Come on, Bella – say what you mean! You don't want to fly off round the world because – what? Because you won't know where the money is being stashed, right?'

'Spot on,' Bella replied.

'And you need to know because you don't actually trust me, do you? Still, you don't trust me! So far I've laid out nearly seven grand of me own money and trusted all of you with that. When the robbery's done and we all head off in our different directions, who'll actually have the money at that stage, Bella? Me? No. You will. The money will be in the back of the getaway car, while I'm in the bleedin' laundry van that we still haven't nicked yet. Have I once doubted your honesty and whinged about the possibility that you could run off with the money immediately after the robbery? No! I wouldn't do that to you. I don't make decisions just for my benefit, I make them to safeguard the lot of you.' Dolly moved towards the three women. Shirley and Linda stepped slightly behind Bella for protection. 'I know you all much, much better than you think,' Dolly continued. 'Do you reckon, after a few drinks, Linda could keep her mouth shut about all that money if she knew where it was? Do you think Shirley might not be tempted to slip her mum a couple of hundred?' Dolly paused briefly to see if any of them would be brave enough to answer . . . they weren't. 'I'm not telling you where the money will be stashed because one slip of the tongue and we'll not only have the law down on us, but every villain in London including the Fishers who, you may have noticed, have gone to ground. Boxer's dead, Carlos was raided – that's why the Fisher brothers are keeping their heads down. They're scared, confused and they don't know what's going on. All they know is that it looks like someone might be out to get them and they don't know who. They think it's Harry – good.'

'Nice speech,' Bella said. 'But this isn't about trust. This is about knowing where the money is if anything happens to you.'

Dolly's face was now red with anger and hurt. 'You think I haven't thought of that after all we've bloody well been through? I've left a letter with my solicitor for each of you in case I die. In the letters is what you're so desperate to know.'

If they were surprised by Dolly's mention of the letters, it also seemed a very convenient addition to the conversation. She could see the doubt in their eyes. 'Believe me, don't believe me,' Dolly said in a weary voice. 'But do the robbery as planned.' As Dolly went to pick up her handbag, Shirley spoke.

'I believe you.'

Dolly pulled a glove on over her blistered finger and winced. She looked at Shirley and smiled. 'Thank you, Shirley.' She headed for the door. Her steps were short and slow; she looked tired and old. 'Run off with the money, eh?' Dolly laughed. 'How would I spend a million on me own?'

Bella shrugged and grinned. 'We got to get our hands on it first, darlin'.'

'You said it, Bella. And it's up to you lot now if we do it or not. Let me know what you decide. Come on, Wolf.'

Wolf was curled up asleep on the office chair and didn't hear Dolly's command. Bella picked him up, caught up with Dolly and handed Wolf to her. 'OK,' Bella said, looking Dolly in the eyes. 'Everything stays as planned.'

* * *

Dolly moved slowly towards the exit, keen to get out before any of them saw how close she was to tears. She hadn't really left any letters with a solicitor; she'd lied to get the girls to trust her. But she would write the letters now, just in case something did happen to her. She felt unappreciated and betrayed by Bella and Linda – and after all she had given them! She hugged her little dog for comfort and kissed his head. 'Let's go home, my little baby, let's go home,' she whispered. As Dolly walked gingerly across the cobbles in the dark, Wolf looked back over her shoulder and gave a low grumble. Dolly glanced back and caught sight of a rat disappearing into one of the lock-ups. 'Ssshhh, Wolf. It's just a rat.' But Wolf's eyes, like huge, dark saucers, were fixed on something else.

* * *

Ten minutes after Dolly left, Bella left. Then Linda and, lastly, Shirley. As Shirley buttoned up her coat, she realised that the big dog from next door hadn't barked when the others left. She shrugged the thought off and, reaching the main door, turned the overhead strip lights off, ignoring the drip, drip of water echoing round the cavernous lock-up. She was about to open the door when she heard a noise, a sort of scuffle that sounded as if it was coming from outside. She listened closer, ear against the door, and started to shiver. She switched on her small torch and shone it round the dark lock-up.

Bill Grant pressed his face against the cold wall as he stared into the garage through the slits in the air bricks. The blonde seemed to stare straight at him. As the torch light moved towards him, he stepped back briefly in case his eyes glistened in the light beam. Once the beam had passed, Grant returned to his vantage point. 'You're beautiful,' he whispered. 'I could keep you safe in the dark, my darlin'. Nice and safe with me.'

Shirley finally braved opening the main door and stepped out into the darkness of the night. She paused, and once her eyes had adjusted, almost ran towards the main road.

'The last one's just left,' Grant said, turning from his spyhole in the wall. He laughed, a chesty, smoker's laugh with a dirty undertone. He leant against the wall, arms folded. 'Who'd have thought it, eh? The chicks are really fuckin' gonna do it.' Standing up from the wall, he brushed brick dust from his coat sleeve. His lock-up was identical to Dolly's, but much dirtier, with lines of wrecked cars covered in dust and pigeon shit. A flashlight shone in Grant's face and he held his hand to his eyes. 'Do me a favour! You can turn the lights back on now they've gone.' The flashlight clicked off.

Harry Rawlins held the straining Alsatian by the scruff of the neck while he untied the rag that was wrapped round its jaws like a muzzle. The dog started barking and snarling, its long shiny white fangs dripping thick spittle. Harry suddenly let the dog go and it hurtled forwards towards Grant, who jumped backwards in fear. The chain round its neck ran out of slack inches from Grant, jerking the animal's head back and stopping it in its tracks. Harry laughed.

'Fuckin' hell!' Grant exclaimed. He was shaking. Harry looked like the animal now, his mouth open with a snarl and his teeth glistening as he sneered.

'She's copying my plans virtually to the letter,' Harry said. 'So she'll be the only one who knows where the money's stashed when the job's done. That's when we move, Bill. It'll be like taking candy from a baby.'

CHAPTER 28

Linda waited nervously in Warrington Crescent within sight of the Colonnade Hotel, a small and elegant Victorian boutique premises in Maida Vale. It was early Tuesday morning just after sunrise and she was cold, even though she had on a thick red sweater and Puffa jacket.

North-west London wasn't Linda's usual stomping ground; there was no one here who would recognise her or even notice her. For the past few weeks, she had visited the area on five different occasions. She'd spotted the Leyland laundry van on her second visit, established the regular drop-off at the Colonnade Hotel on her next two visits – and today was the big day.

Linda rarely got nervous about anything, but as she waited she kept wiping her sweaty palms on her trousers, and she could feel her heart beating out of her chest. She felt frightened but, more than that, she felt excited. Linda had never quite understood the glint in Joe's eyes whenever he set out on a job – but now she did. She checked her watch: the Leyland van was now less than ten minutes away. She felt invincible. The driver had no idea she'd been watching, no idea she was watching now and no idea that he was about to lose his vehicle. *Poor bastard*, she thought to herself.

The driver of the Leyland laundry van pulled up outside the hotel side entrance, just as she had seen him do on the previous occasions. She watched as he carried out his normal routine, stacking baskets of clean laundry onto a trolley and taking them to the side entrance of the hotel. He whistled away without a care in the world as he rang the side doorbell and was let in. Linda had about three minutes to nick the van before he returned with the dirty laundry sacks.

Linda walked over to the van – not too quick, not too slow – and wished that Dolly could see her. Her meticulous planning, her precision timing – yes, Dolly would be impressed. She took a casual look round before jumping in the driver's seat. Pulling a small screwdriver out of her jacket pocket, she rammed it into the ignition barrel and turned it to start the van. It wouldn't budge. Linda didn't panic: she knew what to do next. She'd seen Joe hotwire a car on numerous occasions to get them home after a night out. She'd done it herself three or four times. She prised open the ignition tumbler, ripped out the wires and twisted two together. Next, she pushed her foot on the accelerator a couple of times to inject petrol into the carburettor, then touched the other two wires together to activate the starter. As the engine started, she smiled to herself . . . just like old times.

Linda drove directly to the underground parking area used by Shirley's mum and the other market traders to stash their vehicles, cart stalls, tables and produce. The two-mile drive was thrilling: Linda's eyes darted from the road to the wing mirror to the rear-view mirror and back again. She was hyper-alert, taking in every detail; she even noted a couple of beat cops wandering aimlessly around their patch. She smiled; they were totally oblivious.

When she reached the market, Linda edged her way slowly through the line of trucks and vans delivering fruit and veg to the traders, on the lookout for Shirley. She spotted her, standing outside the car park, waving furiously. Shirley had managed to get two copies made of her mum's key and had cleared a pile of old fruit and veg boxes out of the way to make a space in the far corner to park the van. Linda reversed into the space and Shirley banged on the rear doors when she needed to stop.

Linda was feeling pleased with herself as she showed Shirley round the van. 'It's perfect, nice and big too, look at the size of the rear bumper . . . it will stand up to a tank hittin' it.' Shirley kept schtum as she slid open the driver's door, allowing Linda to enjoy her moment. 'There's only one seat, so Dolly can move fast from here to the rear doors . . . when she's learnt to get out of the harness, that is!'

'You've nicked a good 'un, I reckon,' Shirley replied, encouraging Linda. Then she noticed the damage to the ignition. 'What the hell's happened there?'

'Well, the driver was hardly going to hand me the keys, was he?' Linda said. 'I bought a replacement barrel before I nicked the van – I knew it was likely to get damaged. It's a thirty-minute job to replace it.' Replacing the barrel was actually something Linda had never done before, but she had seen Joe do it. It looked easy enough and now the van was safely tucked away, she had time to work it out.

As the two of them heaved a tarpaulin over the vehicle, to hide the logo on the sides, Linda asked Shirley if she'd brought the false plates.

'Course I 'ave. And some spray paint to go over the logos, just like you asked.' Shirley handed Linda a key. 'That's for the padlock on the gate. Make sure it's all secure when you leave and leave at least ten minutes after me.'

'Yes, Dolly,' Linda mocked and they laughed, releasing some of the tension. 'Go on, then,' Linda said. She released the bonnet and took a look at the engine. 'Sod off and leave me to work.'

Instead of leaving, Shirley stood close to Linda's shoulder and peered at the engine. 'Does she run OK?' she asked anxiously.

'So so,' Linda replied, humouring Shirley. 'But I won't know until I done a bit of work on it, will I? So, if you'd let me get on . . .'

'Sounded like it was on its last legs to me – you sure it'll be all right?'

'I know a lot more about engines than you do, Shirl, and when I've finished givin' it the once-over, it'll run like a Maserati.'

Shirley was fed up with how quickly Linda would go from being nice to being a bitch. 'You're welcome!' Shirley shouted as she stomped off. 'For getting the key cut, and for bringing the paint, and for waiting in the freezing bloody cold all morning for—'

'THANK YOU!' Linda yelled with a huge grin on her face. Shirley shut up mid-sentence, but still left in a huff. Linda returned to the van's engine and her grin slowly faded. *Fuck me. It's a bit different from a normal van . . .*

* * *

Shirley was still tetchy when she arrived at her mother's flat later that afternoon. She let herself in and shouted to Audrey, who yelled that she was in her bedroom and would be out in a minute. At first Shirley thought she'd walked into the wrong flat. It was so neat and tidy – not one dirty mug or dish in sight. Suddenly Audrey swirled into the kitchen, dressed up to the nines, wearing heavy make-up, hair lacquered stiff as a board. Shirley almost keeled over from the strong smell of Revlon's 'Intimate'.

'What ya think of me dress? It come off the back of a lorry – only a fiver!' Audrey paraded in front of Shirley in a sequinned Crimplene evening dress.

Shirley tried to hide her horror at the colour, the shape and, well, everything really. Audrey was so busy swirling, she missed the way her daughter's eyes almost popped out of her head and, by the time she'd stopped swirling, Shirley had composed herself again.

'It's lovely,' Shirley lied. 'Where's Greg? I need him to fix me car, the knob on the gearstick keeps fallin' off.'

'Don't talk to me about him – not after what I caught him doin' . . .'

'Not shaggin' again, Mum?'

Audrey opened the kitchen utility cupboard and out fell the ironing board, a pile of dirty washing, shoes and a bin bag full of rubbish. Far from tidying, Audrey had, in fact, just hidden all the junk. Eventually, she found what she was looking for.

'Your bruvver was sniffin' glue with this thing on,' she said, putting an old gas mask over her face. 'I found him stoned out of his head – didn't know what to do with him!'

Shirley stared at her mother. Audrey's voice through the mask sounded low and deep, with a strange muffled echo. She grabbed at the mask and pulled it off Audrey's head. 'That's awful,' Shirley said, not remotely interested. 'Truly awful.' She kept a tight hold of the mask. 'I'll get rid of this for you, Mum. Don't worry, Greg won't find it.'

'Good!' Audrey said. She caught a glimpse of herself in the kitchen window. The gas mask had made a right mess of her hair. 'Oh, bleedin' 'ell! I'll have to do me hair again! You know that bloke from the market?' she asked Shirley with a huge smile. 'Well, his brother-in-law's mate spotted me the other day and said he fancied a go. He sounds lovely, Shirl. And he's got money.'

'He doesn't sound lovely at all, Mum. And money's not everything. I look after you, don't I?'

'You ain't gonna stick around forever. I have to fend for meself. He's taking me to the Golden Nugget.'

'Do you even know him?'

'It's a blind date. Well – it's a half-blind date. He's seen me but I ain't seen him. The man from the market says he's a looker though. I got to fix me hair, Shirl'. What you up to tonight?'

Shirley was still examining the gas mask. It would be perfect for Dolly. She couldn't wait to get it to her. 'I'm sorting meself out for that holiday I told you about, Mum.'

'Oh, I remember. Couple of weeks in Spain'll do you good. Put a bit of colour back in your cheeks. We can all do with colour in our cheeks, Shirley, my girl. Grab every opportunity that comes your way.'

Audrey was referring to hooking up with some rich bloke in Spain; Shirley was thinking about the robbery. That was the only opportunity she'd be grabbing in the next few weeks. She kissed her mum on the cheek. 'Good luck with your mystery man, Mum.' And, with that, she left.

* * *

Linda had her head buried in the engine of the laundry van when she felt something race by, brushing her leg. She jumped, banging her head on the open bonnet, and there was Wolf, looking up at her with his stupid tail wagging.

'It ain't ready yet,' Linda said as Dolly came into view round the side of the van.

'Looks all right, Linda,' Dolly commented. 'Well done.' Even this compliment annoyed Linda. Dolly sounded slightly surprised, as if she assumed Linda would have nicked a dud.

'I'll give you a hand.' Dolly removed her coat and placed it on a crate of apples in the corner of the car park.

Before Linda could say anything, Dolly had picked up the spray paint, checked no one was watching and pulled the tarp back to reveal the logos in the side of the van. 'We'll meet the others at the lock-up in two hours,' Dolly continued. 'You finish what you're doing. I'll spray and change the plates.'

'I got time to do all that, you know. You can get on with – whatever it is you need to do,' Linda said curtly. The laundry van was her territory.

'I'm the one who's gonna be driving this, Linda, so I'm the one who needs to check everything's as it should be,' Dolly snapped. Then she paused. 'Listen . . .'

A market trader entered the car park. Dolly yanked the tarp back over the van's logo and hid the spray gun. The trader nodded, collected a box of veg and left. Linda waited for Dolly to finish her sentence.

'I'm not here to check anything, Linda. I want . . . I just want us to finish this final piece of the puzzle together. Everything's in place now and I want to know that we're all right. Me and you.'

Linda stared at Dolly. She didn't like her and probably never would, but that wasn't what Dolly was after. She just wanted to know that they were all on the same team; that's all. Never very good with words, Linda picked up the false number plates. 'You spray. I'll secure these.' It was all Dolly needed.

It took three coats of paint to hide the black logo. And although Linda had managed to get her black Puffa jacket covered in white paint while bending to fix the number plates at the back of the van, everything was looking good.

Dolly climbed into the driver's seat, which already had the harness bolted into place.

'It needs a lot of choke to start and then let it in easy,' Linda said from the doorway.

The van started first time. 'Where you gonna sit?' Dolly asked. Linda climbed into the back of the van and plonked herself down into a basket of fresh, clean white sheets – probably from one of the poshest hotels in London. Dolly laughed and they headed out for a test drive to the lock-up.

The van did stall twice on the way, which worried Dolly, but it was nothing to do with the engine, which Linda had fine-tuned beautifully. It was a loose wire contact where she had fitted the new ignition barrel, but, with a bit more electrical tape round it, the wiring was soon secure and the van didn't stall again.

* * *

When Dolly and Linda arrived at the lock-up, there was nervous tension in the air. Bella was busy preparing and checking over the tools and shotguns they needed for the robbery. Shirley had gone over their overalls and balaclavas so many times she knew every inch of them and she was now double checking everyone's passports and flight tickets before putting them into the suitcases that they, apart from Dolly, had each prepared for their flight out of the country. Bella had given her notice in at the strip club, Linda had got herself fired from the arcade quite easily and Shirley had told her mother she was going on a holiday.

No one spoke much. They didn't need to at this stage. Each knew exactly what their roles were during the robbery. Carrying out these final preparations was exciting: they were ready.

Bella had already put the chainsaw in the back of the van Linda would be driving. She now placed a sawn-off shotgun and the sledgehammer in a hockey bag, which she zipped up and put in the back of the laundry van. Tomorrow, Dolly would put the sledgehammer by the rear doors and keep the shotgun up front with her.

Dolly sat in the driver's seat of the laundry van, all harnessed in, while Linda tightened the straps to fit her exact padded-out body shape. 'That OK, Dolly?' Linda asked.

'Feels perfect.'

'Right, now see if you can unclip yourself.' Without looking, Dolly found the buckle on the harness, pressed the release and had got to her feet before Linda could finish her sentence. Linda handed Dolly a spare key for the market stall car park.

'I'll take the van back for you and park it where it was earlier. I'll put the ignition key under the wheel arch.'

'Is it safe in that underground car park?' Dolly asked.

'It will be with me kipping in the back of it.' Linda smiled. 'And remember – lots of choke to start, then let her out easy.'

Shirley put Dolly's overalls, balaclava, plimsolls and rubber gloves in a bag and handed them to her, and then put the rest of the gear in neat piles on top of the work table with three little notes saying whose was whose. Finally, she put the three suitcases in the boot of her Mini estate.

Shirley showed Dolly the gas mask. 'This'll be perfect to disguise your voice, Dolly.' As Dolly put the gas mask on, Shirley added, 'It might smell a bit of glue.'

'Glue?' Linda joked. 'What you been up to?'

'Nothing!' Shirley was defensive. 'I had to fix the mouthpiece cos it was a bit wobbly.'

Dolly picked up a crowbar, held it like a shotgun, stood in the middle of the lock-up and yelled: 'DON'T MOVE!'

'Bleedin' 'ell!' Bella said. 'You don't sound like Bambi no more!'

Dolly pulled the mask up and rested it on top of her head. 'Can you tell if I'm a woman?'

'Definitely not,' Linda confirmed.

Dolly placed the mask in the laundry van next to her other kit. As she caught a glimpse of her own left hand, she noticed her wedding ring for the first time in weeks. She twisted it round and slipped it off, not noticing Bella step up beside her.

'We're ready,' Bella said gently.

Dolly's eyes flickered as she gripped Bella's arm. 'You think we can pull it off?'

Bella, taken aback at how nervous Dolly was, put her hand on top of Dolly's and grinned. 'With you leading us – we can't fail.'

Dolly smiled. 'You'll have to keep your eye on Linda. Don't let her go crazy. I don't want her shooting that gun off.'

Bella shrugged. 'I've changed Linda's shotgun cartridges to some blanks I got hold of from a mate of Oil Head,' she whispered to Dolly with a sly grin. 'If she does pull the trigger there'd be a big bang, but no one'll get hurt.'

Dolly was still twisting the ring. 'Shirley will be scared, but she's up for it and she'll come through. You back her up, Bella, keep her strong. Know what I mean?'

Bella nodded, but she was worried about Dolly. Was she beginning to crack under all the stress? She was, after all, driving the laundry van, on which the entire robbery depended. If she lost her bottle, then the whole job would be screwed.

'I know it's easier for us, Dolly. I mean, we'll be together supporting each other in the rear van. It'll be tough for you on your own up front. But you'll do fine. Out of all of us, you can do that best.'

Dolly's eyes narrowed. 'Don't you worry about me. I won't let you down.' She turned to see Shirley and Linda looking at her, apparently waiting for . . . something. Dolly cleared her throat. 'This is it,' she said to all of them. 'Everything's ready – you're ready. I know it'll be hard, but try and rest up before the big day.' She kept back her parting words until she was almost out of the door, in case she might begin to cry. 'I'm proud of you,' she said.

Then, without looking back, Dolly called for Wolf and left.

As they watched Dolly leave, the three women knew it would be the last time they saw her until the robbery. Once alone, they had a group hug. No one said a word.

They just held on.

CHAPTER 29

On the morning of the robbery, Linda arrived at the lock-up to find Shirley heaving and retching into a small bin.

'You OK?' Linda asked.

'No! Me stomach's churning with nerves,' Shirley replied, appearing at the office door. She was as white as a sheet and her eyes seemed three times their normal size. She hugged the sloshing bin to her chest.

'Bloody hell, Shirl! You eat something funny?'

'I think it's more to do with the armed robbery we're about to commit!' Shirley barked back. She knew Linda must be sick with nerves too.

There was a bit of sick down the front of Shirley's overalls. She'd bandaged her ample chest flat, which gave her a muscular look to the top half of her body, her arms were padded out into bulging biceps, and her thighs looked pretty impressive too. In fact, from the neck down, Shirley looked like a fit bloke . . .

Linda sniffed the air. 'You been smoking?' she asked.

'I had a couple to settle me nerves.'

'You don't smoke! You're always wafting Dolly's smoke away cos the smell sets your stomach churning. No wonder you're being sick, you dozy cow!' Linda pushed past Shirley, grabbed a towel, wet the corner in the office sink and then returned to scrub the sick from Shirley's overalls. She could see how incredibly nervous Shirley was. 'Once your head's in that balaclava,' she said with a wink, 'I might fancy you summat rotten.'

Shirley snatched the cloth off Linda and they both giggled. 'Your turn,' she said.

Linda stripped off, pulled her overall on up to her waist line and tied the sleeves together while Shirley wrapped a bandage round her chest and the upper half of her arms.

'Is this the weirdest thing you've ever done?' Linda asked, and, once again, the women giggled. Neither knew exactly what they were laughing at, but it felt good.

Just then, Bella strode in. She sniffed. It had to be Shirley. 'Morning.' Bella grinned. 'You're both eager beavers, ain't you? Can't wait to get out there, eh?' Shirley was sick into the bin again.

'You OK, Shirl?' Bella asked. Shirley managed a feeble moan.

Linda wanted to distract Shirley. She picked up two pairs of gloves and handed one pair each to Bella and Shirley, then she put her own gloves on. 'OK, from this moment on – gloves. Nobody touches anything without gloves. I wiped everything down so there's no trace of us in the place once we leave.'

'What time is it?' Shirley asked, lifting her head out of the bin.

'Nearly seven,' Bella replied. 'You lost your watch?'

'It's being temperamental. Shouldn't we synchronise them or something?'

Bella smiled a gentle smile. 'We're all in the same van, darlin'. Don't worry about the time. You just stick with me.'

* * *

At 7 a.m., Dolly made her way down the side street to the market traders' car park. The overalls with their heavy padding made her waddle as she walked. Her hair was greased back and flattened to her head and she wore a ski-mask on top of her head. Rolled up, it looked just like a woolly hat, but it was ready to be pulled over her face in an instant.

Two men unloading crates of fruit didn't pay any attention to her, and another man she passed said, 'Morning, mate.' So, he thought she was a fella. Perfect.

Taking the tarpaulin off the laundry van, Dolly chucked it into the back. She then felt for the key beneath the right wheel arch, but couldn't immediately find it. Had Linda forgotten to leave it there? She got down on her knees and looked under the arch, but still couldn't find it. The two men looked over. Dolly tried to control her panic as she felt all round the wheel. Then a glint of metal on the ground under the wheel axle caught her eye. She breathed a sigh of relief and picked up the key.

Dolly got into the laundry van and, taking deep breaths to calm herself, checked the hockey bag containing the shotgun and sledgehammer was still there. She opened the bag, placed the sledgehammer on top a pile of laundry near the rear doors and placed the shotgun under the driver's seat. Next, she climbed into the seat and pulled the harness over her shoulders, buckling it up and pulling the straps as tight as she could. She rocked back and forth to make certain she was secure.

Placing the key in the ignition, she turned it and the engine cranked over but didn't start. She tried two more times without success. '*Come on, come on . . .*' Dolly whispered. Out of the corner of her eye, she could see the two market traders looking over in her direction, but she didn't dare look at them in case they came over to help her. Dolly dipped her head to regain composure. *Oh, Linda . . . I'm gonna kill you if this doesn't start.* Dolly had tested the van, she was familiar with it; why wasn't it working now?

'Pull the bloody choke out and pump the accelerator, mate!' one of the market men shouted. Dolly remembered what Linda had told her.

The engine started instantly and, once ticking over, it sounded good. Dolly raised her hand in thanks. Crunching into first gear, Dolly let her foot off the clutch too quickly, sending the van lurching forwards. She could hear the men laughing at her. 'Fucking idiot!' one of them shouted. She ignored them. She just wanted to get out of there.

* * *

Back in the lock-up, Bella lifted up the chainsaw to test it out one more time. She'd padded up her shoulders so much she looked like a weightlifter on steroids. As she pulled the cord to start the saw, it slipped out of her hand. She'd never tried to start the saw wearing elbow length rubber gloves before and her hands were sweating profusely inside them. After a couple more attempts, she got the hang of it. She noticed Linda looking over at her hands.

'You're obsessed, woman! I got gloves on, for Chrissakes. I got 'em on, all right?' Bella said as she put the chainsaw in the rear of the van.

Linda looked over at Shirley. It wasn't the fact she hadn't put on her gloves yet that angered her. 'You got eye make-up on! You've bloody got eye make-up on!'

'No, I ain't!' Shirley shouted. 'It's no sleep and puking makes me look like this.'

As Bella passed Linda she whispered, 'Lay off her, all right? It'll only take a couple of seconds to wipe it off.'

'It ain't make-up!' Shirley repeated, moving towards Linda so she could see her close up. 'Leave me alone – just leave me alone! I'm not stupid.'

Bella stepped between them, 'Pack it in! You ain't mad with each other, you're stressed. But keep a lid on it, yeah?' Linda put a gentle hand on Shirley's shoulder; no more words were needed.

Linda opened the driver's door of the van, climbed in and tucked her shotgun under the passenger seat.

Bella put her arm around Shirley's shoulders. 'It's time for us to go. Dolly will be on her way to her start position. This is it, ladies . . . you good and ready?'

Shirley nodded, as did Linda. 'Let's do it!'

Bella and Shirley heaved open the garage doors for Linda to drive out, then closed and locked them before jumping in the back of the van. None of them noticed that the garage doors where the Alsatian lived were open, nor saw the dark-haired man in the BMW watching them.

* * *

Eight months ago, to the day, Terry Miller, Joe Pirelli and Jimmy Nunn had driven a van from this very same lock-up to do the very same robbery.

'Let's go!' Terry shouted, and a thumbs-up from Jimmy told him that they were all set. While Jimmy's hand was in the air, Terry clocked Harry's watch on his wrist. 'Bleedin' 'ell! Nice watch!'

Jimmy turned and smiled. 'He said he was trading it in for the latest model as soon as this is all over. Suits me, don't it?' Jimmy turned his wrist to let the light catch the diamond-encrusted face.

Terry looked at Joe and they both smirked. 'That's not the only model Harry's trading in after this job,' Terry sniggered, nodding towards an oblivious Jimmy. 'His missus is a right little raver and Jim can't keep up with her. But Harry can . . .'

Joe laughed as Jimmy pulled out of the lock-up. 'A watch in exchange for his bird. Seems like a good deal to me.'

CHAPTER 30

It didn't take Dolly long to get from the market traders' underground car park to her start point, about two minutes away from the security firm's depot in Battersea. She was now parked up in a side street with the engine running. She could see the depot entrance from where she was and, as the heavy iron gates opened, she knew the security wagon would come out, turn right and then right again at the end of the road . . . towards her. The sky was clear, the roads were clear – conditions were perfect. The rush hour traffic was just getting out of bed and London had no idea what was about to happen.

Timing was imperative, as the gap between the security wagon and the car in front of it widened – this was where Dolly's laundry van had to end up; right in front of the security wagon. There could be nothing in between them.

The security wagon was forty yards away, then thirty. At twenty yards, Dolly calmly pulled out into the road. She had timed it perfectly. The security wagon didn't even have to brake to let her out.

As they travelled along York Road towards Waterloo Bridge roundabout, Dolly realised how important it had been to get the route plan. It would only be a matter of minutes now before they turned left at the roundabout and northwards over Waterloo Bridge towards the Strand underpass. Dolly hoped to God the girls had left the lock-up and were in position.

As they headed towards the Strand underpass, Dolly moved out slightly to get a better view in her nearside mirror. Linda was in position, behind the security wagon. Dolly moved back into lane and slowed to twenty miles per hour to allow the vehicles in front to pull away from her. Then she pressed her foot hard down on the accelerator and watched the speedometer.

The laundry van picked up speed quicker than she expected – thirty, thirty-five, forty, as they entered the underpass. Dolly glanced in the wing mirror; the security wagon was right behind her, right on her tail. Dolly pressed the accelerator further; as the speedometer reached fifty, she saw the glimmer of light at the end of the underpass and pulled her balaclava down over her face. She glanced in the wing mirror again and, judging that the gap between her and the security wagon was just right, she slammed on the brakes. The security wagon smashed into the back of the laundry van, the front of the wagon totally crumpling as it was brought to an instant halt. Dolly was thrown forward, but the harness protected her from the full force of the impact.

Grinding the van's gear into first, she moved sharply forwards a few feet and then hard into reverse, slamming the laundry van's rear bumper into the crippled wagon. Dolly could hear the crunch of metal, the shattering of glass and then the sound of hissing steam coming from the wagon's radiator. She thanked God for the harness – she'd been jerked about so hard she thought her chest would crack open. Undoing the buckle, she grabbed the gas mask from the gear stick and dived into the back of the van. She stood at the rear door, gas mask on, shotgun hanging by her side from the makeshift belt, sledgehammer in hand. Then she kicked the back doors of the van wide open and threw the sledgehammer right at the centre of the security wagon's windscreen. The reinforced glass didn't even crack. Dolly swung her shotgun up into position, chest high, and pointed it directly at the two stunned, panic-stricken security guards.

'DON'T MOVE!' she screamed. Her voice sounding deep, distorted and frightening.

The security guards lifted their hands above their heads. One shouted to the guard in the back: 'They're armed!'

At exactly the same time, Shirley flung open the back doors of their follow van and hurled two smoke canisters at the cars behind them. Instantly, the smoke began to billow and hiss, clouding visibility. She then clambered on top of the security wagon and, removing wire cutters from her pocket, cut the radio aerial.

Grabbing the sawn-off from under the passenger seat, Linda took up position at the rear of the follow van. A man was getting out of his Fiat, but when Linda raised the gun and waved it at him, he quickly got back in and locked the doors, just as another car slammed into the back of him. The second driver put her car into reverse, but it stalled. Linda ran over and smashed the windscreen with the butt of the shotgun. The terrified woman screamed and covered her face, giving Linda plenty of time to grab the ignition keys and throw them away. Then she stepped back to her initial position and stood, legs apart, with the shotgun raised.

Bella leapt from the follow van behind Shirley, ran to the nearside of the security wagon and started up the chainsaw. Hot sparks flew around the side of the van as the saw cut through the metal like butter.

Inside the back of the van, the sound was deafening and the guard trembled in fear as he watched the blade emerge through the metal. He had no idea what was on the other side, no idea what or who was coming through at him, no idea if he was going to live or die.

It took less than thirty seconds for Bella to make a cut big enough to peel the metal back. Shirley handed Bella her shotgun and she stuck it through the hole she'd cut. She waved the barrel of the gun towards the rear doors and the guard opened up.

As Bella stepped into the back of the security wagon, the terrified guard unlocked the money cabinet. She then forced him out of the van. Linda pointed her shotgun at him and indicated that he should lie on the ground. Shaking with fear, the guard did exactly as he was told.

Shirley climbed into the back of the security wagon and started to cut through the interior wire cage with her cutters. This was the slowest part of the process and, after a few seconds, Bella nudged

Shirley out of the way, fired up the chainsaw again and, with one swipe, cut enough of the wire cage away to access the money bags. Shirley then began stuffing them into the open rucksack on Bella's back and, as soon as it was full, she slapped Bella on the shoulder.

Terrified members of the public watched from the safety of their cars as Bella took over from Linda. Holding the shotgun up to keep the public and the guards at bay, Linda ran to the wagon so Shirley could fill her rucksack. Linda's breath heaved, and her wet ski-mask dragged in and out of her mouth. As Shirley filled her rucksack, Linda could feel it getting heavier. Once it was full, she stuffed the rest of the money into Shirley's rucksack.

As Linda and Shirley jumped out of the security wagon, Shirley caught her rucksack on the door latch and dangled there like a rag doll. Linda was already sprinting towards the exit of the underpass on the Strand side, but Bella was quickly at Shirley's side. Once she was unhooked, they both followed Linda as fast as their legs could carry them under the cumbersome weight of a third of a million pounds each.

* * *

Dolly still stood in position in the rear of the laundry van, her heart beating like mad as first Linda and then Bella ran past her. She looked out of the van and saw two men running quickly behind Shirley. One of them dived forward and rugby-tackled her to the ground with a heavy thud. Her padding cushioned her fall, but she twisted her ankle.

Quick as a flash, Dolly leapt from the back of the laundry van and fired a shot into the air. Both have-a-go heroes hurled themselves flat on their stomachs with their hands covering their heads as shattered ceiling tiles from the underpass showered down on them. A shard of tile lodged itself into the neck of one of them and he started screaming that he'd been shot.

Shirley clambered to her feet and ran precariously towards the exit of the underpass. She only managed a few steps before she was in trouble and started to hobble from the pain and instant swelling in her ankle. But she carried on and didn't look back.

Dolly looked at the carnage they were leaving behind and thanked God that they'd not seriously hurt anyone. She'd never been so scared in her entire life. Members of the public were lying down across the front seats of their cars; the guard from the back of the security wagon was face down on the ground, as were the have-a-go heroes. The power was exhilarating – but she had to get the hell out of there.

She glanced up the underpass to see how far Shirley had got. It wasn't far and she was now dragging her injured leg behind her, while Linda and Bella were nowhere to be seen. Behind Dolly, the guards in the front of the security wagon were opening their doors to get out. She still had one live cartridge left in the double-barrelled shotgun and as she leapt into the back of the laundry van she fired it above the roof of the security wagon. The two guards ducked and ran back down the underpass towards the end they'd entered.

Linda and Bella had made it to the parked getaway van with the fake GLC logos on the side, but there was still no sign of Shirley coming out of the underpass. They threw their rucksacks in the back of the van and Bella climbed in after them while Linda jumped in the driver's seat and started the engine. At first Bella thought Linda was driving off without Shirley, but then she shouted: 'Hold on tight!' and screeched across the front of the oncoming traffic. Cars swerved, mounted pavements and hit each other as Linda bounced over the central reservation and headed back towards the underpass. As Shirley hobbled out into the daylight, Linda pulled the handbrake on hard and the van skidded into a 180-degree turn so that the back was now facing Shirley. Bella flung open the rear door and, with her arms outstretched, grabbed hold of Shirley and hauled her in. Linda, with gears grinding and tyres spinning, burning rubber, accelerated away.

Dolly had been right on Shirley's heels in the laundry van and had been about to pick her up when she saw her leap into Bella's arms . . . they were safe! Dolly floored the van and drove off in the same direction as Linda, swerving onto the pavement to avoid the chaos Linda had left behind.

* * *

In the distance, Dolly could hear the sound of police sirens and knew she could be in trouble. The speed of her getaway had been curtailed because of Shirley. It was now or never. Slowing as she reached a side alley, Dolly grabbed her small holdall, slid open the van door and jumped, already running in the air before her feet hit the ground.

The laundry van swerved across the pavement and hurtled straight into a shop window. The glass shattered inwards and two women shoppers ran for their lives. Dolly ran down the side alley, ripping off her gas mask and gloves and throwing them into a pallet bin. As she neared the end of the alley, she slowed to a walk in the hope that she'd have got her breath back by the time she emerged and mingled with the commuters. She rolled her balaclava back up so it looked like a woolly hat again, stepped out into the crowds and headed towards the Victorian underground toilets near the Transport Museum in Covent Garden.

* * *

Linda had driven up Kingsway and then taken a left into the back streets off the Strand, towards the multi-storey car park. She pulled up in Floral Street near Covent Garden market, where it was reasonably quiet. Linda and Shirley handed Bella their balaclavas and she put them in a black bin bag along with hers. Bella jumped out of the back of the van and, checking no one was watching, Bella ripped the magnetic GLC signs from the Escort van and snapped them in half before putting them in the bin bag as well. Next, she removed the two false plates, exposing the real number plates underneath. The false plates were the final things to go into the bin bag, before Bella tied it up and threw it onto a pile of rubbish awaiting collection. There were only a few people about, and none of them seemed to take any notice. *Thank God you're all engrossed in your own lives*, Bella thought to herself as she jumped back in the passenger seat next to Linda.

Shirley was lying in the back of the van surrounded by the rucksacks, sobbing her heart out. Bella turned in her seat and, reaching over, took hold of Shirley's hand and squeezed it tight. 'We did it, Shirley, we did it. We did it!'

* * *

Dolly was gasping for breath by the time she reached the toilets. She gripped the metal safety rail for support as she hurried down the steps, straight into a cubicle and sat down on the toilet seat. She was sweating like mad and felt as if she was about to have a heart attack. As her breathing calmed, she felt so dizzy that she had to brace her hands against the cubicle wall to stop herself from fainting. Dolly closed her eyes and focused on breathing normally. As her body started to calm, her mind was screaming: *I did it! Dear God, Harry. HARRY, I DID IT!*

Dolly took a number of deep breaths, exhaling slowly and, when her pulse rate had subsided enough, she stood up and removed her balaclava, overall and plimsolls. She already had on a dark sweater and trousers under the overall and, opening the holdall, she removed some shoes, a thin waist-length jacket and a scarf. When she had put everything on, she took out her handbag and put it over her shoulder. Checking her watch, she hoped and prayed that the others had made it safely to the multi-storey car park. She was tempted to go straight there as it was so near, but she had to stick to the plan.

* * *

Linda drove the van into the three-storey car park, nervously wondering if Dolly had managed to make a safe getaway. Bella saw the look of concern on her face.

'Don't you waste time worrying about Dolly. She's a tough old cow.'

Linda smiled. Bella was a real smart-arse mind-reader at times.

Dropping Shirley by her Mini estate on level one, Linda parked near Dolly's Mercedes on the upper level and she and Bella loaded the rucksacks full of money into the boot before going over to Linda's Ford Capri. Both women took one last look at their money, all piled up in the boot of Dolly's Merc.

'We gave her such a hard time, Bella,' Linda said. 'But here we are with all the money. We could just as easily put it in my boot as in hers. She never questioned us once and I just feel—'

Bella slammed the boot of the Merc. 'She knows.'

Opening the boot of Linda's Capri, they took some clothes from their suitcases and went down the stairwell to the ladies' toilet on the ground floor to change. There was no sign of Shirley, so they both assumed that she had disposed of her overalls and gone straight off in the clothes she had on underneath.

* * *

Having regained her composure, Dolly left the toilets. As luck would have it, a rubbish truck was held up in traffic, so as she walked casually by the rear of it she threw her holdall into the back. Crossing the market square, she headed up James Street to Covent Garden tube station, which was by now bustling with commuters on their way to work. She bought a day travelcard and headed slowly down the long flight of stairs to the platform. She could hear the rumble of the trains down below. It felt good to have finally stopped running.

* * *

Linda was changed and ready to leave in no time, though her hand was shaking so badly that she'd smudged her lipstick over her cheek and had to redo it twice. Bella and Linda gave each other a big hug before going their separate ways. Bella, now wearing a smart coat and matching chic hat, walked from the car park carrying her suitcase and hailed a taxi on the main road. 'Luton Airport, darlin',' she said as she got in the cab.

The taxi driver couldn't believe his luck. 'Glad to get out of the city, miss,' he said. 'I've had a hell of a morning! Something was up in the Strand underpass first thing. There's been massive traffic jams . . .'

* * *

Dolly got off the tube two stops along at Piccadilly Circus, crossed the platform and took the next tube back to Covent Garden. She stood at the bottom of the deep stairwell and looked up briefly before deciding the lift was a better option: she'd had enough exercise for one day. Once out in the street, she walked casually towards the car park, taking a moment here and there to do some window-shopping. Police cars were patrolling slowly up and down Long Acre, but elsewhere traffic had come to a standstill. It didn't worry her. She'd no need to make a fast getaway now. She was just another woman out on a shopping trip.

* * *

As Linda drove out of the car park along level one, she saw Shirley's car, stopped and got out to see what was up. Shirley was sitting in the driver's seat, still in her overalls, hunched over in agony. Linda opened the car door. This wasn't good. Shirley should have been on her way ages ago. They had planes to catch.

'Come on, girl,' Linda said. 'I know you're in pain, but you gotta work through it for now. At least get that overall off and, when you get to the airport, you can nip to the loo and change.'

Shirley limped out of the car and supported herself on the roof, while Linda helped her out of the overalls and put them in a bin bag.

'I'll bin these for you,' Linda said. 'You pick up the pace now. Let's get back on track.'

Shirley got back in the car, opened the glovebox and removed some make-up. She looked up at Linda through her tears and gave her a weak smile.

Linda laughed. 'No matter what happens, you always have to look your best, don't you?' Returning to her Capri, she drove off.

As she entered the car park, Dolly saw Linda's car drive off down the road. The relief she felt was so overwhelming, she could hardly stop herself running up the stairwell to her Merc. When she reached the top level and opened the boot, she smiled. All three rucksacks were neatly laid together. Once in the car, Dolly opened the glove box, removed a wig and dark sunglasses and donned her second disguise of the day.

On the way out of the car park, she nearly hit Shirley's Mini estate as it lurched out of the parking bay, stopped and lurched forward again, hitting the car park wall and denting the bumper. Dolly screeched to a halt, jumped out and raced across to Shirley. Before Dolly could ask, Shirley had opened the window. She was in floods of tears.

'It's my ankle,' she moaned. 'I can't hold the clutch down properly it hurts so much. I don't know what—'

Dolly didn't wait for her to finish. Pulling the door open, she helped Shirley out of the Mini and supported her as she limped over to the Merc. Dolly opened the passenger door, dropped the front seat down and pushed Shirley onto the back. Shirley winced in pain.

'There's a rug. Cover yourself – right over your head – and hurry. Where're your flight tickets?' Dolly asked.

'In me handbag under the driver's seat . . . and one of me plimsolls just fell off.'

Dolly ran to the Mini, retrieved Shirley's handbag and plimsoll and chucked them on the back seat beside her.

'The keys, the keys, Dolly! They're in the ignition. And my case – what about my case?'

Dolly slammed the passenger door shut and got back in the Merc. 'There's no room for your case and we have to go now. Shut up and cover yourself.'

With Shirley hidden by the blanket and sobbing in the back seat, Dolly began the drive to the airport. All around Covent Garden the police sirens screamed; traffic remained at a standstill. Dolly realised there was no way she was going to get Shirley to the airport any time soon – and in any case being seen at an airport together would be a really bad idea, even if Dolly was only dropping her off. They'd have to go back to Dolly's and work out their next move from there.

* * *

It was 9.45 a.m. when Dolly at last drove into Totteridge Lane, which was deserted apart from a few parked cars. Her heart thumped as she turned into her driveway. As she got out of the car to unlock the garage doors, she whispered to Shirley to stay covered and keep quiet. Shirley, head fully covered by the blanket, had no idea where she was.

Once inside the privacy of her garage, Dolly opened the passenger door and flipped the seat down. 'We're in the garage at my house, darlin'. You can come out now.'

As Dolly helped Shirley out of the car, the sound of the police sirens made them both freeze. They were getting closer and closer.

'Oh, my God, it's the police, Dolly! They got us, Dolly . . . What we gonna do?' Shirley exclaimed, her voice getting higher-pitched with every word.

Resisting the temptation to slap Shirley, Dolly instead put her hand gently over her mouth. 'Ssssh,' she said. Peering through the tiny window in the garage door, she saw a police car pulling up outside her house, blue light flashing. Two uniform and two plain-clothes officers got out and she recognised Detective Sergeant Fuller. Scurrying back over to Shirley, Dolly pushed her back into the rear seat of the car. 'Cover yourself up again, don't move or make a sound,' Dolly whispered. Ripping off her wig and dark glasses, she threw them on top of Shirley, and then covered her up again with the blanket.

Dolly unlocked the adjoining door from the garage into her kitchen. She had to think fast. Pulling off her sweater, she threw it in the utility room laundry basket, then she rummaged around until she found the dirty dressing gown she'd dropped in there the day before. Wolf leapt out of his basket with excitement on seeing her, yapping round her feet and jumping up and down with joy. Dolly flicked on the electric coffee percolator. She'd last used it at 6 a.m. and knew it was still at least three quarters full. 'Not now, darling,' she said to Wolf. 'Mummy's got things on her mind.' Next, she opened a cupboard, took out a packet of cereal, emptied some into a bowl, grabbed a bottle of milk from the fridge and poured some over the cereal. She'd never moved so quickly in her life.

The doorbell started ringing. Someone was keeping their finger on the buzzer. Dolly bet her life it was that arrogant teenager, Fuller.

Wolf ran towards the door, barking and jumping up at the shadows he could see though the stained glass.

Dolly opened a packet of Ryvita, took a deep breath, exhaled and then took a bite of the biscuit. The doorbell continued to ring. Trying to steady her breathing, Dolly shouted, 'All right, all right, I'm comin'. I'm comin'!' Out in the hallway, she snatched Wolf up into her arms before finally opening the door. As she thought, it was Fuller who was ringing. The other officers stood behind him waiting for their instructions.

Fuller walked right past Dolly into her hallway. He didn't even bother to produce his warrant card. He almost pushed Dolly into the living room while one officer headed up the stairs, and the other two began a search of the downstairs rooms.

'Get dressed or put a coat on, Mrs Rawlins. You're coming to the station,' Fuller instructed.

'You've got no right! No bleedin' right. You don't even have a warrant!' Dolly shouted, poking her finger at him.

With a smug grin on his face, Fuller pulled a search warrant out of his coat pocket. 'Want to bet?' he said, and headed towards Dolly's kitchen.

Once Fuller was in her kitchen, only one door stood between him and her garage. Between him and Shirley. But under her dressing gown, she was fully dressed. That would be impossible to explain.

'What are you lot looking for this time?' Dolly asked, stopping Fuller in the hall.

'We'll tell you down the nick, so go get dressed – unless you want to come down the station in a dressing gown?'

Dolly's heart was thumping like crazy as she raced up the stairs to her bedroom. God forbid Fuller should search the Merc: he'd not only find Shirley but the rucksacks full of the stolen money. Keeping up a steady flow of abuse might get her dragged off more quickly, so she grabbed her coat and raced back downstairs just as Fuller laid his hand on the garage door handle.

'What's this all about?' Dolly shouted. 'I'm going to have your badge for this! Take me to the station right now. Let's get it over with. Come on – if we're going.'

Ignoring her, Fuller opened the garage door, leant forward and looked inside. As he fumbled around on the wall for a light switch, Dolly shouted, 'Right!' and stormed off towards the front door.

Fuller whipped round. 'Where you going?'

'To walk my bleedin' dog,' Dolly shouted. 'If you ain't coming right now, I'm off.'

Fuller slammed the garage door shut and paced after Dolly. 'You're not going anywhere other than the station, Mrs Rawlins.'

It was Fuller who now led the way towards the front door, with Dolly in tow, still nagging and badgering him.

'I've had enough of you effin' lot! The sooner you ask your stupid questions, the sooner I can get home to me housework . . . you'd better be bringing me back an' all.'

As Fuller opened the front door, he said, 'Put the dog down, please. He's not coming.'

* * *

Shirley had heard Fuller's voice when he'd opened the door to the garage and, fearful of making the smallest sound, she had bitten down hard on her hand, her teeth almost cutting through the skin. She lay there listening to the commotion, which had now moved outside onto the driveway.

Dolly was still shouting the odds. 'If he's pissed on the carpet by the time I get back, you're getting the cleaning bill!' she yelled. 'And which nick we goin' to this time?'

'The big house,' Fuller replied 'Scotland Yard.'

Shirley edged out of the Merc, limped over to the garage door and peered through the tiny window, like Dolly had done not ten minutes ago. Dolly was pushed into the police car, and then they were gone. In the sudden silence, Shirley leant against the car, her chest heaving up and down. It had been a very close call. If the officers had touched the bonnet of the Merc they would have known that Dolly had been out. Shirley's mind raced as she replayed everything that had just happened and tried to work out what to do next. Dolly had just saved her neck by being so loud and angry and annoying with the police . . . in fact she might well have just sacrificed herself. What Shirley couldn't work out was how on earth the police had got here so quickly. Why? Why had they arrested Dolly and taken her away?

* * *

Eddie Rawlins waited for the police car to leave before he inched back up into a sitting position. Bill had called earlier and told him to get his arse round to Dolly's house and wait for her to come home. When Bill told Eddie that Dolly was doing Harry's raid, he'd almost pissed himself laughing. 'How the 'ell's a bird gonna do a raid like that?' But when Bill mentioned that she had Harry's ledgers, with the plan all laid out for her, Eddie believed it.

As he watched the police car disappear round the corner, Eddie wondered what the hell was going on. How and why had the Old Bill turned up at Dolly's house so quickly? What had gone wrong? Eddie scratched the stubble on his chin. He supposed it was possible that someone grassed her up, but the officers hadn't stayed long and they certainly didn't walk out with bags full of money. Could they possibly have missed it? Was it still in the house or somewhere else? Eddie thought hard about what to do next . . . but he wasn't one for making big decisions. He could go and find a phone box and call Bill, or he could nip into Dolly's house and see if she'd left a million quid lying round anywhere. Eddie went for the easiest option.

Shirley could hear Wolf howling for Dolly in the kitchen. As she limped inside to comfort the little dog, she heard a bubbling sound and, spinning round, saw the electric coffee percolator boiling over. God, she was jumpy! As she bent down to pick Wolf up, he turned his head sharply towards the closed kitchen door that led to the hallway and started to yap. Shirley tried to calm him, but he continued with his yap-yap-yapping at the kitchen door.

Eddie had decided to kill two birds with one stone – he'd break into Dolly's house, take a brief look round and, whether he found anything or not, he could then call Bill from there. No need to find a phone box.

He slowly and quietly forced the French window in the living room with a jemmy and made his way straight to the kitchen in order to get to Dolly's Merc in the garage. If Dolly had indeed just returned home from an early morning armed robbery, unless she'd dumped it somewhere on the way, this was the only place the money could be.

Eddie opened the kitchen door an inch or two to make sure Wolf knew it was him before opening it fully. Eddie knew that even the smallest dog, if frightened, could be a vicious bastard, but Wolf was yapping his welcome. Relieved, Eddie opened the door fully and was stunned to see a blonde standing over by the percolator. Panicked at being rumbled breaking into Dolly's house. Eddie raised his hands and charged towards Shirley. She'd seen his face, and he didn't like that.

For Shirley, it was like the moment when Tony Fisher had been about to attack her. *Not this time, you bastard*, she thought and, screaming like a banshee, she took an almighty swing at Eddie with her right hand.

Eddie had done a bit of sparring back in the day, with Harry. He raised his left hand to defend himself from the punch and then swung with his right at the same time, catching Shirley on the jaw. She was in such a state and her ankle was still so weak that she stumbled on her heels and fell backwards at the same time as Eddie's fist made contact, which turned it into a glancing blow rather than a full-on punch. Shirley was back at him in an instant, scratching at his eyes and kicking him with her good leg for all she was worth. Eddie grabbed her wrists hard and held her arms apart.

'Where's the fucking money, you bitch?' he screamed and, releasing one hand, he slapped her hard.

At first Wolf thought it was some kind of game, and jumped up on his hind legs, yapping and wagging his tail. But the tone of anger in Eddie's voice, followed by the slap to Shirley's face and then her piercing scream, was enough for the little dog. He sank his teeth into Eddie's leg. The little teeth didn't hurt that much, but it took Eddie by surprise, and in that split second Shirley broke from his grip. As she turned towards the kitchen counter she heard Wolf let out an ear-piercing yelp.

Grabbing the coffee pot, Shirley pulled the lid off and threw the still bubbling brown liquid into Eddie's face, aiming for his eyes. He screamed in pain as the boiling coffee burnt and blistered his face and his neck. Half-blind, he turned and ran from the kitchen into the hall, crashing into a table and knocking over a vase of flowers.

Shirley heard the vase break as it hit the wooden hallway floor, then she heard the front door opening and Eddie's heavy footsteps running off down the gravel path, followed by a car starting up then speeding away. In the eerie silence that followed, Shirley crumpled into a heap on a kitchen chair and held her head in her hands. Her jaw ached, her ankle throbbed and her head spun. She began sobbing, a mixture of fear and relief. She had no idea who the intruder was, but he was clearly after the money, which meant he must have known about the robbery. Oh – how she wished that Dolly was with her right now!

Wiping her eyes, Shirley looked round the kitchen. Coffee stains were all over the wall and even on the ceiling by the open door to the hallway, but she didn't think that Dolly would give two hoots about any of that. Then Shirley realised – it was silent. 'Wolf?' she whispered. 'Wolfie?' She staggered to her feet. Perhaps Wolf had followed the man out into the street? But as she glanced towards the corner of the kitchen, she realised that things were far, far worse.

'Oh no, no, no . . . please, God, no . . .'

Wolf lay motionless on the floor. Shirley knelt beside him, silently begging. *Please let him be* OK . . . She touched his little body, but there was no response. A small trickle of blood ran from Wolf's mouth. Shirley sat on the kitchen floor next to the dead body of Dolly's most beloved companion and cried. Stroking Wolf's soft white fur, she realised what comfort he must have brought Dolly every time she held him in her arms. How was Dolly going to cope without him? She had no one in her life to love her now.

CHAPTER 31

Arnie Fisher poured a dose of Bisodol into the plastic cap provided with the bottle, gulping it down and burping loudly. The death of Carlos had shaken him badly. It was not that he genuinely cared about him; it was the rumours being spread. And not just about his connection to Carlos – Tony's assault on Shirley Miller had got about, too. Arnie had attempted to control his brother but now he felt that everything was closing in on him.

Arnie began to sweat. What really terrified him was that Boxer Davis might have been telling the truth about Harry Rawlins. If Boxer was right and Harry Rawlins was alive, there would be severe repercussions. Arnie had been fencing stolen goods for Rawlins for many years, as well as having his hand in various other frauds and robberies. He had to restrain his crazy brother.

Tony chose that moment to kick open Arnie's office door. 'Look,' he said and held up an early edition of the *Evening Standard*. 'Front page: Daring Armed Robbery on a Security Wagon.' He slapped the newspaper down on the desk in front of Arnie. 'The scream's gone up. Four masked men – and they've got away with fuckin' hundreds of thousands. Whether you like it or not, that fucker's wife Dolly Rawlins has gotta have a hand in it. I'm gonna go there and slit the bitch's throat . . .'

Arnie stood up and threw a large glass paperweight at his brother. It missed. He moved in front of the desk and grabbed Tony's shirt collar, sweating profusely. 'You listen to me,' he said urgently. 'We need to back off and go to ground. You've already put the frighteners on her, and I'm not havin' that son of a bitch Harry Rawlins slit *my* throat.'

Pushing his brother away, Arnie went back to his desk and unlocked a drawer. He took out a thick wedge of bank notes.

'Take this and get the first flight out of here, to Spain. Stay there until you hear from me. This time, Tony, you obey me or I swear to God you'll get the same treatment as Boxer Davis.'

Tony smirked and reached for the money, tucking it into the inside pocket of his coat. 'You're the boss,' he said.

Arnie replied softly. 'You'd better believe it, because I'm protecting you. Until I say so, don't show your face here again. I'll make sure the boys in Spain look after you.'

In the past, Tony had always been able to argue with his brother, but he had never seen Arnie so determined. He could almost smell his fear. 'I'll leave tonight,' he said.

'Good boy.' Arnie watched his brother walk out. He hoped this time he would listen, because as soon as he'd seen to some things, he'd be joining him in Spain. Arnie picked up the newspaper and stared at the headlines. With Harry Rawlins dead, Arnie had been free of him and his infamous ledgers. If Harry Rawlins was alive – well, Arnie felt as though he had been given a life sentence.

* * *

Dolly sat in the interview room at Scotland Yard waiting for Fuller. She'd already looked through the pile of mugshots on the table and been asked if she recognised any of them as associates of her deceased husband. Even if she had, there was no way she was going to say anything. It might have got the police off her back, but she didn't want word getting out she was a grass. Dolly looked at her watch: it was eleven thirty. She tapped her foot, hoping to irritate the policewoman standing by the door. She hated her expressionless face and hatchet eyes.

'Is there any chance of a cup of coffee?' Dolly asked. There was no response. The policewoman sucked her teeth. 'Listen, Uri Gellar – you keep staring like that and your handcuffs will start bending!' Dolly said sarcastically. Still the officer didn't flinch.

Dolly lit another cigarette and looked at her watch again. 'It's my dog, you see. He'll be going nuts by now and he can only keep his legs crossed for so long. So can I, as it happens. Oi! I'm talking to you! Any idea how long they're going to keep me here? I mean, what's this all about anyway?' Dolly waved her cigarette around as she pointed at the mugshots in front of her, scattering ash carelessly over the photos. 'I told you I don't know none of these. What's he supposed to have done anyway, this coloured bloke you're after?' Still no reaction. Dolly began to whistle the theme tune from *Dixon of Dock Green*.

DS Fuller walked in and sat down opposite her. The press was going bananas. They were demanding to know what the police were doing about the robbery, whether they had any suspects and whether it was connected to the recent similar robbery where three men died. Fuller hadn't been able to get any sense out of DCI Saunders; he was like a rabbit caught in headlights. The whole office was in pandemonium.

Dolly sucked on her cigarette. 'How long you gonna keep me here?'

Fuller looked at Dolly. 'As long as it takes.'

The door opened again and DCI Saunders walked in. He called Fuller over and they had a whispered conversation by the door. Dolly thought she heard something about bringing in the security guards in case it was an inside job, but she couldn't hear clearly.

'Excuse me,' Dolly said to DCI Saunders with feigned politeness. 'I hate to interrupt your conversation, but I've looked through your mugshots and there's no one I recognise or have seen before, so if you don't mind, I've got a dog at home waiting for me.'

Saunders went over to Dolly. 'Did your husband have any black associates, either as friends or on his payroll?'

Dolly paused as if was thinking about the question. 'No, not that I know of.'

'That's all then, Mrs Rawlins, you can go,' Saunders said, much to Dolly's surprise and Fuller's annoyance. He turned to the policewoman. 'Show Mrs Rawlins out,' he ordered.

As the policewoman opened the door, an officer led in the security guard who had been driving the van. He had small cuts to one side of his face. He passed within inches of Dolly, who stepped back, allowing him to enter the room.

After Dolly had gone, Fuller laid out the mugshots along the desk in front of the security guard. 'Do you recognise any of these men as being involved in the raid this morning?'

The guard was shaking. All he could say was that he thought one of the men had been black because of the colour of his eyes staring through the balaclava. Fuller sat down with a sigh and began going over everything again from start to finish, but he knew it was hopeless. The security guard was still in a state of shock – and all the suspects had been wearing masks.

* * *

Dolly returned to her house in a taxi, paid the fare and almost danced up the drive. She felt so good, so damned good. Opening the front door, she shouted for Shirley. She couldn't wait to reassure her that they were in the clear.

'I'm in the lounge,' Shirley called out.

Dolly launched in, talking nineteen to the dozen, going over everything that had happened, the questions the police had asked her and how they were already linking the robbery to a possible associate of Harry Rawlins. 'One of the security guards was there, Shirl, I mean right *there*. As close to me as you are now – and he never batted an eyelid.' Dolly checked her hair in the ornate gold mirror over the fireplace. 'Bloody hell, I look awful!' She laughed. 'They suspect one of the robbers was black . . . so I pity all the black lags in London tonight.'

'That's good,' Shirley said softly. She sat with her head bent, her bruised eye and cheek turned away from Dolly. She knew she had to tell her about Wolf, but she just couldn't get it out.

Dolly poured herself a large brandy. 'Want one, Shirl?'

'No thanks, Dolly. I do need to talk to you about something, though.'

'Go on, girl. What is it – something wrong?' Dolly asked. Just then the phone rang twice and stopped. 'Hang on a sec, Shirl . . .' Dolly held her hand up. A second later the phone rang again. This time she picked it up.

The person on the other end was clearly telling her a long tale. Eventually, Dolly said, 'Shirley's flight was cancelled, so she'll be with you a bit later than planned. Nothing at all to worry about. Have a nice holiday, love . . . yes, yes, everything's fine here.' Dolly put the phone down. 'That was Linda. She's through passport control and will be in the air soon. Everything's going to be—' As Dolly turned back to Shirley, she saw the cut from where Eddie's ring had dug into her beautiful skin, and the bruise now developing around it.

Slamming her brandy glass down on the telephone table, Dolly moved quickly to Shirley. 'Dear God, girl, what happened to you?' she asked as she sat down and took hold of Shirley's shaking hand.

'Someone broke in . . .' Shirley stuttered. 'They wanted to know where the money was . . .'

Dolly looked worried. 'You saw him?'

Shirley nodded.

'You know him? Did he hurt you, darlin'?'

Shirley shook her head. 'Not really.'

'The money. Did he take the money?'

Shirley looked up at Dolly. 'No, it's still in your car.'

Dolly's whole manner changed. She toughened up and, in an instant, was back to her usual self. 'How the hell did he get in? Did you let him in?'

'No! He broke in through your French doors at the back.'

The telephone rang three times and went silent, then two seconds later it rang again and Dolly picked up. Two rings for Linda, three rings for Bella – that was the code they'd agreed. Bella was also about to board her plane and was checking to see if everything was OK with Dolly. 'Everything's fine. Shirley didn't catch her plane because of her swollen ankle. She's with me and will be flying out in a couple of days. Have a nice time.' Dolly replaced the phone before Bella could ask any more questions and poured herself another brandy.

Shirley turned to Dolly. 'I swear I've never seen him before, Dolly! He just came at me and then he kicked . . .' Still Shirley couldn't get it out. She bent her head and covered her face.

Dolly sat down next to her again and put her hand on Shirley's knee. 'All right, love, just calm down and we'll go over it all. Here, have a sip of my brandy.' Dolly took Shirley's hands and cupped them round the crystal glass. 'You settle your nerves. I'll nip and let Wolf out before he waters the plants for me.'

Shirley had to say something before Dolly got to the lounge door. 'I'm sorry, Dolly. I'm so sorry.' Dolly paused. 'He was protecting me from the man. He bit him and – I didn't see exactly, but Wolf was right in the middle of all the scuffling, biting and barking, and then . . .' Shirley broke down in tears. Dolly's reaction was like nothing Shirley had ever seen from her before. She looked like a lost and frightened child.

'Please tell me he's all right.' Dolly nervously picked at a thread of loose cotton on the seam of her trousers; all she could do was stare at Shirley. 'Where is he?'

'I put him in his basket,' Shirley said, broken-voiced.

Shirley followed Dolly into the kitchen and watched as she knelt beside the motionless little dog. She picked up his limp body, held him close and nursed him in her arms. He was still warm as Dolly nuzzled his neck. Her voice was filled with grief. 'Oh, my little darlin', my poor little darlin'.'

Dolly took two or three minutes to say goodbye to Wolf, while Shirley stood silently in the kitchen doorway. When the moment was right, Dolly visibly seemed to stiffen; her whole body went rigid, her mouth hard and tight. She gently put Wolf down in his basket and stroked his head. Then she got up, opened a drawer and took out a lace table cloth, which she laid out on the kitchen floor. She gently wrapped the cloth round Wolf's body, like a baby at a christening. She picked him up and turned to Shirley.

'Bury him in the garden, in his basket, with his bowls and leads as well. Anything you see belonging to him gets buried with him.' Dolly kissed Wolf's head, handed him to Shirley and picked up her car keys.

'Where are you going, Dolly? Please don't leave me on my own,' Shirley pleaded.

'I've got things to do, but I won't be long. We'll leave the country together in a day or so. There's no reason for me to stay now, not with my baby gone. Close the garage doors for me after I've left.'

Dolly was out of the kitchen door and in the garage before Shirley could ask her anything else. She limped over to the basket, put Wolf in it, followed by his dog bowl and lead, and then carried everything out to the garden.

As she opened the garage doors and stood by her car, Dolly couldn't stop herself. The inner pain and numbing grief was just like the day her baby boy was stillborn in the hospital. Harry wasn't with her at the time – he'd been away on 'business' – and she'd been rushed to the hospital in an ambulance with stomach pains. It was weeks before her due date. Dolly could remember the kind midwife handing her over the still-warm body of her dead son. He was beautiful. His pale skin was perfect and, as she put her little finger in his hand, she sobbed her heart out. She was so proud of her little boy for trying so hard; he'd done so well to make it that far and she thanked him for the time they shared. She told him that he had his dad's features and that she was so very sad not to have known him for longer. The pain of her loss was compounded by having to lie in a ward filled with other women who gently cradled their newborns.

At the time, Dolly hadn't known how she would tell Harry when he eventually turned up at the hospital. He had been so happy when she fell pregnant; their love had grown even stronger and he had been so affectionate, promising to take great care of them both. He'd been immensely proud at the prospect of being a father – especially to a son – and in many ways Dolly was more upset for Harry than herself. She longed to give Harry everything he desired; she loved him so very much. She'd sensed the moment he'd arrived at the hospital; even before he walked through the doors to the maternity ward, she knew he was there.

She dreaded telling him the heart-breaking news but, as he walked through the swing doors and onto the ward, she knew from the look of sadness in his eyes that the doctor had already told him. Harry was never one freely to show emotion, but he did that day. They wept together and they held each other so tight that Dolly could still remember the feel of Harry's strong arms round her shoulders. She also remembered his voice as he whispered in her ear . . . 'Never again, Dolly. I can't lose any more.' And that was the moment that her hopes of a family disappeared.

When she and Harry returned home, he didn't go into work for weeks. He waited on her hand and foot until she was physically well again, bringing trays of food and drink to her bedside and even doing the housework – sort of.

Dolly leant her head against the roof of her car as she recalled how Harry had helped her deal with their tragic loss – the day he had come home with a tiny white bundle of fur and gently placed him on her lap.

'I think we should call him Wolf,' Harry had said with a loving smile. But his eyes had a different message. His eyes said: 'This is an end to it. This is your baby. Subject closed.' He wasn't being unkind; he was being practical. Their lives had to get back to how they were and that couldn't happen with all the sadness and mourning in the air. Life goes on.

Dolly recalled holding Wolf as a tiny puppy in her arms and rocking him like a baby. He had snuggled down and fallen asleep almost immediately. He had been so content – and so had she. But now . . . now she felt the pain of loss bursting her body open. A sound – not a cry, but a deep low sound of anguish and anger inched out of her. Dolly turned towards the garage wall and there was a sickening thud as she smashed her fist against it, then another and another as she punched the wall for a second and third time. Only when she saw the red patch on the wall from her bleeding knuckles did she realise what she was doing and stop. The pain that filled her chest filtered slowly to her hand and distracted her from wanting to curl up and die.

CHAPTER 32

Resnick wiped the remains of the egg yolk with a slice of bread, then sucked on it before swallowing it down and neatly placing his knife and fork on the plate. He slurped his tea and looked round the clean, orderly kitchen. His dirty frying pan and plate were the only things out of place. From upstairs, Resnick could hear the Irish DJ Terry Wogan burbling on his wife Kathleen's radio. Resnick sighed. *Jesus, I hope I'm good at golf.*

It was a long time since he'd played golf, so he set about looking for his set of clubs in the cupboard under the stairs. He had to chuck out Wellington boots, a shooting stick and an old upright Hoover to get to them. Some of the clubs were a bit rusty and his golf shoes were covered in mildew, but they'd be easy enough to clean. If he left them on newspaper on the kitchen table with the polish and brush by their side, Kathleen would clean them for him. That's how his shoes normally got polished.

He got a putter and four golf balls out of the bag. Placing his used tea mug on its side on the hallway floor, he practised putting the balls towards the mug. He was rubbish, but as he stood there, head down and focused, he smiled at the thought of having something to take his mind off work.

Upstairs, Kathleen could hear the golf balls hitting the hallway skirting board. She pursed her lips and called out. 'George! George, what on earth are you doing?'

Resnick hit the next ball hard, it went straight into the mug, spinning it round and breaking the bottom off it. 'Yeah!' Resnick yelled.

'George!'

The mug stopped spinning. The side of it facing him bore the legend: 'Best Boss'. It had been a Secret Santa Christmas present seven years ago. He knew it was from Alice, as she'd filled it to the top with his favourite chocolates and also bought him a quarter bottle of his favourite whisky. She was good like that – he'd mention something in passing, such as his favourite tipple, and she'd remember. Resnick stared at the mug for a moment, then at the skirting board behind it, then at the rest of the hallway. God, it was drab. There was the odd feminine touch here and there, but the paintwork and the decor was boring and unloved.

Resnick picked up his putter and golf ball and went upstairs.

Kathleen lay in bed, the newspapers and morning tea tray at her side. 'I'm going to paint the hallway,' Resnick said, placing his golf ball on the carpet and lining up his first bedroom shot.

Kathleen didn't even look up. She turned a page of the paper. 'Get dressed first, dear,' she mocked.

'I don't mean right this very minute. It'll take planning.'

'That's what you're doing now, is it? Planning?'

'I'm taking golf up again.' Resnick beamed.

'It'll do you good to get some fresh air,' she replied. 'Not to mention get you out from under my feet,' she added under her breath.

Resnick whacked the golf ball hard with the putter, it bounced off the skirting board, flew across the room, hit the wardrobe followed by the dressing table and bounced into Kathleen's slipper.

'Hole in one!' Resnick exclaimed, punching the air.

Kathleen ignored him. He was just trying to irritate her. He was a devil when he was bored. 'What colour? The hallway. What colour are you going to do it?'

'White?' Resnick said. Kathleen would tell him what colour he was going to paint it.

'Peach might be nice,' she said. 'It'll go with the lampshade I've bought and, if you carried it on into the lounge, peach would be the perfect colour to bring out the curtains.'

'Peach it is then,' Resnick said, not giving two hoots what colour the hallway or the lounge were. He fished his golf ball out of Kathleen's slipper and placed it back on the carpet. He was just about to swing his putter when he saw her glaring over the top of her glasses at him. He leant on his putter, like a walking stick. 'What have you got planned for today?' he asked.

Kathleen put her paper down, took her glasses off and smiled at Resnick. It unnerved him; she didn't do it often. 'I expect I'll be putting the under-stair cupboard back into some semblance of order. Then I'll wash up your breakfast things. Then I'll no doubt be polishing your golf shoes – and then, well, if you're painting, I'll be at Marjorie's for the rest of the day.' Kathleen put her glasses back on and returned to her newspaper.

Resnick looked at his wife sitting in their bed. He had more true and honest affection for Alice than he did for her. Alice was good to him; she tolerated his bad habits way better than Kathleen did and she was kind. Resnick couldn't remember when Kathleen stopped being kind. He wondered if she thought the same about him and was momentarily filled with shame that he hadn't noticed their marriage was over. The shame didn't last long: the real tragedy was that he didn't care.

Suddenly, Resnick dived across the bed and turned the volume on the radio up loud.

'The investigation into the armed raid on a security wagon in the Strand underpass earlier this morning is now well under way. Four masked men are said to have escaped with over one million pounds. Police are searching for a white Leyland truck used in the robbery and a white GLC van in which the suspects made their escape . . .'

Ripping off his pyjama top, Resnick started to dress.

* * *

Harry Rawlins was listening to exactly the same broadcast on a small transistor radio. He knew newscasters liked to embellish a story for the public and doubted that over a million was stolen – he reckoned it was probably between six and seven hundred thousand pounds – but even so, he was still angry that he didn't know where the money was. In a fit of fury, Harry swiped at the radio, which flew from the table and smashed against the wall.

Trudie jumped. She was cleaning Eddie's face with cotton wool swabs and disinfectant at the kitchen table. The scalds from the bubbling coffee were now painful blisters and the scratches on his eyelids and ears from Shirley's beautifully manicured nails were a dark, burning red. Eddie winced with the pain as Trudie dabbed at his face, but he never took his eyes off Harry.

Harry was in a volatile state of mind. He lit a cigarette, took a deep lungful of smoke and let it stream out slowly from his nose as he glared at his nervous cousin.

'She just came at me, Harry, like a wildcat. I never seen anything like it! I don't know who the hell she was.'

From the description Eddie had already given, Harry knew exactly who she was, but he didn't tell him. Harry looked at the cheap watch he was wearing and then back at Eddie. 'Your face looks bad. Must be real painful, son.'

'It is, Harry, when I get my hands on that cow she's gonna suffer real bad.'

Trudie looked at Harry. It made her uncomfortable when they spoke about violence, especially towards women. Just then, the baby started crying in the bedroom. Harry looked as if he was about to blow a gasket. He jerked his head for her to go and see to the child, but she continued dabbing Eddie's face. Harry stood up, kicked a chair over and took a step towards her. Trudie scurried into the bedroom and quietly shut the door.

'You sure the filth didn't find the money?' Harry said, leaning over the table towards Eddie.

Eddie gulped. 'I'm almost certain, Harry,' he said in a shaky voice. 'They wasn't there that long before they put Dolly in the patrol car and left. She was givin' 'em a right mouthful and not one of them was carrying any holdalls. In fact, they wasn't carrying anything at all.'

Harry crossed to the window, stubbed his cigarette out between his fingers then flicked it towards the sink. It fell short and landed on the floor. He leant his head against the cold window and clenched his fists. He felt incredibly frustrated. He was used to being in control, total control. As the cold glass cooled his temper, his cheek muscles jumped. Robbery was a man's game and the fact that Dolly seemed to have pulled it off and got away with it infuriated him. All he wanted to do now was get the money and disappear. It wasn't her money, it was his – his plans, his ledgers, his contacts, his brains . . . and she was taking all the credit. A grin crept over his face. He couldn't help but admire her balls. He knew that she'd be running on pure adrenalin right now, and he hoped she knew how to control it. Harry, head still on the glass, laughed out loud. *Shirley fucking Miller*, he thought to himself. And it made sense, therefore, that Linda Pirelli was also involved. Unbelievable. Then he spoke out loud.

'Women, eh, Eddie?'

Eddie had no idea what Harry was referring to, so opted to laugh quietly and cautiously.

Harry turned to Eddie and perched on the windowsill. His voice was quiet, as if he was mulling things over to himself. 'The Old Bill must have searched the house. If she was yappy with 'em, it sounds like she's already hidden the cash somewhere. Even if she ain't, she'll soon find out from the blonde who scalded you that someone's looking for the money . . . You really fucked up, Eddie.'

Suddenly Harry moved across the room and punched Eddie hard on the nose. He fell off his chair and onto the floor with a cry of pain. Harry stood over him like a towering, menacing giant. Eddie braced himself for a beating, but thankfully it didn't come. He sighed with relief as Harry returned to looking out of the window. His nose was throbbing and when he wiped it on his sleeve and saw the blood he thought it might be broken.

'Get Bill. And watch Dolly like a hawk, 24/7,' Harry ordered. 'Don't lose sight of her.'

'Shall we wait till she goes out and then search the place?' Eddie suggested.

Harry spun round. 'Is that what I said? Did I say "search the house", Eddie? Did I?'

Eddie bowed his head and shut his mouth.

'You watch her. You follow her. She's done this by the book so far – *my* book – so I know what she'll be doing next. She'll need to launder the money. There're contacts in the ledgers that she might use. She'll only do this when she's sure it's safe, cos she'll need to have the money out in the open. That's when we pounce. If she doesn't make a move soon, then I'm gonna pay her a visit.' Harry had a nasty glint in his eyes.

'But she thinks you're dead, Harry!'

Harry smiled. 'Well, she's in for a surprise, then, isn't she? Now get out, go on – out.'

Eddie crossed to the door, frightened at what Harry might be capable of. 'I don't want to hurt her, Harry, not Dolly. I couldn't. I feel bad enough about the bleedin' dog, but a person. And a woman—'

Harry interrupted Eddie. 'What about the dog?'

Eddie froze, wishing he'd never opened his big mouth. 'When the blonde went for me,' he stuttered, 'I . . . I'm not sure but I think I might have stood on it. It bit me and she was scratching me face; I punched out at her and I kicked out at . . . well, it was all yap-yap-yapping and then it wasn't.'

Harry's look of hatred made Eddie back out of the living room. When he'd cleared the doorway, he turned to run, but, quick as a flash, Harry had grabbed the scruff of his neck, spun him round and slammed him up against the wall.

'I could kill you, you pathetic worm of a man,' Harry snarled in Eddie's face. 'You can't kill Boxer Davis, but you can kill a poodle. That sums you up, Eddie. Just you remember this – you're the one who led Boxer to that alley, you're the one who put him in front of

Bill's car. If Dolly makes a mistake now cos of losing that dog and things start to go wrong, you're the one going down for Boxer.'

Eddie was terrified. Why the hell was Harry being so threatening? 'It's only a dog,' Eddie whispered.

Harry landed one solid punch to Eddie's gut. 'She's grieving now cos of you,' he hissed. 'And grieving people make mistakes.' He pushed Eddie so hard out of the door he tripped over his own feet and toppled backwards onto his backside. Harry looked at him with disgust. 'Get Bill. Watch Dolly. Nothing more.' And he slammed the door.

Clutching his head in his hands, Harry paced the living room, struggling with a whirlwind of emotions. He hated Dolly for succeeding where he'd failed. He wanted to snatch it all away from her to show her who was boss – but, my God, if Wolf was really dead! The idea of pulling the rug from underneath Dolly when she was on a high, flooded with adrenalin, didn't faze Harry one little bit. She was strong. She'd recover. But snatching her defeat from the jaws of victory if she'd really just lost her baby, well . . . he couldn't handle the guilt, and that was why he wanted to kill Eddie.

Harry had known before his botched robbery that he was going to leave Dolly, which was why he couldn't have cared less about giving his watch away to Jimmy Nunn. His plans were always to go to Spain with Trudie and the baby and stay away for good, but to do that he needed money, lots of money. As he'd driven away from the inferno in the Strand tunnel on that fateful day, he had had no idea what he was going to do next. Dolly going half mad with grief at losing him, then stepping up to the plate and pulling off *his* robbery, was his saving grace. Now all he had to do was get the money.

Trudie came back into the lounge. 'What you hit him for?' she asked.

Harry ignored her and walked into the bedroom. She followed.

'You shouldn't push him too far, you know,' she said. 'What if he turns on you and blabs to Dolly, what d'ya think she'll do then?'

Still ignoring her, he began to undo his shirt.

'I'll tell you what she'll do,' Trudie persisted. 'She'll scarper with all the money and you'll never see her again.'

Harry shrugged his shoulders, pulled off his shirt, threw it in the corner and lay back on the bed with a sensual come and get it grin. He didn't want to do any more talking today.

'Promise me you won't do anything silly, Harry?' Trudie begged, distracted by Harry's toned, muscular body. She could feel the pull of desire inside her; he'd had that effect from the first moment she ever set eyes on him.

Trudie had first met Harry Rawlins over a year before her husband Jimmy Nunn started working for him. She'd been on a girls' night out with Shirley Miller and they'd gone to the Fishers' club for a little flutter on the roulette table. Harry had been there on his own, and Shirley, who had met him a couple of times before, had introduced Trudie. She'd felt an instant attraction and flirted with him, Shirley had told her to back off as he was married and, even if he wasn't, he was not a man to get involved with. Trudie hadn't cared: she wanted him and nothing Shirley said was going to stop her having what she wanted.

Harry had been at the blackjack table when Trudie sat down next to him and deliberately let her thigh brush against his. He looked at her and she smiled seductively. It had the desired effect. His hand moved under the table and he gently pressed and ran one finger along her inner thigh. The tingling sensation that ran through her body was exquisite torture; she didn't want it to stop. When Harry began to move his hand away, she grabbed it and moved it closer to her crotch. The way he made her feel, she'd have let him take her there and then on the blackjack table.

After that first chance meeting, days and nights of illicit passionate sex followed, mostly in cheap hotels, the back of a car, woodland – in fact anywhere they were unlikely to be caught. No matter where or when Trudie was with Harry, she was always putty in his hands.

She remembered Harry's face that one special afternoon in a grubby hotel when she told him she was having his baby. At first, he'd doubted her and asked if it could be Jimmy's child. She assured him it wasn't: she and Jimmy had not had sex for over a month. Harry had held her close. He'd hugged and kissed her and then he'd rested his head on her stomach. Trudie couldn't see his face, but she knew his eyes were wet.

After the child was born, Harry had sat in his car at the hospital, waiting for Jimmy to leave. When he did, Harry snuck up to the maternity ward. He was quiet, almost as if there was something about the maternity ward that disturbed him, and she could see the adoration in Harry's eyes – the boy that Dolly could never give him. But he never said it out loud.

Harry had held the baby close and kissed its soft silky head, but then the smile turned to a scowl and his eyes had narrowed to a glare of distrust.

'Why was Jimmy here if it can't possibly be his?' Harry had asked.

'I lied to him,' Trudie explained. 'All the way through the pregnancy I lied about how far gone I was. I swear to you, Harry, on my life, he's your baby . . .'

Harry had settled down, but she'd never forgotten the look of evil as he stroked the baby's head. 'If I ever find out you lied to me,' he'd whispered, 'you'll regret it.'

Trudie snapped out of her daydream as soon as Harry pulled her down onto the bed and slid his hand inside her dressing gown and onto her breast. He pulled her on top of him and slipped the dressing gown over her shoulders so she was naked. When Harry wanted sex, his smile altered his whole face, softening his eyes. She found it hard to believe this was the same man who, no more than two minutes ago, had frightened her and whacked Eddie.

Harry sat up and started kissing her neck and moved down slowly to her breasts. Wrapping her legs round his waist, she squeezed him tight as her body started to tingle and quiver. None of the men she'd ever had sex with had been able to make her feel the floods of erotic sensation that Harry did. He laid her gently onto her back and began kissing every inch of her body. The weeks of being closeted up with him since his 'death' had made no difference to how much she wanted him. All he had ever had to do was touch her and she needed him inside her. When Harry made love to her, he never spoke a word. He didn't need to, because the sex was that good – but she so wished that once, just once, he would tell her that he loved her.

CHAPTER 33

Once at the convent, Dolly had to work fast in the empty classroom. The children would be coming back from lunch in a few minutes. She was relieved to see that the brightly coloured floor-to-ceiling lockers, which she had bought as a gift for the convent, were now in place and being used. All except the top ones, which were far too high for the children to put their coats and play equipment in. This was where the money from the robbery would live until Dolly was ready to collect. She couldn't think of a better guardian than the Mother Superior.

On her way to the convent, Dolly had taken a diversion to the lock-up. It was a risk, but she needed somewhere to count the money into four equal amounts and fill four identical bags. Dolly had taken a small amount of cash from each of the bags to create a fifth, smaller share – their spending money for the next few weeks.

As she hefted the four bags into four of the lockers, the sweat poured from her forehead and stung her eyes. Each locker had its own key: one for herself and one each for Bella, Linda and Shirley. Once the lockers were secure and the keys were safely in Dolly's pocket, she set to, pasting the back of a series of large nursery posters. Once they were stuck across the doors, no one would know there were any lockers up there at all.

With one more poster to stick in place, Dolly heard the bell ring to indicate lunch was over. She quickly dunked a brush in one of the glue pots she had lined up on the trestle table and smeared the paste over the back of 'Little Miss Muffet'.

'Hello, Mrs Rawlins, not gone on holiday yet?' Sister Teresa bustled in. She seemed surprised.

Dolly accidently knocked a brush off the table and bent over to pick it up. 'Flying off in a day or so,' she said cheerfully. 'I just thought I'd decorate the lockers with some nursery rhyme posters before I go . . .' Dolly noticed the fifth, smaller bag on the floor. It was open and the stacks of bank notes could be seen on the top of it. '*Oh, God . . .*' she muttered, slightly louder than she'd intended.

'Can I help you with anything?' Sister Teresa asked.

Dolly flipped the bag shut and stood up. 'I've just got this last poster to stick up, and then we're done.' Once Dolly had finished, Sister Teresa helped her stick the final poster in place and they both stood back to admire Dolly's handiwork.

'They are fabulous, Mrs Rawlins. It's so kind of you – they'll definitely help the children learn their nursery rhymes,' said Sister Teresa.

Dolly smiled to herself. *Perfect*, she thought. Not one keyhole or join could be seen in the top row. It didn't look as if there were any lockers there.

The classroom filled with laughing, chattering children. One child, a particularly lovely little girl called Isabelle, wrapped herself round Dolly's leg, as she always did. Isabelle never said much but her unconditional affection now reminded Dolly a little of Wolf. She'd miss these children – and the unquestioning generosity of the nuns themselves . . .

Dolly spent the afternoon doing ABCs with Isabelle and the other children, revelling in this particular classroom session: it would be her last one ever. She had loved her time working at the convent – it was so pure, uncomplicated and enjoyable. All the children wanted from Dolly was her time; and this was something she willingly gave. She'd certainly miss the simple certainty of convent life.

At four thirty, Dolly left the convent and headed straight for the nearest travel agent. There, she booked a first-class ticket to Rio leaving the following morning. When asked if she'd like a return ticket, Dolly said that she wasn't sure how long she'd be staying so she would make any return arrangements from Rio. Then Dolly drove a mile down the road to another travel agent, where she pretended to be Mrs Shirley Miller and booked an economy class ticket for Rio on the same flight.

* * *

Resnick had been at home all day, sitting down one minute, getting up the next, pacing round the living room and chain smoking as he waited impatiently for the call from DCI Saunders. The living room ashtray was full, but he still forced his cigarette butt into it before lighting another.

He looked at his watch. It was now 6 p.m. and he could smell the liver and bacon Kathleen was cooking for dinner. The phone rang once and he snatched it up, but it was just Kathleen's bridge partner, Margaret.

'Sorry, Margaret,' Resnick said quickly. 'Kathleen's not in. And I'm going to have to cut you short as I'm waiting for a very important phone call.'

Kathleen appeared behind Resnick and took the phone from him. He gave her a disapproving look, which she ignored.

'Don't talk for long,' he said.

Kathleen pushed him towards the kitchen. 'Go and occupy yourself, George . . . keep an eye on the dinner for me. Go on. Scoot.'

Kathleen finished her phone call five minutes later and returned to the kitchen, where George was picking out bits of bacon with a fork from the liver and gravy and eating them. Kathleen smacked the back of his hand and pursed her lips.

'Stop picking. And don't lie to my friends just because you're waiting on an imaginary phone call.' As she stirred the dinner, she could see that her words had upset him, but she believed in telling the truth. 'You've *retired*, George. Go and play golf or paint the hallway like you said you were going to.'

Resnick's face looked like an abandoned bloodhound.

'Oh, you are stubborn!' Kathleen continued. 'Call them if you want to.'

'It's my case. They'll call me.'

'It's *not* your case, George. Not anymore.' Kathleen drained the potatoes and got the masher from the drawer. Resnick snatched it from her and started to take his frustration out on the pan of potatoes, smashing them into oblivion. Kathleen watched him. She'd never liked her husband being a policeman. He wasn't the sort who could leave his work at the station; he brought it home with him, all knotted up in his stomach, and he was awful to live with at times. *But*, she thought, *George out of the police force was far worse than George in the police force.* She hated seeing him so angry but she couldn't be bothered to placate him anymore.

As Resnick continued to massacre the potatoes, he shouted at Kathleen. 'I told them! I told them these robberies were all connected. All masterminded by the same bloke. Bloody Rawlins! I warned them not to underestimate him. You can never underestimate Harry Rawlins.'

'Harry Rawlins! Harry Rawlins!' Kathleen screamed back at him. 'That's all I've heard for years. Anything and everything that went wrong in your career was always the fault of bloody Harry Rawlins! It couldn't possibly be your fault, could it, George?! No! It's the fault of a dead man.'

Resnick threw the masher into the sink, spraying flecks of potato across the kitchen tiles. He stormed into the hallway to get his hat and coat.

'You have to let go, George!' Kathleen shouted after him. 'I'm not going to stick around to see you in an early grave, do you hear me? I won't do that.'

'Don't then!' Resnick shouted back as he slammed the front door behind him.

* * *

He got into his old battered Granada and made his way to the Rawlins' house. He didn't know why he was going there; the car just seemed to drive itself. Deep down, he knew that no one from his office would call. Why should they? He was a has-been; his opinion had meant nothing for years now. He hoped that all hell was breaking loose at the Yard and that Saunders would get a size-ten boot right up his arse. He smiled at the thought of Saunders being brought down a peg or two.

It suddenly crossed his mind that maybe Saunders and the others had wanted him out so they could take over the case and reap the glory when they found and arrested Harry Rawlins. The more Resnick thought about it, the more he convinced himself he was right. They'd deliberately blocked him along the way because they wanted him out! Well, now he'd show 'em the old two-fingered salute. He'd bloody well sort it out himself! 'There's life in this old dog yet,' Resnick muttered to himself. 'I'm the one who's going to arrest Harry Rawlins. Harry Rawlins is *mine*.'

CHAPTER 34

Eddie adjusted the wing mirror of Jimmy Nunn's car. Bill Grant was slouched in the passenger seat beside him, snoring. Eddie was watching a car pull in and park about fifty yards behind them. The driver got out, lit a cigarette and walked slowly towards them on the opposite side of the street. His pace was too slow to be heading anywhere in a hurry and Eddie was worried. He nudged Bill awake.

'Some bloke behind us is clockin' Harry's place. I can't make his face out yet . . .'

'Keep looking straight ahead,' Bill ordered. 'Shift your wing mirror so I can see him under the next street light. Hurry up.' Eddie did as he was instructed. 'Shit!' Bill whispered as the man's face was temporarily lit up under the street light. 'It's bloody Resnick! He put me away for that last stretch. And he's always had a wasp up his arse about catching Harry.'

'Shall I drive off?' Eddie asked.

'No. Duck your nut so he can't see your face.'

* * *

Resnick had spotted the hand adjusting the wing mirror, but he didn't recognise the car. As he walked past, he paused and looked at the sole of his shoe, as if he'd just trodden in dog shit. Resnick only got a side view of the passenger's face and, although he thought it rang a bell, he couldn't place him at all. But the driver had glanced his way for a split second and he felt sure it was Eddie Rawlins. Resnick made a mental note of the number plate before continuing along the street and past the Rawlins house. The light in the front bedroom was on, but the rest of the house was in darkness.

After looping round the block, Resnick came back to the street where Eddie and Bill were parked, got into his own car and drove away. He pulled up round the corner and wrote down the car's number plate. 'What you up to, Eddie?' Resnick whispered to himself. 'And who you working for? Anyone we know?' He put a cigarette between his grinning teeth and lit up.

* * *

'We should scarper, in case he comes back with more coppers.' Eddie whimpered as Resnick drove off.

'What's he gonna do? Arrest us for sitting in a car? I'll go and see Harry. He'll tell us what to do.' Bill got out of the car and stretched his back out, cracking the bones. 'Stay awake till I get back.'

'Get a cab, otherwise you'll be ages.'

'Walking for miles in a straight line is a luxury I ain't had for years, mate. Don't worry. I'll borrow Trudie's car to come back.'

Eddie didn't feel safe being left alone, but he guessed he felt safer than being with the man who'd crushed Boxer Davis to death without batting an eyelid.

* * *

After visiting the travel agent, Dolly had picked up some food before heading home just after dark. She was so exhausted she hadn't noticed Eddie sitting in Jimmy Nunn's car outside her house. And when Resnick arrived, she'd been in the back garden with Shirley.

The two women had looked at the small mound of freshly dug earth, topped with a bamboo cross and a flower. 'I didn't know if he liked flowers . . .' Shirley said, not really knowing what to say.

'He liked pissing on 'em,' Dolly said. Shirley saw a small smile creep across her face. 'Especially next door's roses.'

'Shall I go and nick one for him, then?' Shirley asked.

Dolly looked at Shirley. She did say some stupid things, but Dolly loved her for that. 'No, darlin'. That one's just fine. Thank you for looking after him for me. I could never have buried him.'

'That's OK.' After a moment, Shirley asked, 'I couldn't have a bath, could I? I'm a bit smelly and dirty after all that diggin'.'

By 9 p.m., they were both exhausted. After her bath, Shirley changed into a nightdress and dressing gown Dolly had loaned her. She looked out of the Dolly's bedroom window through a small crack in the curtains, checking the street.

Dolly came out of her en suite bathroom and crossed to the bed. 'Everywhere locked up?'

Shirley nodded. 'I've bolted every door and window. And made your milk.' She pointed to the bedside cabinet. Dolly picked up the glass, got a sleeping pill from the bottle in the top drawer and swallowed it.

'Want one?' she asked. 'It'll help you sleep with that bad ankle.'

'Yes . . .' Shirley tailed off, still looking out of the window. 'Dolly – this is the third time I've looked out of the window since you got back and each time that BMW has been there with two men in it, but now there's just one. It's too far away to see their faces properly. You think it's the police or . . .' Dolly joined Shirley at the window.

'It'll be the police,' Dolly said reassuringly. 'The man from earlier isn't coming back, love. Not with the coppers right outside.' She didn't want to panic Shirley, but even though she couldn't see the driver's face, she knew the car they were looking at wasn't the usual unmarked police car. 'Right. Sleep,' she went on as she crawled into her bed. 'If I don't sleep, I'm finished. Take your tablet and forget about everything till morning.'

Shirley sat on the edge of Dolly's bed and took the sleeping pill with some of Dolly's warm milk. She noticed a picture of Harry and Dolly on the bedside table. They looked such a happy, loving couple: Dolly in a beautiful designer dress and Harry handsome in a smart, very expensive suit. Better times.

'You done well today,' Dolly said, smiling up at Shirley. 'Brave and strong. I'm very proud of you. Now go on, off to bed and get some sleep.'

Shirley held the milk up for Dolly to take if she wanted more, but she shook her head and closed her eyes. As Shirley sipped she looked at Dolly. It was as if the day's events had aged her ten years; she looked so tired and haggard. Touching Dolly's hand lightly, Shirley whispered, 'God bless.' For a second, Dolly gripped Shirley's hand tight, so tight it hurt, and then she released it.

Shirley took the rest of the milk through to the spare room and placed it on her bedside cabinet. The room was bigger than her bedroom at home and beautifully decorated with pictures of Dolly and Harry on holidays, at parties and with friends. As she finished the milk she walked round the room. 'What a life Dolly's led . . .' she thought to herself. Suddenly she stopped, caught by a photograph on the dressing table. She grabbed it, heart pounding, and ran back through to Dolly's bedroom.

'Wake up!' she said urgently, flicking the bedside light on and shaking Dolly.

Dolly didn't rouse quickly, but when she did open her eyes and saw the look of panic on Shirley's face, she was immediately awake.

'Who's this man in the middle with his arms round you and Harry? Who is he, Dolly?' Shirley was trembling as she held out the photograph.

Dolly rubbed her eyes and waited a second or two for them to focus. 'That's Eddie,' she said. 'Eddie Rawlins, Harry's cousin, why?'

'It was him, Dolly! He was the man who broke in, the one who attacked me and Wolf.'

Dolly sat up and grabbed the photo from Shirley. 'Are you sure?'

'I'm not making it up, Dolly – I swear it was him! I *know* it was him. Wolf acted as if he knew him at first – and of course Wolf *did* know him. What if that's him in the car outside? What if he's coming back?'

Dolly grabbed Shirley by the hand. 'He wouldn't come back here; not after what you did to him. The money is safe. We're safe. It's the police outside, like I said. Trust me, Shirl. You trust me, don't you?'

Shirley nodded. She trusted Dolly with her life.

Dolly took Shirley back into the spare room and tucked her up in bed. 'I'm going to look after you, darlin'. You, Linda and Bella. Please don't worry so much. I know this is all very new to you, but I've lived on my nerves for years, so trust me when I say that everything's going to be OK.' And switching off the bedside lamp, she sat with Shirley till she fell asleep.

Returning to her own bedroom, Dolly picked up the photograph that Shirley had found. She went to the window, eased the curtain back slightly and looked down at the parked car. It was too dark to see the interior, so Dolly patiently waited and watched. Eventually, another car drove past and briefly lit up the face of the man in the driver's seat. It was as if a blade of ice cut through her. 'Oh, Eddie,' she gasped. 'Stupid, *stupid* Eddie.' Tears filled Dolly's eyes as her mind raced. Eddie didn't have the balls to do anything under his own steam, let alone break into her home, attack Shirley and kill poor Wolf in the process. 'So, who's pulling your strings?' she whispered. But she already feared she knew the answer.

The gold Dunhill lighter in Jimmy Nunn's flat.

The brutal murder of Boxer Davis.

Bill Grant, the man at the lock-up, knowing who she was.

Eddie Rawlins doing someone's bidding inside and now outside her home.

Dolly slumped on the edge of her bed, gripping her tired and confused head in her hands. 'It was a rumour,' she said, trying to convince herself. 'It was *my* rumour. It wasn't the truth. It was never the truth!' As unbelievable and terrifying and hurtful as it was, Dolly couldn't shake the thought. 'No, no, no, no! I saw your watch.'

All chance of sleep was gone. Her eyes were wide open now, and her heart felt as though it had seized. 'But I saw your watch,' she cried out loud. '*I saw your watch!*'

CHAPTER 35

Kathleen Resnick could hear George moving about downstairs. She looked at the bedside clock; it was nearly midnight. He'd be drunk, pacing up and down with a whisky in one hand and a cigarette in the other. The last time he had been like this was when his suspension made the headlines. Then, he'd drunk himself into oblivion, fallen asleep with a cigarette in his hand and almost burnt the house down.

Slipping on her dressing gown, she went downstairs to give him a piece of her mind. The front room was full of cigarette smoke. Kathleen was about to speak, but he held up his hand. He was on the phone, the receiver balanced between his shoulder and ear and he was holding a notepad and pen in his hands. He wasn't drunk – far from it. He was bursting with energy.

'Yes, I'm DCI Saunders from the Yard. I've been out on an observation and need to know the registered owner of the car index I just gave you. It's very urgent.'

What on earth was he up to? Kathleen crossed the smoky lounge and stood next to her husband, arms folded. Whatever he was doing, he was clearly not meant to be doing it.

'Sorry, what? James what? Nunn . . . and the address?' Resnick scribbled down the information on the notepad. 'Thank you, officer. Very kind and much appreciated.' George replaced the receiver and opened the address book next to the phone.

'What are you doing pretending to be Saunders?' Kathleen demanded.

Resnick thumbed through the diary. 'I needed a car registration checked on the police computer so I phoned the local nick. I couldn't very well say who I was, could I? Where's Alice's home number? I thought we had it in the address book?'

Kathleen couldn't believe it. 'You can't ring that poor woman at this time of night!'

When George looked up at his wife, his face was hard and cruel. 'Yes, I can! Alice is someone I *can* speak to at this time of night. So, take your disapproving looks back to bed and let me do my job.' He found Alice's number and picked the phone up again.

Kathleen stormed back upstairs. 'You don't have a job,' she yelled as she went.

Resnick waited as the phone rang and rang. He glanced at the clock. Maybe his wife was right . . . but this couldn't wait, it was too important.

'Alice?'

'What's wrong?' Alice wasn't angry at being woken at gone midnight; she was worried that Resnick was in trouble.

'Nothing's wrong, love. Listen, I need you to do me a favour first thing tomorrow morning.'

Alice was sitting at her dressing table with a pen and paper on one hand and the phone in the other. As she jotted down Resnick's instructions, she caught sight of herself in the mirror. God, she looked just like her mother! She had thick cream on her face and was wearing a nightdress that would terrify any man. She thanked God that Resnick had chosen to call and not pop round.

'You mustn't get caught, Alice, you understand? You're the only person I can ask. Will you help me?'

Alice looked at her terrible reflection and smiled. 'Of course I'll help you, sir.'

CHAPTER 36

Trudie had let Bill into the flat and he was now waiting for Harry. He sniffed. The grubby little flat smelt of baby's piss. He was still wincing when Harry came out of the bedroom, wrapping a towel round himself.

'Thought I'd update you,' Bill said, grinning. He thought it was funny that he might have just interrupted Harry and Trudie shagging. Harry wasn't smiling at all. 'Dolly's still indoors,' Bill continued. 'She drove back just after dark and ain't been out since. I rang Ray the Rash, but there's not a dickie about her trying to fence the money anywhere, but he'll keep askin'.'

Harry put his finger to his lips and led the way into the kitchen; Bill followed him and shut the door. Harry put the kettle on.

Harry recapped. 'When she went home after being at the nick, the blonde bit will have told her about Eddie's visit . . . hopefully she just described him as "some bloke" and not my stupid fucking cousin. I don't think Blondie and Eddie have ever met so we might be in the clear there. But then Dolly went out in the car, you say?' Bill nodded. 'Then she's stashed the money, ain't she?' Harry was thinking hard. 'Now where would she have put it?'

Bill shifted his weight. He was getting pissed off with all this hanging round: he couldn't see why Harry didn't just let him pay Dolly a visit and force it out of her. 'That cop Resnick turned up and had a good gander at the house,' he added. 'He was on his own. Only there for a minute or two.'

Harry laughed. 'Don't worry about him. He's an idiot only fit to investigate kids nicking sweets from the corner shop.' He handed Bill a mug of tea and paced round the kitchen, deep in thought. 'If nothing has moved by six a.m., you come back and pick me up and the three of us will go in. I'll deal with Dolly and you and Eddie can keep the other one quiet. Eddie owes her a good slap after what she done to his face.'

'You want my opinion?' Bill chewed his lip and slurped his tea. 'We should have gone in that bloody house hours ago and got what we needed. All this farting about has given your missus time to hide the cash and now—'

As Bill spoke, Harry tightened the towel round his waist and launched himself across the kitchen, grabbing Bill by the scruff of his neck and slamming him against the kitchen wall. Harry already knew what Bill's opinion was; he knew what went on in his warped head. 'I make the decisions, you hear me? And you – you do as I say!'

Bill stood against the wall, tea held out to the side so as not to spill it, and avoided eye contact. Bill wasn't frightened of Harry – they were pretty equally matched when it came down to it – but Harry was the boss and Bill respected that. Harry was the one with the money and the brains, the reputation and the power. Bill had none of that, so he held his tongue. Bill liked to live in the shadows, but those who did know him knew he was a man who got things done. Quickly and quietly. That's why people hired him. Bill had never, and would never, grass on anyone. On the three occasions he'd done some face rearranging for Harry, there had been no trail between Harry and the incident itself. That kind of discretion was worth paying for, and Harry paid well.

As Harry let go of Bill, Trudie walked in holding the crying baby. Harry, still all fired up, turned on her.

'What the fuck do you want now?' he snapped, knowing she was just snooping. Bill took his opportunity to slope out of the open door.

Trudie looked nervous. 'Just a cup of tea and some milk for the baby. That's all.'

* * *

Resnick was waiting outside Jimmy Nunn's flat. He'd stopped just along the road behind some parked cars so he had a decent view without being visible himself. He saw a man walk out of the flats and recognised him as the passenger from the car parked outside Dolly's house; the car that had Eddie Rawlins in the driver's seat.

As the man passed under a street lamp, Resnick got a good look. 'I know you,' he whispered, poking his forehead with his finger, willing himself to remember the name that went with the face. 'How do I know you?'

The man got into a Ford Granada and moved off. Resnick decided to follow and they were soon back in the vicinity of Dolly Rawlins' house. Resnick pulled up round the corner; he was unsure of his next move until he could place the mystery man. *Think, think, think* . . . Resnick closed his eyes and, in his head, he flicked back through all the lags he'd arrested over the years. Occasionally he'd shake his head out of frustration at hitting another dead end. His eyes shot open. 'Fuck. Grant!' he breathed. Resnick rubbed his eyes, dragging his hands down his face, distorting his features for a moment as his brain worked overtime trying to figure out what the hell was going on. He needed someone to talk to . . . he never thought he'd say it, but he wished Fuller was sitting next to him. He was a pious prick, but he was also a decent officer who listened, reluctantly or otherwise, when Resnick spoke; unlike Andrews who had, in all honesty, peaked at traffic duty. 'Right,' Resnick said, as if Fuller was by his side. 'Bill Grant. Why is he watching the Rawlins house? Why has he got Jimmy Nunn's car? How does he know Eddie Rawlins? You're working for someone, Bill Grant . . . I know you . . . you get your hands dirty for the highest bidder.' He wished he could call for backup, wished he could nick Eddie Rawlins and Bill Grant and then search Jimmy Nunn's flat.

Just then, the Granada came back round the corner. Resnick ducked down and, as the car passed, he sat up just enough to get a glimpse of the driver. It was Eddie Rawlins. So, Bill Grant must now be outside Dolly Rawlins' house in Jimmy Nunn's BMW. This was tag-team surveillance: two cars, two foot soldiers obeying orders. But who were they working for? Resnick, of course, in his heart of hearts, knew only too well.

* * *

Unable to sleep, Dolly had gone into the spare room where Shirley was sleeping to get a better view down onto the street. Outside, Eddie was sitting alone in the BMW. She needed to know for definite if he was the man who broke into the house.

Dolly shook Shirley, but she didn't stir. Dolly pulled the covers off. 'Come on, Shirley. Wake up,' Dolly said firmly. Eventually, Shirley's eyes opened and Dolly helped her to her feet.

Together, they peered out from behind the curtains just as Bill Grant pulled up in a Granada and swapped places with Eddie. Shirley was shaking like a leaf. It was obvious that she was terrified at the sight of Eddie. Dolly put her arm round Shirley's shoulder.

'That's Eddie Rawlins, Harry's cousin. He's a coward, Shirley. A runt of a man who slaps women and kills dogs. He's nothing, you hear me? And he won't hurt you again. I can promise you that.'

The sincerity in Dolly's voice made Shirley feel safe – she loved the way Dolly could do that. She wished her mum was as strong.

Shirley didn't recognise the other man, but Dolly did. He was the man who had come to the door of the lock-up and introduced himself as Bill Grant. Dolly screwed her eyes shut and whispered, '*Idiot!*' Every move at the lock-up could have been watched by Grant. If he knew everything, right from the very beginning, then no wonder Eddie had been at the house looking for the money . . .

Dolly needed to think about how they could leave the house with Bill Grant watching, and then lose him if he tailed them. And if Eddie returned, there would be the further complication of two men in separate cars to follow them. Too physically and mentally exhausted to think straight, Dolly felt scared, and this was very new to her. She wished Shirley had got on her flight as arranged: at least if Dolly had a meltdown, she could have had it in private! But Shirley was here and, like a child, needed constant reassurance.

Dolly paced up and down the landing, while Shirley went to make them both something to eat. Dolly didn't want anything, but she needed to be left alone to think. She looked at her watch. It was nearly 2 a.m. and the flight from Heathrow wasn't until midday. They didn't have to be at the airport until 10 a.m. at the latest and the airport was, at best, an hour away. Dolly sighed. Leaving the house in daylight was not a good idea and she knew that the sooner they were out under the cover of darkness, the better chance they had of losing a tail.

After a while, Dolly had an idea. It was only a partial plan and it was a bit outrageous, but what the hell – she had become used to outrageous over the past few months! She headed for the kitchen.

'I thought I'd make a fry up, Dolly, do you want—'

'We need to leave here between four and four thirty a.m.,' Dolly interrupted. 'Can you trust your mum?'

Shirley turned the gas off on the stove. 'Yes, of course.'

'Can she drive?'

'Yes,' Shirley replied, waiting for Dolly to reveal her plan.

'And you've got a brother, that right?'

'Greg. He lives with Mum.'

'Right,' Dolly said, pointing her finger at Shirley. 'Get Greg to go to the car park in Covent Garden and get your car. Tell him to park it in Mount Close – that's the large cul-de-sac off the second street down if you go right out of my driveway. Tell him to leave the driver's door unlocked, the keys under the seat and to ring here when it's done.'

Shirley looked doubtful. 'At two a.m., he'll either be pissed as a fart somewhere or comatose in his bed. If he's in, I'll definitely get Mum to wake him. But if he's out . . .'

'Well, let's hope he's in bed, then. Tell him, if your car's gone, if it's been nicked, then he'll have to use his imagination and find us something else. But, no matter what, I need a car, *any* car, parked in that cul-de-sac by four a.m. at the very latest. There'll be a hundred quid in it for him. And get your mum round here as soon as. I'll give the money to her to pass on to your brother. You got all that?'

'Got it,' Shirley confirmed. She got a plate out of the cupboard and picked up the frying pan to dish up her breakfast.

Dolly moved swiftly across the kitchen, got two slices of bread from the bread bin and slammed them down on Shirley's plate, leaving deep finger marks in the soft white dough. 'Make a sandwich.' Dolly glared. 'Eat as you dial.'

* * *

Five minutes later, Dolly leant over the banister and shouted down to Shirley, who appeared from the kitchen, sandwich in hand.

'The phone just keeps ringing and ringing,' Shirley reported. 'I'll keep trying . . .'

Five minutes after that, Dolly leant over the banister again. She was holding a pair of scissors.

'No luck,' said Shirley. 'Me brother may be at his girlfriend's and I haven't got a number for her, and Mum sometimes wears earplugs at night . . .'

'Well, keep bloody trying,' Dolly said, pointing the scissors at Shirley.

'You cutting your hair?' Shirley asked.

'What?'

'Like a disguise. I don't have to cut mine, do I?'

'Honest to God, Shirley, I don't know how your brain works sometimes. Would you rather go to prison for life or cut your lovely blonde curls? Choose!'

Shirley stood in the hallway, running her ringers through her hair and mulling over what she might look like with a bob cut. Dolly rolled her eyes and stormed back upstairs.

'We ain't cutting our hair! Phone your mum!'

Shirley rang her mum's house again and, this time, the phone was answered, but there was silence at the other end. 'Mum, is that you?' Shirley shouted.

'Nah, it's me . . .' Greg's response was slurred. 'What you doin' ringing home this time in the morning?' He'd been drinking and probably been sniffing God knows what as well; but he soon sobered up when Shirley mentioned the hundred pounds.

Shirley shouted up to Dolly. 'I'm going to get dressed, Dolly. Greg's doing what you said and Mum's on her way round.'

Upstairs, Dolly closed her eyes and sighed out of sheer relief. She was in the master bedroom setting light to the last few pages of the ledgers. She'd used the metal bin from Harry's study. The leather covers wouldn't burn but, as she watched every page turn to ashes, she cut them up with the scissors.

She'd been in two minds about bringing the ledgers home after her last visit to the bank but she was glad she had, as she'd never have got another chance to collect them. She'd kept the location of the ledgers from the girls for their own protection; after all, what they didn't know couldn't hurt them.

Standing at the dressing table, Dolly smiled to herself. She looked at the array of beautiful cosmetics and designer perfumes, and then she swept them all onto the floor with one hard, fast swipe of her arm. She was ready; she felt good.

She glanced down at the ashes in the metal bin. Harry's only means of protecting himself and blackmailing other villains were gone. One way or another, she'd make sure that word got out.

Taking one last look around the bedroom, her eyes fixed on the bedside cabinet and the photo of her and Harry. She picked it up, placed it face-up on the floor and stamped her foot down hard, gouging and twisting with her heel and grinding the broken glass into the photo. '*Bastard*,' she muttered through clenched teeth. Then she picked up two suitcases and left her bedroom for the last time.

Dolly carried her suitcases into the lounge and sat down. She picked up her handbag and got out the flight tickets, then she opened one of the suitcases and began to remove some of the men's clothes packed neatly inside and stack them on the arm of the chair.

Shirley finished putting on her lipstick and checked her hair in the dressing table mirror. She looked pretty damn good considering it was the early hours. As she walked down the stairs, the smell of breakfast was mixing with Dolly's heavy perfume. In the lounge, Shirley found Dolly and her two red suitcases, one of which was open. The base was covered with rows of bank notes. 'There's over a hundred thousand in here,' Dolly announced. 'Spending money for Rio. Enough to keep us living well for two months or so. Sit down, love, I need you to listen carefully to this.'

Shirley sat down obediently.

'Two identical suitcases, right? One with a red tag, one with a blue tag.'

'Right,' Shirley agreed, her forehead frowning with concentration. The suitcase with the red tag was the one open on the floor with the money inside.

'The case with the red tag has been cleaned from top to bottom, inside and out, so there're no prints on it from either of us. Not one. You don't touch this suitcase without gloves on.' Dolly handed Shirley a pair of stunning cream silk gloves.

'Red case, red tag – the one with the money in it – is clean. I'm not to touch it without gloves on,' Shirley repeated. 'These are beautiful by the way,' she added.

'Consider them a gift,' Dolly replied, getting quickly back on track. 'The red case with a blue tag is mine. The red case with the red tag has the money at the bottom and will have men's clothes at the top.'

'Got it,' Shirley confirmed. 'I think . . .'

Dolly continued. 'You take the money case and your own case—'

'What if my car's been nicked?' Shirley asked in a panic.

'Then we buy you another suitcase and clothes to go in it. But your car'll be there. I can't see any respectable thief nicking that old crap heap. Listening? Right, I take the red case with the blue tag – that's full of my clothes – and I go through check-in as normal. You take the money case and your own case. You hang about in the check-in area, looking for a bloke – a decoy, someone we can use.'

'Like a pigeon!' Shirley exclaimed.

'More like a stoolpigeon, but yes, you've got the idea. It must be a man.'

'Yes, I got that. Male clothes, right? And then only *his* prints will be on the case if customs try it on. I'm right, aren't I?' Shirley was proud of herself for picking up on the plan so quickly.

'Bang on, Shirl. So, you're looking for a man who's travelling light. You tell him you didn't realise there was a weight allowance, play the dumb blonde, tell him that with two cases, you're overweight and don't want to pay the excess baggage fine. Flutter your eyelashes and get him to check the money case in for you in his name.'

Shirley was now chewing her fingertip through the silk glove.

'Don't chew them – they was an anniversary present!' Dolly shouted.

'Sorry,' Shirley said, forcing her hands down by her side and mouthing the entire plan back to herself.

'When we land in Rio,' Dolly continued. 'The money case –'

'Red tag,' Shirley whispered to herself.

'– and my identical case –'

'Blue tag.'

'– will be on the carousel together. I'm going to pick up the money case and take it through customs.'

'So, do I take your case?' Shirley asked, getting very confused.

Dolly was about to explode, but she had to keep her calm in order to keep Shirley calm. 'No, not right away . . . you leave it on the carousel and watch me. If customs stop me and open the case, I act all surprised that there's men's clothes inside, and even more surprised if they dig down as far as the money. I say I must have picked up the wrong case. I go back to the carousel and pick up the suitcase with the blue tag. My case, my clothes. And I deny all knowledge of the other one.'

Shirley was staring, hands clasped together between her heaving bosoms, taking huge deep breaths. She looked like a rabbit caught in the headlights. But she was listening . . . really listening. A tornado could have swept through the lounge and Shirley wouldn't have taken her eyes off Dolly's face.

'Now, listen hard,' Dolly continued, slow and exact. 'If, and *only* if, I get through customs safely, then you pick up my case. If you get stopped there's no problem because both of your cases are full of women's clothes.' Dolly ended with a triumphant smile. Her plan was brilliant!

Shirley's mind had gone to putty. She slumped into an armchair. 'I'll never remember all that!'

Dolly controlled her temper and sat on the arm of the chair. The last thing she needed was for Shirley to lose her bottle. 'Course you can do it, darlin'. Look at everything you've done so far! The case switch is a doddle compared to the robbery. So, in your own time, go over it once again, just to be sure.'

Shirley began again, but Dolly wasn't really listening; her eyes were on the clock. Where was bloody Audrey? As Shirley talked the whole plan through again, Dolly got up, crossed to the window and pulled the curtains back very slightly. Bill Grant was still there, still watching.

'I don't see why we're taking such a risk, Dolly,' Shirley was beginning to whine. 'I mean, why do we have to take this amount of money with us? It's crazy! We don't need all this. What if you're caught?'

Dolly clenched her fists and her face twisted. 'It's me taking the risk!' she snapped. 'Me carrying it through Rio customs, not you. You've got bloody sod all to do except to carry your case and mine through. If the customs officers don't believe me then I'm the one that gets arrested, so shut your face and do as I ask!'

Shirley was close to tears, not because Dolly had shouted at her, but because she was so stressed the slightest thing might tip her over the edge. She picked up Harry's clothes and threw them into the case.

'Is that how you pack for a holiday?' Dolly demanded. Shirley stopped what she was doing and shook her head. 'Then please pack them properly,' Dolly went on. 'Because if customs do open the case, I don't want them to suspect anything out of the ordinary.'

Shirley pulled Harry's clothes back out of the suitcase and folded each item before putting it into the case, covering the money bit by bit. 'What do we do if you get arrested?' she asked quietly from her position on the floor. 'Me, Bella and Linda will have no money and no way of getting back home.'

Dolly was suddenly livid. She had been forking out thousands of pounds from the get-go and now all Shirley was thinking of was herself and the other girls. The girls saw her as a goddamned bank, churning out cash as and when they needed it. What they didn't realise was that *she* didn't have any more money – or, at least, not any she could get her hands on quickly. That suitcase contained everything she had right now. If Dolly did get arrested, they'd all be in huge trouble – but at least they'd be in huge trouble by a swimming pool.

Shirley sniffed pathetically as she continued to pack Harry's clothes on top of the money. Dolly knew she was frightened and she knew that Shirley, out of all the girls, was the least selfish. She'd never been the one to question where the money was stashed or when they'd get their cuts. Shirley was just scared and needed to know that everything was going to be OK. Dolly spoke kindly.

'I gave Bella and Linda a large sum of money each before they left. That'll be enough to see them and you through if I do get caught.'

Shirley let out a quiet laugh. 'Knowing those two, they'll have blown the money already.'

'You might be right,' said Dolly. 'Look – if I had any money left, darlin', I'd give it to you, but right now I'm out of hard cash. Why don't you take a couple of grand out of the money case and stick it in your handbag just in case it all goes wrong? How does that sound?'

Shirley lifted up some of Harry's clothes and looked at the money in the case. She was conflicted – she knew exactly what Bella and Linda would say if they were here. Then she spoke. 'It's not just your money, Dolly. It belongs to all four of us. Maybe risking losing a hundred thousand isn't the right thing to do? Maybe we should both just take a couple of thousand in our handbags?'

Dolly held her temper. She could understand Shirley's concerns, but she wasn't the brightest thing on two legs. She was prepared to explain this as many times as was necessary while they waited for Audrey to show her face, because Dolly needed Shirley to be bang on her game from this moment forwards.

'We'll need a lot of money, much more than a couple of thousand here and there, because we won't be coming back to England for quite some time,' Dolly explained. 'Not until the heat dies down back here. The more we take out, the safer we'll be.'

Shirley tightened her lips and continued with the packing. Eventually, she asked Dolly if she'd like a cup of tea or something to eat; she'd had nothing for hours. Dolly didn't reply, she just crossed to the drinks cabinet, poured herself a brandy and sat down.

'Go and phone your mum again,' said Dolly. 'And if she answers, ask her why the hell she hasn't left her flat yet.'

With Shirley out of the room, Dolly dug her heel into the plush cream carpet and looked round the room. She'd get a good price for the house, not to mention all the furniture and antiques. She twisted her heel, digging it further into the carpet, imagining it was the smashed photo of her and Harry from the bedroom. Then, her leg relaxed and her eyes filled with tears: she could almost feel Wolf snuggled by her feet, his warm body against her ankle. Sadness turned to anger and Dolly made her decision there and then. Everything belonged to her now. If she was playing the part of the grieving widow, she'd tell her lawyers to sell the lot.

She got up, went to Harry's study and looked in his desk drawer for the deeds to the house, which she then folded up and placed in her handbag. This desk was so tidy, so unused and so . . . sterile. It was beautiful and ornate, but, when it came down to it, it could belong to anyone. There was nothing about this desk that screamed 'Harry Rawlins'. No personality, nothing to tell you anything about the man himself. The rest of the house said so much about them as a couple, but, Dolly now realised, this was mainly her doing. She was the one who had filled the house with beautiful things and made it into a home. She was the one whose personality was stamped across every room. Harry Rawlins had left little trace of himself anywhere. He was a mystery. 'How can you have been so stupid for so long?' Dolly whispered to herself.

Once again, Dolly was filled with a sense of clarity. She rifled through the small filing cabinet in the corner of Harry's study and found a copy of his will and his latest bank statements. She put everything into her bag along with the deeds to the house. She was the one and only beneficiary named in Harry's will and he, on paper, was dead and buried. Once her lawyers had got rid of the house, she'd have all the money transferred to a bank in Rio. She'd make at least £150,000 on the property alone.

And once she was settled in Rio, she'd stop any unnecessary bank transactions. The first to be cancelled would be the monthly rent on Iris Rawlins' flat in St Johns Wood! There was no way Dolly was going to continue sending money to a woman she loathed. Iris would have to fend for herself and Dolly rather hoped she would have to sell the flat and go into an old people's home. The very thought of Iris in a home made Dolly smile. But the thought of Harry finding out that Iris was in a home made her stop smiling. Dolly's actions today were irreversible. Harry, once he and Iris were both homeless and penniless, would kill Dolly if he ever saw her again.

Dolly's heart ached for the days when she was happy and when she was ignorant of her husband's betrayals. Harry had let her believe he was dead, he'd let her mourn and he'd let her bury a stranger – a man she now assumed was Jimmy Nunn. After all, if Harry was shacked up in Trudie's flat, then Jimmy couldn't still be on the scene. And that baby . . . Was it Harry's baby? Dolly screwed up her eyes, trying to squeeze the thought right out of her head. But it wouldn't go.

Through her tightly closed eyelids, the tears found their way out and rolled down her cheeks. If Harry had simply found the life he truly wanted with another woman and left Dolly, she could have forgiven him. It would have been heart-breaking of course, but she'd have understood because she, too, would have done anything to have a family. But Harry didn't just leave her for another woman; he'd torn her apart in the process with his lies and deceit and cruelty. How could she ever know what was true and what had been a lie?

* * *

Shirley stood by the study door and repeated herself for the third time. Dolly was miles away. 'There's no answer at me mum's, so she must be on her way.'

Dolly swigged back the brandy. It hit her stomach hard, warming her as she looked at the clock. Almost 3.15 a.m.

Shirley and Dolly went back through to the lounge. Dolly poured herself another brandy and sat opposite Shirley, who told her to go easy as it wouldn't be a good idea to turn up at the airport pissed. Dolly swung one leg over the other, tapped the carpet with the toe of her shoe, got out a cigarette and lit up.

'Chuck one over, Dolly,' Shirley said.

Dolly threw a cigarette like a dart at Shirley and it landed neatly on her lap. 'Wasn't long ago you hated the stench of smoking,' Dolly remarked.

'We've all changed these past months, Dolly. Hard not to.'

The telephone rang and Dolly nearly jumped out of her skin. They both listened, frozen to the spot – one ring, two rings, three rings, four. On and on. 'It'll be Greg,' Shirley said. She answered the phone cautiously at first, but then relaxed; she kept saying 'yes' and nodding. Then she put the phone down. 'He's parked my car in the cul-de-sac outside number fifteen; the keys are under the seat. He said don't forget to give me mum the money for doing it.'

Dolly just dragged on her cigarette and swigged her brandy.

'Seems funny Greg worrying about a hundred quid, considering how much I'm worth now.' Shirley smiled. 'How much you reckon, Dolly?'

'You're worth about two hundred and fifty grand, darlin'. I took off what I laid out for you each so far from my own pocket . . . but still. A real tidy sum.' Dolly got up and peered out of the curtains again. 'Shit!' she exclaimed. 'Eddie's back.' Shirley joined her at the window and they watched Eddie and Bill standing close to each other and talking in whispers. 'Two of them complicates things.'

'Why?' Shirley asked, wide-eyed and vacant.

Dolly turned away from Shirley. Quite how Shirley had got through life so far was baffling, but then she'd always had Terry to look after her. Dolly sat down, lit another cigarette from the stub of the one she had on the go and threw it into the ashtray; her foot was now jerking up and down, twitching all the time.

The two sat in silence, the clock ticking away on the mantel. Shirley watched Dolly out of the corner of her eye. Her lips were moving, as if she was talking to herself. 'What are we going to do, Dolly? How can we lose two of them?'

'Where in God's name is your mother?' Dolly was sick of having to have the answers to stupid questions.

Shirley moved to the window again. Bill was sitting on the bonnet of the BMW and Eddie was standing next to him. 'What's to stop them from coming into the house?' Shirley asked. 'What's to stop them looking in the case and finding the money?'

Questions! Always questions! Dolly wanted to scream at Shirley. 'Harry! Harry's stopping them from coming into the house!' Bill and Eddie must be under orders to watch and nothing more, otherwise they'd have come in by now. Course, those orders could change in the blink of an eye but, right now, there was a stand-off.

Shirley was winding herself up. 'Once they saw that money, they'd want the rest! They'd want it all. I can't imagine what they'd do to get it.'

'Don't, then!' Dolly shouted. 'Don't stand there imagining what *might* happen.' Dolly took a breath. She had to calm Shirley down. 'The money's safe, love. They'll never find it.'

'But only you know where it is – and if anything happens to you, what then?'

Dolly closed her eyes and looked away from Shirley.

Shirley was getting herself into a state. 'Why are they just watching? Why don't they do something?'

'Calm down.'

'Calm down! How are you so calm? So cold? Stone cold. What aren't you telling me?' Dolly couldn't believe that Shirley was choosing this moment to grow a pair of balls and turn into Linda. 'Who's that man with your Harry's cousin? Another relative?'

'My God,' Dolly exclaimed. 'Your brain's working overtime all of a sudden, ain't it?'

'Well, you don't seem scared by the fact that they could burst in here at any moment and kill us both! And that's because you know they're not going to, isn't it? You *know*. How? You've got an arrangement, haven't you?' It hardly seemed possible, but Dolly's face was becoming even more stern, her lips narrowing and her jaw twitching. Shirley was on a roll, fuelled by fear. 'You and Eddie got plans? Did I stop him from getting the money last time, did I? I'm feeling very outnumbered here, Dolly, and I want to know where the rest of the money is, right now!'

Dolly had her arms tightly folded so as not to slap Shirley's stupid head right off her shoulders. But then Shirley opened her frantic mouth one more time. 'If you've got Eddie lined up to step into your Harry's shoes, I want my money first!'

Face twisting with uncontrollable anger, Dolly launched herself forwards and slapped Shirley hard across the face. Shirley took it without flinching, and returned the slap so hard Dolly had to step back to stop herself from falling over.

'What I just said about you and Eddie having an arrangement was out of order,' Shirley said. 'But I want to know where the money is, Dolly. I want to know for me, for Linda and for Bella.'

Dolly was at breaking point. She'd lost the will to argue or to defend her actions. If it all went wrong, she wanted to be the only one the police could possibly lean on for the money – but right now, she couldn't give a damn.

'The money's at the convent,' Dolly said. 'There's a row of new lockers in the kiddies' playroom. The top four lockers, well out of reach, are covered with nursery rhyme posters. That's where the money is. Four lockers, four bags, four equal shares. All ready for when it's safe to come home.' She sat on the sofa and opened her handbag. 'I've got a key for each of you. When the time comes to collect, just mention my name.' Dolly stood and looked Shirley square in the eyes as she handed her the keys one by one. 'Here's Linda's key. And Bella's. And yours.' There was such disappointment in Dolly's eyes, Shirley didn't know what to say.

The silence was broken by the doorbell.

'That'll be Mum,' Shirley whispered.

All they could do now was stick to the plan. They needed each other. Everything else would wait.

* * *

Eddie watched the woman, dressed in a tatty coat, boots and headscarf, standing on Dolly's doorstep. When the door was opened and she was let in, Bill and Eddie looked at each other.

'Maybe it's the cleaner?' Eddie speculated.

'That'll be it,' Bill said sarcastically. 'My cleaner starts at four in the morning as well. It could be one of the other women who done the robbery. I'm going to go tell Harry.' He got into the BMW and drove off.

Eddie climbed back into the Granada and resumed his watch.

* * *

When Shirley and Audrey entered the lounge, Dolly had recovered her composure and was sitting, smiling, with her fourth brandy in her hand.

'You know Mrs Rawlins, Mum?'

'Lovely home you've got,' Audrey said, putting on a posh voice and trying to pretend she'd been inside a house like this before.

'Sit down.' Dolly waved her hand at an armchair. She got out her purse. 'Here's one hundred pounds for your Greg and two hundred for you, for your trouble.'

'Bleedin' 'ell!' Audrey exclaimed, taking the money. Shirley rolled her eyes at how quickly her mum's classy façade had slipped.

'What I'd like you to do, Audrey, is drive my Mercedes into London and then go south, through Croydon and onto the A23 towards Gatwick,' Dolly explained as though it was the most natural thing in the world to ask a stranger to do at four o'clock in the morning.

Audrey stared at Dolly, jaw dangling so low she was in danger of dribbling down her coat. 'I'm not sure I quite understand—'

'Mum,' Shirley interrupted, dragging on a newly lit cigarette. 'Just do as Dolly asks. Please.'

'Since when have you smoked?' Audrey shouted.

'Mum!'

'The other thing is, Audrey,' Dolly continued, getting back on track, 'that a man in a Ford Granada will probably follow you. If you could do your best to try and lose him around the Croydon area, that'd be best. Now,' she got to her feet, 'would you excuse me for a moment?"

As Dolly left the room, Audrey leapt to her feet. 'What the bleedin' 'ell's going on, Shirl? Are you going away with her? How come?'

'Please, Mum. She's got some heavies after her and I'm helping her out, that's all.'

'That's all! That's *all*? That's enough, my girl. She dragging you into trouble, is she? Cos we can leave now . . .'

'No, Mum.' Shirley bowed her head, recalling the row she and Dolly had just had. 'She's my friend and I want to go with her.'

Audrey took the cigarette from Shirley and took a huge drag, then puffed the smoke out in a circle as she turned to admire the ornate room. 'A Merc!' Audrey laughed. 'Bet you didn't tell her I ain't passed my test yet.'

* * *

When Dolly came back downstairs, she was carrying a designer dress, patent leather shoes and a headscarf of her own. 'There's a cloakroom just by the front door. Go and get changed.'

Bewildered by the request, Audrey did as she was asked for Shirley's sake. Dolled up – and from behind – Audrey looked surprisingly like Dolly. From the front, she still looked like a market trader, but with Dolly's headscarf, make-up and glasses, the disguise would be good enough to fool Eddie.

Audrey's own coat looked awful and ruined the entire effect, so Dolly went to the hallway closet and returned with the long black mink coat Harry had given her for their eighteenth wedding anniversary. Eddie had been at that party and had commented on how amazing it was. This would definitely fool him.

Dolly held the coat up and Audrey carefully slipped her arms into the sleeves. 'Oh, this is lovely,' Audrey said, completely distracted. 'Lovely. Ain't it, Shirl?' Audrey stroked her own arms – the coat felt like silk. She felt like the bee's knees.

Shirley and Dolly stood back and examined Audrey from top to toe. Although things were still strained between them, they both knew this part of the plan had to go smoothly. If Eddie doubted for a second that Audrey was Dolly, he wouldn't follow her and they wouldn't be able to escape.

Dolly's an odd sort of woman, Audrey thought, *very exact, yet edgy*. Mind you, Shirley seemed very jumpy too. She couldn't figure out why her daughter was going away with the much older Dolly Rawlins. Couldn't figure out how or why they'd be friends or even know each other, really. She knew they had dead husbands in common, but the women themselves had never been pally. Above all, Audrey wondered who was after Dolly and why Shirley was willing to put herself in the firing line. As for Audrey's part in all of this – she'd have danced naked on the doorstep of the local nick for £200, so driving a Merc about dressed in a mink coat was nothing but a pleasure.

Dolly and Shirley nodded at each other. Audrey was as ready as she'd ever be. Dolly handed Audrey the car keys to the Merc. 'You can keep the mink,' she said, then, 'Shirley, love,' she went on, 'would you grab my dark glasses from the dressing table drawer, please?' When Shirley left the room, Dolly turned back to Audrey. 'I need you to do one other little thing for me, please.' She handed Audrey an envelope. Seeing the stupid woman's eyes light up, she leant slowly towards her. 'I need you to buy a stamp and post this for me. Today.'

Audrey was clearly disappointed, but as she slipped the envelope into the pocket of the mink coat, she smiled. *I post a letter and get a mink coat for me troubles*, she thought to herself. *Not a bad day's work, Audrey. Not a bad day's work at all.*

What Audrey didn't know was that the letter contained the deeds to the house, a copy of Harry's will, and a letter of instruction for Dolly's lawyers to sell the house and everything in it. The lawyer would then bank the money in a new account. This was it for Dolly. No turning back.

* * *

As Shirley entered Dolly's bedroom, the smell of burning was still in the air, although there was no sign of fire or anything burnt. The contents of the dressing table still lay scattered across the bedroom floor where Dolly had thrown them. A bottle of nail varnish had smashed against the wall near the wardrobe and the deep plum coloured contents had slowly seeped out and onto the cream carpet. Shirley was shocked to see such a mess in an otherwise pristine house and blamed it on one of Dolly's meltdowns. Searching the drawers of the dressing table, she eventually found Dolly's dark glasses and was about the leave when she noticed a stray scrap of material on the carpet. She slowly opened the wardrobe door and gasped. There wasn't a single article of clothing in Harry's wardrobe that hadn't been cut to shreds. Even his shoes were slashed or stained with a rainbow of nail varnish colours. How tormented Dolly must have been to be so destructive and how strong she must have been to hide it all morning. Shirley realised that there was much more going on inside Dolly Rawlins than she could never imagine.

Back in the lounge, Dolly handed Audrey her own tatty coat and woolly boots. 'Stick them in the boot of the Merc,' Dolly instructed.

'I might have to wear the boots, actually. I'm no good on the clutch in high heels.'

'There is no clutch,' Dolly replied. 'The Merc's an automatic.'

'A what?'

Oh, God, thought Dolly. *I'll have to give the stupid woman a crash course in how to drive!* 'Come through to the garage. I'll show you.' She was being as patient as possible, considering that it was now almost 4.30 a.m. and they needed to get to the airport so as not to miss their flight to Rio.

Audrey got into the driver's seat and Dolly explained the two pedals and shift stick. Dolly could see that Audrey was getting her left and right mixed up, so she punched her hard in the left thigh. 'Don't use the leg that hurts, all right, love?'

* * *

They headed back into the house, where Shirley handed her mum the dark glasses to complete her disguise. Audrey took some deep breaths; this was the most exciting thing she'd ever been asked to do.

'Well,' she said to Shirley. 'Have a nice time away. And I suppose I'll see you when you get back.' Audrey leant forwards to kiss Shirley on the cheek, but Shirley grabbed her and hugged her tight.

'Bye, Mum,' Shirley whispered.

'Come on. We got to go.' Dolly didn't want Audrey to start thinking there was something wrong.

'I love you . . .' Shirley added, turning quickly away from her mum. She went out of the front door to open the garage doors from the outside, so Eddie could see her.

* * *

Audrey put the Merc into reverse and started to back it down the drive. Shirley waved from the front door step. 'See you later, Dolly,' she called and started to close the garage doors. A nervous Audrey put her foot down a bit too hard on the accelerator and the car lurched backwards at speed into the road. Audrey hit the brake and turned the wheel at the same time. The car screeched: the rear wheels skidded off to the right and in a panic Audrey slammed it into drive. It lurched forward and took off at high speed down the wrong side of the road, but Audrey soon righted herself and off she went.

Eddie had watched all of this unfold. As soon as Dolly's Merc fired up, Eddie had started the Granada. It was unusual for her to kangaroo down the road as clumsily as she did, but Eddie figured that she was in a hurry. *Maybe she's cracking up*, he thought. If so, then taking the money from her would be like taking candy from a baby. Eddie smiled to himself as he thought about all the money he, Bill and Harry would end up with. 'Stupid bitch,' he muttered as he took off after Dolly's Merc. 'You done all that hard work for nothing. Cos now we're coming for you, Dolly Rawlins.'

* * *

From the living room, Shirley watched Eddie's car turn the corner. Behind her, Dolly stood, all ready to go, holding the two suitcases.

'He's gone.' Shirley took one suitcase from Dolly and they both headed for the front door.

'Come on then, Shirl – move it. The way your mum drives, we might not have as long as we need.'

Dolly and Shirley ran as fast as they could down the road towards the cul-de-sac where Shirley's Mini estate was parked up. Shirley's ankle was still bruised and every step was agony. 'You still there?' Dolly shouted back without looking.

'I'm right behind you,' Shirley replied, battling through the pain. Then the adrenalin started to take effect and Shirley found her stride, closing the gap between her and Dolly. When they reached the car, they threw the two identical cases into the boot on top of Shirley's suitcase.

Shirley bent down by the driver's seat and reached underneath to find the keys. Dolly impatiently tapped the roof of the car with her hand.

'Come on, darlin',' Dolly said. 'Your mum'll probably have crashed by now and Eddie will have figured out that she ain't me.'

'I can't find—' Shirley froze. 'What would he do to her?'

Dolly realised her joke was a mistake. 'Nothing, Shirl, I promise. He's a coward.'

'That's not what you called him earlier,' Shirley replied, still searching for the keys. 'You said he was a runt who slaps women and kills dogs. Well, she's a woman, Dolly, and if he lays one finger on her . . .' Shirley stood up with the car keys in her hand.

Dolly took the keys and spoke gently. 'I know, love . . . you'll kill him.'

Shirley stared at Dolly. Strong and fixed. 'No, Dolly,' she said. 'Not him.'

Shirley walked round to the passenger door, leaving Dolly staring into space. She'd probably lost Shirley completely now. Dolly had used Audrey and Greg to get what she wanted. What she needed. Greg could have ended up in prison and Audrey could still end up dead. Shirley, the girl who had once looked at her like a mother, hated her.

But Dolly would make it right. Once they were safe, she would make it right.

CHAPTER 37

Alice knew she could get into trouble if she got caught, possibly even lose her job, but she was doing it because George Resnick had asked her to.

She'd been in the office since 6 a.m.; no other admin staff were about this early to see what she was up to. Picking up the files and the neatly typed notes from her desk, she put them all into a plastic bag, hurried off down the corridor and out of the station. None of the night shift officers gave her a second look as she passed them.

As arranged, Resnick was waiting for Alice in the greasy spoon round the corner. He was slurping on a coffee and eating a sausage and egg sandwich covered in HP sauce when she arrived. He waved to the waitress as Alice sat down. 'Nice to see you, girl.' He smiled, showing little bits of sausage skin between his teeth.

'And you, sir,' Alice replied, eyeing the brown sauce dribbling down Resnick's fingers. If he got any of that on the files, everyone would know exactly who'd been handling them. Resnick was forever spilling things on important paperwork and all his files had been decorated with coffee rings from his dirty mug.

The waitress brought a pot of tea to Alice and Resnick beamed. Alice hated tea, but she accepted it with thanks: it was rare that Resnick bought anyone anything. She got up and collected a pile of napkins from the counter and handed them to Resnick, waiting until he'd obediently wiped his mucky hands before handing him the first file. Then she gave him a summary of the most important bits of information.

'You won't find much there about Jimmy Nunn. He's got no criminal record so I got everything from the Social. He'd had high hopes of being a racing driver, and he's got two traffic convictions for reckless driving and speeding. Married to Trudie, one child aged six months. Receiving Child Benefit, non-taxpayer, unemployed for two years and, according to the dole office, he hasn't claimed for the past two months.'

'Why hasn't he claimed, Alice?' Resnick asked. 'Prison? No. Travelling? Probably not if he's got a six-month-old kid. Employed? Doubtful, after two years of skiving. Dead?' He glanced up at Alice and she could almost hear the cogs turning.

Alice passed Resnick the second, larger file. 'William Grant was released from Brixton prison nine months ago,' she said. 'GBH, robbery, arson.'

'Murder?' Resnick asked.

Alice poured herself a cup of tea. 'No murder convictions. But you'll see that his crimes are – what's the word?'

'Random?' Resnick suggested.

'Yes. Often no connection to the victim, nothing stolen . . . it's as though he was acting on behalf of someone else and getting his money that way.'

Resnick smiled again. He loved the way Alice's brain sometimes worked like his. She had superb gut instinct. 'You're right, Alice. He's a hired thug. The last time I put him inside, he was "no comment" from the get-go.' Resnick looked at the photo. It was definitely the same man he had seen leaving Jimmy Nunn's house.

'And now . . .' Alice passed Resnick the third file – the file on the latest security wagon raid.

Resnick read fast. It was page after page of textbook Harry Rawlins MO. He *knew* it was Harry bloody Rawlins. He couldn't keep the grin off his face. 'I've got him, Alice. We've only bloody well got the bastard!'

Alice checked her watch. Any moment now the day shift could come in for their morning fry-up. 'Sir – you're not going to do anything stupid, are you?' she asked.

Resnick closed the file and handed it back to Alice, who put all the files back into the carrier bag. He smiled again. 'I'm on my way back, Alice. They were all wrong about Harry Rawlins being dead. And I'm going to show them.' He looked at Alice's worried face, her big hands clutching the plastic bag to her bosom. He leant across the table and placed a big wet kiss on her cheek. 'Don't worry about me. I don't like to see you worried – especially about me.'

Alice managed a quivering smile before she got up and left the cafe. Her heart was pounding; partly because she knew Resnick was now going after Harry Rawlins on his own and partly because she could still feel his warm, sticky lips on her cheek.

* * *

Instead of going straight to tell Harry about the arrival of the mystery woman at Dolly's house, Bill Grant had taken a detour via the lock-ups by Liverpool Street. He reasoned that the mystery woman had to be part of the robbery team. Harry was preparing to come out into the open and confront Dolly at the house. If the money was there, Bill would get his measly cut and Harry would get the lion's share. But if the money was at the lock-up and Bill found it on his own – well, then, screw Harry Rawlins.

He didn't realise how much time had passed as he searched every nook and cranny of the lock-up. He'd found nothing, and when he'd looked at his watch, he'd realised it was after 7 a.m. He was an hour late: he'd been supposed to pick up Harry at six . . .

When he got to Trudie's, Bill parked up and ran from the car up the stairs to the flat, breathing heavily as he knocked on the door.

Trudie opened it. She looked him up and down as if he was low-life. 'Come in,' she said. 'Harry expected you an hour ago.'

Bill tapped his watch as he entered the lounge. 'Sorry, Harry. This thing's on the blink again. Nothing's happening at your place anyway: they're like sitting ducks.'

'Really?' Harry said. 'Then someone's lying.' He was dressed in a pair of blue jeans, white crew neck T-shirt, blue jumper and trainers.

'What do you mean?' Bill said nervously.

Harry closed in on Bill, his stare menacing. 'Where you been, Bill? What you been up to?'

'I did grab a quick bit of shut-eye after I left Eddie – I'm knackered, Harry.' Bill didn't dare tell him he'd been to the lock-up. He saw the look of simmering anger on Harry's face. 'What's happened?'

Harry's eyes lit up with rage. 'While you was kippin', Doll pulled a fast one on the pair of you! She got someone to dress up as her and drive away in the Merc. That prick Eddie fell for it and now we don't have a fuckin' clue where Dolly's gone. And you can guarantee the money ain't in the house now.'

It was beginning to dawn on Bill that he'd messed up big time. 'So, where's Eddie now?'

'He phoned me earlier, his car's knackered so he's making his way here by bus. When he arrives, we're all going to the house to tear it apart. There'll be something there; some clue as to where Dolly's gone or where she's stashed the money.'

* * *

Dolly pulled up outside Victoria bus station to drop Shirley off. Shirley would get the bus to Heathrow and Dolly would continue by car, so nobody would suspect they were travelling together. The street was pretty busy, even at that time of the morning, and the idea of being jostled about by strangers with a hundred grand in a suitcase was sending Shirley into a panic.

'I can't do this, Dolly. I want to stay with you.' All her earlier bravado had disappeared.

Dolly, on the other hand, was now back in complete control. 'I'd like us to stay together as well, darlin',' she lied. 'But you know why we have to split up. We can't be seen arriving at the airport together in the same car. No one can suspect we even know each other. Come on.'

She got out of the car, opened the boot and heaved the money case and Shirley's case out onto the street, setting them down just outside the passenger door. Through the window, Dolly could see that Shirley had her head dipped and was crying. *Bleedin' 'ell,'* Dolly thought to herself. *She's all I need!* Getting back into the car, she said in a loving voice, 'Go on, darlin'. Couple of hours and we'll be in the air. This time tomorrow, we'll be by the pool with Linda and Bella sipping – well, sipping whatever the hell they drink in Rio.'

Shirley looked at Dolly with her puppy-dog eyes. 'All right,' Dolly said finally. 'You can stick with me. Go and put the cases back in the boot.'

As soon as Shirley was out of the car, Dolly chucked her handbag out after her, slammed the passenger door shut, started the engine and was off up the road before Shirley realised what was happening. She was about to shout and curse after Dolly . . . then she looked around and decided against it. The idea of drawing attention to herself was even more frightening than the idea of making her way to Heathrow all on her own.

* * *

Eddie arrived at Jimmy Nunn's, exhausted and sweating. The bus hadn't come and he'd had to run over a mile. When Harry opened the door, he dragged Eddie in by his scarf, tightening it so hard that Eddie's face went blue. Eddie feebly pushed at Harry's solid shoulders, but Harry didn't shift an inch.

Harry spoke calm and low. 'You're a fucking waste of skin, Eddie, you know that? If I killed you right here and now, who'd miss you? Eh? The bookies. And that's only a maybe.' Eddie's eyes bulged in his head as his face turned purple and his hands screwed Harry's jumper up in his fists. Harry stared into Eddie's eyes and waited for him to stop moving.

From behind Harry, Bill spoke. 'This ain't a good place to remove a body from, Harry. Way too busy.' Harry released his grip on the scarf and Eddie fell to the floor, gasping for breath. Bill helped him up onto the sofa and sat beside him.

Harry paced up and down in front of them, taking deep breaths to calm himself down. 'If she's gone – if the money's gone – I'm going to kill the pair of you. Starting with you.' Harry pointed his finger at Eddie.

Eddie was terrified. Inadvertently, he let out a small giggle. Harry tore across the room, ready to beat him to death. Bill stood up and stepped in between them to catch Harry. With all his might, he pushed the furious man backwards.

'I said not here!' Bill shouted, hoping to God that Harry would listen. 'I'm trying to help you, Harry! He might be a useless piece of shit, but this is your home. Your girl and your kid are just through there. If you want him dead, fine, I'll do it meself when all this is over. When we got the money and Dolly's got what's coming to her for making you look like a fool. It's her you're angry at, Harry, not him. He's nothing.'

The red mist faded, Harry slowly calmed down and turned away from Eddie to stop himself losing it again. Bill glanced at Eddie and gave him a small wink. It was like being smiled at by a crocodile before heading in for a swim.

'We're going to go back to the house,' Harry said, 'and we're going to tear it apart.' He snatched up his coat. 'COME ON!'

From the bedroom, Trudie raced out and grabbed Harry's arm. 'Please, Harry! It's daylight. I'm begging you not to go out. If anyone sees you, that's it. It's all over.'

Harry lurched towards Eddie and grabbed his scarf again. Eddie nearly pissed himself on the spot but Harry put the scarf round his own neck, pulling it up to cover his nose and mouth.

For a split second, it had occurred to Bill that he and Eddie might stand up to Harry together: he couldn't take the two of them on in a fight. The thought was short-lived as he watched a quivering Eddie rub his sore neck and attempt to walk in a straight line, and the two of them followed Harry out of the flat.

Trudie ran to the window just in time to see the three men get into Jimmy's BMW. As Trudie watched Bill drive off, she noticed a car parked a short distance away pull out at the same time. It stopped and didn't move off again until another car was sitting between it and the BMW. At the end of the road, the BMW turned left, the car immediately behind it turned right but the suspect car waited for a van to pass and sit behind the BMW before it pulled out, also turning to the left.

Trudie slammed her hands on the window. There was nothing she could do. She didn't even know where Harry had lived with Dolly.

The baby screamed from the bedroom. Trudie knew exactly how he felt: she too wanted to open up her lungs and let it all out. It was all going horribly wrong. Harry had been so careful for so long, and then Dolly soddin' Rawlins had to go and do one of his robberies! The stupid cow. The stupid, old, ugly cow!

Trudie raced into the bedroom and shouted, 'SHUT UP!' The baby, who was sitting in his playpen, howling for no apparent reason, turned up the volume. Trudie felt as if her world was about to collapse around her and she suddenly snapped and slapped the child hard. Instantly mortified, she picked him up and squeezed him tight. Shaken by the slap, the baby fell silent, while Trudie sobbed her heart out.

* * *

Shirley waited nervously at Heathrow as the bus driver lifted the cases from the luggage compartment. *Just wait till I see her*, she thought angrily to herself. *I'll tell her what I think. And I'll tell the girls that she left me in the street. Linda will hate her even more when she hears that!* She realised that she sounded like a petty, sulky child but, right now, this anger was helping her keep her focus.

She got a trolley, placed the two cases on it and, entering the terminal, checked the illuminated notice board for the Rio flight check-in desk. Pushing her trolley over to the check-in queue, she took some deep breaths and got down to the job of looking over the passengers for an appropriate stooge. '*Young bloke, very little luggage . . .*' she repeated to herself. The thought of flirting with a total stranger filled her with dread. She was surprisingly bad at flirting, except with judging panels at beauty competitions. She took a moment to get her head straight and then practised fluttering her eyelashes.

After about twenty minutes, she began to feel scared. Everyone in the queue so far had big cases – and she hadn't spotted Dolly anywhere. What if the plan failed at the first hurdle because she couldn't find a single gullible man travelling light?

Shirley wheeled the trolley up and down, watching and waiting. Fifteen more minutes passed with no one suitable joining the queue. She began to get edgy: she might have to risk taking the case herself and paying for the excess luggage with the cash she'd put into her handbag. She didn't want to do that as the serial numbers on bank notes could be traced.

Suddenly she saw a likely candidate. A scruffy-looking young man with only a rucksack had joined the end of the queue and was checking over his flight papers. Shirley grabbed her ticket and passport out of her handbag, quickly pushed her way in behind him and clipped his heel with the trolley.

'Oh, I'm so sorry! I didn't mean to bump you. Is this the queue for the Rio flight?' Pretending to be flustered, she dropped her ticket and passport. He bent to pick them up for her and handed them back. 'I've been such a silly thing,' Shirley continued, playing the dumb blonde beautifully. 'I'm a model and I'm doing my very first foreign magazine shoot in Rio. I didn't realise there was a weight restriction on the luggage and I've brought two cases filled with dresses and bikinis. Now I'm worried that I'm way over the allowance and I can't think what on earth to do because I've got no money to pay for extra luggage. I really do need seventeen bikinis though and . . .'

She didn't even have to finish her sentence. 'Why don't you let me help you out?' the young man said, and moved to grab Shirley's own case from the trolley. She put her hand on top of his.

'The other one's a little heavier,' she said, 'so if you don't mind . . .?'

He clearly didn't mind. He gave her a quick wink and picked up the money case as he shuffled forwards.

Feeling very chuffed with herself, Shirley kept up the polite chat as they queued for check in. He smelt of body odour, looked unwashed and unkempt, but his voice suggested that he was well educated, although clearly not very streetwise. She was relieved to watch her new friend, who told her his name was Charles, check in and put the money case on the conveyor belt. The attendant placed a sticky luggage tag around the handle and Shirley watched her hundred grand head for the plane.

When it was Shirley's turn to check in, she whispered to the lady at the desk, 'Please can you make sure I'm not sitting near that man?' The lady glanced at Charles, smiled her understanding and with female solidarity sat Shirley a good ten rows away from him.

Charles hovered around her through passport control and into the departure lounge. He rambled on about how he travelled to different destinations and how he had hitchhiked his way across countries, sightseeing and doing all sorts of jobs to pay his way. His parents were wealthy but he refused to sponge off them and always found the cheapest and most economical ways to travel. *Oh, my God!* Shirley thought to herself as she sipped the champagne Charles had bought her, *he's* so *boring!* Eventually, she made her excuses and said that she had some important calls to make to her agent prior to boarding.

Shirley looked in every restaurant, burger bar, pub and wine bar – even the bathrooms – but she couldn't see Dolly anywhere. It was as if Dolly wasn't taking the flight to Rio at all. Shirley knew she couldn't turn back, not now the money bag was on the plane: she'd have to go to Rio and tell Bella and Linda that they'd all been stiffed! She took deep breaths as she thought through her plan of action. They'd all have to return to London on the next flight and go to the convent and – oh, God, what if the rest of the money wasn't there? What if it was never there? What if – Shirley's head was about to explode when she suddenly saw the one area of the airport she hadn't searched. And there, in the window of the first class lounge, was Dolly bloody Rawlins, eating her breakfast.

* * *

Bill Grant adjusted the mirror again and looked behind them. 'It ain't an Old Bill car, but he's definitely keeping one vehicle in between us and him.'

'Classic filth technique.' Eddie sounded panicked.

Harry checked out the car, sat back in his seat and shook his head. 'No matter how many times you swat some flies, they always come back for more.' There was real hatred in Harry's voice. The other two didn't ask for further details.

'Do I keep going?' said Bill. Going to Dolly's house in broad daylight was a bad idea, especially if someone was tailing them.

'Nothing changes,' Harry growled. He looked in the rear-view mirror again, just to be sure, and spoke through gritted teeth. 'Jesus Christ, I thought I'd done his legs and seen the last of him years ago. He followed me about for years like a bloodhound on the scent of his biggest kill. He got close, real close.'

'And now he's back . . .' said Bill.

Harry wondered how on earth Resnick could be on to him. How could he know he was still alive? Maybe he didn't . . . maybe he was watching Eddie and Bill over the murder of Boxer Davis? Harry pulled the scarf a little further up his face.He was confident he hadn't been seen when they left Jimmy's flat and he doubted Resnick would recognise him from just his eyes, not after so many years. He smiled behind the scarf. If Bill and Eddie got nicked for Boxer, that wasn't his problem.

Bill couldn't hold back any longer. 'He's filth then, is he?'

'The bloke on our tail is none other than the infamous Detective Inspector George Resnick.'

'Shit! What we gonna do, Harry?' Eddie bleated.

'Don't worry, son, Resnick's luck just ran out for good,' Harry said.

Bill pulled up a good fifty yards from Dolly's house and Resnick had no choice but to drive on past them. His intention was to go round the block, double back on himself and park up at a safe distance without, he thought, being seen. But as Resnick drove past,

Harry taunted the old man by pulling the scarf down to his chin, revealing his face. The inside of the car was too dark for Resnick to be certain; but the speed at which his heart rate increased told him that the man he'd just seen was Harry Rawlins . . .

Harry was quick to bark his orders. 'Eddie, open the garage. Bill – he's all yours.' Eddie raced across the street as instructed; Bill got out of the car and hid behind the hedge; Harry slipped across to the driver's seat and drove the BMW into the garage.

Now parked opposite, Resnick sat staring at the Rawlins house. His fists gripped the steering wheel and, when he unclenched them, his hands trembled like jelly. He watched Eddie close one garage door behind the BMW, and then another man came out of the garage and closed the second door. This man paused, looked straight at Resnick and lit a cigarette. Briefly, the flame illuminated every feature of the face Resnick had been chasing for so many years. 'Rawlins!' Resnick whispered. A broad smile crept across Resnick's face. He was right! He was always right!

He was taken completely by surprise when the driver's door was yanked open and blow after blow from Bill's knuckleduster rained down on his face. Trapped by the steering wheel, Resnick couldn't get away or defend himself properly. He raised his hands to try and deflect the punches but it was too late. His head reeled backwards and forwards from the savage attack and then he felt a hand grab his hair and repeatedly smash his face into the steering wheel. As he started to slip into unconsciousness, lights flashed before his eyes, reds, blues, yellows, a mass of bright rainbow colours. He heard the sound of his nose crunching and breaking as Bill's fist slammed into his face again. And all Resnick could do was wait to pass out, so the terrible pain would end.

Eventually, he went limp and he fell sideways, his upper body hanging partially out the car. Bill stepped back and kicked out as hard as he could at Resnick's head, causing it to snap back and shift over towards the passenger's seat. Looking up and down the street, Bill slammed the car door shut, slipped his knuckleduster back into his pocket and casually crossed back towards the house. The vicious attack on Resnick had taken less than thirty seconds.

Although Bill thought he'd slammed the car door shut, Resnick's right arm had been caught in it. The blood streamed down his fingers, his face was covered in blood, but he felt no pain now, just the cool air as the door slowly, inch by inch, swung open and away from his shattered fingers. He couldn't move, he couldn't cry out. Unable to open his swollen, bleeding eyes, Resnick simply sat and waited to be found.

As Bill jogged across the road and disappeared into the darkness of Dolly's garage, a man out walking his dog headed towards Resnick's car.

* * *

When Bill slipped in through the gap in the garage door, Eddie was already searching.

'Harry's upstairs,' he said to Bill.

Bill went through to the lounge, where he opened a flick knife and started to cut into the sofa and cushions, the same cushions that had already been slashed by Tony Fisher and neatly sewn up again by Dolly. Bill was getting Resnick's blood on the fabric, but he figured that didn't matter now.

Upstairs, Harry stood in the doorway of the empty nursery. There wasn't a scrap of furniture left; only the pale blue wallpaper with dancing teddy bears told him that this had been his son's bedroom. His nostrils flared as a strange and painful anger filled his soul. Wherever Dolly was, he now knew that she had no intention of ever coming back. This room had meant everything. Wolf had meant everything. *He* had meant everything. All gone. She had nothing to come back for.

In the guest room, the unmade bed told Harry that blondie had stayed the night. He searched, but found nothing. He was seething with fury: he had to find something quickly now, anything that would lead him to the money. Dolly had a clear head start and she was covering her tracks well; if he didn't find some clue as to where she'd gone – and fast – then the game was up and he'd be left with nothing.

In the master bedroom, he was confronted by a smell of burning and a picture of destruction – the strewn cosmetics, the smashed and trampled photo frame. Dolly was naturally such a pristine woman. He knew this room like the back of this hand but now couldn't tell if anything was out of place, because *everything* was out of place. Harry picked up a spilt bottle of face cream and set it back on the dressing table, and then he picked up the smashed photo frame and put it back on the table next to Dolly's side of the bed. He crossed to her wardrobe, opened it, and saw there were clothes and shoes missing. Then he crossed to his own wardrobe, and discovered that everything had been slashed, torn or stained with nail varnish. '*Bitch!*' he hissed. Not because of the lost clothes, but because of the hatred Dolly must have felt for him as she destroyed the designer labels he valued so highly. This was the act of a betrayed woman, a woman in pain – and a woman with nothing left to lose. There was no doubt Dolly knew he was alive.

The last remnants of Harry's old life hung in tatters before his eyes. As he slammed the wardrobe shut, the mirror on the outside of the door shattered.

'Seven years bad—' Standing in the bedroom doorway, Eddie shut his own mouth before Harry shut it for him.

Harry followed his nose to the metal waste bin and saw charred paper at the bottom. It wasn't at all clear what this was, but the cut-up leather book covers could only mean one thing. He reached into the bin, picked up a handful of ashes and let them fall between his fingers like black snow. His ledgers. His ledgers were gone. He clenched his fists; he wanted to scream at the top of his voice. He had *nothing* and Dolly, it seemed, had everything. How dare she? How fucking dare she do this? 'I'll kill you,' he whispered. 'I swear to God I'll kill you, *myself*.'

Eddie couldn't hear Harry's words and had no idea what he had just discovered. 'I'll carry on searching, shall I?' he said. 'Don't worry about the mess, Harry. Your Trudie will have this ship-shape in no time at all. And your nursery will finally get a bit of use—'

Harry erupted in sheer, uncontrolled anger and kicked Eddie in the balls, sending him crumpling to his knees. He wanted to kill Eddie, wanted to rip his heart out and feed it to him, but the weaselly little runt wasn't worth the effort. Harry spun round, let out a huge roar and slammed his fist into the wardrobe door, punching a hole straight though the wood. Splinters shot into his hand, but he didn't feel a thing.

As Eddie whimpered from the carpet, Bill ran up the stairs.

'Harry, come and see . . .' Bill stopped at the sight of Harry standing, shoulders hunched, chest heaving and blood dripping from his knuckles. His hooded eyes were as angry as the devil himself. Bill thought Harry had flipped beyond the point of no return and, if he had, then Bill was out of here – he was a cautious thug, never killing or maiming in anger, always controlled violence. He said what he'd come up to say, in case Harry was capable of snapping back to reality. 'I found something in the garden. Something buried. You interested or do you just want to kill everybody?'

Harry's eyes blinked and the glazed look disappeared. He was just stepping over Eddie, who was still on the floor nursing his balls, when the phone rang. Harry froze. He took his time to cross the bedroom and, two rings in, the phone stopped. Harry stopped. The phone rang again and, this time, it kept on ringing. He stood over the phone, his hand outstretched towards it. He knew it was Dolly; it had to be. He didn't want to give her the satisfaction of answering, but he had to. He sat on the bed and slowly picked up the receiver. No one spoke, yet through the echo of eerie silence he could sense her. 'That you, Doll?'

The line went dead.

Harry ripped the phone from the socket and hurled it across the room.

CHAPTER 38

Linda's hand was shaking as she replaced the receiver on the hotel room phone. She felt numb and the hairs on her arms were standing on end, as if a blast of ice-cold air had struck her body. She looked up at Bella, who was standing at the bathroom door in yet another creation she had bought from the hotel boutique store the night before. This time, she was wearing a green and white silk dress and she was swathed from head to foot like a Greek goddess in a matching body scarf.

'Right, tell me straight, Linda, do you think I should change this dress for the blue one, or treat myself and buy both?'

Linda was staring at the wall. That voice – she knew that voice . . .

Bella was oblivious as she plonked a sequin-covered hat at a jaunty angle on her head. 'What do you think? Does the hat go with the outfit or not?'

They'd only been in Rio for a matter of hours, but Bella had been going spend-crazy in the hotel boutique. The money Dolly had given her had gone in the blink of an eye, and her bed was covered in dress boxes, handbags, shoes and bathing suits. The hotel staff were already treating Bella as if she was Shirley Bassey, and so they should: she had so far spent thousands on hotel credit and was still going strong.

Bella looked over to Linda. She was beginning to get on her nerves. 'You been phoning London again? Shirley will be here when she's here. Stop worrying. If you call again, I'll chuck the phone in the pool.'

While Bella had been spending herself silly, Linda had been drinking herself silly. She'd drunk all the bottles of miniatures from the fridge and had been on to room service so often last night that they'd stopped asking her what she wanted; they just brought her 'usual'. She'd been drunk all night, barely slept, and now she was getting neurotic and imagining all sorts of terrible things had happened to Shirley.

Bella threw one of her new swimsuits at Linda and it hit her on the head. 'Come on, Linda, stop worrying about Shirley. Dolly told me her ankle was bad and she'd fly out later. Let's go for a morning dip – there were some good-looking guys down by the pool last night.'

Linda was looking confused. 'Dolly told me that Shirley's flight was cancelled; she never said anything about her ankle being too bad to fly. Why give each of us a different story? Something's happened.'

'Like what?' Bella asked sarcastically.

'Like – I don't know. But I'm really worried about her now.'

'Don't be stupid, Linda. All that booze is mushing your brains.' Bella began to strip off to change into one of her new bikinis. She held it up for Linda to see. 'What do you reckon – skimpy and sexy, yet classy and upmarket, right?'

Linda didn't reply.

'Listen, sweetheart, if we go round lookin' like a couple of well-to-do rich bitches then we'll be treated as such. If you look like a slag, you'll be ignored. Let's enjoy ourselves, have a swim and then later we can get some dinner at the rooftop restaurant.'

'I just called Dolly's house,' Linda finally said. 'A man answered. He said . . . "That you, Doll?"'

Bella was stunned. 'It can't be,' she gasped.

'He's the only one who calls her "Doll". She told us that herself.'

Bella desperately tried to be the voice of reason. 'You ever heard his voice before? Think, Linda, have you ever heard Harry Rawlins' voice before?'

'Not sober . . . me, that is, not him.' Linda laughed feebly, trying to think straight. 'He had a deep voice, like velvet. Joe always said that the deep tone of Harry's voice could melt chocolate. It was him, Bella. I know it was. "That you, Doll?" Calm as you like. That bastard's still alive and Dolly's with him.'

'So, where's Shirley?' Bella was now as worried as Linda.

Linda leapt to her feet. 'You're a bloody idiot, Bella! You've got a bedroom full of fancy gear that you can't carry and no cash! We've got to get out of here!'

'Hang on, hang on!'

'Hang on? Shirley could be dead and buried in Dolly's back garden for all we know – or worse, she could be with the cops right now. She won't last two minutes in a police interview! We're stuffed. Well, if I'm going to do time, I ain't doing it in a Rio jail.' Linda moved quickly to the bedroom window, then the door, then the mini-bar – empty – then a silver-domed room service tray. She lifted the dome, no booze left.

'Linda!' Bella shouted. 'Just stop! If Dolly's double-crossed everyone with Harry, how come he's at the house answering the phone like he doesn't know where she is? Why are they not hot-footing it to the other side of the world? It *can't* have been Harry. It'll be the cops. Sitting there like idiots because they don't know what else to do. Dolly and Shirley will be on their way. You'll see.'

Quite unexpectedly, Linda began to cry. Bella gave her a hug.

'Listen, love. If they're not here in a day or two, we'll do a runner. Just like we did from that curry house when we was young and skint.'

Linda leant heavily against Bella's shoulder. 'Oh, Bella. We ain't meant to be lucky, are we?' She sighed. 'All I ever wanted to do was be a racing driver and be the first female World Champion. I was going to give James Hunt a good seeing-to – on and off the track.'

Bella laughed and Linda, letting go of all her tension, laughed too. Through the open balcony window, the pool band started up and Ike and Tina Turner's 'River Deep, Mountain High' filled the air. Linda was the first to join in, quietly at first, and then she turned the volume right up.

Bella joined in and they reached a crescendo together, singing at the top of their voices, jumping around and waving their arms in the air. As the song came to an end, they slowed to a stop and they got their breath back. It was not knowing that was killing them.

'Me and you'll be all right, won't we, Bella?' Linda asked.

'We all will.' Bella was a dab hand at reassuring paranoid drunks. 'Let's get room service.'

As she waited for someone to answer, Bella's smile dropped. The man who had answered the phone at Dolly's house was a real worry. If it was Harry, then Dolly had done them over for sure. If it was the cops, then Bella reckoned Dolly and Shirley were already in cells. And if it was someone working for the Fishers – then God knows where Dolly and Shirley were. Whatever the truth, Bella would take all her new gear back to the shop and get refunds on everything. She would give Dolly and Shirley one more day – and then she'd take Linda and run.

CHAPTER 39

The police had parked cars at either end of the Dolly's street, blocking any access in or out. The local man was hugging his dog tight as he repeated his story once again for DCI Saunders. He had come across the badly injured man in the car; he was passing in and out of consciousness but had managed to mumble that he was a police officer. 'Is he dead?' the man asked.

'No,' said Saunders quickly. He had no time to talk. 'Go with the uniformed officers now, please, and they'll take a full statement.' He ushered the man towards the nearest police car.

Glancing along the dark road, Saunders could just make out DS Fuller kneeling by Resnick's car door. Saunders looked away almost in shame. He'd seen the mess Resnick was in and, even now, through all of the pain, Resnick had said just one word: 'Rawlins.' Saunders was certain of it. Of course, he could have been delirious, hallucinating or even brain damaged . . . so Saunders decided to get proof before repeating anything.

As the DCI plucked up the courage to head back towards Resnick, he grabbed a uniformed officer. 'I need to make sure that DI Resnick's safely out the way before we move into the Rawlins house. Get on the radio and chase that bloody ambulance up. Tell them no bells and horns. Silent approach.'

Resnick was slouched in the driver's seat, blood streaming down his face from numerous deep gashes in his skin. His breath was coming in terrible guttural gasps.

Saunders leant into the car. 'Ambulance is on its way, George, you hear me? It's on its way, so hang in there.'

Resnick's chest made a rasping sound as he heaved for breath, but he nodded just slightly. Saunders shook his head, stepped back and whispered to Fuller.

'What on earth was he doing out here alone playing super cop?'

Fuller had no answer he cared to share. No answer he needed to share. They both knew exactly why Resnick was on his own – because that's the corner they'd forced him into.

Resnick's chest rasped as he tried to speak, followed by a gurgling of the blood in his mouth and a cough that sent blood spattering across the windscreen. Saunders winced.

'You need to clear his airway, Fuller. See if he's got any false teeth. Don't let him choke to death, for God's sake. Not in the street. Stay with him and if he says anything, write it down. Someone's going to swing for this, and it's not going to be me.'

'Of course . . . sir,' Fuller replied. The pause before the 'sir' was exactly the same disdain Fuller had once shown for Resnick. As Saunders walked away, Fuller shook his head in disgust. Saunders was the sycophantic, arse-covering bastard Resnick had always said he was.

Fuller knelt back down and looked at the pitiful, broken figure of Resnick. He had hated this man for so long, but he wasn't looking at an enemy right now: he was looking at a victim. A brutalised victim who deserved respect and care. He got some clean, sterile gauze from a first aid box and leant into the car.

Resnick's eyes opened slightly and he looked at Fuller through the crimson haze of blood.

'Sir,' Fuller started. 'I'm gonna clean your mouth to help you breathe more easily. You got false teeth?'

Resnick managed a slight nod, so Fuller slipped his finger into his mouth and felt around. Suddenly, a couple of real teeth that had been knocked loose during the assault fell out onto Resnick's lap. Fuller eased the plastic bridge out. It was a plate with two side teeth on it.

'I'll put everything in your pocket. The fake ones will be waiting for you when you're ready; the real ones you can put under your pillow for the tooth fairy.' Fuller smiled and he swore that the old man's eyes creased slightly. It could have been a smile; it could have been a flinch of pain.

Taking his coat off and gently draping it over Resnick's shoulders and chest, Fuller said kindly, 'Don't want you getting cold, do we? I'm so sorry, George,' he went on. 'You're a fucker of a man to work for, but this isn't right in anyone's book. And I'm sorry. I'll get him for you. Whoever did this – I'll get him.'

Resnick's breath rattled; the blood dripped from his mouth and nose as he tried to turn his head towards Fuller. He gasped and lifted his broken hand, the fingers black and blue, the blood seeping down inside his coat sleeve. He pointed to his left breast and tried to speak, but Fuller couldn't understand what he was trying to say. Resnick managed to lift his hand a little further, to his left breast, and patted it twice.

'Is it your heart? Are you having a heart attack?' Fuller asked.

Resnick pulled Fuller's jacket down from his shoulders and pointed with his finger to inside his coat. Then, from sheer exhaustion, his head slumped to one side and he passed out.

Fuller searched Resnick's inside coat pocket and took out a crumpled sheet of paper. As he started to read it, he saw the ambulance crew running towards him with a stretcher. Fuller moved out of their way, pocketing the paper at the same time. At the other end of the street, Saunders gave the thumbs up for everyone to move towards the Rawlins house.

* * *

Harry stood behind Bill as, shovel in hand, he dug down into the soft earth beneath the willow tree. None of them had noticed the bamboo cross which had fallen flat on the soil and was now covered by Bill's clumsy digging. Before too long, Bill hit a white lace table cloth. 'Trust a bird to neatly wrap a million in cash before she buries it!' He laughed and tore at the cloth, desperately trying to get to the contents.

As Bill got closer, Eddie suddenly realised what was buried in the cloth and backed away. 'Oh, fuck!' Bill shouted as he broke through the cloth and the stench hit him smack in the face. He leapt to his feet, hands covered in soil and crap.

Harry picked Wolf's body up by the scruff of his neck and held him up towards Eddie, fury filling his eyes. 'Look what you made her do! You made her bury her baby! AGAIN!' Harry thrust Wolf towards Eddie's face, wiping dog shit across his cheek. Eddie backed off, heaving and vomiting into the shrubbery.

Suddenly, they heard the sound of the front door being struck with a sledgehammer. 'POLICE – OPEN UP!' Bill raced towards the kitchen to try and fight his way to the BMW. Eddie froze and then hurtled after Bill.

Harry didn't panic. He moved quickly to the far corner of the garden and inched his way behind the blackberry bushes. He scratched his body with every step, the trailing thorns cutting into every part of exposed skin, but he remained silent. He stood by the seven-foot wall and looked up, raised his hands, lowered his weight and jumped. As his palms gripped the shards of glass he'd cemented into the top of the wall years ago, the pain ripped through his body. He wanted to scream but he hung there with his forehead against the bricks and his eyes screwed tight shut.

Behind him, Eddie suddenly reappeared, running down the garden. Harry knew the police would be right behind, so he pulled himself upwards, grimacing through the pain. Eddie saw Harry as he reached the top of the wall. 'Harry!' he screamed. 'Harry, help me!' Eddie, looking up at his cousin, didn't see Wolf's body on the ground. He tripped over the little dog, fell into the mud and the police were on him.

From the top of the wall, as Harry silently manoeuvred round as much of the glass as he could, he glanced down at Eddie, barely visible under three uniformed officers. He looked at Wolf's body and smirked to himself. *Revenge is sweet, Wolfie boy . . .* Harry disappeared over the wall and into the darkness of the alleyway behind.

Outside in the street, Bill had slipped his knuckleduster on and was fighting for his life. He had too much to lose: there was no way he was going to roll over and just let himself be caught. He kicked and punched for all he was worth, keeping two officers easily at bay. Even when they were joined by two more policemen, Bill stood his ground. Eventually one of them got in a lucky hit to the side of Bill's head, dazing him for long enough to allow the others to take control. The next moment, Bill was on the ground, curled up into a ball with his arms above his head, as four truncheons rained down on his head and body.

As officers walked the bleeding, battered and still swearing Bill Grant towards the police van, handcuffed and struggling, Fuller watched from just outside the back of the ambulance where Resnick, wrapped in blankets, was being looked after by paramedics. Fuller hadn't been part of the arrest team; he'd chosen to stay with Resnick. If he did say anything, Fuller wanted to make sure that his words were recorded properly. He wasn't going to let Saunders twist anything or blame Resnick for anything that wasn't his fault: there'd be enough about this mess of a case that *was* Resnick's fault . . .

As the officers passed Fuller, one of them handed him Bill Grant's knuckleduster. The congealed blood and hair had been smudged by the inside of Bill's pocket, but was still visible. Fuller looked at the fit, young, fighting man restrained by four police; and at the fat, wheezing old man in the ambulance. He was suddenly filled with an uncontrollable combination of fury and guilt. Every other day of his life, he'd hated the idea of sitting in a smoke-filled car with Resnick, but tonight – tonight he wished he'd been right by his side. Resnick didn't deserve this beating. No one deserved this beating.

Before he knew it, he'd slipped the knuckleduster onto his right hand, strode across to Grant and punched him hard in the kidneys. He managed to land one more blow before being pulled away.

As Fuller climbed into the back of the ambulance with Resnick, he saw Eddie being marched towards a police car. He was blubbering and squealing. 'I've got a right to be here! It's me cousin's place! I'm keeping an eye on it for him. I ain't done nothing wrong.'

In the ambulance, Resnick's head lolled towards Fuller as he sat down beside him. The dark blood was now congealing round his mouth and nose. His eyes, like a wounded animal's, stared at Fuller.

'I gave him something to remember you by,' said Fuller. 'The one who did this. He won't forget you in a hurry.'

But Resnick didn't seem to care. As he tried to speak again, more blood spluttered from his mouth. The paramedic put an oxygen mask over it and he closed his eyes.

* * *

Harry Rawlins crouched low behind the thick privet hedge of his rear neighbour's garden. He had ripped out the pockets of his trousers and put them on his shredded hands, which he had squeezed into fists to stem the flow of blood. He could still feel tiny shards of glass buried deep in his palms. From his hiding place, he watched as the ambulance left, followed by the police van and, one by one, all the police cars and bystanders, until the street was clear. Even then he waited another half an hour just in case the police returned. Eventually, when he was satisfied the coast was clear, he moved out onto the street and looked around: it was as if the circus had left town. Taking Eddie's scarf from his coat pocket, he wrapped it round his neck and pulled it up over his mouth and nose. He then put his hands in his coat pocket and casually walked off down the road.

CHAPTER 40

Shirley stepped onto the plane clutching her ticket and, unsure where her seat was, turned left. A stewardess standing by the galley asked if she was travelling first class and Shirley held up her ticket. The stewardess looked at it, gave her a cheesy smile, and said economy seats were to the right. As the stewardess politely shuffled Shirley back towards economy, Shirley saw Dolly sitting by the window in first class, sipping champagne and reading *Vogue*. 'Bloody typical,' Shirley muttered.

To make it worse, Shirley was in an aisle seat where people would bump into her and, worse still, she discovered Charles sitting right next to her.

'I swapped seats to be next to you!' He beamed. 'Now we can get to know each other better!'

It had been hours since she'd eaten anything, so Shirley enjoyed the in-flight meal. After eating, she put on her headphones and settled back to watch the movie; she wasn't really interested in it, but anything was better than having to listen to Charles drone on and on about all the countries he'd been to.

Shirley had fallen asleep during the film when, yet again, she felt someone bump into her. She whipped off her headphones, and was about to give whoever it was a piece of her mind, when she saw Dolly standing there. Dolly apologised as if Shirley was a complete stranger, before walking on towards the toilets. Checking that the toilets were all vacant, Dolly took a cigarette out the pack she was holding and lit up as Shirley joined her, the headphones still dangling round her neck. As the women talked, they kept smiling at each other, as if they were simply passing the time of day.

'We got trouble,' Dolly said quietly. 'The customs system at Rio is different from ours. There's no red and green area: everyone goes through the same exit. They just swoop on anyone they feel like searching. We have to risk it, though. You OK with that?

Shirley's heart sank. 'No, I'm not OK,' she hissed. 'It's crazy to risk it! The Brazilian customs officers will be watching for the slightest twitch and you know how nervous I get.'

'I'll be the one taking the risk by carrying the money bag,' Dolly pointed out. 'Without it we'll soon have nothing left to survive on in Rio – or to get us out of the bloody country if we need to. All I need you to do if you see a customs guy stop me is create a diversion.'

Shirley nervously twisted the wire on the headphones. She knew Dolly was taking the biggest risk. She had no choice but to back her up.

'I'll take your silence as a yes, then?'

'What sort of diversion should I create?'

'You'll think of something. You've still got six hours before landing,' Dolly said as she walked off.

Shirley went into the toilet. She held her head in her hands, feeling sick. When she got back to her seat, the film was just ending. They had caught the villains on the Costa Brava with the stolen cash. Shirley ordered a large brandy to calm her nerves and settle her brain. Closing her eyes, she pretended to sleep.

* * *

Harry moved softly round the darkened bedroom, trying not to wake Trudie. His hands had stopped bleeding, but he was still feeling the pain from the cuts as he packed a holdall and then opened a drawer in the dressing table. Taking out his passport, he searched around for the fifty quid Dolly had given Trudie for the baby. The thought of Dolly made him twist inside with hate. He would pay her back for this: he would find her and, even after he'd got his money, she'd suffer for doing this to him. He fumbled around in the drawer, wincing with pain when he caught the palm of his hand on a stiff hairbrush. One of the larger cuts reopened, he sucked in air through his teeth and let out a small sigh.

Trudie woke and all she could see was a dark figure searching through the dressing table. Harry moved in an instant to the bedside and put his hand over her mouth. 'It's me, Harry,' he whispered, and she relaxed. She grabbed his arm and pulled it from her face. She could feel something wet round her mouth. As she switched the bedside light on, she saw the blood from Harry's hand.

'Quiet, keep it shut, don't wake the kid,' he said, wiping his blood from her face.

Trudie looked at Harry's hands and saw the numerous cuts and blood. 'Where have you been? I've been awake for hours waiting for you! What have you done?'

Harry stood up. 'Where's the fifty quid she gave you?' Trudie opened her mouth to ask why, but Harry made a 'cut it' gesture.

'You didn't find the money, did you?' she said, realisation dawning. 'And where're Eddie and Bill?'

Harry ignored her, picked up her purse and took out the fifty quid, plus what was left of her child benefit. He stuffed it into his pocket and then pulled out his bedside drawer. Taped to the underside was the false passport Bill had got for him. He stuffed it into his holdall and walked out of the bedroom.

Trudie got out of bed and followed him. 'Where are you going? Harry? Where are you going? You're not leaving me, are you?'

Harry shook his head, but Trudie ran to the door and positioned herself in front of it. 'Are you going back to Dolly? Do you still love her, or is it for the money?'

Harry stood face to face with Trudie and spat the words out. 'Don't even say her name. She's gone . . . gone forever!'

Trudie grabbed hold of him. 'The money – what about the money?'

Harry pushed her to one side and wrenched the door open. Trudie clung onto him tight.

'I love you so much, Harry. Please stay. I need you here with me . . . I love you.'

Harry held her tightly and pulled her head into his shoulder as she began to cry. He lifted her chin up and stared down into her eyes as he whispered, 'I know, but I can't stay. We went to the house. Neither Dolly nor the money was there. Then the police turned up and all hell let loose. Eddie and Bill got nicked and we both know there's no way Eddie will keep his mouth shut once he's been roughed up a bit in a cell. I have no choice. I have to go.'

Trudie let out a howl and Harry covered her mouth with his hand.

'I'll be back for you, I promise, but I just got to make it on me own for a while.'

He moved out onto the landing. Sobbing, Trudie held onto his coat, pulling him backwards. Harry stopped, and jerked his hand backwards to get her off him.

'I won't let you go; I won't let you!' she said, weeping so hard she was shaking.

Harry held her cheeks and squeezed them hard. 'The kid – he's mine isn't he? Isn't he?'

Trudie winced as his grip tightened. 'Of course he's yours,' she said, looking into his hard and cruel eyes.

'He'd better be; he'd better be mine! I'll be back for you both.' He turned. Trudie's grip on him was so tight that he had to jerk his hand sharply away and, as he did, he knocked her backwards.

He was off, running down the stairs as Trudie fell and cracked her head against the wall, but he didn't look back. Trudie felt sick as she crawled to the banister.

'Harry, you bastard!' she screamed as she hauled herself up and looked down the staircase. 'You run to her – go on, RUN TO HER! She was the brains behind you all along and you never even knew it!' Slumping onto the stairs, she wept even harder.

Mrs Obebega came out of her flat below and looked up. 'You all right, Mrs Nunn? Mrs Nunn, you OK?' she asked, coming up the stairs towards Trudie.

Below them, they heard wood cracking and splintering as the front door was smashed in against the inside wall, and the sound of heavy boots running up the stairs.

Detective Sergeant Fuller was leading the raid. Jimmy Nunn's address had been barely legible on the blood-soaked scrap of paper Resnick had given him. Seeing Trudie on the floor, Fuller waved his warrant card at her and then ran past her. 'Where is he? Tell me right now, where is he?' Fuller shouted over his shoulder.

'He's gone . . . he's gone . . . now GET OUT!' Trudie screamed over and over again, becoming ever more hysterical.

Tenants were coming out their flats as uniformed police entered and swarmed the building. Back on the top landing, Fuller hauled Trudie up from the floor by her dressing gown as the uniformed officers stomped into the flat. One of them kicked open the bedroom door and woke the baby, who began to howl.

Fuller held Trudie by the arm and pulled her towards her front door. 'Where's Jimmy? You'd better tell me where he is, Mrs Nunn, or I swear I'll nick you as well.'

Trudie could hear herself laughing, a crazy sound. Like a needle stuck on a record, she just kept repeating: 'I don't know anything, I don't know anything, I don't know anything.'

CHAPTER 41

The queues at passport control in Rio airport were long. Dolly and Shirley stood in different lines and at no time so much as glanced at each other. The waiting had made some passengers irritable and tetchy, but when they complained, the Brazilian immigration officers delayed even further.

Dolly and Shirley made their separate ways to luggage collection, where some passengers were already wheeling and heaving their cases towards the customs control. The air conditioning made the vast room cold, the muzak was a repetitive heavy drumbeat samba and, combined with the excited chatter of Brazilian passengers and a long flight, the whole experience was exhausting.

Shirley could just see Dolly's blonde head above the group of passengers who pushed and shoved their way towards the luggage carousel. At the only exit was a row of trestle tables with a customs officer standing at either end and a further two officers standing by the exit doors. They were all armed and were watching the passengers like hawks. Shirley could feel the sweat begin to trickle down her forehead as she fought her way towards the carousel.

As she waited for her suitcases, Shirley glanced over to the trestle table, where a line of passengers was waiting to go through. Her heart lurched: every passenger's case was being searched. Articles of clothing were strewn out across the whole length of the tables as passengers and customs officers argued loudly. Shirley pushed closer to Dolly and eventually squeezed in behind her. She whispered in Dolly's ear, her voice hardly audible above the din.

'They're searching everyone. Don't do it.'

Dolly didn't turn round. 'You know what to do – now get away from me.'

Up came one of their red suitcases, but they couldn't see if it was the one with the red tag or blue tag. As they watched and waited for the case to get closer a hand came forward and dragged it off the carousel. Dolly was about to have a go, when Shirley kicked her foot.

Charles, rucksack on back, smiled at Shirley. 'Your case, I believe? Do you want me to carry it for you?'

'No, I'm fine, thanks. I've got to wait for me other one anyway.'

He pressed closer towards her, his BO smelling much worse after the long flight. 'I don't mind waiting with you . . . I wondered if maybe we could have dinner, do some sightseeing or just stay in together?'

Shirley had to get rid of him. She turned on him and spoke softly but plainly. 'No way . . . just piss off!'

Charles wasn't expecting such a sudden rejection and, taking a step back, trod on a fat woman's foot. She squealed and pushed him hard; he started to fall backwards and as he turned to regain his balance, his rucksack hit another woman, who swore at him in Portuguese. Apologising to everyone around him, he skulked off with his head held low.

Shirley turned to tell Dolly to leave the case. She wasn't there, but the case was. Shirley couldn't bring herself to pick it up; but then she noticed it was the case with the blue tag. While everyone was looking at Charles, Dolly had lifted the other red case off the carousel, swapped it with the money case and casually walked off.

Shirley's mouth was dry, and her hands sweated. When she looked over to see Dolly in the queue by the trestle tables, the money case by her side, Shirley thought she'd faint. Dolly seemed so calm as she inched closer to the customs officer, kicking the money case along as she moved. Figuring that, as Dolly hadn't lifted the money case up yet, she wasn't next to be searched, Shirley turned back to the carousel to see if she could get her case – but it had just gone past her for the second time!

Charles's rucksack was on the trestle table next to Dolly. Two officers were dealing with him, going over every nook and cranny of his clothing looking for drugs, before they decided to take him off for a strip search.

A customs officer pointed at Dolly and then her case. Trying hard not to show how heavy it was, she lifted it onto the table and laid it on its side, then quickly placed her small holdall on top and rested her hands on it. The officer stared at her, held his hand out and snapped his fingers.

'Passport.'

She handed it over; he took a quick look and put it down beside him. 'You'se have anythings to declares?' he asked in broken English.

Dolly smiled sweetly and shook her head.

'Any foods or plants wiz you?' he asked, still staring.

'No, but I do have a duty free bottle of gin and some cigarettes in my holdall. Do you want to see them?'

'Yes … Tell me why you are here? Business or holiday?' He seemed to be looking for any involuntary signs of nervousness.

'Holiday,' Dolly replied calmly as she slowly unzipped her holdall. Her head was spinning like mad and she was controlling every nerve in her body to keep herself from showing any sign, any twitch, any flicker of emotion that might make the officer more suspicious than he already was. She didn't have a clue what was going on behind her or where Shirley was, but she wished to God she'd hurry up and put whatever distraction plan she'd decided on into action.

Shirley had now retrieved her cases and was standing in the queue waiting for customs. Looking over at Dolly, she saw the customs officer taking the booze and fags out of her holdall and then rummaging through the contents. He lifted the holdall off the case, handed it back to Dolly and started to turn the case round so the lock catches were facing him. Shirley knew it was now or never. She unzipped her handbag, put her hand inside and started screaming.

'Help me! Oh, my God, help me! Someone's stolen my passport!' She rummaged round her handbag, tipping it sideways so the contents fell to the ground. 'It's not here, it's not here! I've been robbed. I've been robbed.'

Everything came to a standstill and all eyes were on Shirley. The two officers at the exit door stepped forward to see what the rumpus was, the man behind Dolly threw up his arms in despair, then started shouting something in Portuguese and pointing at his wristwatch. The officer dealing with Dolly told him to be quiet, but he wouldn't let it go and even Dolly knew what he meant when he called the officer *idiota*.

The officer, now very angry, handed Dolly her passport, pushed her case to one side and signalled for her to get out of the way. He then turned to the man behind her and slammed his hand on the table.

Dolly slid her suitcase off the table. It was over. All eyes were still on Shirley, further back in the queue, who was still screaming while on her knees, frantically looking through her strewn handbag contents. Dolly melted into the crowd and slowly walked through the automatic exit doors.

It was not until the doors closed behind Dolly that Shirley waved her passport above her head, indicating she'd found it. The customs officers took her off to a room, with her suitcases, to speak to her. Now that Dolly had got through, Shirley didn't feel nervous: she had nothing to hide or declare in either of her cases.

Unbeknownst to Shirley, Charles was being spoken to in the next-door cubicle about the commotion he had caused by the luggage carousel. He was in tears as he explained that at Heathrow he'd helped a lady with an overweight case by saying it was his and then offered to carry it for her after landing in Rio. He had been hoping to get his leg over and was very disturbed by her sudden rejection.

One of the officers who had spoken to Charles came in to join the two who were questioning Shirley. He spoke good enough English to report what Charles had said. 'I'm ever so sorry,' Shirley said, with a little pout. 'I didn't have enough to pay the luggage excess, so I'm afraid I was a bit naughty. It was a silly thing to do and I am ever so sorry. It wasn't my idea to lie though – that man said it was perfectly OK and no one would mind really. Was that wrong? Oh –' Shirley exclaimed, getting into full dumb-blonde mode – 'do you think he had other ideas?'

An officer told her to wait and he left the room. Shirley was now beginning to feel nervous, as she had thought that she'd be free to go by now. The officer returned a few minutes later, sat down opposite her at the table and glared into her wide blue eyes.

'Why you tell the young man you do a shoot for a magazine in Rio?'

'I lied,' she said, bowing her head to pretend she was ashamed, but also to hide her nerves. 'I sort of fancied him and wanted to impress him and—'

The officer banged the table, making Shirley jump. 'Then why you tell him piss off when you land in Rio?'

Shirley leant forward confidentially. 'Well, on the plane he was sitting next to me and I could smell how bad his body odour was. When he approached me in the luggage collection area it was awful! I didn't mean to hurt his feelings, but I had to be honest.'

The customs officers all burst out laughing.

'He does smell bad!' said one of them. 'Especially in a small interview room! Off you go, missy.' Opening the door for her, he ushered her out.

* * *

Alice found Resnick in a side room off the main hospital ward. He made a surprisingly small figure on the high bed, motionless, hooked up to a drip, his face so puffy and bruised he was barely recognisable. As she went over to him, she noticed his false teeth lying in a saucer on the locker and had to suppress a sob. Drawing up a chair as close as she could to the bed, she settled down to wait.

* * *

On her way to the hotel, Shirley looked out of the taxi window as Rio whizzed by, and thought of Terry. She had never known such an exhilarating feeling before. It was over, all over and she was free – free to do what she wanted, be what she wanted. She was rich. Very rich. She so wished that she could share this part of her life with the man she had loved. This was his dream too – well, maybe not Rio exactly, he was more of an East End boy – but being able to do anything they wanted. Shirley could hardly believe where she was and she certainly couldn't believe how she'd got here. She couldn't wait to see Linda and Bella again, she had so much to tell them.

For the first couple of minutes, there were no words, just squeals of joy, laughter, lots of hugging and lots of tears. Shirley had never been held so tight: it was as if they never wanted to let her out of their sight again. Although she had pictured Linda and Bella having loads of fun by a heated pool, they had pictured her in a police interview room being leant on by some unscrupulous copper. They were incredibly relieved to be back together.

Hours later and the chatter was still in full flow, as was the champagne. The suite looked more like a Harrods' sale room, with boxes of beautiful designer gowns and dresses everywhere. The three young women were like excited children racing around, whooping and dancing in the small hours, champagne corks popping.

Next door, Dolly lay in the bath. She could hear the girls shouting and laughing and was glad they were happy. She had arrived about half an hour after Shirley, but her reception had been more reserved. Dolly wished she could evoke emotion, in herself and in others, but she'd always been so tightly wound she didn't know how to express herself. *I think they know how fabulous I think they are*, she thought as she lit another cigarette and sipped on her champagne. *They must know how proud I am of them?* When Dolly had divvied up the £120,000 from her suitcase, the girls' eyes had almost popped from their heads.

Dolly looked at the cigarette between her wrinkled fingers. She'd been in the bath long enough for the water to be only just lukewarm now, but she didn't care. As the tension seeped from every muscle in her body, she didn't care about anything. Dolly closed her eyes.

'Come on, Dolly!' Linda shouted from the living room.

Dolly smiled. How she'd missed those dulcet tones. A cork popped and the girls shrieked as though it was the first of the day, even though it must have been the fourth. Touching the soft, fluffy soap suds, she was reminded of Wolf. She felt sick and then, as she tried to get up, she felt dizzy and slid back into the bath, the cigarette dropping from her fingers. As Dolly watched it disappear beneath the water, she wanted to cry. Her emotions were so close to the surface but they refused to come out. Whether her sadness was for Wolf, Harry or herself, she wasn't certain – but, naked and alone, she felt so incredibly vulnerable.

* * *

Nearly 6000 miles away, holed up in his stinking lock-up with only the vicious Alsatian for company, Harry Rawlins felt equally vulnerable, but for very different reasons. He had never felt so powerless or so alone. He was a dead man: he couldn't surface, he couldn't touch the cash in any of his bank accounts, he couldn't even go home. He'd have to leave the country, but he didn't know how long he would have to wait before he could do that safely. *Dolly* . . . He clenched his fists at the thought of her. Years ago, he had wept with her for their stillborn son. He had betrayed her – but she had beaten him at his own treacherous game.

But it wasn't over, no, not by any means. No one beat Harry Rawlins . . .

* * *

Shirley was in the bedroom looking at herself in the long mirror, wondering if she should have put on the blue dress. *No*, she thought, *the silver one is perfect.* She stepped back to admire her slender body. *Boy, do I look good . . . In fact, more than good – I look absolutely beautiful.*

Bella walked in through the adjoining bedroom door. She shimmered, draped from head to toe in a black sequin dress. 'Nice bum!' she commented to Shirley and they both laughed. She shouted to Dolly to come out and join the party.

'Come on, Dolly!' Shirley added. 'We're all waiting for you!'

Shirley's money was in bundles on the coffee table. Linda's was piled in her lap and she was singing at the top of her voice. Bella's money was thrown, carelessly, on an elegant armchair. She sang along with Linda, belting out their own dodgy version of 'My Way'. Shirley swirled round the room, loving the feel of her dress as it spun out and showed her knickers. Bella, not to be outdone, went into a Shirley Bassey stance and began singing 'Goldfinger' over the top of Linda. The atmosphere was electric as the girls let loose, without a care in the world.

Shirley gulped more champagne, lit a cigarette and began parading up and down the room as if she was on a catwalk. Linda stood up with a hairbrush in her hand and pretended it was a microphone.

'An' now we have Miss Shirley Miller! And what are your hobbies, Miss Miller?'

'Well, I likes children and ROBBIN' BANKS!' Shirley shrieked as she threw a wad of her money into the air.

* * *

Dolly knotted the dressing gown round her waist, wiped the steamy mirror clear, and stared at her face. Her wet hair hung down like rats' tails. She looked – and felt – haggard and old. She pressed her forehead against the cold mirror. The tears wouldn't come now. *That it?* she thought to herself. Crying done. All dried up and sealed back inside.

Linda helped herself to some caviar from the room service trolley and fingered Dolly's pile of notes, which were in her small holdall on the sofa. Dolly had explained that she'd split the money equally, and that the rest was hidden in the convent. She'd also explained that she'd taken back £5000 from each of them to cover all their up-front expenses. Everyone had been more than happy with the deal, but something else was now on Linda's mind. She stood close beside Bella.

'Shall I tell Shirley about the phone call?' she whispered.

Bella spun round and gave Linda a dirty look. 'No. Just forget it. You don't know it was him for a fact. You agreed you must have been mistaken, so forget it.'

Shirley poured herself another glass of champagne. 'What were ya both talking about?'

Linda gave Bella a quick look, then sat on the sofa. 'I put a call into London . . . to Dolly's house. I know we weren't supposed to, but, well, I did cos I was worried about you.'

Shirley shrugged her shoulders. 'Dolly never said anything to me.'

Linda looked down. 'Dolly never answered. Harry did.' Before Shirley could speak, Linda carried on, 'I know it was him. It was Harry.'

Bella poured herself a drink. 'I'm not arguing with you, sugar, we've been over it a dozen times already.'

Shirley couldn't take in what Linda had just said. She looked towards the bedroom. 'Are you sure? Are you sure it was him, Linda?'

'He was the only one who ever called her "Doll".' Linda was getting uptight. 'The man said, "Is that you, Doll?" It had to be him. He used to call for Joe and his voice sounded the same. I'm tellin' you – Harry Rawlins is alive.'

They sat in silence, looking at each other. Was Harry alive and, more importantly, did Dolly know all along? Shirley was the first to break the silence. She told them everything: Harry's shredded clothes in the wardrobe, Eddie watching the house day and night, Eddie breaking in and killing Wolf, Eddie beating her up. She leapt to her feet as if she'd had a sudden revelation: 'I knew it! Well, actually, I thought she might be shacking up with Eddie, but Harry makes much more sense. So, she never lost him.'

Linda was on her feet in a split second, her face tight and ugly. She kicked the money case. 'This is a kiss off! To keep us sweet. And who do you think's getting the rest? Eh? Harry will be emptying them convent lockers as we speak . . . if the rest of the money was ever there in the first place.'

Bella put her glass down and stood up too. 'Just take it easy. We don't know if any of that's true. We don't even know if he's really alive; I mean, if he is, why would she come here?'

None of them heard Dolly come out of the bathroom.

She was dressed in a hotel dressing gown that was at least two sizes too large for her and she looked like someone's old grandma. They didn't know if she'd heard what they had said, but she said nothing. She just went to the money case and started to move all of Harry's clothes into a hotel laundry bag.

The girls looked to each other and Bella gave Linda the nod.

'I put a call into London this morning, Dolly, to your place.' Linda started cautiously.

Dolly appeared not to hear. She just opened her own case and, rummaging through, held up a grey dress. 'I could wear this. Won't be as dressy as you lot, but I could wear this. Or I've got a cocktail dress, I think I put it in here somewhere.'

'Is Harry alive?' Linda asked.

Dolly lifted out her cocktail dress, held it against her body. 'What do you think?'

Linda stepped forward and snatched the dress from her hands. 'Harry answered the phone. He's alive, ain't he?'

Dolly's eyes glazed over. She had no fight left and no will to go on. She felt as if someone had kicked her hard in the pit of her stomach. The burning feeling began to spread outwards and upwards, engulfing her entire body, but when she spoke her voice was calm. 'If you say so, Linda,' she said, still with her back to them all.

'I do say so, Dolly. And you know he is.' Linda asked the question on all of their lips. 'What about the rest of the money? What you really done with it? Harry got that now, has he?'

Dolly was burning up, her mouth incredibly dry. She swallowed hard. 'You think I'm working with Harry? You think I knew?' she said, still not turning to face them.

Bella held Linda back as she tried to grab Dolly's arm. 'We just need to know what's going on, Dolly,' she said calmly.

Dolly turned and looked at each girl one by one. She was trembling as she moved over to the drinks trolley. She put out a hand to reach for the bottle and her hand shook so much she couldn't lift it. Then her whole body started to shake uncontrollably.

'Is he alive, Dolly?' Linda persisted. Dolly was shaking like a frail old lady. Bella and Shirley looked at each other, worried that something was terribly wrong.

The sudden, frightening explosion of emotional anger took them all by surprise. Over went the drinks trolley, glasses, food, anything Dolly could lay her hands on she hurled across the room. She grabbed her holdall, pulled handfuls of her money out and flung it at the three women. Her voice was like a low growl to begin with; then it got louder and louder as she snarled like a mad dog over and over: 'YES, YES, YES, YES, YES!'

The girls stood huddled together. They'd never seen Dolly like this before – they'd never seen anyone like this before! They had no idea what to do, how to help, how to comfort, how to make the pain she was in go away.

When Dolly had nothing left to throw, her face twisted and she began pulling at the dressing gown, trying to rip it with her nails. Her head shook backwards and forwards as she glowered at them like a rabid animal. It was a terrifying thing to watch. She pulled the dressing gown off her shoulders and began to scratch at her bare arms. Deep red welts appeared and her voice rose higher and higher. 'You want to know what it felt like?' Dolly yelled. 'What it felt like to find out? It was like a raging fire inside me. It's still inside me: he's inside me . . . *out*, get him out of me, dear God get him out!'

Dolly's scratched her arms deeper and harder until the blood ran down to her fingers.

Linda's eyes almost popped out of her head, Shirley's face began to pucker like a frightened child, but it was Bella who took action. Linda thought she was going to slap Dolly out of her hysteria, but she grabbed her in a bear hug and held her as tight as she could. Dolly struggled, her arms pinned at her sides by Bella's huge strength. Dolly sobbed in Bella's arms and, as she loosened her grip, Dolly slid to the floor and landed on her knees.

No one knew what to do.

The tears Dolly had wanted to cry for so long finally came in floods. She wept as she had never done before. She had wept for Harry many times, but these awful wrenching sobs were different, and although the pain was excruciating, they were a welcome release.

Hardly able to stand it, Shirley stepped forwards to comfort Dolly, but Bella stopped her. Dolly had to let it all go, because keeping it all inside was killing her. The sobbing went on and on and on until finally Dolly was so exhausted that she had nothing left. Helping her to her feet, Bella gently held her again, rocking Dolly back and forth and whispering to her that it was all right. It was all right now. It was all over.

None of them could believe that this was the strong-minded woman they had fought and argued with for months and months. Linda felt so guilty she couldn't look at Dolly and just sat clenching and unclenching her hands. Shirley lit a cigarette, bent down and held it out to Dolly, but she was too exhausted even to lift her hand to take it. Shirley held it to her lips and Dolly drew on the hot smoke, pulling at the cigarette like a baby with a dummy, filling her lungs and slowly letting the smoke drift out.

The tears rolled down Dolly's face, but she made no effort to wipe them away. She tried to stand, but was too weak, so Bella guided her to a chair. Dolly sat motionless, the front of her dressing gown wet with tears and the sleeve wet with blood.

The girls waited.

Eventually Dolly spoke. Her speech was a stream of disjointed thoughts as she tried to piece it all together.

'I suspected when I went to Jimmy Nunn's place . . . but not for certain . . . and . . . I didn't want to believe it was possible . . . I thought I'd buried him, but it was Jimmy Nunn. I buried Jimmy Nunn . . . I cried for Jimmy Nunn . . . Harry must have been driving the front van . . . I'm so sorry. He was the fourth man and I'm so very, very sorry for what happened to your fellas.'

'But Harry's watch. Was Jimmy wearing it?' Linda asked sincerely.

Dolly shook her head. 'Only Harry knows . . .'

She held out her hand for another cigarette and Shirley handed one to her. Dolly sat and smoked in silence. Then her face suddenly twisted, her body shaking as she spoke. 'The way that Trudie looked at me when I introduced meself! It was as if I was a piece of dirt. I think he was there. Hiding. Wolf knew, I think. Wolf could smell his dad in that grubby little dump of a flat. Just like he smelt him in the lock-up.' Dolly held her head in her hands in disbelief. 'I loved him so much. He was my life, I loved him from the first moment I saw him.' She took a moment to try and calm herself. 'Even when I pieced it together, I still – I still wanted him back.' She lowered her head with shame. 'I still loved him then, I wanted to be with him, but I couldn't tell you, I couldn't tell you that. I was too ashamed.' Dolly wiped her nose with the sleeve of her dressing gown and looked up at the girls. 'I wouldn't have let him touch your money,' she said. 'He would have had to kill me first.'

Dolly stood up, tall and straight. She tightened her dressing gown belt and ran her hands through her hair. She was a fighter: she always had been and there was still plenty of fight left in her.

'I've left him nothing,' she told them. 'No money, no ledgers, nothing, not even a roof over his head. I've sold the house and everything in it from under him. On paper he's dead, so there's nothing he can do about it. All he can do now is go on the run. And keep running.'

Bella put up her hand as if she'd heard enough. 'Take it easy, Dolly, you don't know for certain he's alive – none of us do. But even if he is, why sell everything so quickly and leave yourself with nowhere to live?'

Dolly smiled and calm spread over her face.

'What are you going to do, Dolly?' Shirley asked.

'Buy twenty years of my life back.' She walked towards the bedroom.

'That's it, Dolly. You have a lie down,' Linda said.

Dolly turned, her hands spread against the bedroom doorframe as she regained her strength. 'I'm not tired. I'm going to get a new face, a new body even. They can do wonders nowadays, and God knows I'm rich enough. I'll buy youth with my share, and I'll soon look as good as any one of you.'

She stared at them, swaying slightly, then turned and walked into the bedroom. She needed to be alone.

Bella recalled Dolly that day at the beach when they were rehearsing the robbery. She remembered the way Dolly had punished herself, desperate to be as good as them, putting on a show of bravado that she was as fit as they were. Bella knew she was acting her socks off then, just as she was now, and she was damned good at hiding her true feelings: she was feeling old and out of place. Looking at Shirley and Linda, Bella saw they were taken in by the act and believed Dolly was going to have a facelift.

Shirley followed Dolly. 'Come on. Get into your nice dress! The table's waiting – best club in Rio.'

Dolly stopped for a second, braced herself and turned to Shirley. 'I'm going to stay here, but you go. Enjoy yourselves. I've got a new life to plan.'

Bella picked up the cocktail dress, a few others from Dolly's case and some more that Linda and Shirley had bought. She walked into the bedroom, placed the dresses on the bed and stood with her hands on her hips. 'We ain't takin' no for an answer, darlin',' she said to Dolly. 'So, get out of that oversized dressing gown and slip into one of these.'

Dolly looked at Bella and Bella could see the longing to be young again in her eyes. 'Your new life starts right here, right now, Dolly,' she whispered. 'It don't take no planning.' Then she spoke louder so that Linda and Shirley could hear her. 'Linda'll do your hair.'

Linda raced to the bedside drawer and pulled out a hair dryer. 'I do a cracking blow job!' she announced. As the girls laughed, a smile crept over Dolly's face.

Bella chipped in again. 'And to round it off, Shirley, our very own professional model and catwalk star, will do your make-up. By the time we've finished, you'll look twenty years younger.'

Shirley pulled Dolly over to the dressing table, while Linda ran to her bedroom and got her heated rollers. Dolly had a childlike look on her face as she sat in front of the mirror: Cinderella about to go to the ball.

'What you want – the silver lamé or the sequins?' Bella asked as she picked up two evening gowns from the bed.

Dolly looked at her through the mirror. 'Be a bit of a mutton in that, won't I?'

Bella laughed and chucked the lamé to one side. 'The sequins will be just fine!' She caught Dolly's eye in the mirror and gave her a wink, but looked away as she saw Dolly's mouth begin to tremble. She didn't want to set her off again. Dolly had done the emotional abandon bit . . . now she needed to get pissed and let her hair down.

As Linda began blow-drying Dolly's wet, matted hair, she didn't even realise that she was lightly squeezing and affectionately stroking Dolly's shoulder with her thumb. But Dolly knew. It was the first time Linda had ever shown any real sign of friendship and Dolly felt so moved that she couldn't help but touch Linda's hand. Linda closed her fingers around Dolly's and, looking in the mirror at their reflections, Dolly could see the guilt in the younger woman's eyes. 'Leave it all behind, eh, Linda?' Dolly said quietly. 'All the cold, and the rain and the mistakes.' This was Linda's pardon from Dolly – and Linda accepted it with a smile. There was, at long last, an understanding between them all.

The room gradually filled with laughter and chit-chat about hairstyles, dresses and make-up. Dolly felt loved in this moment and, whether it lasted or not, she was going to enjoy every second of it. Their friendship warmed her, strengthened her and made her feel wanted. For now, she was one of the 'girls', but unlike Shirley and Linda, Dolly was not a widow. Not anymore. And she would never forget what Harry Rawlins had put her though.

One day she'd see him again. One day he'd have to face her.

Harry was still alive and she would find him. Wherever he might be.

THE END

Lynda La Plante

Readers' Club

If you enjoyed *Widows*, why not join the LYNDA LA PLANTE READERS' CLUB by visiting www.bit.ly/LyndaLaPlanteClub?

Dear Reader

Thank you very much for reading *Widows*. I hope you have enjoyed the story of Dolly and her 'girls' – they are very dear to my heart! *Widows*, as many of you may know, was my first ever TV show, commissioned by Verity Lambert of Euston Films for Thames Television and it remains a special favourite of mine. In the wake of the phenomenal TV success – it became one of the highest rating series of the early 1980s – I turned the screenplay and script into a tie-in novel, which was first published in 1983.

The original *Widows* ran to two series on ITV and went on to have a sequel set ten years later – *She's Out*. Since then I have produced many TV series, films and novels. However, I was particularly delighted when award-winning film director Steve McQueen chose to buy the rights to *Widows* to adapt my story for a major movie that is planned for release in autumn 2018. It prompted me to re-read my original tie-in novel and to edit and reshape it for a new audience – and I've loved every minute of it.

Dolly Rawlins was the first of my heroines to emerge into the limelight on screen and on the page. She was followed by, among others, Anna Travis and most famously Jane Tennison. Like Dolly, Jane is a strong, independent woman making her way in a tough male world – although, unlike Dolly, she is on the right side of the law! *Murder Mile*, the fourth in the Jane Tennison series in which I explore the influences that made Jane the iconic character she becomes in *Prime Suspect*, will be published in hardback in autumn 2018. It's set in Peckham, in south London, in 1979 where a series of murders takes place within a one-mile radius – although the police can find no pattern or connection linking the female victims. When another victim is found, this time a young male, Jane Tennison must fit the pieces of the jigsaw together in time to stop the murderer from striking again.

If you have enjoyed *Widows*, please do read the first three novels in the Jane Tennison series: *Tennison*, *Hidden Killers* and *Good Friday*, all of which are available in paperback or ebook. And if you would like to hear more about *Murder Mile*, or about the brand new series I'm working on at the moment, you can visit **www.bit.ly/LyndaLaPlanteClub** where you can join the LYNDA LA PLANTE READERS' CLUB. It only takes a few moments to sign up and there are no catches or costs. We'll keep you up-to-date with news about my books and give you exclusive early access to material from future books.

We promise to keep your data private and confidential, and it will never be passed on to a third party. We won't spam you with loads of emails, just get in touch now and again with news about my books, and you can unsubscribe any time you want.

And if you would like to get involved in a wider conversation about my books, please do review *Widows* on Amazon, on GoodReads, on any other e-store, on your own blog and social media accounts, or talk about it with friends, family or reader groups! Sharing your thoughts helps other readers, and I always enjoy hearing about what people experience from my writing.

Thanks again for your interest in *Widows*, and I hope you'll return for *Murder Mile*, the fourth in the Jane Tennison series.

With my very best wishes,

Lynda La Plante

Turn the page for the first chapter from Lynda La Plante's new book in the brilliant Jane Tennison series, *Murder Mile*.
Coming August 2018.

CHAPTER ONE

Jane Tennison, recently promoted to sergeant, looked out of the passenger window of the CID car at the snow, which was falling too lightly to settle. It was 4.30am on a freezing Saturday morning in mid-February 1979 and recently the overnight temperatures had been sub-zero. The weather reports were calling it one of the coldest winters of the century.

Apart from a couple of minor incidents, Jane's CID night shift at Peckham had been remarkably uneventful, due to the bad weather. She looked at her watch: only another hour and a half to go before she finished her week of night duty and could get home to a warm bath, good sleep and some time off. She'd be back at Peckham on Monday for day shift.

Detective Constable Brian Edwards, an old colleague from her Hackney days, had been her night duty partner throughout the week. He was so tall he had the driving seat pressed as far back as it could possibly go, but his knees were still almost touching the steering wheel.

'Can you turn the heating up?' she asked, as they drove along East Dulwich Road.

'It's already on full.' Edwards moved the slider to be sure, then glanced at Jane. 'I meant to say earlier – I like your new hairstyle . . . sort of makes you look more mature.'

'Is that a polite way of saying I look older, Brian?' Jane asked.

'I was being complimentary! It goes with your smart clothes, makes you look more business-like . . . especially now you've been promoted.'

Jane was about to reply when Edwards suddenly slammed his foot on the car brake bringing it to an abrupt halt. They both lunged forward, Edwards banging his chest against the steering wheel and Jane narrowly avoiding hitting her head on the windscreen.

'What – what's up?' Jane asked, startled, staring at Edwards.

'A rat . . . A bloody rat!' He pointed at the middle of the road in front of them.

Illuminated by the car headlights was a massive rat, a piece of rotting meat between its sharp teeth. The rat suddenly darted off across the road and out of sight. Edwards shook his head.

'I hate rats. They give me the creeps.'

'Well, that's obvious! And yes, thank you, Brian, I'm OK – apart from nearly going through the windscreen.'

'I'm sorry, Sarge . . . I didn't mean to hit the brakes so suddenly.'

'I'm just touched that you didn't want to run the rat over, Brian,' Jane said.

Edwards pointed over towards Peckham Rye to a pile of rubbish-filled plastic black bin and shopping bags. They were piled up five foot high and stretched over twenty feet along the side of the park. The stench of rotting rubbish slowly permeated its way into the stationary car.

'It's thanks to Prime Minister Callaghan and his waste-of-space Labour government that the bin men and other public-sector workers are on strike,' grumbled Edwards. 'Everyone's dumping their rotting rubbish in the parks and it's attracting the rats. No wonder they're calling it the "Winter of Disconnect".'

'It's "Discontent",' Jane corrected him.

'You're quite right – there's not much to be happy about! Mind you, if Maggie Thatcher wins the next election we might get a pay rise. She likes the Old Bill.'

Jane was trying hard not to laugh. 'It's the "*Winter of Discontent*"! It comes from Shakespeare's Richard III: "*Now is the winter of our discontent, made glorious summer by this sun of York . . .*"

Edwards looked sceptical. 'Really?'

'I studied Richard III for A level English.'

'All that Shakespeare lingo is mumbo jumbo to me. I left school at sixteen and joined the Metropolitan Police Cadets,' Edwards said proudly.

'I didn't know you'd been a "Gadget",' said Jane, somewhat surprised. A 'Gadget' was affectionate force jargon for a cadet.

'It was all blokes when I first joined the Gadgets,' Edwards went on. 'We lived in a big dormitory and got work experience on division alongside the regulars. It gave me a better understanding of police work than your average ex-civvy probationer who went to Hendon – no offence intended,' he added hastily.

'None taken. If I'd known what I wanted to do at sixteen I'd probably have joined the cadets – though my mother would have had a heart attack.' Jane liked Edwards, but he wasn't the brightest spark. He'd been transferred to various stations and hadn't lasted long on the Flying Squad. In her estimation, he'd likely remain a DC for the rest of his career.

'Tell you what – head back to the station so we can warm up with a hot drink and I'll type up the night duty CID report,' she said.

Edwards snorted. 'That shouldn't take long – we haven't attended a crime scene or nicked anyone all night.'

Their banter was interrupted by a call over the radio. 'Night duty CID receiving . . . over?'

Jane picked up the radio handset. 'Yes, Detective Sergeant Tennison receiving. Go ahead . . . over.'

'A fruit and veg man on his way to set up his market stall has found an unconscious woman in Bussey Alley. Couldn't rouse her so he called 999. There's an ambulance en route,' the comms officer said.

'That's just off Rye Lane.' Edwards made a sharp U turn.

'Yes, we're free to attend and en route,' Jane confirmed over the radio, switching on the car's two-tone siren.

'If she's been out drinking she's probably collapsed from hypothermia in this bloody weather. Or maybe she's been mugged?' suggested Edwards.

'Let's just hope she's OK,' Jane said.

Rye Lane ran between the High Street and Peckham Rye. In its heyday it had rivalled Oxford Street as a major shopping destination and was known as the 'Golden Mile'. It was still a busy area, with a large department store, Co-op and various small shops and market traders selling home-produced and ethnic goods from their stalls. During the 1970s, Peckham had gradually become one of the most deprived areas in Europe, with a notorious reputation for serious crime, especially muggings, which were a daily occurrence.

Jane and Edwards arrived at the scene within two minutes. A man who looked to be in his mid-fifties was standing under the railway bridge at the entrance to Bussey Alley, frantically waving his hands. He was dressed in a dark-coloured thigh-length sheepskin coat, blue and white Millwall football club scarf and a peaked cap. Edwards pulled up beside him and opened the driver's window.

'I thought you might be the ambulance when I heard the siren.' The man crouched down to speak to them. 'Poor thing's just up there. She's lyin' face down and ain't moved. I put one of me stall tarpaulins over her to keep off the sleet and cold. I was hopin' she might warm up and come around . . . '

Jane put on her leather gloves, got the high-powered torch out of the glove box and picked up the portable Storno police radio.

'There's quite a lot of rubbish been dumped on one side of the alley, just up from where she is – be careful of the rats,' the market trader said as they got out of the car.

Jane grinned at Edwards. He hadn't looked too happy at the word 'rat'. 'You get the details,' she said. 'I'll check on the woman.'

She turned on the torch, lighting up the dingy alley. The narrow path ran alongside the railway line. In the arches underneath were small lockups where the market traders stored their stalls and goods. Jane walked at a brisk pace, until about forty feet along she could see the green and white striped tarpaulin. Crouching down, she lifted it back and shone the torch. The woman beneath was wearing a thigh-length blue PVC mac, with the collar up, covering the back of her neck.

Removing her right glove, Jane put her index and middle fingers together, and placed them on the side of the woman's neck, in the soft hollow area just beside the windpipe. There was no pulse and the woman's neck felt cold and clammy. Jane felt uneasy. She stood up and slowly shone her torch along the body revealing dried blood smears on the back of the blue mac. The woman's knee-length pleated skirt was hitched up to her thighs revealing suspenders and black stockings. Near the body the torch beam caught three small shirt buttons. Peering closely at one of them, Jane could see some white sewing thread and a tiny piece of torn shirt still attached. It looked as if the button had been torn off, possibly in a struggle.

A little further up the alleyway Jane noticed a cheap and worn small handbag. Wearing her leather gloves, she picked it up and opened it carefully, looking for any ID. All she found was a lipstick, handkerchief, a small hairbrush and a plastic purse. Inside the purse were a few coins and one folded five-pound note. There were no house or car keys inside the handbag or purse. Jane picked up the handbag and placed a ten pence coin down on the spot where she'd found it; it would go in a property bag later to preserve it for fingerprints.

Next, Jane shone the torch around the body. It was strange: she couldn't see any blood on the pavement around or near the victim, or on the back of her head. She crouched down and slowly lifted the collar on the PVC mac back, revealing a knotted white rope round the victim's neck and hair.

Shocked Jane got to her feet and pulled out the portable radio.

'WDS Tennison to Peckham Control Room. Are you receiving? Over.' She spoke with confidence and authority, despite the fact she'd only been promoted and posted to Peckham a few weeks ago.

'Yes, go ahead, Sarge,' the comms officer replied.

'Cancel the ambulance . . . The woman in Bussey Alley appears to have been strangled. I've looked in a handbag for possible ID, but can't find any. I need uniform assistance to cordon off and man the scene at Rye Lane, and the far end of Bussey Alley, which leads onto Copeland Road.'

'All received, Sarge. A mobile unit is en route to assist.'

Jane continued. 'Can you call DCI Moran at home and ask him to attend the scene? I'll also need the laboratory Scene of Crime DS here – oh, and the Divisional Surgeon to officially pronounce life extinct . . . Over.'

The Duty Sergeant came on the radio. 'Looks like a quiet week just got busy, Jane. I'll call Moran and tell him you're on scene and dealing . . . Over. '

Jane ended the transmission and replaced the tarpaulin over the body to preserve it from the sleet that was still falling, although not as heavily. Then she walked back to Rye Lane.

Edwards was still speaking to the market trader, and making notes in his pocket book. As she approached him, she gave a little shake of her head to indicate this was more than a collapse in the street or hypothermia and went to the rear of the CID car. Taking out a plastic police property bag, she placed the handbag inside it.

'Is she all right?' the trader asked.

She shook her head. 'I'm afraid she's dead, sir. Did you see anyone hanging about or acting suspiciously before you found her?'

The man looked shocked. 'No, no one . . . Oh, my – the poor thing. What's happened to her?'

'I don't know, sir, I'm afraid. Further investigation is needed,' Jane did not want to reveal more.

'Can I get me gear out the lockup and set up for business?'

'Sorry, not at the moment, but maybe in an hour or two,' she said. 'We'll need to take a more detailed statement off you later.'

Jane took Edwards to one side.

'I take it you're thinking murder?' he whispered.

Jane nodded. By now their hair was soaking and their coats sodden. 'Looks like she's been strangled and maybe raped. I've spoken with the Duty Sergeant who's informing DCI Moran. The market man's up a bit early – does his account of how he found her sound above board to you?'

'Yeah. His name's Charlie Dunn, he's sixty-two and he's been working the markets since he was twelve. He's always been an early bird. He said he's just been over to Spitalfields fruit and veg market to get fresh stock for the day. That's his white van under the railway bridge. He was unloading it to his archway lockup in the alley when he saw the woman on the pavement. I checked his van, it's full of fresh goods. He also showed me the purchase receipt for the fruit and veg and his market trader's licence. He sounded and acted legit to me.'

'Well, she's stone cold, so it looks like she's been dead a while anyway.'

'Any ID on her?'

'Nothing in the handbag I found, not even keys. I haven't had a chance to check her coat pockets yet. I want to get both ends of the alleyway sealed off and manned by uniform first – all the market traders will be turning up soon and wanting access to their archway lockups.'

Edwards nodded and blew into his freezing hands. He didn't question her authoritative tone; on the contrary, he liked the fact WDS Tennison was taking responsibility for the crime scene.

The market trader went to his van and returned with a Thermos flask.

'Hot coffee? You can have it if you want. I'm going to go home and come back later.'

'Thank you!' Edwards took the flask and poured some coffee into the removable cup and handed it to Jane. She took a mouthful, swallowed it, then let out a deep cough and held her chest.

'There's more brandy in that than coffee!'

Edwards promptly held the flask to his lips and took a large gulp.

'So there is,' he said with a grin.

'Put it in the car, Brian. We don't want Moran smelling booze on us – you know what he's like about drinking on duty.'

Edwards took another gulp, then put the flask in the back of the car and got a packet of lozenges out of his pocket.

'"Be prepared", as we used to say in the scouts. You see I remember some famous quotes as well.' Edwards took one for himself, and offered the packet to Jane.

'What are they?' Jane asked.

'Fisherman's Friends. They'll hide the smell of the brandy and warm you up at the same time. I take them fishing with me when it's cold like this.'

Jane reached into the pack, took out one of the small, light brown, oval-shaped lozenges, popped it in her mouth and immediately began taking deep breaths. The menthol flavour was so strong her eyes began watering, her nose started running and her throat tingled.

'They taste awful!' she exclaimed spitting out the lozenge and placing it in a tissue to throw away later.

Just then, two police constables arrived in an Austin Allegro panda car. They got out and approached Jane.

'What do you need us to do, Sarge?'

'I need the Rye Lane and Copeland Road entrances to the alley sealed off with tape and one of you to stand guard at each end.'

'Will do, Sarge.' They both set off and then one of them turned back. 'Oh – the Duty Sergeant said to tell you DCI Moran's been informed and is on his way with DI Gibbs.'

Edwards looked at Jane. 'I thought DI Gibbs wasn't due to start at Peckham until Monday?'

Jane shrugged. 'That's what I thought as well.'

'Maybe Moran wants him to run the investigation.'

'Why? Moran's the senior officer – he's in charge of the CID at Peckham,' Jane pointed out.

'Don't tell anyone I told you this,' said Edwards. 'But I was in the bog cubicle when I overheard Moran talking to the Chief Super. Moran said his wife was suffering from the "baby blues". Apparently, the baby was crying a lot and he didn't know what to do for the best. The Chief suggested he take some time off when DI Gibbs arrived – so maybe Moran's called Gibbs in early to familiarise himself with everything before he steps back to spend time at home.'

'I didn't know his wife had had a baby.'

'Yeah – about a month before you started at Peckham,' Edwards paused. 'I've not seen Spencer Gibbs since our Hackney days, but I heard he went off the rails a bit after Bradfield was killed in the explosion during that bank robbery by the Bentley family.'

Jane immediately became tight-lipped. 'I worked with Gibbs in the West End at Bow Street when I was a WDC and he was fine,' she lied. At the time Gibbs was drinking heavily to drown his sorrows, but managing to hide it from his other colleagues. She had always had a soft spot for Gibbs and didn't like to hear his name or reputation being tarnished. She suspected he must have overcome his demons, especially if he'd been posted to a busy station like Peckham. She also knew DCI Moran would have had to agree to Gibbs's transfer.

Jane and Edwards returned to the alley. Edwards went over to look at the body, while Jane picked up the coin she'd used as a marker and replaced it with the handbag, now inside the property bag. Then they both checked to see if there was anything in the victim's pockets to help identify her; there was nothing.

Edwards pulled up the left sleeve of the victim's PVC mac.

'She's wearing a watch,' he said. 'Looks like a cheap catalogue one, glass is scratched and the strap's worn. There's no engagement or wedding ring – they might have been stolen?'

'Possibly,' said Jane, 'but there's no white patch or indentation on the skin to suggest she was wearing either. Plus the handbag was left behind with money in it.' Jane got the radio out of her coat pocket and handed it to Edwards.

'Call the station and ask them to check Missing Persons for anyone matching our victim's description. I'll replace the tarpaulin, then we'll do a search further up the alley towards Copeland Road to see if there's anything else that may be of significance to the investigation.'

Edwards hesitated. 'What should I tell Comms?'

Jane gave a small sigh. 'Brian – just look at the victim and describe her when you speak to them, OK?'

'Oh, yeah. OK, I see.'

Jane watched Edwards disappear down the alleyway, leaving her alone with the body. It was still dark and now the initial adrenalin rush was wearing off she was even more aware of the cold. She stamped her feet and flapped her arms across her chest to generate some warmth. A sudden noise made her jump, and swinging her torch round revealed a rat scurrying from a pile of rubbish that had been left rotting in front of one of the arches. She thought about the woman lying on the ground in front of her. What had she been doing here? Had she been on her own, like Jane was now, or was her killer someone she knew?

Footsteps approached from the Rye Lane end of the Alley. Jane looked up, shone her torch, and saw Detective Sergeant Paul Lawrence from the forensics lab approaching. He was accompanied by a younger man in civilian clothes. Even if she hadn't seen Paul's face, she'd have guessed it was him. As ever, he was dressed in his trademark thigh-length green Barbour wax jacket and trilby hat.

Paul Lawrence was renowned as the best crime scene investigator in the Met. He had an uncanny ability to think laterally and piece things together bit by bit. Always patient and willing to explain what he was doing, Jane had worked with him several times and felt indebted to him for all that he had taught her. Now she felt relief at the sight of his familiar figure.

Paul greeted Jane with a friendly smile. 'I hear it's Detective Sergeant Tennison now! Well done and well-deserved, Jane. As we're the same rank, you can officially call me Paul.' He laughed. She had always called him Paul when not in the company of senior officers.

'You were quick,' Jane said.

'I'd already been in the lab typing up a report from an earlier incident in Brixton,' he said. 'Victim stabbed during a fight over a drugs deal. Turned out the injury wasn't as serious as first thought and the victim didn't want to assist us anyway, so there wasn't much to do. No doubt there'll be a revenge attack within a few days.'

Jane explained the scene to him, starting with the market trader's account and exactly what she and DC Edwards had done since their arrival at Bussey Alley.

'Good work, Jane. Minimal disturbance of the scene and preservation of evidence is what I like to see and hear. Peter here is the Scene of Crime Officer assisting me. He'll photograph everything as is, then we can get the victim onto a body sheet for a closer look underneath.'

The SOCO set to work taking the initial scene photographs of the alleyway and body. He stopped when the Divisional Surgeon appeared. Although it was obvious, the doctor still checked for a pulse on her neck, before officially pronouncing she was dead. As he was getting to his feet, Detective Chief Inspector Moran arrived, carrying a large red hard-backed A4 note book, and holding up an enormous black umbrella. Dressed smartly in a grey pin stripe suit, crisp white shirt, red tie, black brogues and thigh length beige camel coat, he nonetheless looked bad-tempered and tired.

‘So, DS Tennison,’ he said. ‘What’s happened so far?’ He sounded tetchy.

Jane had worked with DCI Nick Moran when she was a WPC at Hackney in the early seventies, and he was a Detective Inspector. She knew to keep her summary brief and to the point so as not to irritate her superior.

‘The victim was found in here by a market trader. Edwards spoke with him and is satisfied he wasn’t involved. I called DS Lawrence to the scene and the Divisional Surgeon who’s pronounced life extinct. From my cursory examination it appears she’s been strangled and may have been sexually assaulted. I haven’t found anything to help us identify who she is, though a handbag was nearby which I checked – ’

Moran frowned. ‘I had expected you to just contain the scene until I arrived. It’s my job to decide who should be called and what action should be taken. You should have left the handbag in situ as well. It’s not good to disturb a scene.’

Jane felt Moran was being a bit harsh. She, like everyone else, was working in the freezing cold and soaking wet. He should have realised she was trying to obtain the best evidence and identify the victim. She thought about saying as much, but wondering if his mood was connected to a sleepless night coping with the new baby, decided to say nothing.

Lawrence looked at Moran. ‘It’s standard procedure for a lab sergeant to be called to all suspicious deaths and murder scenes at the earliest opportunity. Preserving the handbag for fingerprints showed good crime scene awareness by WDS Tennison.’

Moran ignored Lawrence and spoke to the Divisional Surgeon. ‘Can you give me an estimation of time of death?’

The doctor shrugged his shoulders. ‘There are many variables due to the weather conditions, breeze in the alley and other factors which can affect body temperature. It’s hard to be accurate, but possibly just before or after midnight.’

Just about managing to keep his umbrella up, Moran wrote in his note book. Jane could see Lawrence was not pleased. She knew his view was that Divisional Surgeons were not experienced in forensic pathology or time of death and should confine their role to nothing more than pronouncing life extinct.

Lawrence looked at Moran. 'Excuse me, sir, but now the sleet's stopped, it would be a good idea to get a pathologist down to see the body in situ. He can check the rigor mortis and body temp – '

Moran interrupted him, shutting his umbrella. 'The weather's constantly changing, and more snow is forecast, so I want the body bagged, tagged and off to the mortuary as a priority for a post mortem later this morning.'

Lawrence sighed, but he didn't want to get into an argument about it. Opening his forensic kit, he removed a white body sheet and small plastic ring box and latex gloves. Using some tweezers, he picked up the three buttons beside the body and placed them in a plastic property bag. Then he unfolded the body sheet and placed it on the ground next to the body.

Lawrence looked up at Jane and Edwards. 'I want to turn her over onto the body bag. If one of you can grab her feet, I'll work the shoulders. Just go slow and gentle.'

Jane took a step forward, but Edwards said he'd do it and grabbed a pair of protective gloves from Lawrence's forensic bag. As they turned the body over, Jane shone her torch on the victim, lighting up her contorted face and the rope round her neck. The strangulation had caused her tongue to protrude and her eyes were puffed and swollen. The victim wore little makeup, and looked to be in her late twenties to early thirties. She was medium height, with brown shoulder length hair parted down the middle, and was wearing a pink blouse, which was torn, and her bra was pulled up over her breasts.

Lawrence pointed to the pavement area where the body had been lying. 'It's dry underneath her,' he observed.

‘The sleet started about 3a.m.,’ Jane said.

‘Then it’s reasonable to assume she was killed before then.’

‘How can you be sure it was 3 a.m., Tennison?’ Moran snapped, tapping the ground with the steel tip of his umbrella.

Jane got her note book out of her inside coat pocket. ‘We’d just stopped a vehicle and I recorded the details and time in my note book. I remember the sleet starting as I was taking the driver’s details . . . Let me find it.’ She flicked through the pages. ‘Ah – here it is. Time of stop, 3.03 a.m.’

‘Well, I want it checked out with the London weather office in case it becomes critical to the case,’ said Moran. ‘The body is a stone’s throw from Peckham Rye railway station. She might have been out late Friday night and attacked in the alleyway if using it as a cut through to Copeland Road.’

Lawrence shrugged. ‘She might have thrown it away, but there was no train ticket on her. She may have been walking from the Copeland Road end and heading towards Rye Lane. The fact there were no house keys on her could suggest she was returning home and expecting someone to let her in.’

Moran nodded. ‘We can put out a press appeal with the victim’s description and ask if anyone recalls seeing her on the train Friday night. Also we can run a check with Miss Pers for anyone matching her description.’

‘Already in hand, sir.’ Jane said, without receiving so much as a thank you back. She glanced at Edwards, reminding herself to check exactly what description he had given to Miss Pers.

Lawrence crouched down next to the body, looked at Moran and pointed to the victim’s torn blouse. ‘There’s four buttons missing. I only recovered three beside the body and there’s no more underneath her.’

Edwards raised his finger. ‘Tennison and I had a good look up and down the alley before DS Lawrence arrived and we didn’t see any more buttons.’

Lawrence stood up. 'Best we check the soles of our shoes in case one of us has accidently trodden on it and it's got lodged in the tread. It won't be the first time something has unintentionally been removed from a crime scene in that way. When you see the market trader who found her, check his footwear as well.' Everyone checked the soles of their shoes.

'Someone tread in dog shit?'

Jane turned around. Spencer Gibbs was wearing a trendy full-length brown sheepskin coat. His hands were deep in the pockets, pulling the unbuttoned coat around his front to keep out the cold. He had a big smile and Jane could instantly see he was looking a lot better now than when she last saw him, almost younger in fact. His hair had changed as well. It no longer stood up like a wire brush, but was combed back straight from his forehead.

Gibbs' smile widened when he saw Jane.

She held out her hand. 'Hello, Spence, you look well.'

'Jane Tennison – long time no see!' He pulled her forward to give her a hug.

Jane noticed that DCI Moran didn't seem too impressed and wondered if Gibbs' jovial mood was due to drink, although she couldn't smell any alcohol.

Gibbs walked over to Moran. 'Good morning, sir,' he said, and they shook hands. Gibbs' coat fell open to reveal a blue frilled shirt, tight leather pants, blue suede shoes and a large 'Peace' sign medallion. Everyone went quiet.

Moran frowned. 'So you really think that sort of outfit is suitable for a senior detective, DI Gibbs?'

'Sorry, guv. I did a gig in Camden town with my band last night then stayed at the girlfriend Tamara's pad. Thankfully I'd added her phone number to my out of hours contact list at the old station. I didn't want to waste time by going home to change when I got the call out, so after a quick dash of Adidas aftershave, I came straight to the scene by cab.'

Gibbs' looks and patter had become even more 'rock and roll' than they used to be.

'Your band do Glam Rock, guv?' Edwards asked trying not to laugh at Gibbs' dress sense.

'No, we're more progressive . . . Serious rock and roll. Girlfriend's in the band as well, looks like Debbie Harry from Blondie – she's a real stunner.'

'Well – you look like a real poofter in that gear,' Edwards replied, earning a playful slap on the back of his head from Gibbs.

Moran coughed loudly to get Gibbs' and Edwards' attention. 'Show a bit of respect you two. We're supposed to be investigating a murder, not discussing bloody music!'

'Sorry, sir,' they said in unison.

'What have you got so far?' Gibbs asked Moran.

Moran frowned. 'A murder, obviously. I want you to organise house-to-house enquiries DI Gibbs. Start with any flats in Rye Lane, and all the premises in Copeland Road. Tennison and Edwards can return to the station to write up their night duty report then go off duty.'

Jane knew that organising house-to-house was normally a DS's responsibility and she was keen to be part of the investigation team.

'I should have the weekend off, sir, but I'm happy to remain on duty and assist the investigation. You've got a DS on sick leave, one at the Old Bailey on a big trial starting Monday, and one taking over nights from me tonight. House-to-house is normally a DS's role so I could – '

Moran interrupted her. 'I'm aware of all that, Tennison. If you're willing to work for normal pay and days off in lieu, as opposed to costly overtime, then you can head up the house-to-house. Edwards, same rule goes for you if you want to be on the investigation.'

Jane and Edwards agreed. Earning extra money was a bonus, but never a big deal when it came to a murder enquiry; it was more about being part of a challenging case.

Moran closed his notebook and put his pen back in his jacket pocket. 'Right, DI Gibbs will be my number two on this investigation. We'll head back to the station. I'll get more detectives in from the surrounding stations and contact the Coroner's Officer to arrange a post mortem later this morning. Tennison – you head back to the station with Edwards. Do your night duty report first, then prepare the house-to-house documents and questionnaires. You can get uniform to assist in the house-to-house, as well as the Special Patrol Group. DS Lawrence and the SOCO can finish bagging the body and examining the scene. If possible, I'd like to know who the dead woman is before the post mortem.'

'I'll take a set of fingerprints while I'm here. Uniform can take them straight up the Yard for the fingerprint bureau to check. If she's got a criminal record they'll identify her,' Lawrence said.

Moran nodded his approval. As he walked off with Gibbs, Edwards turned to Jane.

'He could have poked someone's eye out the way he was swinging that umbrella! I reckon he's in a mood because the baby kept him up, and his wife gave him a hard time about being called in.'

Jane said nothing, but she suspected there was some truth in Edwards' comment. Just as she was about to follow him back to the CID car, Paul called out.

'Can you grab the large role of sellotape from my forensic bag?'

He and the SOCO had wrapped the body in the white body sheet and twisted each end tight. Jane knew the procedure and helped by rolling the tape several times around each twisted end to secure them. She always found it surreal that a bagged dead body ended up looking like an enormous Christmas cracker.

'Thanks, Jane.' As the SOCO moved away, Lawrence asked, 'Is Moran always so tetchy these days?'

'Wife had a baby recently; sleepless nights are probably getting to him.'

'Well, he was wrong to have a go at you and ignore my advice. He should have called out a Pathologist.'

'He was probably just asserting his authority to let us know he's boss.'

'He might be in charge, but he's spent most of his career on various squads like vice, so he's not had a lot of experience in major crime or murder investigations.'

'He did solve the Hackney serial rape cases and that murder committed by Peter Allard the cab driver,' Jane pointed out.

'Yes – but I also recall he was accused of faking Allard's confession. If it hadn't been for your dogged work in that case, he wouldn't have solved it. He showered himself in glory because of you, Jane. He seems to have forgotten that you stuck your neck out for him that night in the park acting as a decoy. You were the one that got attacked by Allard, not him.'

'I know, Paul, but I think he's mellowed since our Hackney days. Apart from this morning he's been OK towards me.'

'Well, I'd be wary of him, Jane,' warned Lawrence. 'He likes to think he knows best, which puts not only the investigation at risk, but the officers on it as well.'

This was not the first murder. The body count began to mount, the killings became more gruesome, no suspects and no witnesses, and all within a stone's throw of each other.

TENNISON

The sensational thriller behind the hit ITV show, *Prime Suspect: 1973*, starring Stefanie Martini, Sam Reid, Alun Armstrong and Blake Harrison

The Kray twins may be behind bars but the streets of London are still rife with drugs, robbery and murder.

1973, in the East End of London, a young WPC Jane Tennison joins the toughest ranks of the Hackney police force as a probationary officer.

When her first case comes in, a woman savagely beaten and strangled to death, Jane is thrown in at the deep end. But the victim's autopsy is just the beginning of Tennison's harsh initiation into the criminal world . . .

Praise for the Jane Tennison series:

'Classic Lynda, a fabulous read'
MARTINA COLE

'La Plante excels in her ability to pick out details that give her portrayal of life in a police station a rare ring of authenticity'
SUNDAY TELEGRAPH

'A terrific, gutsy back story for the heroine of TV's *Prime Suspect*'
WOMAN & HOME

HIDDEN KILLERS

The second brilliant crime thriller in the Jane Tennison series by Lynda La Plante.

When WPC Jane Tennison is promoted to the role of Detective Constable in London's Bow Street CID, she is immediately conflicted. While her more experienced colleagues move on swiftly from one criminal case to another, Jane is often left doubting their methods and findings.

As she becomes inextricably involved in a multiple rape case, Jane must put her life at risk in her search for answers.

Will she toe the line, or endanger her position by seeking the truth?

Praise for the Jane Tennison series:

'An absorbingly twisty plot'
GUARDIAN

'Enthralling'
HEAT

'Vintage La Plante'
INDEPENDENT

GOOD FRIDAY

In the race to stop a deadly attack just pray she's not too late . . .

March, 1976. The height of The Troubles. An IRA bombing campaign strikes terror across Britain. Nowhere and no one is safe.

When detective constable Jane Tennison survives a deadly explosion at Covent Garden tube station, she finds herself in the middle of a media storm. Minutes before the blast, she caught sight of the bomber. Too traumatised to identify him, she is nevertheless a key witness and put under 24-hour police protection.

As work continues round the clock to unmask the terrorists, the Metropolitan police are determined nothing will disrupt their annual Good Friday dinner dance. Amid tight security, hundreds of detectives and their wives and girlfriends will be at St Ermin's Hotel in central London. Jane, too, is persuaded to attend.

But in the week leading up to Good Friday, Jane experiences a sudden flashback. She realises that not only can she identify the bomber, but that the IRA Active Service Unit is very close to her indeed. She is in real and present danger. In a nail-biting race against time, Jane must convince her senior officers that her instincts are right before London is engulfed in another bloodbath.